DOCTOR WHO

THE ESSENTIAL
TERRANCE DICKS
VOLUME TWO

T0332832

BBC
─ĐOCTOR WHO─

THE ESSENTIAL TERRANCE DICKS VOLUME TWO

TERRANCE DICKS

BOOKS

BBC Books, an imprint of Ebury Publishing
20 Vauxhall Bridge Road, London SW1V 2SA

BBC Books is part of the Penguin Random House group of companies
whose addresses can be found at global.penguinrandomhouse.com

Doctor Who and the Genesis of the Daleks
Original television script copyright © Terry Nation 1975
Novelisation copyright © Terrance Dicks 1977

Doctor Who and the Pyramids of Mars
Original television script copyright © Stephen Harris 1975
Novelisation copyright © Terrance Dicks 1976

Doctor Who and the Talons of Weng-Chiang
Original television script copyright © Robert Holmes 1977
Novelisation copyright © Terrance Dicks 1977

Doctor Who and the Horror of Fang Rock
Original television script copyright © Terrance Dicks 1977
Novelisation copyright © Terrance Dicks 1978

Doctor Who – The Five Doctors
Original television script copyright © Terrance Dicks 1983
Novelisation copyright © Terrance Dicks 1983

Daleks created by Terry Nation
Cybermen created by Kit Pedler and Gerry Davis

Doctor Who is a BBC Wales production for BBC One.
Executive producers: Chris Chibnall and Matt Strevens

First published by BBC Books in 2021
Paperback edition published by BBC Books in 2022

www.penguin.co.uk

A CIP catalogue record for this book is available from the British Library

ISBN: 9781785947360

Printed and bound in Great Britain by Clays Ltd, Elcograf S.p.A.

The authorised representative in the EEA is Penguin Random House Ireland,
Morrison Chambers, 32 Nassau Street, Dublin D02 YH68

Penguin Random House is committed to a sustainable future for our
business, our readers and our planet. This book is made
from Forest Stewardship Council® certified paper.

CONTENTS

DOCTOR WHO AND THE PYRAMIDS OF MARS

DOCTOR WHO AND THE TALONS OF WENG-CHIANG

DOCTOR WHO AND THE HORROR OF FANG ROCK

DOCTOR WHO – THE FIVE DOCTORS

FOREWORD

All readers are travellers in time and space. A story takes our imagination on a journey through strange lands, meeting strange people and doing things we would never do in our ordinary lives. For as long as we are holding that book, whether we are floating down the River Mississippi in the 1860s (*The Adventures of Huckleberry Finn*) or roaming around a forest in India in the 1890s (*The Jungle Book*) or hiding in the library of an Oxford College in a parallel universe in the 1990s (*Northern Lights*), books make Time Lords of us all. It's just that, you know, reading a story whilst sitting in a comfortable chair tends to be less hazardous than climbing up a giant radio telescope to do battle with the Master.

I was nine years old when Tom Baker's Fourth Doctor said, 'It's the end, but the moment has been prepared for.' (*Logopolis*) He reached out to the ghostly figure known as the Watcher, and as the two merged, the Doctor regenerated into his fifth incarnation. This one was played by Peter Davison and from that moment forward I would be a *Doctor Who* fanatic, or 'fan' as we are more usually known. It became clear very quickly that I was going to need a heftier dose of this time-travelling adventurer than BBC TV could supply in twice-weekly instalments; that's where Terrance Dicks stepped into my life.

If I told you that Terrance Dicks taught me to read then I would be exaggerating. But not much. Yes, Coningsby Junior School had done a bang-up job at enabling me to, for example, tell the difference between 'though', 'thought' and 'through' (I mean, I still had to concentrate quite hard just then – English remains a crazy ride, my friend) but practice makes all the difference and the thing about reading is, you only get good at it after quite a lot of … well, reading. And when you're reading something you love as much as your favourite TV show, and when it is written with all the excitement, clarity, wit, suspense, economy and fun that you get from Terrance Dicks, then you're going to end up ploughing through those Target books like, ooh let me see, like a Dalek through a patrol of lightly-armed Thals.

This was important because I didn't grow up in a house where there were many books lying around. I knew that reading was A Good Thing but before *Doctor Who*, it wasn't something I did much of in my spare time. The world of books seemed like an exotic and sophisticated foreign land, and I needed a trusted guide to help me negotiate the terrain. So, reading stories that I had already watched on TV was for me a gateway into the world of literature. Those of us who came to books in this funny way tend to be super-grateful to the authors who bridged the gap.

Inevitably, it wasn't long before I was reading stories that I *hadn't* already seen. Impatient for each new clutch of adaptations to be published – as well as being a nine-year-old on a budget – I raided the local library for earlier stories, especially the ones involving the Fourth Doctor (e.g. *The Talons of Weng-Chiang* and *Pyramids of Mars*) because I had a vague memory of the crazy tall guy with the teeth and the curls. This meant that I was now, rather daringly, trusting the author alone to supply my imagination with the story.

So it was through Terrance Dicks, as well as the other *Doctor Who* authors, that I formed a voracious reading habit that I know made a huge impact upon my education and life. For the joys of discovering English literature at university and becoming a professional writer, I have a long list of people to thank. The name 'Terrance Dicks' is near the top of that list.

To turn a TV serial into a short novel is not an easy task and I hope I know enough about writing these days to see that Terrance Dicks went about his work with considerable skill. The stories can stand alone without the need to have seen the original or even to have that much pre-existing knowledge of *Doctor Who*. His language is accessible but he never patronises his young readers; in fact, most of us came away from each book with our vocabulary broadened and enriched by his crisp style. More than anything, he knows he is writing an adventure: there is always enough atmosphere to set the scene but then the story clips along with great verve. Just what you want from *Doctor Who*!

Reading fiction of any kind is a form of play – it's a fun way to work out how to do this 'life' business. To read a story is to ask yourself enjoyable but also useful questions. Such as, 'What would I do in this situation?' and 'What must it be like to be this other person?' And the questions don't become less real just because the situations and characters are out-of-this-world. 'What would I do if I had the power to wipe out the Daleks before they became a menace to the universe?' is a pretty important ethical dilemma. Would you make the same choice as the Doctor? Hmm …

Such are the time-and-space-travelling pleasures of all stories but especially the ones about *Doctor Who*. This volume contains some of my favourites and I hope you enjoy the trip as much as I did. Bon voyage!

Robert Webb

DOCTOR WHO AND THE GENESIS OF THE DALEKS

1

SECRET MISSION

It was a battlefield.

The ground was churned, scarred, ravaged. Nothing grew there, nothing lived. The twisted, rusting wrecks of innumerable war-machines littered the landscape. There were strands of ragged, tangled wire, collapsed dugouts, caved-in trenches. The perpetual twilight was made darker by fog. Thick, dank and evil, it swirled close to the muddy ground, hiding some of the horrors from view.

Something stirred in the mud. A goggled, helmeted head peered over a ridge, surveyed the shattered landscape. A hand beckoned, and more shapes rose and shambled forwards. There were about a dozen of them, battle-weary men in ragged uniforms, their weapons a strange mixture of old and new, their faces hidden by gas-masks. A star-shell burst over their heads, bathing them for a moment in its sickly green light before it sputtered into darkness. The thump of artillery came from somewhere in the distance, with the hysterical chatter of automatic weapons. But the firing was some distance away. Too tired even to react, the patrol shambled on its way.

A man materialised out of the fog and stood looking in bewilderment after the soldiers. He was a very tall man, dressed in comfortable old tweed trousers and a loosely-hanging jacket. An amazingly long scarf was wound round his neck, a battered, broad-rimmed hat was jammed on to a tangle of curly brown hair. Hands deep in his pockets, he pivoted slowly on his heels, turning in a complete circle to survey the desolate landscape.

He shook his head, the bright blue eyes clouded with puzzlement. This was all wrong, he thought. It was all terribly wrong. The transmat beam should have taken him back to the space station. Instead he was here, in this terrible place. How could it possibly have happened?

'Greetings, Doctor.'

The Doctor spun round at the sound of the voice behind him. A tall, distinguished figure in flowing robes stood looking at him quizzically. A Time Lord! The Doctor knew all about Time Lords—he was one himself. He had left his own people untold years ago to roam through Space and Time in his 'borrowed' TARDIS. He'd rebelled against the Time Lords, been captured and exiled by them, and had at last made his peace with them. He had served them often, sometimes willingly, sometimes not. These days their hold on him was tenuous. But it was still a hold, a limitation of his freedom, and the Doctor never failed to resent it.

He glared at the elegant figure before him. 'So! I've been hijacked!' he said indignantly. 'Don't you realise how dangerous it is to interfere with a transmat beam?'

'Oh come, Doctor! Not with our techniques. We transcended such simple mechanical devices when the Universe was young.' The languid voice held all the effortless superiority that the Doctor always found so infuriating.

He controlled himself with a mighty effort. 'Whatever I may have done, whatever crimes I committed in your eyes, I have made ample restitution. I have done you great services, and I was given my freedom as a reward. I will not tolerate this continual interference in my lives!'

The Time Lord looked thoughtfully at him and began to stroll across the battlefield, with the air of someone taking a turn on the lawn at a garden party. The dull rumble of gunfire came from somewhere in the distance. '*Continual* interference, Doctor? We pride ourselves we seldom intervene in the affairs of others.'

'Except mine,' the Doctor said bitterly. He hurried after the Time Lord.

'Ah, but you are an exception, Doctor—a special case. You enjoy the freedom we allow you. Occasionally, *not* continually, we ask you to do something for us.'

The Doctor came to a halt, his arms folded. 'I won't do it,' he said obstinately. 'Whatever you want—I won't do it!'

The Time Lord spoke one word. 'Daleks.'

4

The Doctor spun round. 'Daleks? Well, what about them?'

The Time Lord paused, as if collecting his arguments, then said, 'Our latest temporal projections foresee a time-stream in which the Daleks will have destroyed all other life-forms. They could become the dominant creatures in the Universe.'

'That has always been their aim,' agreed the Doctor grimly. 'Go on.'

'We'd like you to return to Skaro at a point in time just *before* the Daleks evolved.'

Immediately the Doctor guessed the Time Lord's plan. 'And prevent their creation?'

'That, or alter their genetic development, so they evolve into less aggressive creatures. At the very least, you might discover some weakness which could serve as a weapon against them.'

The Doctor tried to look as if he was thinking it over. But it was no more than a pretence. He couldn't resist the idea of a chance to defeat his oldest enemies once and for all. 'Oh all right. All right. I suppose I'll have to help you—just one more time. Return me to the TARDIS.'

'No need for that, Doctor. This is Skaro.' The Time Lord gestured at the desolate scene around them. 'Skaro—after a thousand years of war between Kaleds and Thals. We thought it would save time if we assumed your agreement.' He tossed something to the Doctor, who caught it instinctively. He found himself holding a heavy, ornately-designed bangle in a metal that looked something like copper. It wasn't copper, of course, any more than the object was the simple ornament it appeared to be. 'A Time Ring, Doctor. It will return you to the TARDIS when your mission is finished. Don't lose it, will you? It's your life-line. Good luck.' The Time Lord vanished as suddenly and silently as he had appeared.

'Just a minute,' yelled the Doctor. 'What about my two human companions?'

As if in answer a voice called from the fog. 'Doctor? Where are you?'

'Sarah?' The Doctor began running towards the sound. Almost immediately he lost his balance and skidded down a long muddy slope. Sarah Jane Smith and Harry Sullivan were waiting for him at the edge of a big shell crater.

Sarah was a slim, pretty girl in fashionable clothes. On Earth she was a journalist, though that life seemed very far away now. Harry was a square-jawed, blue-eyed, curly-haired young man. He had the rather dated good looks of the hero of an old-fashioned adventure story. Harry was a Naval man, a doctor. He was attached to UNIT, the Security Organisation to which the Doctor was Scientific Adviser. Harry had made the mistake of doubting the power of the TARDIS. This amazing device, in appearance an old-fashioned police box, was in fact the machine in which the Doctor travelled through Time and Space. Harry had rashly accepted the Doctor's challenge to 'come for a little trip'. Now, after a number of terrifying adventures, he often wondered if he would ever see Earth again.

The Doctor's two companions looked at him indignantly. 'I say, that was a pretty rough landing,' protested Harry.

Sarah had known the Doctor for longer than Harry; her travels had accustomed her to rough landings and unexpected destinations.

'All right, Doctor, where are we? This isn't the beacon.' They were supposed to be returning by transmat beam to the space station, where the TARDIS was waiting to carry them home.

The Doctor looked at her apologetically. 'I'm afraid there's been a slight change of plan …'

There was a sudden whistling sound. The Doctor wrapped his arms around his two friends and threw himself into the crater, dragging them with him. They raised their heads to protest—then lowered them hurriedly as heavy-artillery shells roared overhead. One thudded into the rim of the crater, showering them with mud.

The barrage went on for an appallingly long time, but at last it died away. The Doctor lifted his head and looked cautiously out of the crater. 'Not what you'd call a very friendly welcome.'

He turned at a muffled scream from Sarah. She pointed shakily. They were not alone in the crater. A raggedly-uniformed soldier crouched on the other side, his rifle aimed straight at them. Nobody moved. Then the Doctor walked cautiously towards the soldier. The man didn't react. The Doctor touched him on the shoulder and the soldier pitched forward, landing face-down in the mud.

The Doctor knelt beside him. 'It's all right, Sarah, the poor fellow's dead.' The Doctor examined the body, noticing the strangely shaped gas-mask, the holstered hand-blaster, the ancient projectile rifle. He pointed out the last two items to Harry. 'You see? These two weapons are separated by centuries of technology.'

Sarah joined them. She pointed to a small dial sewn into the ragged combat-jacket. 'What's this thing, Doctor?'

'A radiation detector.'

'Worn with a gas-mask straight out of the First World War?' asked Harry incredulously.

Sarah examined the uniform more closely. 'That combat-jacket's some synthetic fibre—and the rest of the uniform seems to be made of animal skins!'

The Doctor nodded. 'It's like finding the remains of a stone-age man with a transistor radio.'

Harry chuckled. 'Playing rock music, eh?' Even in the most macabre circumstances, Harry could not resist a joke. He looked at the others, hurt at their lack of reaction. '*Rock* music—cave-man—get it?'

Sarah threw him an impatient look and said, 'What does it all mean, Doctor?'

'A thousand-year war,' the Doctor said sadly. 'A once highly-developed civilisation on the point of total collapse. Come along, you two.'

He jumped out of the crater. Sarah scrambled after him. 'Where are we going?'

'Forward, of course.'

The Doctor set off at a great pace, Sarah and Harry following. They were picking their way through a very nasty clump of barbed wire when the Doctor stopped. His keen eyes had seen a sinister shape, half-buried in the mud.

'What is it?' asked Sarah.

Apologetically the Doctor said, 'I'm afraid we seem to be in the middle of a mine-field. Keep close behind, and follow in my footsteps.'

'You sound just like good King Wenceslas.'

The nightmare journey continued. Fog swirled around them, gunfire rumbled in the distance, and their feet squelched through clammy, clinging mud. In between studying the ground beneath his feet, the Doctor swept occasional glances about the desolate landscape.

'What is it, Doctor? Have you seen something?' asked Harry.

'I'm not sure. I keep getting the feeling we're being watched.'

'Me too,' said Sarah. 'Ever since we set off …'

'Rubbish,' said Harry vigorously. 'There's nothing out there except mud and fog.'

'Then let's hope it's just my over-active imagination.' Still looking around him, the Doctor took another step forward. Suddenly he stopped. Beneath the mud, his foot was jammed against something round and metallic. Silently the Doctor pointed downwards. Harry and Sarah looked.

All three held their breath. Slowly the Doctor started to withdraw his foot, then stopped at once as he felt the movement of the mine. He spoke in a quiet, conversational voice. 'Harry, this mine seems to be resting on something solid. If I move my foot it will tilt—and that could be enough to detonate it.'

Harry edged cautiously forward and dropped to his knees beside the half-buried mine. He began clearing mud and gravel away from the mine's surface. The Doctor stood motionless, like someone caught in a game of 'Statues'.

'Seems to be a rock underneath,' said Harry slowly.

Sarah spoke in a whisper, as though the very sound of her voice might be enough to explode the mine.

'Can't you wedge it, Harry? Jam something underneath to make it firm?'

Without looking up, Harry said, 'That's what I'm trying to do, old girl.' He groped round the surrounding area and picked up a suitably-sized lump of rock. Very slowly he slipped it between the mine and the rock on which it rested, holding the mine steady with his free hand. 'All right, Doctor, give it a try. Sarah, you back away—and keep to our footsteps.' Sarah obeyed—it was no time to argue.

'You get back as well, Harry,' said the Doctor.

Still crouching at the Doctor's feet, Harry shook his head. 'No. You'll have a better chance if I hold the mine steady while you move.'

'Don't be stupid, Harry.'

'Don't waste time arguing, Doctor. Just move that foot—gently.'

The Doctor moved it. Nothing happened. He watched as Harry Sullivan took first one hand and then the other from the mine. It didn't shift. The Doctor let out a long sigh of relief. 'Thank you, Harry.'

'My pleasure, Doctor,' said Harry Sullivan, a little shakily.

(As they moved clear of the minefield, a huge twisted figure in a shapeless fur hood slipped after them through the fog. The Doctor's and Sarah's instincts had been right. Something was following them across the battlefield …)

The Doctor trudged to the top of a long steep rise. He stopped and pointed. 'Look!'

Harry and Sarah joined him. There in the distance they saw— what? A giant, semi-transparent dome, fog swirling around its base, odd shapes just discernible beneath it.

'A protective dome,' said the Doctor softly. 'Large enough to cover an entire city.'

Harry gazed at it in wonder. 'If these people can build something like that, why are they fighting a war with barbed-wire and land-mines?'

'Why indeed,' replied the Doctor.

Sarah looked at him curiously. 'Doctor, isn't it time we had a few explanations?'

The Doctor sighed. 'Yes, of course it is. I must begin with an apology …' Briefly the Doctor told them how the Time Lords had intervened to prevent their safe return to the TARDIS, and of the vital mission that had been imposed on him. 'I'm only sorry you two were caught up in their high-handed action.'

He seemed so genuinely distressed that Sarah said, 'That's all right, Doctor. Not your fault is it, Harry?'

'Of course not. If these Daleks are as bad as you say, it'll be a pleasure to help scuttle 'em.'

The Doctor grinned, spirits restored by Harry's cheerful confidence.

'So where do we begin?' asked Sarah, sounding a good deal braver than she actually felt.

The Doctor pointed towards the dome. 'There!' he said. And they started moving towards the distant city.

But *getting* to the city wasn't so easy. It was guarded by an elaborate system of interconnecting trenches, similar to those that had covered Europe during the First World War. Fortunately the trench network appeared to be completely deserted. The Doctor and his companions were going through a kind of maze, moving, they hoped, ever nearer to the mysterious city.

'Maybe all the troops have been withdrawn,' suggested Harry.

'Or killed,' said the Doctor. 'See here.'

They followed him round a corner and found themselves in a large trench, floored with wooden planks and barricaded with sandbags. It was lined with men, propped up along its edge as if awaiting attack. 'Even the dead have a part to play in this war,' said the Doctor. 'They've been stood here to make the trench look fully manned.'

They moved along the row of silent figures. Harry examined one more closely. 'Same scrappy uniform as that chap in the crater. Seems to be different insignia though.'

'Different side, Harry,' the Doctor said. 'He was one of the attackers. These are defending the city.'

Sarah shivered as she glanced at the line of dead men, their sightless eyes staring out into the fog. She wandered further along the trench. Set deep into the rear wall was a heavy metal door. 'Look at this,' she called out.

Harry and the Doctor joined her. 'We must be getting near the city,' said the Doctor. 'That's probably the entrance to some kind of service tunnel.'

Harry heaved on the door, but it wouldn't budge. 'Seems to be locked solid,' he grunted.

Suddenly there was a whistling sound, followed by a thud from over the rim of the trench. Cautiously the Doctor looked out. A metal projectile lay half-buried in the mud. Evil-looking green smoke was welling out of it, and creeping slowly towards the trench.

The Doctor jumped back. 'Look out,' he yelled. 'Poison gas, and it's coming this way!'

2

PRISONERS OF WAR

The Doctor was already reaching for one of the propped-up bodies. 'Get gas-masks, quickly!' he shouted. Sarah and Harry ran to obey.

It wasn't particularly pleasant grappling with the stiff, cold corpses, but things were too desperate for any fastidiousness. All three pulled tight the straps of their gas-masks, just as green smoke began creeping into the trench.

There was a sudden burst of rifle fire. Bullets sprayed the edge of the trench, thudding into the sandbags and whining over their heads.

The Doctor peered cautiously out. A small group of ragged soldiers was pelting towards them, yelling and firing as they came. He turned to shout a warning to Sarah and Harry, but it was already too late. Troops leapt over the sandbags and dropped into the trench. Seeing the gas-masked forms of the Doctor and his companions, they hurled themselves upon them.

They had no chance to explain their neutrality. Within minutes they were engaged in savage hand-to-hand fighting. Luckily the trench was so packed with struggling bodies that the attackers had no chance to use their weapons, not daring to shoot for fear of hitting each other. The Doctor and Harry closed ranks to defend Sarah. They put up a splendid fight. Harry had boxed for the Navy in his time and he dealt out straight rights, lefts and uppercuts in the best traditions of the boxing ring. The Doctor fought in a whirl of long arms and legs, using the techniques of Venusian Aikido to drop one opponent after another. But so heavily were the two outnumbered that the sheer weight of bodies soon bore them down.

Crouched in one corner of the trench, Sarah heard a grinding noise. Peering through the struggling mass of bodies, she saw the heavy metal door slide open. A fresh contingent of soldiers appeared. They were better uniformed than the first attackers, and better armed too. There was a sudden fierce chattering of automatic weapons. Sarah jumped up to warn the Doctor, but a wild swing from a rifle-butt caught her on the temple. She collapsed face downwards.

The Doctor heard the chatter of machine-guns and realised that the character of the battle had changed. These new arrivals had no hesitation in shooting. 'Down, Harry!' he yelled, and flung himself to the ground. As the two dropped down, heavy shapes began falling on top of them—the now bullet-ridden corpses of their first attackers.

Shielded by the bodies of their former opponents, the Doctor and Harry laid low.

The rattle of machine-gun fire ended at last. The leader of the victorious soldiers saw that the green gas had drifted away. He pulled the gas-mask from his face and took in great gulps of the foggy air. He was very young. As the others pulled off their gas-masks it could be seen that they too were little more than boys.

Pushing aside the dead body which held him down, Harry began struggling to his feet. Instantly the nearest soldier raised his gun. The Doctor struggled up, shouting, 'No ...'

Then came the sound of more shooting from outside the trench, the yelling of a fresh wave of attackers. The leader indicated the Doctor and Harry. 'Into the tunnel with them—quick!' Harry and the Doctor were clubbed down and dragged unconscious through the metal door. The leader followed his men, and the door clanged shut behind them.

Outside the trench the sounds of yelling and shooting faded as the attack moved on to another section of the line. Hidden beneath a pile of bodies, Sarah lay unconscious, a trickle of blood running from her temple.

Harry and the Doctor were carried along a dark tunnel into a small, concrete-walled room at its far end. The place was primitively furnished with wooden tables, benches and a couple of bunks. One of the tables held some kind of field communications equipment. On the far side of the room was an arched opening in which stood a small passenger trolley. The trolley was on rails which disappeared into the blackness of the tunnel. It looked like the terminus of a miniature underground railway.

As the patrol crowded into the room, Harry and the Doctor were dumped casually on the ground. The soldiers began struggling out of their equipment.

Looking at his two prisoners with a satisfied air, the young patrol leader wrenched the gas-masks from their faces. His expression changed to one of puzzlement. 'They don't *look* like Thals ...' He thought for a moment. 'Stick them in the transporter, I'll take them to Command Headquarters.' A couple of soldiers grabbed the two prisoners and threw them into the trolley. The patrol leader climbed in after them and operated controls. The trolley rumbled away into the darkness.

Harry and the Doctor recovered to find themselves rattling through pitch darkness at terrifying speed. The trolley shot into a big, well-lighted area and jolted to a halt. Armed guards swarmed round and dragged them along more concrete corridors and into a large room.

By now the Doctor had recovered enough to take an interest in his surroundings. They were in some kind of central command post. Maps covered the walls, there was more communications equipment, and in the centre of the room was a huge map table holding a relief map, a kind of model landscape. It seemed to depict *two* dome-covered cities, with the trench-riddled battle-field between them. A fitting image for the present state of Skaro, thought the Doctor. He noticed that the guards were smartly uniformed here, their weapons modern and well cared for. Strange how all wars were the same, thought the Doctor. The staff back at H.Q. always had better conditions than the men actually out fighting ...

A tall, very young officer, elegant in his gold-braided uniform, was shifting symbols on the relief map. He straightened up and looked coldly at the patrol leader. 'Well?'

'Two prisoners, General Ravon. Captured in section one-zero-one. For interrogation.'

The officer smiled. 'Excellent. I enjoy interrogations.'

The Doctor looked at him. The young face was hard and cold. 'Yes,' he said cheerfully, 'I must say, you look the type.'

A blow from the rifle-butt of one of the guards sent the Doctor staggering. 'Insolent muto,' said Ravon. He turned to the patrol leader who stood rigidly to attention, obviously waiting to speak. 'Well, what is it?'

'My section totally destroyed the Thal attackers, sir, except for these two prisoners. But—well, the men are exhausted, and ammunition is running low.'

'Your men will fight until they are relieved. As for ammunition, conserve it. Use the spears and knives you were issued with whenever possible. Return to your patrol.'

'Sir.' The patrol leader saluted wearily and marched out, taking the guards with him. The Doctor glanced quickly round the room. Except for the soldier manning the communications unit, they were now alone with the General …

As if guessing the Doctor's thoughts, Ravon drew his blaster and covered the two prisoners. 'So—the Thals have degenerated to recruiting mutos, have they? Turn out your pockets!'

The Doctor shrugged. 'Why not? I always try to turn them out every year or so!' He began piling up an incredible assortment of junk on the edge of the map table—a yo-yo, a bag of jelly babies, several lengths of string and a miscellaneous collection of scientific instruments. As he did so, he took the opportunity to study the relief map.

Ravon noticed the Doctor's interest.

'Take a good look,' he sneered. 'In a few weeks we're going to change the shape of that map for ever. We shall sweep the Thals from the face of Skaro!' A note of hysteria was in his voice.

The Doctor studied him thoughtfully. Basic insecurity there—or why would he bother to boast to a couple of prisoners. In tones of deliberate provocation the Doctor said, 'Oh yes? And how are you going to do that—with worn-out soldiers, no ammunition and boy generals?'

Ravon reacted with hysterical rage. 'You've been warned about your insolence—'

Harry Sullivan, who had been watching all this with keen if baffled interest, felt a pressure from the Doctor's foot on his own. He tensed, ready for the next move.

The Doctor gave Ravon one of his sudden, brilliant smiles. 'I'm sorry, General. But you do seem to be having problems with this final campaign.'

14

Ravon felt he had to convince this infuriating prisoner. 'When victory is ours, we shall wipe every trace of the Thals and their city from this planet. We will avenge the deaths of all the Kaleds who have fallen. Our battlecry will be, "Total extermination of the Thals".' Ravon's voice had risen to a ritual chant. He was repeating a lesson drummed into him since childhood. Deliberately the Doctor made his own voice low and soothing.

'That's very impressive, General. You mean you're going to *sweep* across these trenches ...' The Doctor suited his actions to his words, flinging one arm out in a sweeping gesture. At the end of it, the edge of his hand hit Ravon's wrist in a precisely timed blow. Ravon's hand opened, the blaster flew through the air. Harry Sullivan caught it with the skill of a born cricketer. The Doctor turned to Ravon, who was rubbing his hand. 'Did I hurt your fingers, old chap?'

The soldier at the communications set turned round to find Harry covering him with the blaster.

'You won't get out of here alive,' Ravon blustered feebly. The Doctor ignored him. He crossed to the communications set, took the blaster from the startled soldier and put the set out of action with a few well-aimed blows. Outraged, the soldier jumped him—and the Doctor silenced him with a swift tap from the blaster. He lowered him gently to the floor with genuine regret.

The Doctor's expression hardened as he swung back to Ravon. 'Now then, Alexander the Great, you're going to take us out of here.'

Ravon struck a heroic attitude. 'Never!'

Harry jammed the blaster under his chin. 'You won't get any medals for being stupid, General. In fact you won't get any more medals for anything—ever.'

Ravon looked from the Doctor to Harry. These two ruffians were obviously desperate men. Surely his own life was too valuable to risk? It wasn't as if they stood any real chance of escaping ...

'All right. Where do you want me to take you?'

'Back to where we were captured,' said the Doctor. 'We left a friend behind.'

'In the Wastelands?' said Ravon. 'Yes, I suppose that's home to you mutos, isn't it? Well, come on. I can promise you won't get far.'

The Doctor and Harry fell into step beside Ravon, the stolen blasters concealed in their pockets. Ravon led them out of the room and along the corridor. Passing guards glanced curiously at them, but no one dared question the actions of the General.

They followed him along one corridor after another, twisting and turning until Harry at least had lost all sense of direction. He gave Ravon a jab. 'Where are you taking us? This isn't the way we came.'

'There's a platform lift at the end of this tunnel. You know what a lift is, don't you, muto?'

'Yes, but I don't know what a muto is,' said Harry. 'You're making a mistake, General.'

'If you come from the Wastelands, you're mutos!' Clearly that settled the matter for Ravon, and Harry didn't bother to argue. The lift appeared at the end of the corridor. Ravon touched a control beside it, and they all stood waiting.

Harry gave the Doctor a worried look. 'I hope Sarah's still there.'

Ravon couldn't resist the opportunity to sneer.

'If you're *not* mutos, then you won't last long up there.'

There came the sound of jackbooted feet on the concrete floor. Someone was walking along the corridor towards them. Harry gave Ravon a warning jab with the hidden blaster in his pocket. 'Just remember we're your friends, won't you?'

The newcomer was a slightly built, thin-faced man. His black uniform was plain except for silver insignia, and seemed somehow different from Ravon's. Not a soldier, thought the Doctor, but some kind of policeman. Ravon's greeting confirmed the Doctor's theory. 'Greetings, Security-Commander Nyder.'

Nyder's reply was equally formal. 'Greetings, General Ravon. I was just on my way to see you.' He stared curiously at the oddly assorted trio. The Doctor beamed, and Harry managed a curt nod. Nasty-looking customer, he thought.

Ravon coughed nervously. 'Perhaps you would be kind enough to go to my office and wait. I shall only be a few minutes longer.'

Nyder nodded, but made no attempt to move on. He looked more closely at the Doctor and Harry. 'You're civilians?'

The Doctor nodded. 'Just here on a brief visit to our old friend General Ravon. Don't let us detain you.'

'You won't.' As if satisfied with this riposte, Nyder started to walk away. Then suddenly he jumped back, drawing a pistol. 'Ravon—get down!' he shouted.

Ravon flung himself to the ground as Nyder fired at the Doctor. The bullet sang past his head, chipping concrete fragments from the wall. The Doctor yelled, 'Run for it, Harry,' and the two fugitives disappeared round the corner.

Nyder produced a pocket communicator. 'Alert all guards. Two Thal intruders in command complex. Sound the alarm.'

A few seconds later, a high-pitched siren began to blare through the corridors. Nyder looked at Ravon, who was shamefacedly picking himself up. 'You're a fool, General Ravon,' he said dispassionately.

Ravon tried to justify himself. 'They took me by surprise.'

'What kind of soldier allows two unarmed prisoners to overpower him in his own headquarters?'

Stung by Nyder's scorn, Ravon said, 'Those weren't ordinary prisoners. There's something different about them. They're not mutos and they're not Thals.'

Nyder looked at him sceptically. 'No? Well, if they *are different*—we'll find out when they're recaptured.' There was total confidence in his voice.

The Doctor and Harry sprinted along a corridor with no idea where they were going. Their one thought was to escape the pursuing guards. Unfortunately more guards appeared ahead, and only a providential side-corridor saved them from capture. Shots ringing all round them they turned left, then right, ran down an even smaller corridor and found themselves in a dead end. The corridor ended in a pair of lift doors like the ones where they'd left Ravon and Nyder. They turned to go back, but heard guards running towards them. Instinctively the Doctor pressed the lift controls. The running feet came nearer. As guards appeared in the corridor the lift doors opened and Harry and the Doctor dived inside. The soldiers raised their guns, the Doctor stabbed frantically at the controls, and the lift doors closed—just in time to save Harry and the Doctor from a hail of bullets.

Nyder arrived to see what had happened. He snatched out his communicator. 'Alert surface patrols to watch for intruders in lift area seven!'

The high-speed lift whisked Harry and the Doctor to the surface in a matter of seconds. The doors opened on a featureless stretch of open country—Wasteland as Ravon had called it. As yet no soldiers were in sight. Harry stared out into the drifting fog. 'Where to, Doctor?'

Figures loomed out of the fog, then came the sound of shouted orders. 'Just keep running,' called the Doctor, and shot off across the battlefield like an ostrich, Harry close behind. The Kaled patrol lumbered after them.

The Doctor and Harry tore across the churned-up landscape leaping over pill-boxes, dodging barbed-wire, stumbling in and out of shell holes. In their frantic burst of speed they left the patrol far behind. It began to look as if they had succeeded in making their escape. But the battlefield held more dangers than pursuing soldiers. Stumbling down a muddy slope the Doctor's foot caught some kind of buried trip-wire. He gave Harry a tremendous shove, yelling 'Mine!' and threw himself in the mud beside him. There was a muffled 'crump', and a fountain of mud shot up in the air as the long-buried mine was detonated. Harry and the Doctor escaped the flying shrapnel but they were close enough to be deafened and half-stunned by the blast.

Dizzily they stumbled to their feet, shaking their heads to clear the ringing in their ears. The Doctor rubbed the mud from his eyes and glanced round.

They were completely surrounded by the Kaled patrol, covered by a ring of rifles. The Doctor looked round at the circle of hostile faces. Slowly he raised his hands. Now what was it they said on Earth, back in the Kaiser's day?

The Doctor smiled round at the soldiers. 'Kamerade?' he said hopefully. No one smiled back. The soldiers began to close in.

3

THE SECRET WEAPON

The Doctor and Harry were marched across the Wastelands, into the lift, through the corridors of the Command Centre and back into the room they had just left. Security-Commander Nyder and General Ravon were waiting for them. Nyder was turning over the odds and ends taken from the Doctor's pockets. He held up a small, complex instrument surmounted with a dial. 'What is the function of this object?'

The Doctor leaned forward and examined it. 'Very interesting little gadget, that,' he said chattily. 'Actually it's an etheric beam locator—but you *can* use it for detecting ion-charged emissions.'

Clearly Nyder was none the wiser. 'It is not of Thal manufacture.'

'Well, of course not. My friend and I don't come from your planet.'

Nyder turned the instrument over in his hands. 'I have heard Davros say there is no intelligent life on other planets. And Davros is never wrong—about anything.'

'Then he must be an exceptional man. Even I am occasionally wrong about *some* things. Who is Davros?'

Nyder looked at the Doctor keenly, then realised that the question was genuine. 'Davros is our greatest scientist. He is in charge of all scientific research in the Bunker.'

Ravon, who had been standing by in the background, made an attempt to assert himself. 'They could be mutos, Commander Nyder. Mutos who've managed to develop some kind of technology ...'

Nyder gave him a look of silent contempt, but said nothing. Harry, equally silent up to now, burst out, 'Look here, I wish you wouldn't keep calling us mutos. We don't even know what they are.'

Nyder looked wonderingly at him. 'Mutos are scarred and twisted monsters created by the chemical and radiation weapons used in the early part of this war. They were banished to the Wastelands, where they scavenge like the animals they have become.'

'In other words, you just abandon your genetic wounded?' There was horror in the Doctor's voice.

'The Kaled race *must* be kept pure. The imperfect are rejected, sent into the Wastelands. Some of them survive.'

'That's a very harsh policy.'

Nyder shifted uncomfortably. 'Your views are unimportant,' he said dismissively. 'General Ravon—I am taking these two prisoners for interrogation by the Special Unit.'

'But they are prisoners of the Army ...'

'You will release them to me. The Special Unit will get more out of them than your crude methods.'

Ravon crumpled before the cold authority in Nyder's voice. 'If you insist ...'

'I do insist.' Nyder produced a sheaf of papers from inside his tunic. 'I have a list of supply requirements here. All these items are to be delivered to the Bunker immediately.'

Ravon scanned the list with growing resentment. 'I simply cannot spare this amount of equipment. Your spare-parts requisition alone would take over half my available supply.'

Nyder smiled coldly. 'General Ravon, you will notice that the requisitions are counter-signed by Davros himself. Perhaps you would prefer to discuss the matter with him?'

Ravon shuddered, and shook his head. 'I'll have the supplies at the Bunker by dawn.'

'By midnight, General. The orders specify midnight.'

'Very well. Midnight.'

Nyder turned to the guards. 'Bring the prisoners.'

As they were marched away after him, the Doctor thought that it had been a very interesting demonstration. It was clear that the real power among the Kaleds lay not with the army, but with Davros, and those who served him.

*

Sarah had one of the most horrifying awakenings of her life. Buried beneath a pile of rapidly stiffening corpses, she could feel her face wet with blood. At first she felt confusedly that she must be dead too, or at least badly wounded. But as she struggled groggily to her feet she realised that the blood came from a shallow cut on her forehead. Miraculously, she was more or less unharmed.

She looked around. Along the line of the trench lay still more bodies, sprawled in the grotesque and ungainly attitudes of sudden death. The metal door was closed. There was no sign of the Doctor or Harry. Sarah began to move along the trench calling softly, 'Doctor? Doctor, are you there? Harry?' There was no answer. She paused, thinking. It would do her no good to stay here. She started to climb out of the trench.

Sarah wandered across the Wastelands for what seemed a very long time, with no clear idea of where she was going or why. The grey half-light, combined with the drifting fog, made visibility very low. She stumbled in and out of shell holes, and disentangled herself from clumps of rusting barbed wire. Occasionally she heard distant gunfire, but saw no soldiers. Clearly the battle had moved away from this section of the line. All the time she had a feeling of something following her, of unseen forms creeping towards her. It was this, as much as any real hope of finding the Doctor, that kept her staggering wearily on her way.

As the darkness deepened, the following shapes moved closer. Sarah told herself it was all imagination, but she knew very well it was not. At last she paused exhausted, and a hideous shapeless *something* loomed out of the darkness, reaching for her. Sarah screamed and ran. The shapeless thing pursued her and soon others joined in the chase. She was hunted across the Wastelands, soft footsteps thudding behind her. Fear gave her fresh energy and she ran blindly at full speed, taking no care where she was going. Suddenly the ground vanished beneath her feet … She felt herself falling. It wasn't a long fall, something like five or six feet, and luckily she landed on soft ground. But it was enough to knock the breath out of her. She lay gasping, pressed close to the ground, and to her relief heard the sounds of pursuit pass by.

Scrambling to her feet, Sarah began to take a look at her surroundings. Close by she could just distinguish the outline of a broken wall. She moved towards it and felt her way along. It seemed she had fallen into the basement of a ruined house. She decided she might as well stay. At least the ruins offered a chance of rest and safety. She made her way out of the basement, climbing some broken steps. As she reached the top, Sarah suddenly drew back. She was in a ruined entrance hall. She could see the sky through the broken roof. Light was streaming from a room on the other side of the hall. Sarah crept up cautiously, feeling that she was more likely to meet enemies than friends on this dreadful planet.

Flattening herself against the wall, she peeped into the room. It was a large room, and might once have been some kind of conference chamber. A space had been cleared in the centre of the rubble littered floor, and a portable field-lamp made a central pool of light. On the far edge of the cleared area, a man was setting up a target, a life-sized, wooden cut-out in the shape of a soldier. The man wore the white coat of a scientist. He was tall and thin, and his features had the dark, thin-faced intense look, so typical of most Kaleds.

There was another man in the room, but Sarah was unable to see him clearly. He was on the near side of the pool of light, his back to her, and was almost hidden by shadows. All Sarah could see was the back of an elaborate wheelchair. A withered right hand hovered constantly over the controls built into the chair arm.

The man finished setting up the target. 'I am ready, Davros.' He walked over to stand beside the man in the chair, his back to Sarah.

'Observe the test closely, Gharman, my friend. This will be a moment to live in history.' The voice was almost inhuman, filtered through some mechanical reproduction system. It had a harsh, grating quality that Sarah found familiar. She saw the claw-like hand touch a switch. There was a whirring sound from the outer darkness and something moved into the pool of light. It was a gleaming metal creature with a rounded base. The body was constructed of heavily-studded metal panels, the top was a dome from which projected a lens on a metal stalk. Sarah recognised the creature at once. It was a Dalek.

True, it wasn't a fully-evolved Dalek, the kind she had seen in ruthless action on the planet of the Exxilons. The movements were jerky and the arm with the curious sucker-like tip was missing. But the gun was there, and the eye-stalk ... This must be an early model, a kind of prototype. Sarah realised that the calculations of the Time Lords had been accurate. The Doctor and his friends had been brought to Skaro as the Daleks were about to be born.

Davros was putting the Dalek through its paces. 'Left, left, forward ... now right. Stop.' The Dalek obeyed, its movements faltering and uncertain. Sarah realised now why the voice of Davros had sounded so familiar. It was just like that of the Dalek he had created!

At last Davros had the Dalek position to his satisfaction. It stood in front of his chair, opposite the target on the other side of the room. 'Now,' grated Davros. 'EXTERMINATE!'

The Dalek's gun roared, and the target exploded in flames.

'Excellent,' said Davros. 'Locomotion is still faulty, and we must improve the sense-organs. But the weaponry is perfect. We can begin!'

As Davros's chair swivelled round Sarah jumped back into hiding. Crouched low she saw the shape in the chair glide past her, followed by the Dalek. Gharman came last, carrying the field-lamp. Sarah watched the bobbing light move away across the Wastelands.

She leant against the wall, thinking hard. Obviously she had stumbled on some kind of secret test, and she ought to get the information to the Doctor. But where to look for him? Presumably in the city. Sarah decided to follow Davros. As she started to get up, a huge, misshapen hand reached out of the darkness and touched her lightly on the shoulder. Sarah turned to see the black bulk of a hooded creature looming over her. The shock was too much, and she fainted dead away.

To their surprise, the Doctor and Harry were marched out of the domed city and across several miles of Wasteland. Soon they saw lights ahead, and the shape of a small, low-lying building, a kind of blockhouse. Nyder halted the party by a massive metal door. A voice spoke from a metal grille. 'You will announce your name, rank, serial number, purpose of visit and authorisation reference.'

Nyder glared irritably into what the Doctor guessed must be a hidden camera. 'All right, Tane, use your eyes. This is Security-Commander Nyder with prisoners and escort.'

'Yes, sir,' squawked the voice in evident alarm. Nyder was obviously a character to be feared. The heavy door slid open and they marched through.

They found themselves in a largish ante-room. One wall was filled with complex scientific equipment, and another metal door faced them. Two black-clad officers stood waiting stiffly to attention, one beside the door, the other at a kind of control console. More black-clad guards lined the walls.

Nyder nodded to the first officer. 'Captain Tane, I want these two screened and passed to Ronson. Full interrogation. Here are their belongings.' Handing over a sealed plastic envelope, Nyder turned. The second officer hurriedly touched a control. The inner door opened, revealing a tunnel stretching downwards. Nyder disappeared along it, and the door closed after him. The Doctor gave Harry a reassuring grin. Any situation that started with Nyder leaving couldn't be all bad! He nodded affably to Tane.

'That's a relief. Any chance of a cup of tea?' Tane glared at him speechlessly. 'Any light refreshment would do,' the Doctor added helpfully. 'We've been through some very trying experiences, haven't we, Harry?'

'Very trying, Doctor.' Harry's agreement was heartfelt.

Tane pointed to a sort of upright coffin surrounded with complex instruments. 'Step into the security scan.'

The Doctor glanced at Harry. 'No tea,' he said sadly.

Tane's voice was coldly angry. 'Let me point out to you that you have no rights here. I have full authority to execute any prisoner who does not obey orders.'

Two soldiers seized Harry and shoved him into the scanning device. As soon as he was inside a powerful light shone from above, seeming to pin him down. Harry went rigid, white lights flashed and instruments buzzed all round him.

The lights went out, and Harry staggered out of the machine on the point of collapse. A soldier grabbed him, propped him against the nearest wall, then pushed the Doctor into the machine. Once again the light flashed and the instruments buzzed. But this time there was a new noise; a high-pitched, warning shriek. Tane glanced at the instrument panel. 'Scan detects power-source on prisoner's left wrist.'

The scan was concluded, the machine switched off and the Doctor stepped out. At a nod from Tane two guards grabbed him. 'Remove object on the left wrist of the prisoner.' One of the guards started to wrench away the bangle.

The Doctor struggled wildly. 'You can't have that. It isn't a weapon, and it's of no possible interest to you …'

A brutal blow from the rifle-butt of one of the guards choked off his protest. Tane took the bracelet, then dropped it into the plastic envelope with the Doctor's other odds and ends. The officer in charge of the scanner gave Tane a sheaf of cards, and he put them in the envelope without looking at them.

As he caught hold of the collapsing Doctor, Harry hissed in his ear, 'Stop making a fuss, Doctor.'

'That Time Bracelet is our only hope of getting back to the TARDIS. We've *got* to get it back.'

'I know that,' whispered Harry. 'But we don't want *them* to know, do we?' The Doctor subsided.

Tane turned to the nearest guard. 'These prisoners are to be given over to the custody of Senior Researcher Ronson. Take this with you.' He handed over the plastic envelope.

The two prisoners were taken through the inner door and down the long tunnel. They were led along endless buttressed corridors and into an enormous underground room. Looking around in interest, the Doctor guessed he was in an advanced research laboratory. Or rather a collection of laboratories. The place was sectioned off, and in different cubicles and enclosed areas white-coated scientists were hard at work. They were taken across the room to a corner desk, where a haggard, grey-haired man sat wearily studying some figures. The guards handed over the envelope and the prisoners, then marched away.

Harry and the Doctor stood waiting before the desk. The grey-haired man tipped out the contents of the envelope and examined them. The Doctor's eyes gleamed at the sight of the Time Bracelet and he took a pace forwards, but Harry nudged him, looking round significantly. The huge room had many doors, but armed guards stood at every one.

The man behind the desk looked up. 'My name is Ronson,' he said. 'Do sit down.' Harry and the Doctor, taken aback by the first kind words they'd heard on Skaro, pulled over a couple of metal chairs and sank into them gratefully.

'Thank you. I take it you're not with the military?' the Doctor asked hopefully.

'I am a member of the Special Scientific Division.'

'Excellent. Perhaps we can have a conversation that isn't punctuated by rifle-butts.' The Doctor rubbed his aching back.

A little shamefacedly Ronson said, 'That depends. If you don't answer my questions satisfactorily, I must hand you back to the Security Guards.' As if glad to leave a distasteful subject, he turned to the objects on his desk. 'Where did you get these things?'

The Doctor smiled. 'Oh, here and there. Different places, different times.'

'If I didn't know better,' said Ronson slowly, 'I would swear they were produced on some other planet. But it's an established scientific fact that Skaro is the only planet capable of supporting life.'

'Suppose there are more planets than you're aware of?' suggested the Doctor gently.

Ronson picked up the batch of coded cards. 'When you went through the scanner the instruments checked your physical make-up—encephalographical patterns, physiological composition and so on. So if you are from another world ...' His voice faded away as he studied the cards.

'You were saying?' asked the Doctor politely.

Ronson looked up with awe in his eyes. '*His* make-up,' he nodded towards Harry, 'is comparable to ours, with a few minor differences. But yours ... Nothing conforms to any known life-form on this planet. *Nothing*—except the external appearance.'

'Just goes to show—you should never judge by appearances.'

Ronson leaned forward. 'Who are you? Where do you come from? Tell me.' The Doctor recognised pure scientific curiosity in Ronson's voice.

'It's a very long story. Do you have any knowledge of the Theory of Space Dimension Co-related to Relative Time?'

The Doctor was interrupted by a low gonging sound. Every single scientist, Ronson included, reacted with eager attention. The sound stopped and a voice said, 'Davros will address the Elite Scientific

Corps in the main laboratory assembly.' Almost at once more white-coated scientists began to enter the room, workers from the adjoining laboratories.

'Our session will have to wait,' Ronson said. 'Davros is coming.' His voice was hushed with reverence.

'I gather Davros is your Chief Scientist?'

'Our Chief Scientist and our supreme commander. He must have something of importance to tell us.'

'I shall be interested to meet him,' said the Doctor politely. But even he was not prepared for the strange apparition that glided into the room. The Doctor was seeing, at close range and in clear lighting, the strange being Sarah had only glimpsed during the secret test in the ruined building.

Davros was no more than the shattered, ruined remnant of what had once been a man. He glided along in an advanced form of wheelchair that moved under its own power. The withered husk of a body was swathed in a high-collared, green plastic overall, and surrounded by a variety of life-support systems. The Doctor guessed that both heart and lungs were mechanically operated and maintained. Only the right hand was visible, a withered claw hovering constantly over the controls built into one arm of the chair. But the most horrifying thing about Davros was his face. Parchment-thin skin clung to the outlines of the shrivelled skull. The eye-sockets were blank and sunken, the mouth a lipless slit. A helmet-like arrangement of wires and plastic tubes surmounted the head, supporting a single lens that rested in the centre of the forehead. Speech, sight and hearing must be mechanically aided too, thought the Doctor.

Harry Sullivan looked at Davros in horror. 'What happened to the poor devil?'

'An atomic shell struck his laboratory during a Thal bombardment,' whispered Ronson. 'His body was shattered, but he *refused* to die. He clung to life, and himself designed the mobile life-support system in which you see him.'

Harry said nothing. To himself he thought that death would surely be preferable to the kind of existence Davros must be leading now.

Davros had taken up his position in the centre of the far wall, flanked by the black-clad figure of Security-Commander Nyder.

Davros spoke. 'If I may have your attention ...' There was utter and complete silence. Helpless in his chair, Davros should have been pitiful. Instead, he was terrifying. The Doctor could almost feel the burning intelligence, the powerful, inflexible will that radiated from the crippled form. 'For some time,' Davros continued, 'I have been busy on a top secret project. There is still much to be done. However, I am anxious that you should see the remarkable progress made so far, and to that end I have arranged this demonstration.' Davros wheeled his chair to face the door by which he had entered. His withered hand dropped to touch a control, and seconds later a metallic shape glided into the room. Like Sarah before him, the Doctor had no difficulty in recognising a Dalek. Armless, weaponless, but still unmistakably a Dalek.

As the machine glided up to Davros, his metallic voice commanded, 'Halt.' The Dalek stopped.

'He's perfected voice-control,' breathed Ronson. 'That's magnificent.'

'Move left. Halt. Move forward. Halt. Circle. Halt.' Obedient to Davros's commands the Dalek moved jerkily about the room.

'Nyder!' The Security-Commander stepped forward. He took a sucker arm and a gun, and fitted them on to the Dalek. 'As you see,' grated Davros, 'our machine is now fitted with a tactile organ and a means of self-defence. I shall turn the machine over to total self-control. It will then be independent of all outside influence. A living, thinking, self-supporting creature.'

Davros touched a switch. For a moment the Dalek did nothing. Then, slowly and uncertainly, it began to move around the room. Davros followed in his wheelchair. Somehow the two were curiously alike. Suddenly the Dalek seemed to see the Doctor. It moved slowly towards his corner, halting just in front of him. The Doctor stood quite still.

'Alien,' croaked the Dalek suddenly. 'Exterminate ... exterminate ... exterminate!' Slowly the gun stick raised until it was pointing straight at the Doctor.

4

ROCKET OF DOOM

Nobody moved. It was clear to everyone in the room that the Dalek intended to kill the Doctor. Suddenly Ronson darted forward and flicked one of the switches on Davros's console. Immediately the Dalek 'switched off', gun arm and eye-stalk drooping.

Davros was furious. 'You dare to interfere! You have the audacity to interrupt my experiment!'

Ronson was clearly terrified but he made himself speak out. 'It was going to destroy him.'

'And you consider his worthless life more important than the progress we have made? My creature showed a natural instinct to destroy everything alien—and you interceded.'

'Davros ... I'm sorry,' pleaded Ronson. 'But this is no ordinary prisoner. I believe he has invaluable information. Let me interrogate him first—then your creature can do what it likes with him.'

Davros considered. 'Very well. You will be punished later for your insubordination. Meanwhile you may interrogate your prisoner until the end of this work-period. After that, I shall resume my experiment.'

Davros wheeled and glided away. Ronson heaved a sigh of relief. The Doctor took a deep breath. 'Thank you,' he said simply.

Ronson seemed hardly able to believe his own temerity. 'I was simply doing my duty. Now you must co-operate with me. If you don't provide knowledge to justify what I have done, Davros will resume his experiment as threatened.'

Nyder crossed over to them. 'Take the prisoners to the cells. You can finish the questioning there. Davros wants them kept safely.'

As the guards bustled them away, the Doctor glanced longingly behind him. The Time Ring still lay among the odds and ends on Ronson's desk ...

Sarah's faint lasted only a few minutes. She awoke furious with herself—she'd always believed she was the sort of girl who never fainted. As consciousness returned, she heard low whispering voices. She decided to fake unconsciousness a little longer. Two cloaked and hooded figures were crouched beside her, one huge and massive, one thin and spindly. The big one touched her cheek with a misshapen hand. Sarah lay perfectly still. When the figure spoke, its voice was deep and gentle. 'She is beautiful ... no deformities or imperfections.'

The smaller figure had a shrill whining voice. 'She is a norm, Sevrin. All norms are our enemies. Kill her.'

'Why?' asked the deep voice sadly. 'Why must we always destroy beauty, kill another creature because it is different?'

'Kill her,' the other voice insisted. 'It is the law. All norms must die. If you will not kill her, I will.' The creature produced a knife from under its cloak and long, incredibly thin arms snaked out towards Sarah.

Sevrin moved protectively in front of her, grabbing the knife-wrist. For a moment the two creatures struggled. They broke apart as they heard footsteps and muffled voices. 'A patrol,' muttered Sevrin. 'They're sure to check the building.'

The smaller creature squeaked in panic. 'We must get away.'

'No,' said the deep voice authoritatively. 'Keep still. If you move they'll see you.'

But the slighter figure was already on the move, scuttling spider-like along the wall. From the darkness a voice yelled, 'Halt!'

The glare of a spotlight pinned the shuffling figure. 'Don't move,' ordered the voice, and the sound of booted feet came closer. Suddenly the spindly creature made a run for it. A single shot rang out and it dropped to the ground. Two fair-haired Thal soldiers came forward, one carrying a hand-beam, the other an old-fashioned single-shot rifle. The first shone his light on their kill. 'Only a muto. You wasted your ammunition.'

The soldier with the rifle began to reload. His companion swept the torch-beam along the wall. 'Here, there's a couple more of 'em.'

The torch-beam lit up Sevrin crouching over Sarah's body. The soldier with the rifle took aim, but the other stopped him. 'Hold it. Remember orders. They need expendable labour for the rocket loading.' He shone the torch on Sevrin, pulling the mutant to his feet. 'This one's not so bad. Got all it needs to walk and carry.' Sevrin stood meekly, making no attempt to resist. The soldier shone the lamp down on Sarah. 'No reason this one can't work. Looks almost a norm.' He poked her in the ribs with his foot. 'Come on you, up you get.'

Sarah got slowly to her feet. So much had happened since she'd come to that she was still confused. She staggered a little as she stood up. The soldier with the rifle called, 'No good, this one's too weak and slow. Better let me finish it off.' He raised his rifle.

Sevrin stepped in front of Sarah, shielding her. 'She'll be all right, I promise. I'll help her.'

The soldier hesitated, then nodded. 'All right. Then move.' He gestured with the rifle. Sarah stumbled into the darkness, Sevrin supporting her.

She felt better once she was moving, and was soon able to walk unaided. The soldiers herded them across the Wastelands for what seemed a very long way, until at last they came to within sight of a huge dome-covered city. It was very like the one Sarah had seen earlier with the Doctor and Harry, though the design was slightly different. She nudged Sevrin. 'Where's that?'

He looked at her in surprise. 'It is the city of the Thals.'

They were taken through a guarded access tunnel, along endless concrete corridors, and herded into a huge, bare cell. Small groups of prisoners like themselves were scattered all over the room. Most were cloaked and hooded like Sevrin—mutos, as the soldiers had called them. But there was also a sprinkling of raggedly-uniformed, dark-haired Kaled soldiers. Sarah supposed they must be prisoners of war.

Sarah and Sevrin joined the rest of the prisoners, slumping down on the floor, backs against the wall. Sarah looked round and shivered. 'I wonder why they've brought us here?'

'I heard the soldiers say they needed workers for their rocket project. I don't mind working. They may even feed us.'

A nearby prisoner leaned across to them. He was a Kaled soldier, very young with a bleak, bitter face. Although neither of them realised it, he and Sarah had met before. The Kaled had been leader of the patrol which had emerged from the Kaled dome to capture Harry and the Doctor. Later he had been captured himself by a Thal raiding party. He gave Sevrin and Sarah a pitying look. 'You'll work all right, muto. On the kind of job that kills you just as sure as a bullet will.'

'What work?' asked Sarah.

The young Kaled seemed to take a gloomy pleasure in breaking the bad news. 'The Thals have built a rocket. Used up the last of their manpower and resources in one final gamble. If they manage to launch it they'll wipe out the Kaled city and most of the Kaled race in one blow.'

Sarah gave him a puzzled look. 'So what are we needed for?'

'They're packing the nose-cone of the rocket with distronic explosives. To reduce weight, they're using no protective shielding. Every load we carry exposes us to distronic radiation. After two or three shifts you feel weaker. Eventually you die!'

Sarah looked at him in horror. Before she could speak a siren blared out and the prisoners shuffled wearily to their feet. She turned to the Kaled. 'What's that?'

'Rest period's over—time to start loading again.'

A Thal guard came over and prodded them to their feet with his rifle. 'All right,' snapped Sarah. 'No need to push!' She joined the long line of prisoners shuffling out of the door. Already her mind was busy with thoughts of escape.

The prisoners were marched through corridors and tunnels and finally into a huge concrete enclosure.

Sarah caught her breath. Towering far above them was the deadly silver shape of the Thal rocket. The base of the rocket was supported by a framework of scaffolding, its nose-cone touched the roof far above their heads. Sarah guessed that a section of the dome would slide back at the moment of firing. Meanwhile the rocket was securely hidden inside the Thal city dome.

Sarah noticed that the guards in here wore all-over radiation suits, gauntlets and masks. She saw too that there was a dial inset in one wall, and that the final third of it was shaded red—presumably for the danger zone.

A steel door slid back and a small lifting-truck emerged, driven by a radiation-suited guard. The truck was loaded with ingots of some dull, silvery metal, and as soon as it entered the rocket silo, the needle on the radiation dial began climbing slowly towards the danger area.

By now the prisoners had been formed into a line, with Sarah and Sevrin somewhere near the end. One by one the prisoners lifted an ingot from the truck and, hugging it to their bodies, staggered over to the doors in the base of the rocket. When it came to Sevrin's turn, he lifted the ingot with ease and set off with it. Sarah was next. She hesitated, reluctant to touch the ingot, but a guard threatened with his rifle, and she was forced to pick it up. It was astonishingly heavy for its size and she had to hug it to her body to carry it. The ingot in her arms, Sarah stumbled towards the rocket doors.

In a tiny windowless cell in the Kaled bunker, Harry Sullivan sat on a bunk and waited. It seemed ages since they had taken the Doctor away. The longer Harry waited, the more worried he became. At last he heard the thump of booted feet in the corridor outside. The cell door clanged open and the Doctor was shoved in by a guard, who promptly shut and locked the door behind him. The Doctor threw himself on the bunk with a groan of relief. Harry perched on the metal stool beside him. 'How did you get on, Doctor? Are you all right?'

The Doctor gave him a weary nod.

'Did you tell them anything?'

The Doctor managed to grin. 'I told them *everything*, every bit of scientific gobbledygook I could think of. They took *reams* of notes. Their scientific experts will be confused for *weeks!*' The Doctor chuckled. 'I learned more from them than they did from me!'

'What about this Bunker, Doctor? Where are we? What's it all for?'

'Most of the place is underground, like these cells. It's a few miles from the main Kaled dome, bomb-proof and completely impregnable to attack.'

'What are they all doing here?'

The Doctor yawned and stretched, rubbing his bruises. Harry guessed that the security guards had given him the occasional thump to loosen his tongue.

'Years ago the Kaled Government decided to form an Elite Corps. All their leading scientists, plus security men to protect them. Over the years, this Elite has become so powerful that now it can demand anything it wants ...'

The Doctor stopped talking as they heard someone approaching outside. 'Perhaps it's the tea,' he said hopefully.

The door opened and Ronson appeared in the doorway, a guard behind him. He entered the cell and turned to the guard. 'It's all right, you needn't wait.' The man hesitated and Ronson snapped, 'I am armed. You can stay on duty outside.' The guard nodded and closed the door. Ronson looked at the Doctor stretched out on his bunk. 'I hope they didn't hurt you too much. I'm afraid I was unable to interfere.'

The Doctor waved a dismissive hand. 'I'm all right. The main thing is that you saved me from being the very first victim of a Dalek!'

Ronson started. 'How did you know that name? Just a few minutes ago, Davros announced that his new device would be known as a Dalek—an anagram of Kaled, the name of our race.'

'I have a certain advantage, in terms of time,' said the Doctor solemnly. 'In fact the reason I came was because of—well, let's say *future concern* about the development of the Daleks.'

Ronson sank wearily on to the end of the bunk. 'I too am concerned,' he confessed. 'Others feel the same, but we are powerless.'

The Doctor sat up, leaning towards him. 'Perhaps I can help. But you'll have to trust me.'

Ronson glanced towards the cell door and dropped his voice. 'We believe that Davros has changed the direction of his research into something immoral. The Elite Corps was formed to produce weapons that would win this war. But soon we saw that was futile. Already the weapons used had begun to cause genetic changes. We were forced to turn our attention to the survival of our race.'

The Doctor nodded grimly. 'Meanwhile the early products of these genetic changes—the mutos—were banished to the Wastelands?'

'That's right. Davros believed this trend was irreversible, so he decided to work *with* it, to produce accelerated mutations in an effort to find our final mutated form. He produced what he calls the ultimate creature.' Ronson rose to his feet. 'Come with me, Doctor.' He rapped on the door and the guard opened it. 'I require the assistance of these prisoners in certain top-secret experiments. You will release them into my custody.'

The guard looked doubtful, but the habit of obedience to the Scientific Elite was too strong in him. Dismissing the guard, Ronson led Harry and the Doctor in another direction. He took them along dimly-lit passages to a short corridor. The roof was supported by heavy buttresses jutting out from the walls. The corridor ended in a massive metal door in which was set a small viewing-panel, covered by a shutter.

Ronson pulled the shutter to one side, revealing a thickly-glassed window. From inside it came a pulsating green glow. 'Take a look, Doctor.'

The Doctor peered through the little window then hurriedly stepped back. Harry saw the look of revulsion on his face but couldn't resist taking a quick look through the panel. He caught a fleeting glimpse of long rows of tanks, holding twisted, hideously deformed shapes. Then the Doctor moved him aside, sliding the shutter closed. 'I shouldn't, Harry. Not unless you want to lay in a permanent stock of nightmares.'

Ronson looked at them, and Harry saw the bitterness in his face. 'You see, Doctor? If Davros has his way, that is our future. *That* is what the Kaleds will become!'

In the big communal cell, Sarah was trying to whip up a spirit of revolt. 'Look,' she said fiercely. 'We have to do something *now*. A few more shifts and we won't have the strength. We've *got* to get out of here.'

The young Kaled patrol leader glanced across at the doors. 'That's just not possible.'

Sarah looked at the guards. They were leaning against the doors, rifles held casually in the crooks of their arms. 'Oh yes, it is. Those guards aren't expecting any trouble—not from a group of worn-out slave-workers.'

'Supposing we do get out—we'll only be in the rocket silo. The exit from that goes through a Thal command point—and that'll be crawling with troops.'

'There's another way out from the silo,' replied Sarah. 'Straight up! The scaffolding goes right up to the nose-cone of the rocket. From there we could get out on to the surface of the dome, then climb down to the ground.'

Beside them the giant mutant Sevrin sat huddled beneath his all-concealing cloak and hood. 'Climb that scaffolding,' he protested mildly. 'It's very high.'

'I know,' said Sarah gently. 'I don't exactly fancy it myself. But it's our only chance to survive.' She had endured one long work-shift lugging the metal ingots into the rocket's storage chamber. The Kaled soldier had explained that while the first few shifts produced only normal fatigue, further exposure would begin a dangerous build-up of radiation effect in the body. Sarah was prepared to face any risk rather than that.

The patrol leader had already endured several shifts, and his face was grey and drawn. 'Why not,' he muttered. 'Better to take a chance than rot away here.'

'All right,' whispered Sarah. 'Now—move round among the others. Recruit as many as you can!'

Guards came in with cauldrons of grey, mushy porridge, food providing the absolute minimum of nourishment, just enough to enable the prisoners to work. Bowlfuls of the stuff were passed out and the prisoners ate greedily with their fingers, afterwards licking the bowls till they were clean. During the general confusion produced by this 'feeding time', Sevrin and the young Kaled moved among the prisoners, explaining their plan for a breakout. Some prisoners fled from them in terror, others just stared blankly. But here and there they found some willing to listen. There were still a few whose spirits were not completely broken.

When feeding was over and the bowls handed in, the three conspirators met in a corner. 'Well?' asked Sarah.

The Kaled soldier nodded fiercely. 'Some of my men were captured with me. They'll fight. So will most of the other soldiers.'

Sevrin however shook his head. 'The mutos are too frightened,' he explained sadly. 'We are always frightened. But I will help.'

'We'll just have to do the best we can,' Sarah said. 'Once we get started the rest will probably join in.'

The first part of the breakout was surprisingly easy. Sarah, Sevrin and the more aggressive prisoners all drifted slowly towards the door. When Sarah was opposite the nearest guard she stumbled and fell against him, pretending to faint. Instinctively the guard grabbed her—and the Kaled soldier chopped him down from behind. Before the second guard could react Sevrin sprang upon him, lifted him high in the air and dashed him to the ground. He stood looking at the motionless body as if astonished by his own daring.

'Come on,' yelled Sarah. 'Quickly!' She threw open the doors and the prisoners streamed out, overwhelming the guards on the other side. The breakout had begun!

5

ESCAPE TO DANGER

The Doctor, Harry and Ronson were hurrying along the corridors beneath the Bunker. From time to time a passing guard glanced curiously at them, but the presence of one of the Scientific Elite proved a good enough passport. They talked in low voices as they walked. Ronson went on with his explanations. 'Davros says that having evolved our ultimate form, he then created a travel machine in which to house it.'

The Doctor nodded. 'And the two combined have produced a living weapon—the Daleks! He's created a monster utterly devoid of conscience. Are you prepared to help me stop him?'

'I must,' said Ronson simply. 'There are those in the Kaled government who may still have the strength to act. If they knew the full truth they could end Davros's power, close down the Bunker and disband the Elite. I myself am not allowed to leave the Bunker ... But you two might make it.'

'Help us to escape,' urged the Doctor. 'Give me the names of the men you speak of and I promise you I'll make them listen.'

Was it going to be as easy as that, Harry wondered. He turned to Ronson. '*Can* you really get us out?'

'One of the ventilation-system ducts leads to a cave on the edge of the Wastelands. The exit is barred, but you might get through. But there's an added danger ...'

'I knew it,' said Harry. 'Go on.'

'Some of Davros's early experiments were with our wild animals. Horrific monsters were created—some of them were allowed to live as a controlled experiment.'

'Don't tell me—they're in this cave we go through?'

Ronson nodded. Harry sighed. It certainly wasn't going to be so easy!

Ronson led them through smaller and smaller corridors, until they came to a short rock-walled tunnel. It ended in a blank wall into which was set a ventilation-duct, just large enough to admit a human body. A metal hatch covered the duct. It was stiff with disuse, and it took the Doctor and Harry quite a time to wrench it open.

As they worked, Ronson was scribbling rapidly in a plastic-covered notebook. The hatch creaked open and he handed the book to the Doctor. 'I've written down the names of all the people you should try to contact giving the facts about Davros's research, and I've added a note of introduction to confirm your story ... If anything goes wrong ...'

'Don't worry, I'll see it's all destroyed.' The Doctor knew that with the notebook Ronson was placing his life in their hands.

Harry jumped up to the opening and wriggled through into the cramped tunnel. Ronson helped the Doctor to climb in after him. 'Hurry,' he gasped. 'I think someone's coming. Good luck!'

The Doctor's long legs disappeared into the duct and Ronson slammed the hatch-cover closed behind them.

He turned and hurried back down the tunnel. At the point where the tunnel joined the main corridor, he ran straight into a patrolling guard. The guard was surprised to see an eminent scientist leaving what was essentially a maintenance area, but Ronson looked haughtily at him, and the man went on his way. Concealing a sigh of relief, Ronson headed back to his laboratory.

In the ventilation duct, Harry and the Doctor edged their way through total darkness. Harry didn't know which to worry about most, the perils behind them or the dangers ahead.

A yelling crowd of prisoners burst out of the cell and milled round the base of the giant rocket. Some began running blindly towards the exits, only to encounter Thal guards running out from their command posts. The guards started shooting wildly into the crowd.

Sarah saw the young Kaled soldier fall early in the mêlée, but the giant form of Sevrin was still at her side. Together they pushed their way to the scaffolding and began climbing. Up and up they climbed, hand over hand until Sarah's arms were aching and the sounds of shooting and yelling seemed faint and distant. Gasping for breath, Sarah made the mistake of looking down. She hadn't realised how far they'd come, and the dizzying drop below her made everything spin round. Luckily Sevrin was close enough to lean across and grab her arm. 'Don't look down, Sarah. And keep climbing.'

Something bounced off the metal scaffolding near Sarah's head and whined away into space. She looked down and caught a brief glimpse of a Thal guard, his rifle pointing upwards. 'They're shooting at us,' she gasped. 'Come on.'

By now other prisoners were following their example, swarming up the scaffolding like monkeys. Many were picked off by the rifles of the Thal guards and crashed to the ground at the base of the rocket. Others were luckier, and the Thal Guard Captain soon realised there was real danger that many of his prisoners might get away. As more reinforcements arrived to deal with the prisoners, he slung his rifle over his shoulder and assembled a small group of reluctant soldiers. 'Come on—we're going up after them.' The soldiers began to climb.

High on the scaffolding, the nose-cone very close now, Sarah hung gasping. 'It's no good. I can't climb any more.'

Sevrin was close behind her. There seemed to be enormous strength in the great twisted body, and he could swing ape-like along the scaffolding with no sign of fatigue. 'You must go on, Sarah. See, they are coming after us.'

Sarah glanced down to see Thal soldiers swarming up the scaffolding in pursuit. Stronger and better fed than their escaping prisoners, they were catching up rapidly. Sarah started to climb again, but her tired sweating hands slipped on the scaffolding. She felt herself dropping into space. A sudden jerk arrested her fall. Sevrin had caught her arm, taking her whole weight with one hand while he clung to the scaffolding with his other. Sarah swung back close to the scaffolding and managed to find a fresh hold. She glanced down again. Because of the delay, the pursuing Thals were now much closer. Yet the narrow escape had stiffened Sarah's determination not to be recaptured; she began climbing even higher. There wasn't far to go.

At the top of the scaffolding, Sevrin was waiting for her. They were right by the nose-cone of the rocket, and the roof of the dome was only a few feet away. 'Look, Sarah. There's a section of the dome that slides away. We could reach it from the tip of the nose-cone and get out!'

'How do we get on to the nose-cone?'

'We'll have to jump for it—I'll go first, then I can catch you.'

Sevrin poised himself for a moment, then leaped like a giant spider across the gap between the scaffolding and the nose-cone. He landed spread-eagled on the very tip of the rocket, hands scrabbling for a hold on the smoothly polished metal. When he felt secure he yelled. 'It's all right, Sarah. Jump and I'll catch you.'

Sarah looked across. The gap seemed enormous, and stretching down below her was the entire length of the huge rocket. The figures round its base seemed like tiny moving dots. She clung to the scaffolding, shivering with fear.

'You've got to do it,' called Sevrin. 'Jump!'

Sarah looked down again. The pursuing Thal soldiers were very close. She jumped. She hit the nose-cone with a thump, and immediately started sliding off, but one of Sevrin's huge hands caught her and dragged her to safety on its rounded tip. A narrow ledge gave a foothold. 'We're nearly there,' he muttered reassuringly. 'Just a bit more and we'll be on the dome surface. We'll be safe.' Slowly Sevrin climbed to his feet. Balancing precariously on the very tip of the rocket's nose-cone he slid back the panel in the dome. Sarah felt a rush of cold air and saw the night sky through the gap. Sevrin had one hand on the edge of the gap, and was reaching down to pull Sarah through when a voice called out, 'That's far enough.'

The Thal soldiers had caught up with them. The Guard Captain was clinging to the scaffolding with one hand, levelling his rifle at them with the other. Close to him, the rest of his men were doing the same. 'Right,' he ordered. 'Back on the scaffolding.'

Sevrin sighed. Releasing his grip on the opening he took a flying leap and landed back on the scaffolding. Immediately a Thal soldier jammed a rifle in his ribs. 'Start climbing. No tricks, or you'll go down the quick way.' Obediently Sevrin started to descend.

The Guard Captain turned to Sarah. 'Now you.'

Hanging grimly on to the nose-cone, Sarah didn't dare move. 'All right,' said the Captain softly, 'I'll come and get you.' He leaped confidently across the gap and landed on the rounded tip of the rocket where Sevrin had stood a moment earlier. 'Take my hand,' he ordered. Sarah reached up and he grasped her wrist. Suddenly he jerked. Sarah's feet slid from her precarious foothold. She was dangling over empty space supported by the Captain's hand.

The Guard Captain knew he would be punished because of the prisoners' revolt, and the knowledge made him cruel. He grinned down at Sarah. 'All I have to do is slacken my grip ... They say people who fall from great heights are dead before they hit the ground. I don't believe that, do you?' He pretended to let Sarah go and she moaned in fear. Tiring of his game the Captain pulled her back to safety. 'Don't worry, you're going back to work. Before long you'll wish I *had* let you drop.' He called across to one of the soldiers. 'Better throw a rope over, or this one will never make it down.' As the rope was lashed round her Sarah felt only relief. The escape had failed—but she was still alive.

Harry felt the journey through the cramped dark tunnel was never going to end. Maybe they were lost, he thought, maybe they'd die here in these tunnels. Suddenly he felt cold, damp air, and saw a dim glow of light. 'I think we're nearly there, Doctor,' he called behind him. The tunnel widened a little towards its end, which was blocked by heavy wire mesh.

The Doctor squeezed up beside Harry. 'That must be the entrance to the cave. So all we've got to do is ...' A snuffling grunt came out of the darkness.

'Must be one of Davros's little pets,' Harry whispered nervously. They waited in silence. Something big and shapeless brushed past the other side of the grille, and they heard it shamble away into the darkness. They waited a moment longer.

'Well, whatever it was, it's gone,' the Doctor said cheerfully. 'Give me a hand, Harry.' Using their combined strength, they managed to prise off the grille.

'After you, Doctor,' said Harry politely.

The Doctor grinned and slipped into the cave. Harry followed him. The cave was very dark, and he was aware of little more than a dank rock wall close beside him. But there did seem to be a lighter patch somewhere in the distance. The Doctor tapped his shoulder. 'Keep close to the wall, Harry, and make for the light.'

As they shuffled along, Harry was almost grateful for the darkness. Whatever was in the cave, he thought he'd be a lot happier if he *didn't* see it. They reached the light source without incident. It proved to be a very small barred window looking out on to the Wastelands.

'We've made it,' said Harry exultantly. 'Come on, Doctor.' He hurried towards the window. The Doctor was peering cautiously at the ground just beneath the window. A giant round shape was half-buried in the ground.

'Harry, be careful—' the Doctor called. But he was too late. The hump seemed to split into two separate halves. They widened like gaping jaws and clashed down on Harry's leg. Harry let out a howl of pain and the Doctor ran to his side.

Harry's leg was gripped tight by what appeared to be a kind of giant clam, several feet across. Hissing fiercely the creature was trying to drag Harry into the darkness of the cave, no doubt hoping to digest him at leisure. The Doctor grabbed a chunk of rock and hammered at the shell, but it was iron-hard. Remorselessly the sliding horror dragged Harry further away. The Doctor glanced round for a weapon. He saw a jagged spear-like piece of rock projecting from one wall. Using his rock as a hammer he broke it away, ran back to Harry and jammed the improvised spear into the gap in the giant shell. He rammed the sharp stone deep inside the clam, using all his strength. With a hiss of pain, the 'jaws' sprang open. Harry fell backwards, free, and the creature slithered away in the darkness.

The Doctor knelt beside Harry who was moaning and clutching his leg. He made a brief examination. 'Nasty bruise there, but nothing seems to be broken,' he said briskly. 'You had a lucky escape, Harry. That must have been one of Davros's nastier experiments.'

Harry rubbed his leg tenderly. 'Why is it always me who puts his foot in it?' he grumbled.

The Doctor slapped him on the back. 'You'll be all right, Harry. Can you walk yet?'

'Just about.' Harry hobbled a few steps.

'Then we'd better get out of here. It's not a place to hang about.'

As they wrenched at the rusting bars in the window Harry said, 'When we're out in the Wastelands, Doctor, can't we have a look for Sarah?'

The Doctor shook his head. 'At the moment we're just a couple of fugitives. We'd be shot or imprisoned in no time. There's still a war going on, remember. But if we warn the Kaled Government about Davros—well, they'll owe us a favour, won't they? We can ask for an official search.'

Harry looked worried and the Doctor gave him a reassuring grin.

'Don't worry, Harry, we'll find her, I promise you. But one problem at a time. And our problem now is to get past these bars.'

In the Bunker's main laboratory, Davros was holding a demonstration. This time *two* Daleks were gliding backwards and forwards along the laboratory. They completed a complicated sequence of evolutions, then came to a halt before Davros's chair. The granting voice of the nearer one said, 'We await your commands.'

Chillingly like that of his creation, the voice of Davros spoke, 'No further command. Disengage automotive circuits.' The lights on the Daleks' heads went out, their guns and sucker-arms drooped. 'Excellent,' said Davros in a satisfied voice.

One of his retinue of scientists, a plump, smooth little man called Kavell, leaned forward obsequiously. 'They are perfect, Davros. A truly brilliant creation.'

The rasping voice corrected him. 'A brilliant creation, yes. But not perfect. Scientist-Technicians!' Davros raised his hand and a group of younger men hurried forward. 'Improvements must be made in the optical systems and the sensory circuits. Their instincts must be as accurate as any scientific instrument. Work will begin at once. You will carry out the following adjustments ...'

As Davros's voice droned on, Kavell slipped away from the group and moved across to the corner desk where Ronson sat working. He peered over Ronson's shoulders as if checking his results, and said quietly, 'Does Davros know that your two alien prisoners have escaped?'

Ronson glanced up quickly, then went on with his work. 'As far as I know the prisoners are in their cell.'

'Don't worry, Ronson, I won't betray you. You're not the only one worried about Davros's plans. Now answer me. Does Davros know?'

'The prisoners are in their cell,' repeated Ronson. He didn't trust Kavell enough to make any damaging admissions.

The plump little man chuckled. 'I have some news for you, Ronson. Your two prisoners have managed to cross the Wastelands and make contact with certain members of the Government.'

'How do you know that?'

Kavell smiled complacently. 'There are still some advantages to being in charge of the communications system.' He looked across the laboratory to where Davros sat surrounded by his admiring assistants. 'All we can do now is hope that your friends manage to convince our leaders that Davros's work must be ended.'

Kavell walked away, and Ronson buried his head in his hands. 'They must succeed,' he muttered to himself. 'They *must*!'

In the Kaled City, Harry Sullivan sat in a luxurious underground conference room, scarcely able to believe what was happening. Only the Doctor could possibly have managed it, thought Harry. No one else would have the cheek!

When the window bars had finally given way, the Doctor had led Harry across the Wastelands to one of the main entrances to the Kaled City. Marching straight up to an astonished sentry, the Doctor had demanded to see his superior officer. Then he had bullied his way up the chain of command, intimidating a Captain, a Colonel and finally a full-blown General, with impressive but vague talk of a vitally important top-secret mission, and repeated demands to be put in touch with certain important members of the Kaled Government, dropping their names freely, as if they were old friends.

Several times Harry felt that various officers had been on the point of having them shot, but the Doctor's bare-faced audacity had at last succeeded. They had been granted an interview with Mogran, one of the names on Ronson's list.

Mogran had listened sceptically at first, then with increasing concern. He had studied the letter and the details of Davros's experiments in Ronson's notebook. Finally he had summoned a secret meeting in this hidden conference room.

Now Mogran was addressing his fellow councillors, while the Doctor waited beside him. Harry was amused to see that Ravon, the young General from whom they'd first escaped, was also at the meeting, puzzled to find his former prisoners being treated as honoured guests.

Mogran, an impressively robed figure with silver hair, was concluding his speech, '... and it is only because I am personally convinced of both the accuracy and importance of the Doctor's information that I ask you to listen to him now. Doctor?'

The Doctor stepped forward, as relaxed and authoritative as the guest-of-honour on some state occasion. 'Some of what I am about to tell you concerns events in the future. Events not only on this planet, but on other planets whose existence is not even known to you ...'

A murmur of surprise went up from the audience. The Doctor raised his hand. 'I realise that may be hard to accept, but my knowledge is based firmly on scientific fact. I *know* that Davros is creating a machine creature, a monster that will terrorise and destroy millions. He has given this vile creature a name—a name that is a distortion of that of your own race—DALEK! The word is new to you, but for a thousand generations it will bring fear and terror.' The Doctor paused impressively. 'Davros has one of the finest scientific minds in existence. But he has a fanatical desire to perpetuate himself in his creation. He is without conscience, without soul and without pity, and his creations are equally devoid of these qualities ...'

As the Doctor went on with his speech, Harry slumped down in his seat. Would the Doctor be able to convince them? The fate of this world, and of many more, depended on his success ...

6

BETRAYAL

Davros watched with satisfaction as a team of scientists and technicians toiled to make the improvements he had demanded for his Daleks. Through the vision-lens that provided him with sight, he saw Security-Commander Nyder enter the laboratory and come towards him. Davros wheeled his chair to a secluded corner, and Nyder joined him. He leaned forward urgently, keeping his voice low. 'Davros, I've just had word from one of our supporters in the Government. Your old enemy Councillor Mogran has called a meeting. Only known opponents of your Scientific Elite have been invited to attend.'

Davros clenched and unclenched his withered hand. 'I want a full report of everything that's discussed. I don't care how you get the information ... just get it!' After a moment he went on more calmly. 'I don't think we need be too concerned. Many times in the past fifty years opponents in the Government have tried to interfere with my research. They have always failed – they will fail again.'

'There's something else,' Nyder said. 'The two alien prisoners left in Ronson's charge. They are attending the meeting.'

Davros turned his chair so that he could see Ronson working in the corner. Nyder followed the direction of his gaze. 'What action shall I take concerning the traitor Ronson?' The lipless mouth of Davros twitched in what might have been a smile.

'For the moment, none. I shall deal with him in my own way.'

The meeting was drawing to its close. The Kaled politicians were talking among themselves, occasionally glancing across to the Doctor and Harry. General Ravon, who seemed to take no part in the deliberations, was standing nearby. Harry wondered if he was guarding them. The suspense was getting on his nerves. 'Do you think you convinced them, Doctor?' he whispered.

'I'm not sure, Harry, I tried, but sometimes words just aren't enough.'

Harry saw a bustle of movement on the other side of the conference room. 'Looks as if they've reached a decision.'

With muttered farewells the other councillors were hurrying away, leaving Mogran behind. He came over to the Doctor, who jumped eagerly to his feet. 'Well, what have you decided?'

'It has been agreed that an independent tribunal will investigate the work being carried out at the Bunker.'

'That could take months,' protested the Doctor. 'Davros has prototype Daleks ready for action *now*!'

Mogran held up his hand. 'It has also been agreed that pending the result of the investigation, Davros's Dalek experiments will be suspended.'

The Doctor brightened. 'Now that's more like it—though mind you, it's less than I'd hoped for …'

Mogran gave him the reassuring smile of a politician. 'I assure you, Doctor, if your allegations are borne out the Bunker will be closed down, and Davros dismissed. Meanwhile, you are welcome to remain here as our guests.'

'I'm afraid we haven't time for that,' the Doctor said briskly. 'One of my companions was lost in the Wastelands almost as soon as we arrived. I'd be very glad if you'd give us some help in finding her.'

Mogran looked ill-at-ease. Glancing round for a solution he caught sight of General Ravon, and passed the buck with polished skill. 'I'm afraid that's outside my sphere. But General Ravon here will give you all the help he can. I must go and inform Davros of my Committee's decision.' Mogran left the room, and Harry turned aggressively to Ravon. He didn't much fancy leaving Sarah's fate in the hands of one who'd so recently been their enemy.

'Well, General,' he demanded, '*can* you help us?'

'As a matter of fact, I believe I can,' Ravon replied surprisingly. 'One of our agents inside the Thal dome sent a report about a newly arrived girl prisoner who led some kind of breakout among the slave-workers. Gave the Thals a lot of trouble before she was recaptured.'

Harry said eagerly, 'Well, that certainly *sounds* like Sarah. What's all this about slaves?'

'The Thals are using prisoners to load their last great rocket. It's their super-weapon. They think they'll win the war with it.'

'You don't seem very worried.'

Ravon smiled confidently. 'No matter how powerful the rocket, it will never penetrate our protective dome. Davros had it reinforced with a protective coating, a new substance with the strength of thirty-foot concrete.'

'Congratulations,' said the Doctor drily. 'Now how can you help us find Sarah?'

Ravon looked doubtful. 'One of my agents could get you into the service shafts under the Thal rocket silo. But after that, you'd be on your own.'

'Understood,' said the Doctor. 'Let's be on our way.'

He seemed ready to set off at once. Harry caught his arm. 'I'm as anxious to rescue Sarah as you are, Doctor, but do you think there'd be time for a bite to eat first? It's been all go since we arrived.'

The Doctor looked at Ravon who said, 'Yes, of course. Come with me and I'll arrange it.'

As they followed him from the room Harry said, 'I suppose we'll have to cross those Wastelands again.'

'That's right.' The Doctor smiled. 'And then our troubles will really begin.' You might almost have thought he was looking forward to it.

Councillor Mogran was an extremely worried man. Somehow everything was going far too smoothly. He'd expected fiercely determined opposition from Davros. Instead he was encountering an unnerving degree of co-operation. 'An investigation?' Davros was saying. 'But of course, Councillor Mogran. I welcome your inquiry into my work here. The Kaled people sacrifice much to give us the materials we need. They have a right to know how our work is proceeding. My only hope is that when they learn of our achievements their patriotism will be re-fired.'

Mogran could say little in face of such sentiments. 'I am grateful for the way you have accepted this decision, Davros. There is one thing more—until the inquiry is concluded, all work on the Daleks must be suspended.'

'If that is your wish, then I must obey. It will take time to close down certain equipment. Shall we say twenty-four hours?'

The request was so reasonable that Mogran did not dare to refuse it entirely. 'Shall we say *twelve* hours?' he countered.

'It will be difficult—but it will be done.'

Mogran prepared to leave. 'Then it remains only for me to thank you for your co-operation.'

Davros bowed his ghastly skull-like head. 'It is simply my duty. The investigation will reveal only my loyalty and total dedication to our cause.'

Mogran left the laboratory. Nyder, who had been a silent witness to the confrontation, leaned over Davros's chair. 'We cannot allow this investigation. The stupidest councillors cannot fail to see that the Daleks will give *you* total power. They will end the experiment.'

'There will *be* no investigation,' Davros answered. 'Mogran has just signed the death-warrant of his city. Only we, the Elite, will go on.'

Nyder looked at him in astonishment, but said nothing.

'I want twenty of the genetically-mutated creatures installed in the machines immediately. They will be our shock-troops in the battle for survival.'

'They're still erratic, mentally unstable,' Nyder protested.

'They will not be allowed *total* self-control. I shall prepare a computer programme to limit their actions. Come, Nyder. We are going on a journey!'

The Doctor and Harry were close to their destination—the Thal rocket silo where they hoped to find and rescue Sarah. After a hasty meal, Ravon had handed them over to one of his agents, a weasel-faced man who spoke only when strictly necessary. Disguised in the hooded cloaks of mutos, the Doctor and Harry had been led by way of hidden paths and abandoned trenches across the central Wastelands to the outskirts of the Thal dome. Shifting a carefully-hidden hatchway, the agent had then gone underground, leading them through an interminable series of cramped tunnels and passageways where mysterious machinery hummed and throbbed. Finally he had stopped in a corridor junction, pointing to a ladder, bolted to the wall, which gave access to a hatch-cover. 'You're right underneath the silo now. That's all I can do for you. Here's your map!' And with that he had slipped away into the darkness.

Harry and the Doctor stripped off their muto disguise. 'Well, might as well get on with it,' said the Doctor. He climbed the ladder till he was high enough to raise the hatch-cover a few inches and peep through the gap. 'Seems clear enough. Come on, Harry.' Carefully the Doctor lifted the hatch and climbed through, reaching down to help Harry after him. They replaced the cover and looked at their surroundings.

They were in a featureless concrete corridor. Nearby was a door, the top-half glassed in. A notice read, 'Launch Control'. The Doctor checked his map. 'We seem to have surfaced in the administrative block,' he whispered. 'But we're pretty near the rocket.'

Impelled by his usual curiosity, the Doctor couldn't resist a swift peep through the glass panel in the Launch Control door. He stiffened in sudden surprise and beckoned Harry over. Harry joined him. The place was crowded with all the paraphernalia of a rocket control room, but now it was full of people too. Some wore military uniform, others robes like those of Kaled councilmen, though of different design. They were surrounding two central figures, who were set apart from the rest. To Harry's astonishment he saw Davros, in his wheelchair, Nyder beside him. He nudged the Doctor. 'What's the chief scientist of the Kaleds doing in the Thal rocket base?'

The Doctor touched a finger to his lips. With infinite caution he opened the door the merest crack, and Harry heard the metallic, inhuman tones of Davros. '... my concern is only for peace, for an end to the carnage that has virtually destroyed *both* races.'

Davros was talking to a high-ranking Thal Minister, summoned specially for this incredible meeting. Like his Kaled opposite number, Mogran, the Minister was a tall, imposing man with an air of great authority. There was scepticism in his voice. 'Why not try to convince the Kaled government to make peace?'

'I have tried, time and time again. They will settle for nothing less than total extermination of the Thals.'

Davros's deliberately provocative announcement was greeted with angry murmurings. 'Then they deserve to perish,' the Minister replied coldly. 'And perish they shall. Our rocket—'

'—will be a total failure.' The voice of Davros completed the sentence. 'The Kaled city dome cannot be penetrated. It is protected by a special material of my invention. Your rocket will hardly scratch it—unless you accept my help.' Nyder produced a sheaf of papers and held them out. 'This is the measure of our sincerity. A simple chemical formula. Load the substance into normal artillery shells and bombard the Kaled dome. The dome will be weakened, its molecular structure made brittle. Then your rocket will penetrate with virtually no resistance.'

The Minister took the papers and looked at them incredulously. 'Why do you give us this information, when it means the end of your city?'

'No price is too great for peace,' Davros said solemnly. 'When the war is finally over, I ask only to be allowed to take part in the reconstruction of our world. And, remember, by dawn tomorrow this planet could be at peace.'

The Minister spoke slowly, 'If you would give me a moment to confer with my colleagues alone?'

Davros's chair began moving towards the door. The Doctor and Harry ducked back, and disappeared round the corner. After a moment they heard Nyder's lowered voice. 'Do you think they believed you, Davros?'

'They are hungry for victory. They will use the formula, and fire their rocket, no matter what they think.'

The door opened and again they heard the Minister's voice. 'A barrage of shells containing the formula will begin at once. The rocket launch will follow immediately. I shall see that you are given safe escort from the city.'

As the Minister led his two visitors away, the Doctor and Harry emerged from hiding. 'We'll have to warn the Kaleds,' muttered the Doctor.

'Not before we find Sarah,' Harry said firmly.

'Of course not,' agreed the Doctor. 'Come on, Harry, don't just stand there.'

Guided by the Kaled spy's map, they made their way along the corridors towards the rocket. Suddenly the Doctor heard footsteps approaching from an intersecting corridor. He peered round the corner and saw two Thal guards, both dressed in anti-radiation suits, marching along the corridor towards him. He ducked back, whispered a few words to Harry, and then stepped blithely round the corner. Hat on the back of his head, long scarf dangling, the Doctor had passed the two guards before they had time to take in his extraordinary appearance. As soon as it did register, both guards spun round, rifles levelled. 'Hey,' called one of them. 'Who are you?'

The Doctor walked back towards them, his eyes wide and innocent. 'Well, as a matter of fact I'm a spy. I wonder if you could help me—I'm looking for this rocket of yours ...'

The astonished guard gaped at him—giving Harry Sullivan time to fell him with a rabbit-punch below the ear. The first guard dropped, the second turned—and the Doctor knocked him out. They dragged their victims round the corner and out of sight.

Beneath the towering bulk of the huge rocket, the motley band of slave workers were coming to the end of their task. Sarah staggered wearily as she came out of the rocket. Sevrin caught her by the arm, supporting her. One of the guards laughed. 'Don't worry, that was the last consignment. You can have all the rest you need now.'

As the prisoners came out of the rocket they were bunched into a group under the rifles of a couple of guards. The rest of the Thal soldiers marched away. Sarah looked at Sevrin. 'If the rocket is loaded, why are they keeping us here?'

The giant muto shrugged. 'Why should they bother to move us?'

Sarah looked up at the rocket. 'But when that thing goes off, we'll all be killed.'

'Our lives are of no more interest to them.'

Sevrin seemed resigned to his fate, but Sarah certainly was not. Their second shift on the rocket had been a fairly short one, and so far Sarah was feeling no ill effects other than normal tiredness. She was fairly sure her exposure had been too short to do serious damage, and she was by no means ready to abandon hope of escape.

She looked round. Only two guards now—they could always have another go at breaking out. Her heart sank as two more guards in radiation suits walked into the silo. They walked up to the soldiers guarding the prisoners, then suddenly jumped them. There was a flurry of blows and the Thal soldiers were knocked out. The new arrivals started removing their radiation suits. To her amazement and delight, Sarah found herself looking at the Doctor and Harry Sullivan.

The Doctor ran across and gave her a hug. 'Are you all right, Sarah?'

'I am now,' she said. 'But we've got to get out of here. The Thals are just about to set this rocket off.'

'I know. Sarah, you've got to go with Harry. Harry, here's the map, you can find a way out. Get to the Kaled dome and tell General Ravon what we've learned. He must evacuate at once.'

Sarah looked at the Doctor sadly, realising that their reunion was to be very brief. 'What are you going to do?'

'I'll try to sabotage the rocket and delay the launch. There's no time to argue, off you go!' He turned to the other prisoners. 'Go on, all of you—you're free. Escape while you can.'

Dazedly the prisoners began stumbling off. Sarah noticed a bewildered Sevrin staring about. 'You come with us, Sevrin,' she called. The muto moved over to join them.

The Doctor waved his arms. 'Off you go, the lot of you—I've work to do.'

Sarah still hesitated, but he was obviously quite determined. Harry took her arm. 'Come along, old girl, or we'll all be caught.' Sarah allowed him to lead her away.

Harry took Sarah and Sevrin out of the silo and along the corridors. His eyes were on the ground and he stopped when he saw a hatch like the one they'd emerged from. 'This'll do.' With Sevrin helping, Harry lifted the hatch and sent first Sevrin, then Sarah down into the darkness of the service tunnel. Just as he was about to climb down himself, Thal soldiers ran round the corner, firing as they came. Harry bolted through the hatchway, bullets whizzing over his head, landing on top of Sarah and Sevrin. 'Come on, they're after us,' he yelled. The three disentangled themselves and set off along the tunnel at a run.

In the silo the Doctor heard the sound of firing and hoped his friends were still safe. Then he dismissed them from his mind, reserving all his concentration for the task at hand. He studied the rocket thoughtfully. Perhaps if he started by severing the exterior fuel lines ... The Doctor took a knife from the body of an unconscious guard and purposefully approached the massive tail fin of the rocket. He leaned forward, jabbed with the knife ... there was a sudden shower of blue sparks, and a crackling noise. Twisting in agony, the Doctor's body was thrown clear across the silo. He crashed to the ground and lay still.

In the Rocket control room, a technician studied a flickering dial. 'Better check the silo,' he called to a guard. 'Someone's trying sabotage.'

The Thal Minister, waiting to watch the launch, said anxiously, 'Any damage?'

The technician shook his head. 'He ran into our electrical defence system. Probably dead by now.'

In the silo, guards were running towards the motionless body of the Doctor.

7

COUNTDOWN TO DESTRUCTION

The Doctor heard a voice moaning and muttering. 'Must stop rocket … warn …' To his surprise he realised the voice was his own.

There came another voice. 'Still alive is he? A shock like that should have killed him immediately.'

Then a gruffer voice, 'What do we do with him, Minister?'

'Oh, I've no time now,' said the first voice fussily. 'Leave him where he is till after the launch. I'll interrogate him myself if I've time. Otherwise you chaps can have him.'

The Doctor opened his eyes cautiously, then closed them again, since the whole room was spinning like a Catherine wheel. He made a mighty effort and tried again, first one eye then the other. He was in the rocket control room, the room in which he'd watched Davros betray his people not so long ago. But he couldn't move …

The Doctor realised that he had been lashed by the arms into a wheeled metal chair and shoved into a corner, a piece of unimportant, unfinished business to be dealt with later. The room was a bustle of activity as civilian and military VIPs got in the way of the technical staff desperately preparing for the countdown.

The Minister was looking at a monitor screen which showed a picture of the Kaled City beneath its protective dome. The dome was in a bad state now, broken in several places, with a creeping stain spreading over its surface. 'It's working,' said the minister exultantly. 'The Kaled dome is breaking up. Start the countdown!'

Helpless in his chair the Doctor shouted, 'No—you mustn't.' No one took any notice—except for the guard, who gave him an absent-minded cuff to silence him. Everyone was intent on the big digital clock which dominated the main control panel. It was counting down from fifty—forty-nine, forty-eight, forty-seven …

Other monitors were alive now, showing the missile on its launch-pad. The clock was still counting down, through the thirties, twenties, into single figures … ten, nine, eight, seven, six, five …

Using the wall behind him as a lever, the Doctor kicked fiercely backwards, sending his wheeled chair skidding into the main control console. He lashed frantically with his feet at the instrument panel, but the guard pulled him back, and the Doctor's feet flailed uselessly in the air. Two … one … blast-off! Helplessly the Doctor watched as the missile lifted from its pad and set off on the brief journey towards the Kaled dome.

Now everyone's attention shifted back to the monitors showing the dome as, battered and broken, it awaited final destruction. There was a blinding flash, a distant explosion that shook the control room. When the smoke cleared the Kaled dome had disappeared.

Flames roared in the crater that had replaced it, like those of some newly-born volcano.

Cheers and shouts echoed through the Thal control room. Only the Doctor sat silent, his head slumped on his chest, appalled as always by the corrupting brutality of war. Thousands of their fellow-creatures dead, and these people were cheering. On top of that, there was his own, personal loss. He had sent Sarah and Harry back to the Kaled city—the city that was now no more than a guttering inferno on the monitor screen.

The same terrible picture was seen on another monitor screen, this one in Davros's Bunker, some miles from the Kaled city. The Bunker had been far enough away, and sufficiently deep underground to escape the effects of the rocket. Davros and his Elite Corps of scientists and security men were quite unharmed.

Davros wheeled his chair away from the screen. 'Switch it off,' he ordered, and one of the scientists hurried to obey. Davros turned to the awe-stricken group around him. 'Never fear, my friends. We shall avenge the destruction of our city with retaliation so massive and so merciless that it will live in history.' He touched the control on his chair-arm and a group of three Daleks glided into the laboratory. They formed a line before Davros, awaiting his commands. Davros looked round the room. 'Let our vengeance begin with the destruction of the Thal agent, Ronson. It was he who betrayed us to the Thals. He gave them the formula which made possible the destruction of our beloved city.'

Gliding smoothly, the line of Daleks swung round to encircle Ronson, who cowered back into his corner. 'No, no,' he babbled. 'It isn't true ...'

Viciously Davros hissed, 'Exterminate! Exterminate! Exterminate!'

The Dalek guns blazed and Ronson was hurled across the room. His body collapsed, a charred and smoking ruin, against the far wall. Davros spoke, not to the horrified Thal scientists, but to the Daleks. 'Today the Kaled city and much of the Kaled race has ended, consumed in the fires of war. But from the ashes will rise the supreme creature, the ultimate conqueror of the Universe—the Dalek!'

No one moved or spoke. Still ignoring the scientists, Davros addressed his creations. 'Today you begin a journey that will take the Daleks to their destiny of universal and absolute supremacy. You have been programmed to complete a task. You will now begin.'

In response to Davros's speech the leading Dalek spoke only two words. But in them was the whole of the Dalek creed. In that grinding, metallic voice, so hideously like Davros's own, it said, 'We obey.' The Daleks turned and glided from the laboratory.

In the Thal rocket control room, the rejoicing went on. Wine was produced, toasts were drunk. No one thought about the Doctor, slumped head-down in his corner.

The Minister was in the full flood of his eloquence. 'A thousand years of war, and now it's ended. Listen to the people, they know already.' From outside the control room came a growing rumble of distant cheering, as the good news spread through the Thal City. 'I must speak to them,' said the Minister. 'There must be a victory parade. Come, there is much to be done ...'

He began to lead his fellow VIPs from the room. As they passed the Doctor, one of the Minister's special aides, a tall, severe-looking girl called Bettan, asked, 'What about him?'

The Minister glared indignantly at the Doctor. 'He must be punished, executed …' The Minister broke off. He was a kindly man at heart, and he really wasn't in the mood to think about such distasteful matters as executions. 'No—let us show that although ruthless in war, we Thals can be merciful in victory. All political prisoners will be freed, and all charges dropped. Release him!' The Minister swept out, and at a nod from Bettan the guard began untying the Doctor. He rose and stretched his tall figure, his face sad. Bettan turned to go, then hesitated. There was something curiously compelling about this odd-looking man in the strange clothes.

'You had friends in the Kaled City?' she said gently.

'Two people very dear to me. The worst of it is, I sent them back into—that.' He glanced at the monitor where the ruined remains of the Kaled city could be seen, still burning fiercely.

'What will you do now?'

'Start again. Try to complete what I came here to do.'

'What was that?' Bettan asked curiously.

'Stop the development of the Daleks, the machine creatures Davros has created. Creatures as evil as he is himself.'

'Davros is interested only in achieving peace. *He* told us how to destroy the Kaled dome,' Bettan protested.

The Doctor shook his head emphatically. 'The Kaleds themselves realised the danger of Davros's experiments. They were about to stop him. Rather than let that happen, he betrayed his own people.'

'You'll never convince the Thals that Davros is evil,' said Bettan. 'He's become a popular hero!'

The Doctor nodded, lost in thought.

'You're *free* now,' said Bettan. 'You can go where you please.'

'Thank you,' the Doctor said absently. With a sudden, charming smile, he wandered away.

Bettan was an efficient and hard-working young woman, with an important official position. Arrangements for the victory celebrations kept her busy during the next few hours. But she often found herself thinking of the strange man in the control room. She had no idea of the terrifying circumstances under which she was to meet him again.

*

'And there you have it, gentlemen. That outlines the chromosomal variations to be introduced into the genetic structuring of the embryo Daleks. They are to be implemented at once.' Through his vision-lens, Davros looked irritably around the small group of leading scientists. Their faces did not hold the approval and adulation to which he had become accustomed. Instead they looked shocked, disapproving even. It was Gharman, the group leader, who spoke for the rest.

'Davros … the changes you outline will create enormous mental defects.'

'They will not be defects—they will be improvements,' snapped the metallic voice.

'It will mean creatures without conscience. No sense of right or wrong, no pity. They'll be completely without feeling or emotion.'

'That is correct. That is the purpose of the changes. See that they are carried out—without question, Gharman.'

No one dared object further, and the scientists left to begin their tasks. Nyder, who had entered in time to witness the end of this scene, smiled thinly and went over to Davros. 'The Dalek task-force is in position,' he said. 'They await your order.'

'I see no reason for further delay.' The withered hand dropped down on a control. Miles away, on the edge of the Thal city, Daleks began to move forward.

The Doctor made his way with difficulty through the rejoicing Thal city. The place was completely roofed-in, like one enormous building. Corridors, streets, squares and walk-ways were jammed with excited revellers, all celebrating the end of a war which had been going on their whole lives. It was rather like being forced to attend an enormous noisy party when not really in the mood. People hugged the Doctor, slapped him on the back and even tried to kiss him. Others pressed food and drink on him, and urged him to join parties in their homes.

Slowly the Doctor forged ahead, accepting some refreshment, but smilingly refusing all other invitations. At last, as he came to the edge of the city, things were a little quieter. The Doctor was looking for a way out into the Wastelands. He intended to make his way to Davros's bunker, though he had no very clear idea what he would do when he got there.

Dodging a group of revellers dancing in a city square, the Doctor moved on. He could still hear the sound of shouts and laughter behind him. Suddenly, silence fell. Then there were screams, shouts of terror. The Doctor ran back the way he had come. Turning into the little square he stopped appalled. The bodies of the dancers were strewn all over the square, contorted in attitudes of sudden death. A Dalek was methodically shooting down the fleeing survivors. A second Dalek glided out to join it. Across the square came the familiar hated voices. 'Exterminate! Exterminate! Exterminate!'

The Doctor turned and ran back towards the gate. There was nothing he could possibly do here. It was all the more urgent that he tackle the evil at its source.

As the Doctor ran he heard shouts and screams of terror from all over the city. He could easily guess what was happening. The happy, careless Thals, the sinister shapes gliding from the shadows, the cries of 'Exterminate!' and the blazing Dalek guns ... Then the heaps of charred, smoking bodies as the Daleks moved off to continue their dreadful work...

The main gate of the Thal city stood open and unguarded. No wonder the Daleks had entered so easily. As the Doctor ran up to the gate he collided with a fleeing figure. It was Bettan, the girl he had seen in the control room. She clutched his arm. 'There are—*machines* all over the city. Killing everybody without mercy. Are those the things you told me about, the things you said Davros made?'

The Doctor grabbed her and pulled her into the shelter of a doorway. A line of sinister metal shapes glided into the square, driving before them a group of running figures. Dalek guns opened fire, the fleeing Thals twisted and fell. The Doctor and Bettan froze motionless in their doorway. The Daleks surveyed the square a moment longer, then turned and glided back into the city. Only then did the Doctor answer Bettan's question. 'Yes,' he said softly. 'Those are the Daleks. Come on, we'll be safer in the Wastelands than here.' They made their way out through the gates and across the Wastelands.

Soon the city was invisible behind them, lost in the perpetual fog and darkness of the Wastelands. They found an abandoned trench and sat down to rest. Bettan was still unable to take in what had happened.

'Davros didn't need to go that far. When our leaders saw they were beaten they would have surrendered.'

'Perhaps they tried,' said the Doctor. 'The Daleks accept no terms. Davros has conditioned them to wipe the Thals from this planet.'

'Some of us will survive,' Bettan said fiercely. 'And we'll fight back.'

The Doctor looked hard at her. 'Do you mean that? Are you really prepared to help me?'

'I'll do anything I can.'

'Even go back to the city?'

Bettan winced, but her voice was steady. 'Even that ... if it'll really help.'

The Doctor leaned forward. 'To destroy the Daleks, we must destroy Davros himself,' he said urgently. 'I'm going to go back into the Bunker and do whatever I can. But I need the backing of some kind of fighting force.' Bettan looked puzzled.

'What can I do?'

'You said yourself, there are bound to be *some* survivors. If you could organise them, find arms and explosives, make an attack on Davros's Bunker—it could be the diversion I'll need. As yet there aren't so many Daleks in existence. If you stay out of their way there's a chance. Will you try it?' Bettan nodded. She stood up. 'Goodbye—and good luck.'

Bettan slipped out of the trench and began retracing their steps, back towards the city. As she came within sight of the main gate she saw Daleks gliding through the streets, illuminated by the flames of the burning buildings. Dodging from one hiding place to another, she made her way back to the city centre, steeling herself against the horrors she would find inside.

The Doctor meanwhile moved across the Wastelands in the opposite direction. He was working his way along a slit-trench that seemed to run in the right direction, when suddenly a cloaked form sprang down and grappled with him. Of all the times to run into a hostile muto, thought the Doctor despairingly. Enemies to everything but their own twisted and abandoned kind, the mutos attacked all strangers on sight. The Doctor disposed of his attacker fairly easily, but soon realised that he had more than one to deal with. More and more cloaked and hooded figures piled on top of him, and soon the Doctor was spread-eagled on his back in the mud, held powerless in the grip of many hands. One of the mutos, evidently a leader, looked round for some weapon to finish him. There was a jagged rock on the ground nearby. The muto lifted it up, raising it above his head with difficulty. He stood there, poised, ready to crash the rock down on the Doctor's head ...

8

CAPTIVES OF DAVROS

The Doctor struggled desperately to escape, but too many bodies were holding him down. Just as the rock seemed about to fall, a burly figure shoulder-charged the muto, sending him flying. The Doctor looked up into the face of Harry Sullivan! The jagged rock thudded into the mud close to the Doctor's head. Then a huge figure started plucking the other mutos from the Doctor, throwing them through the air in all directions.

Terrified by the sudden assault, the band of mutos scuttled off into the darkness. The next thing the Doctor knew, his two friends were helping him to his feet. The Doctor greeted them in astonished delight. 'Sarah! Harry! I don't believe it. I thought you'd been blown up in the Kaled City!'

'We never got there,' explained Sarah. 'Halfway across the Wastelands we were attacked by a band of wandering mutos. While we were fighting them off—the rocket blew up the Kaled city.'

'You could see the flames clear across the Wastelands,' Harry said. 'The poor old mutos were so scared they just ran for their lives.'

The Doctor shook his head wonderingly. 'Then what are you all doing here?'

Harry grinned. 'We knew you'd try to get back into the Bunker through the cave. We came to help.'

'Must you really go back?' Sarah asked.

'I must, Sarah. There's still a chance I'll manage to complete my mission. What's more, there's another very good reason.'

'To recover the Time Ring?'

'That bracelet the Time Lord gave me is our lifeline. Without it, we'll never get away from this planet.'

That was reason enough to convince even Sarah. They made their way out of the trench, across more Wastelands, until they reached the window in the rock wall through which they'd emerged earlier.

The Doctor moved aside the broken bars and helped Harry through. Sevrin was about to follow when the Doctor laid a hand on his arm. 'Will you do something for us, Sevrin—something important?'

'If I can,' Sevrin spoke in his deep, gentle voice.

'Over in the Thal city there's a girl called Bettan. She's trying to organise a resistance group. Will you round up any of your people who can fight, and join her? She's going to stage an attack on the main gate of the Bunker. The attack probably won't succeed, but it will keep the Elite troops occupied while I try to complete my mission.'

'Very well, Doctor. I will do what I can.'

Sarah took one of Sevrin's great hands in both of hers. 'Goodbye, Sevrin—and thank you.' The muto slipped away into the darkness. The Doctor helped Sarah through the gap and climbed through after her. Harry was waiting on the other side.

'We'd better stay close together, Sarah,' warned the Doctor. 'This cave is full of Davros's rejected experiments.'

Sarah shivered. 'Did you have to tell me that?'

Harry chuckled. 'Not scared, are you, Sarah?'

'Of course not!'

'Well you should be,' said the Doctor severely. 'One of them nearly had Harry for lunch!' With these consoling words the Doctor moved off into the darkness, Sarah and Harry following close behind.

The Doctor's Time Ring lay still unnoticed on Ronson's desk. No one was particularly interested in odds and ends taken from some mysterious alien, and the desk had been left undisturbed since its owner's death.

The plump communications scientist called Kavell was working at his own desk nearby when Gharman, Davros's chief assistant, came over to him. He cast a quick glance at the Elite guards on the door, and held up a piece of electronic circuitry. 'I'm having a problem with the dimensional thought circuit,' he said loudly. 'I wonder if you'd have a look at it.' Kavell looked up in surprise. The problem was completely out of his area. He was about to say so when Gharman whispered, 'Kavell—we've got to stop the Daleks!'

Kavell took the circuit and pretended to examine it. 'I want no part of it, Gharman. You saw what happened to Ronson. Davros will have us killed too, if he thinks we're plotting against him.'

'If we plan carefully he won't suspect.'

Kavell nodded towards the guard. 'What about the Elite Security Guards—they'll stay loyal to Davros.'

'That isn't important—not if the whole of the Scientific Corps turns against him. We can demand that the Dalek project is halted. Every day I become more convinced that this whole project is evil and immoral. These latest genetic changes—'

'What do you expect me to do?' whispered Kavell. He had no wish to prolong the conversation.

'Spread the word. Help me to convince the others that it's vital the whole Dalek project is ended.'

'I'll do what I can. I promise nothing—'

Kavell broke off short as Nyder came into the laboratory. Gharman snatched back his equipment and returned to his place. Kavell bent over his papers, working furiously.

Nyder seemed to have noticed nothing. He had a brief discussion about security matters with the guard on the door, then walked back to his own cubicle. As he sat behind his meticulously tidy desk, Nyder's mind was working furiously. He could very easily guess the kind of conversation Kavell and Gharman had been having. The only question in his mind was—what should he do about it?

Some time later, Nyder came back into the laboratory. Kavell was no longer there, but Gharman was still working at his desk. Nyder walked across to him. 'Gharman, I must talk to you. It's very important.'

Gharman didn't look up. 'You can see I'm busy ...'

'Then soon,' insisted Nyder. 'Not here, somewhere private.'

Gharman looked up curiously. There was strain in Nyder's voice. 'What's all this about, Commander?'

Nyder seemed to be groping for words. 'Look, Gharman, you know me ... I've served Davros faithfully for years, just as you have. I've never questioned anything he's done until now.'

'Go on,' said Gharman cautiously.

'He's become a megalomaniac. He's ready to sacrifice all of us just so his Dalek project can be completed.'

Gharman felt a sudden exultation. If even Nyder was coming round to his way of thinking ... With him on their side victory was certain. 'Don't worry, Commander,' he said reassuringly. 'You're not alone in your fears. Where can we talk safely?'

Nyder answered thoughtfully, 'There's the detention area on the lower level. Davros never goes there. We could use one of the cells.'

'Very well. I'll meet you down there as soon as I can.' Gharman bent over his papers, and Nyder walked quietly away.

Deep beneath the Bunker, Sarah held Harry's hand as she walked through the dank and dripping darkness of the caves. She kept her eyes tight shut most of the time. Various unpleasant hissings and gruntings came from all around, and Sarah had no wish to see what was making them. Harry's other hand was gripping the end of the Doctor's scarf, as the Doctor led them unerringly through the darkness. At least Harry *hoped* it was unerringly ...

'Not much further,' whispered the Doctor. 'The entrance to the ventilation duct is just along here.'

Harry stopped and looked around. 'Are you *sure*, Doctor? I don't remember passing this little lot.' A colony of the giant clam creatures was clustered by the cave wall. They gave them a wide berth, but Harry couldn't resist giving the nearest one a passing kick—a gesture instantly regretted as the creature slid towards him, hissing loudly and jaws gaping wide.

Sarah screamed and backed away—straight towards the opening shell of another clam which gaped eagerly to receive her ...

The Doctor pulled her to one side just as the clamshell clanged shut. Harry jumped away from his clam, and all three ran off into the darkness. The clams followed, hissing loudly, then suddenly subsided, waiting for another victim to pass by. Sarah shuddered. 'I'll never eat oysters again.'

'Lucky for us they're not very mobile,' said the Doctor. 'Maybe that's why Davros discarded them. Well—we've arrived.' He pointed to an opening in the cave wall—the other end of the ventilation duct.

Nervously Sarah said, 'Doctor, suppose there's something nasty waiting for us in there?'

'That's a thought,' the Doctor said cheerfully. 'Tell you what, we'll send Harry in first.'

Harry grinned, knowing full well that if the Doctor had suspected danger, he'd have gone in first himself. Harry crawled into the tunnel, then turned and helped Sarah to follow him. The Doctor took a last look round the cave and climbed after them. Harry in the lead, they began working their way down the narrow tunnel.

When Gharman reached the lower level, he found Nyder waiting for him. Without saying a word Nyder led the way through the detention area and into an empty cell.

In a low voice Gharman began, 'We'd better make this as quick as possible. We don't want to be missed.'

Nyder said, 'Tell me your plan.'

'Quite a number of scientists feel as we do. When we've collected enough support, we can give Davros an ultimatum.'

'What kind of ultimatum do you suggest?'

Gharman had worked it out in his mind. 'We shall only continue work on the Daleks if he restores *conscience* to the brain-pattern. The creatures *must* have a moral sense, the ability to judge between right and wrong ... all the qualities that we believe essential in ourselves.'

Nyder nodded thoughtfully. 'And if he doesn't accept this ultimatum?'

'We will destroy all the work that has been done so far—everything! It will be as though the Daleks had never been created!'

'Excellent,' Nyder said crisply. 'I shall do my best to get some of the Security Corps on our side.' Casually he asked, 'Who can you count on among the scientists?'

Gharman considered. 'Kavell to begin with. Frenton, Parran, possibly Shonar ...' He reeled off about a dozen names. 'All those have already been sounded out, and there are plenty of other likely ones we haven't spoken to as yet ...'

'Thank you, Gharman. That is exactly what I needed to know.'

Gharman stared at him. There had been a sudden change in Nyder's tone. Then Gharman heard an all-too-familiar whirring sound. Davros was coming through the cell door, a squad of security men behind him. 'Davros will be most interested in your information,' added Nyder coldly.

Gharman stared round wildly. He was trapped in the little cell. There was nowhere to run. In a sudden frenzy he launched himself at Nyder, who sidestepped neatly and dropped him with one short chopping blow. Gharman collapsed in front of Davros's chair. Davros looked down at the sprawled body. 'A pity. He had a good scientific mind.'

Nyder drew his blaster. 'Shall I kill him?' he asked mildly.

'No. A little brain surgery will remove these stupid scruples, and we shall still have the benefit of his inventive skills.'

Nyder holstered his blaster regretfully. 'And the people he named?'

'The same for them.'

'I'll arrange for the arrests.'

'Not yet. We must move carefully. First we must learn exactly who are our allies, and who our enemies.'

Nyder snapped his fingers and a couple of security guards dragged Gharman away. Nyder was about to follow when he saw that Davros had not moved. 'What is it?'

'I heard something—in there.' Davros's withered hand gestured towards a tiny ventilation duct high in the cell wall.

Nyder could hear nothing. But he knew that Davros's electronically-boosted hearing was far better than his own. He put his ear close to the little grille. Was there something—a faint scuffling sound? 'I think there's someone in the ventilation system,' he whispered.

Harry pushed aside the already-loosened hatch-cover and slithered out. 'Everything's quiet, Doctor,' he called, looking along the little tunnel. He helped Sarah out, and then the Doctor jumped down. Harry was just about to replace the hatch-cover when a dazzling spotlight illuminated the three of them. Behind it the Doctor could make out Davros, Nyder and a squad of black-uniformed security guards.

'Welcome back, Doctor,' said Davros.

The Doctor sighed, and turned to Sarah. 'There *was* something nasty waiting for us after all.'

The security squad marched the three captives to a room in the detention area. Various oddly-shaped pieces of electronic equipment lined the walls. There was something indescribably sinister about the place. The Doctor guessed the room was a kind of electronic interrogation chamber. Its equipment was designed to loosen the tongues of those unwilling to speak, and to check the truth of their stories.

The guards worked swiftly and efficiently. The Doctor was strapped into a metal chair, heavy straps holding his wrists and ankles. A metal helmet was lowered over the top of his head. He assumed that the contraption was some kind of lie-detector. What worried him far more was to see Sarah and Harry strapped to metal tables. These had clamps at each corner, holding the prisoners helpless. Electrodes were taped to their temples. Leads from the two tables were plugged into the control-console on the arm of Davros's chair.

Their work finished, the security men stood back. Davros wheeled his chair directly in front of the Doctor. Nyder, as always, was at his master's shoulder. There was a recording machine on Davros's other side.

Davros was leafing through a sheaf of computer print-outs. 'I have read the reports of your initial interrogation. The suggestion that you had travelled through Space and Time was rejected by the computer.'

The Doctor shrugged. 'Computers are limited. It had probably never been programmed for such a concept.'

'Such travel is beyond my scientific comprehension,' stated Davros. 'But not beyond my imagination. Why did you come here, from this future of yours?'

The Doctor saw no point in evasion. 'To stop the development of the Daleks. In what is to you the future, I have seen the carnage and destruction they will create.'

'So—my Daleks do survive?'

'As machines of war, weapons of hate.' The Doctor leaned forward, straining against his bonds in his urgency. 'There is still time to change that. You could make them a force for good in the Universe.'

'You have seen my Daleks in battle?' Davros demanded. 'Do they win? Do they always win?'

'They have been defeated many times—but never utterly. The Dalek menace always returns.'

'If they are the supreme war-machine, how *can* they lose?'

'Many reasons. Overwhelming opposition, poor information, simple misfortune ...'

'You must tell me, Doctor. Where do the Daleks fail? What mistakes do they make?'

The Doctor shook his head. 'No, Davros. That is something the future must keep secret.'

Davros glided his wheelchair closer to the Doctor. 'You *will* tell me what I want to know because you have weaknesses. Ones that I have eliminated from myself, and from my Daleks. You are afflicted with a conscience, Doctor, and with compassion for others.'

The Doctor said nothing.

Davros went on remorselessly, 'Let me tell you what is going to happen, Doctor. You will answer all my questions, carefully and precisely. The instruments to which you are attached will instantly detect any attempt to lie.'

'And if I refuse to answer?'

'Your friends are attached to rather different instruments, Doctor.' Davros waved a hand towards Harry and Sarah. 'At the touch of a switch I can make them feel all the torments and agonies ever known.'

The Doctor's voice was hoarse with strain. 'If I tell you what you want to know, I betray the future. I can't do that.'

'You can and you will, Doctor,' said Davros gloatingly. 'You will tell me the reason for every Dalek defeat. With that knowledge I can programme my Daleks so there will be no errors, and no defeats. We shall change the future.'

The Doctor looked from Davros to Harry and Sarah. It was the most agonising decision he had ever faced. Davros was becoming impatient. 'Doctor! Either tell me about the Dalek future, or watch the suffering of your friends. Which is it to be?'

Slowly Davros moved his withered hand towards the switch ...

REBELLION!

The Doctor knew he was beaten—at least for the time being. 'All right, Davros, all right. Just leave my friends alone.'

Davros kept his hand poised over the control. 'Then begin, Doctor.'

The Doctor paused, collecting his thoughts. In a flat, hopeless voice he began a catalogue of Dalek defeats, and the errors which had caused them. 'The Dalek invasion of Earth in the year Two Thousand was foiled because of an over-ambitious attempt to mine the core of the planet. The magnetic core of the planet was too strong, the human resistance too determined. On Mars the Daleks were finally defeated because of a virus which attacked the insulation cables of their electrical circuits. The Dalek war against the Venusian Colonies in the Space Year Seventeen Thousand was ended by the intervention of a rocket-fleet from the planet Hyperion ...'

The Doctor's voice went on and on, every word recorded by the tape-recorder at Davros's elbow. Sarah and Harry listened in horror, relieved to have been spared the torments with which Davros had threatened them, realising how much it must cost the Doctor to place such priceless information in the hands of his enemy.

The Doctor talked till he was hoarse, dredging every possible scrap of Dalek history from his memory. At last his head slumped on his chest and he mumbled, 'That's all—all I can remember for now.' At the same moment the tape-machine clicked to a halt, its recording spool exhausted.

Davros nodded slowly. 'This seems an opportune moment to end this particular session. We can always resume later, under the same conditions. Commander Nyder, take the Doctor's two friends to the detention cell.'

Security guards unstrapped Sarah and Harry, lifted them down from the tables and dragged them away. The Doctor too was unstrapped from his chair. He slumped back exhausted. As the guards came to fetch him, Davros waved them away. 'I must thank you, Doctor. All this information will be programmed into the Dalek memory banks.' Davros slipped the tape-spool from the machine and handed it to Nyder. 'Commander, you will place this in the safe in my office. Its security is your personal responsibility. Remember, its value is beyond computation.' The Doctor's eyes followed the tape longingly as Nyder put it inside his tunic and left the room. He and Davros were alone now, though the Doctor guessed there would be more guards outside. He let himself slump deeper in the chair, doing his best to give the impression of utter defeat. But in his heart, or rather hearts, the Doctor was far from giving in. Characteristically, the Doctor wasted no time in regrets. He had given Davros the information he needed because there had been no alternative. He couldn't have allowed Sarah and Harry to suffer. What was done was done, the important thing now was to retrieve the situation.

With his enemy broken and defeated, Davros was in a relaxed, almost genial mood. 'Now, Doctor,' he said. 'Let us talk for a while, not as prisoner and captive, but as men of science. It is seldom that I meet someone whose intelligence even approaches my own ...'

Sarah and Harry were marched along the corridor to a guarded cell and thrown inside. A tall, thin man in the uniform of one of Davros's Scientific Elite was stretched out on the bunk. He jumped to his feet and helped them to pick themselves up. 'Are you all right?' he asked anxiously.

'Just about,' said Sarah.

The man looked at Harry more closely. 'Forgive me, but aren't you one of the prisoners who escaped?'

Harry nodded. 'That's right. Who are you?'

'Until a little while ago I was a senior member of Davros's Scientific Elite. My name is Gharman.'

'And now you're a prisoner like us?' asked Sarah. 'What happened?'

Gharman told them of his attempt to rally the opposition to Davros, and his mistake in trusting Nyder. 'What's happening up there? I suppose the whole place is in an uproar.'

'We didn't get a chance to see very much,' said Harry. 'But as far as I could tell, everything seems to be running smoothly.'

Gharman began pacing about the cell. 'Yet Davros knows we're planning action against him. I should have expected mass arrests, executions ...'

'Maybe that's too obvious for Davros?' suggested Sarah.

Gharman looked at her hopefully. 'He's being too clever for his own good. Every moment he delays our movement grows in strength. A *majority* of the scientists now want to end the Daleks. If they act now, they could break Davros's strength.' Gharman pounded his fist against the wall in an agony of frustration. 'If only I could get in touch with them.'

In the corridor outside, the plump little communications scientist, Kavell, was walking towards the cell door. The guard covered him with his rifle. 'Halt!'

Kavell glared back indignantly. 'I wish to question the prisoners.'

'No one may see the prisoners without a pass signed by Davros.'

'I'm aware of that. I have one here somewhere ...' Kavell moved closer to the guard, his fingers reaching for the truncheon concealed inside his tunic ...

Davros was still enjoying the spectacle of the Doctor's defeat. His prisoner's will seemed completely broken and he slumped dejectedly in his chair. 'I have committed the greatest act of treachery ever perpetrated,' groaned the Doctor. 'I have betrayed the unborn millions. Davros, I beg of you, stop the production of the Daleks.'

'Too late, Doctor. My automated workshops are already in full production of Dalek machines.'

'It isn't the machines that are evil, it's the minds of the creatures inside them. Minds that you created.'

'Evil?' said Davros thoughtfully. 'No, Doctor, I will not accept that. When all other life-forms are suppressed, when the Daleks are the supreme power of the Universe, then we shall have peace. All wars will end. The Daleks are the power not of evil but of good!'

The discussion seemed to revive the Doctor a little. He leaned forward in his chair. 'Evil that good may come, eh? Tell me, Davros, if you had created a virus in your laboratory, one that could destroy all life—would you use it?'

Davros seemed fascinated by the concept. 'To know that life and death on an enormous scale was within *my* choice ... that the pressure of my thumb breaking the glass of a capsule could end everything ... such power would set me among the Gods ... yes, I would do it! And through the Daleks I shall have such power!'

The Doctor abandoned any faint hope he might have had of reasoning with Davros. He knew he was looking upon the face of utter madness. In one swift movement he sprang from his chair and grasped Davros's single wrist. 'Release me,' croaked the metallic voice.

The Doctor ignored him. With his free hand he reached for the row of controls on Davros's chair-arm. 'I imagine these switches control your life-support system. How long would you survive if I turned them off? Answer me, Davros!'

'Less than thirty seconds.'

The Doctor moved his hand closer to the switches. 'Order the complete close-down of the Dalek incubator section.'

'Destroy the Daleks? Never!'

With one sweep of his hand, the Doctor flicked an entire row of switches into the 'off' position. The body of Davros slumped forward, like a puppet whose strings have been cut. The Doctor waited a few seconds, then turned the switches on again. Eerily, Davros jerked back into life. When he was sure Davros could hear him the Doctor said, 'Next time I press those switches, they stay pressed. I mean it, Davros. Now—give the order!'

The lens in the centre of Davros's forehead seemed to glare at the Doctor. 'Even if I obey, there will be no escape for you.'

'That isn't important.'

Davros realised the Doctor was sincere. Tonelessly he said, 'Press the communicator switch—the red one at the end.' The Doctor did so. Leaning forward to a built-in microphone, Davros said, 'Davros to Elite Unit Seven. All survival maintenance systems are to be closed down. The Dalek creatures are to be destroyed.'

'Tell them the order is final and cannot be countermanded,' said the Doctor urgently. Davros hesitated. 'Tell them!' The Doctor's hand hovered over the switches.

Reluctantly Davros began, 'This order cannot ...' Intent on his battle of wills with Davros, the Doctor realised too late that someone had entered the room. Nyder's truncheon took him across the back of the neck and he pitched to the floor. Again Davros leaned forward, almost gabbling in his haste. 'This is Davros. My last order is cancelled, repeat cancelled. No action is to be taken.' He sat back with a sigh of relief.

Nyder prodded the Doctor's body with the toe of one polished jackboot. 'What shall I do with him? It would be safest to kill him now.'

'Not yet. He still has knowledge that is vital to our future success. I shall wrench every last detail of it from his mind—and then he dies! Now, what of our rebellious scientists? How are they progressing?'

'Feeling against you is rising fast. Many of the Scientific Elite speak openly against you since the destruction of the city. Now some of the military are joining them.'

'It is as I expected.'

Nyder's face showed that he did not share his leader's calm. 'The rebels already outnumber those still loyal to you. Let me take a squad of Elite Guards to deal with them. I could wipe out their leaders in an hour.'

'You think like a soldier, Nyder. Rebellion is an idea. Suppress it too soon and it hides away and festers, bursting out elsewhere. My way is best.'

'As you wish.' Nyder hauled the semi-conscious Doctor to his feet. 'I'll take this one to the detention cell myself.' He kicked the Doctor brutally with his boot, 'Come on, you—move!' Nyder heaved the half-dazed Doctor to his feet and shoved him from the room.

Davros leaned towards his microphone. 'All Dalek Units. All Dalek Units. This is Davros ...'

The Daleks swept through the burning Thal city killing all before them. As a party of them shot down some fleeing Thals another Dalek glided into sight.

'Davros has commanded all Dalek units to disengage and return to the Bunker immediately.'

'We obey.'

The Daleks spun round and glided towards the city gates.

Just outside the city, the girl Bettan and a ragged group of Thals crouched in a trench, watching their city burn. Bettan tensed, 'Quiet, there's something moving out there.'

The giant cloaked shape of a muto appeared over the edge of the trench. Bettan raised her rifle but a deep voice rumbled. 'No, do not shoot. I am a friend.'

The muto jumped into the trench, hands stretched out appealingly. 'You are the Thal girl called Bettan?'

'That's right. How did you know?'

'My name is Sevrin. The Doctor sent me to find you. He asked me to raise a band of my people to help you.'

'Well—where are they?'

Sevrin bowed his head. 'My people will not fight. The old hatreds are too deep.'

Bettan nodded, unsurprised. 'Then we'll have to manage alone.'

Sevrin looked at the tattered little group. They were a mixture of soldiers and civilians, clutching a motley assortment of weapons. 'This is all of you?'

'All I could find alive,' Bettan said simply. 'I covered most of the city. We managed to raid the armoury, though. We've got plenty of arms and ammunition. Explosives too.' Sevrin saw that some of the Thals were clutching bombs and packs of explosives.

'You plan to attack the Bunker, with so few?' he asked doubtfully.

'Why not? At least we can die fighting.'

'Then I will help you,' Sevrin said determinedly. 'I am not afraid to fight.'

'Well, there's no point in delay.' Bettan began rousing her small group. 'Come on—it's time to move out!'

Nyder half-dragged, half-carried the semi-conscious Doctor towards the detention cell. He was pleased to see that the guard on the cell was alert. As soon as the guard saw Nyder approaching with his prisoner he turned to unlock the cell door. The door swung open and the guard turned round. Only then did Nyder realise that the 'guard' was Harry Sullivan.

Immediately Nyder threw the sagging Doctor at Harry and sprinted off down the corridor. Harry caught the Doctor, who was rapidly coming to, and led him into the cell. 'Things didn't go quite as planned,' he said apologetically.

Shaking his head to clear it, the Doctor saw that the cell held Sarah and two members of Davros's Scientific Elite. On the bunk was a guard, stripped of his uniform and bound and gagged with torn-up blankets.

Sarah helped the Doctor to sit down. 'He's still a bit groggy,' Harry said.

Sarah saw the Doctor looking at the two scientists. 'They're called Kavell and Gharman,' she explained. 'Kavell helped us escape. He and Gharman are leading the opposition to Davros.'

Gharman started to leave the cell. 'Come on, Kavell, we've a lot to do. We must act quickly…'

'Wait,' said the Doctor. 'I think Davros knows about you. Just as I was coming to, I heard him talking to Nyder.'

'Then why hasn't he taken more action against us?'

'Perhaps he doesn't care?' suggested Kavell. Knocking out the guard had given him new confidence. 'Davros knows we are too many for him.'

The Doctor shook his head, then winced as a stab of pain shot through him. 'I think he has some trap ready for you. Be careful.'

Gharman too seemed to be filled with confidence. 'Thanks for the warning, Doctor, I think we can take care of Davros.'

'That's right,' agreed Kavell. 'We're too many for him now.'

Eagerly the two scientists bustled out of the cell, hurrying off to rally their fellow conspirators.

The Doctor sat for a moment, head in his hands. He was summoning all the powers of his resilient Time Lord body to overcome the effects of his recent blow. Suddenly he rose and stretched, apparently as good as new. Sarah looked dubiously at him. 'I suppose it's no good telling you to rest for a while?'

'No, it isn't. For one thing this place isn't safe. For another, there's too much to be done. First, we've got to recover that Time Ring. Remember, we'll never get off this planet without it. Second, I *must* find and destroy that tape Davros made. The knowledge it holds could make the Daleks totally invincible.'

Full of his old determination, the Doctor led Harry and Sarah from the cell.

*

Outside the Bunker armoury, two of Nyder's Security Elite stood on watch, immaculate in their black uniforms. A head popped round the corner of a nearby corridor, and then popped back. It was Gharman, three more scientists behind him. 'Now remember,' he whispered, 'we resort to violence *only* if there is no other way.'

Chatting idly among themselves, the scientists strolled round the corner. The guards paid no particular attention as they drew level. Suddenly Gharman drew a hidden pistol and jammed it into the nearest guard's ribs. The second guard reacted instantly. Grabbing the nearest scientist as a shield, he hurled him into Gharman, who was knocked to the floor. Raising his rifle, the guard shot down another scientist, then crumpled and fell himself as Gharman fired from the floor. By now the third scientist had produced a gun, and disarmed the remaining guard. Gharman got to his feet, looking at the two bodies. 'A stupid waste of life,' he said sadly. 'Our intention is to make a bloodless revolution.' He waved towards the captured guard. 'Take him away and lock him up with the others. Get his keys first.'

Gharman unlocked the armoury door and they went inside. The plain metal room was lined with racks of weapons, and shelves holding detonators and explosives. Gharman turned to the scientist. 'Take as many weapons as you can carry and pass them out to our people.' At that moment Kavell hurried into the armoury.

'Well done, Gharman!' Before Gharman could reply the little man went on excitedly, 'They're coming over to our side in droves. Security Guards too. We have the backing of at least eighty per cent of those in the Bunker. We're winning, Gharman, we're winning ...'

Gharman took a rifle from the rack and passed it to Kavell. He took another for himself. Holding the unaccustomed weapon awkwardly, he made for the door. 'Very well,' he said. 'Let's finish it off ...'

In the huge emptiness of the main laboratory, Davros sat alone in his chair. From the corridors all round, he heard the sounds of shooting, the bustle of running feet, even the occasional burst of cheering. Davros showed no reaction. He just sat there, silently, waiting, a faint smile on the thin, lipless mouth ... Slowly the fingers of his one withered hand began drumming on the arm of the chair.

10

DECISION FOR THE DOCTOR

Nyder ran into the laboratory, blaster in hand. His uniform was dishevelled, and his usual cold manner replaced by an air of terror. 'Davros, they're taking over. Soon they'll be in total control. *Everyone's* turned against us, even men I thought I could trust ...'

Davros didn't answer. The only sound was the drumming of his fingers.

Nyder's voice rose in panic. 'Listen, I've got a squad of men in section nine. If I order them into action now, they might stay loyal. Davros ...'

The metallic voice was so quiet as to be almost inaudible. 'I hear you, Nyder.'

'Then tell me what to do!' Nyder had grown so used to the support of Davros that without it he felt lost and abandoned.

'Find their leaders. Hand over your weapons to them. Order all members of your Security Guard to do the same. Tell the rebel leaders that *I* have given these orders to avoid bloodshed. Tell them I will submit to their demands.'

Nyder shook his head incredulously. 'We admit we're beaten? We simply surrender?'

'That is what they will believe.'

The evasiveness of this answer gave Nyder new hope. 'You mean to—'

Davros interrupted him. 'Nyder! You—and the rebels—will find out what I mean in good time. Now—carry out my orders.'

*

The route followed by the Doctor and his friends took them past the armoury. The doors gaped open, and Harry couldn't resist taking a look inside. 'Hang on, Doctor. This might come in handy.'

They followed him into the armoury. There were still plenty of weapons on the shelves. Harry grabbed a rifle for himself and offered one to the Doctor. The Doctor shook his head absentmindedly and began hunting around the wall cupboards. Sarah saw that he was filling his pockets with small waxed cartons, spools of wire, and a variety of other objects. 'That's explosive, isn't it, Doctor?' she asked.

'Explosives and detonators,' agreed the Doctor. 'Seems almost providential.'

'What are you going to use it for?'

The Doctor sighed. 'The Time Lords gave me three options. Discover the Daleks' weakness—if they have one. Alter their genetic development, so they become less evil. Or destroy them entirely. Now only the last option is still open.' As the Doctor looked down at her, Sarah was surprised to see the sadness in his eyes. 'I'm going to kill everything in that incubator room. I'm going to destroy the Daleks for ever.'

Davros sat silently in the empty laboratory. Nyder entered, still under strain, but calmer now. 'Everything has been done as you ordered. They are on their way.'

Davros nodded, but said nothing. Nyder took up his usual position behind Davros's chair. A few minutes later Kavell and Gharman entered. They made a strangely incongruous picture, one short and plump, the other tall and thin. Davros spoke, 'You have something to say to me?'

Hesitantly Gharman stepped forward. He knew that he had won, that Davros was in his power, yet the habit of years made his voice respectful. 'Davros, no one questions that under your guidance we have made incredible progress ...'

Ruthlessly Davros interrupted. 'You did not come here to flatter me. You came to deliver an ultimatum. Do so.'

'Very well. Initially the Dalek was intended as a life-support system for the creature into which we Kaleds must ultimately evolve. However we feel the concept has been perverted. You have tampered with the genetic structure of your forced mutations to create a ruthless power for evil. This must not continue.'

'What do you suggest?'

'All work on the Daleks will cease immediately. Those created so far will be destroyed. If you agree to these terms we shall be proud to work under your guidance on the rebuilding of our society.'

'And if I refuse?'

Gharman's voice hardened. 'The Daleks will still be destroyed. You will be imprisoned, and we shall continue under a democratically elected leader.' Davros was silent. After a moment Gharman said nervously, 'Well?'

'At least do me the courtesy of allowing me time to consider.' Davros spun his chair and wheeled it to the other end of the laboratory. Gharman and Kavell looked nervously at each other, wondering how they had lost the initiative. After a long and agonising pause, Davros wheeled his chair back to them. 'I have made my decision. I will accept your ultimatum—on condition that I am first allowed to speak to a full meeting of the Elite, both Scientific and Security. When I have finished, a vote will be taken. I will abide by the decision of the majority.' Taken aback, the two delegates said nothing. 'Well?' snapped Davros. 'Do you agree? You wish to be "democratic", do you not?'

Gharman looked at Kavell, who shrugged. Both knew that ninety per cent of those in the Bunker were now against Davros. What harm could it do to let a once-honoured leader save his face? 'Very well,' Gharman said. 'It is agreed.'

Davros retained control till the last. 'The meeting will take place immediately. Arrange it. You may go now.' Dismissed, Gharman and Kavell turned and left. Once they were out of the room, Davros spun his chair to face Nyder. There was fierce exultation in the metallic voice. 'Victory is ours, Nyder. Democracy, freedom, fairness …' Davros spat out the words like oaths. 'Achievement comes through power, and power through strength. *They have lost!*'

Concealed in a trench near to the Bunker, Bettan and her small force crouched in hiding. Outside the trench a long line of Daleks was sweeping past. Bettan looked up as they disappeared from sight.

'The blockhouse is just over the next rise. That's where they must be heading.'

Sevrin tapped her on the shoulder. 'Keep down. There are more coming.'

Another line of Daleks glided by. When they were gone Sevrin said, 'Will you still attack the Bunker now the Daleks are back?'

Bettan nodded slowly. 'Why not? Davros and his Daleks will soon be inside the Bunker together. We're going to make sure they stay there—for ever!'

The Doctor, Harry and Sarah stood outside the heavy door with its glass viewing panel—the door to which Ronson had earlier brought the Doctor. The Doctor slid back the panel-cover and a greenish light spilled over his face. 'Are there really Daleks in there?' asked Sarah.

'The flesh and blood part of them—if indeed it is still flesh and blood after Davros's genetic tampering.' He began busying himself with detonators, explosives and coils of wire. Harry plucked up courage and looked through the panel.

Morbid curiosity made Sarah ask, 'What do they look like?'

Harry peered into the dim light. 'They seem to be in different stages of development. Some are in jars and tanks ... others seem to be able to move around. Maybe they're fully grown ones ...'

The Doctor, his preparations completed, passed Harry a large spool of wire. 'Pay this out to me slowly, will you?' He put his hand on the door.

'You're not going in there, Doctor?' asked Sarah.

'Only for a moment—the creatures are harmless—I think. Just rather unpleasant ...'

Harry braced himself. 'Do you want me to come in with you?'

To his relief the Doctor said, 'No need, Harry. It's just a matter of setting the charges where they'll do most damage. Shouldn't take long.' Unwinding wire from Harry's spool as he went along, the Doctor disappeared inside the Incubator Room.

After a time the tugging on the spool stopped. Evidently the Doctor had all the wire he needed. Nothing happened for quite a while. All they could do was wait.

Inside the Incubator Room, the Doctor bent his head over his work, paying no attention to the horrors all around him. Greenish light from the tanks filled the room. Inside those tanks ghastly-shaped creatures twisted and writhed in agitation, while in the darker corners of the room other monstrosities cowered away timidly. The Doctor moved from place to place, planting packets of explosives, connecting his central wire to the terminal on each packet. He didn't notice that out of the darkness something shapeless was oozing across the floor towards him …

In the corridor Sarah looked worriedly at Harry. 'What's taking him so long?'

'It's a pretty delicate job, planting explosives.'

'Well he *should* be finished by now. I'm going to take a look.' A choking cry from inside the room sent them running through the door. In the dim green light, they could see the Doctor swaying wildly. Something like a coating of live black tar was covering his legs, flowing steadily upwards as if to engulf him …

'Harry, help me,' yelled Sarah. She dashed into the room and grabbed one of the Doctor's arms. Harry grabbed the other, and they heaved him free of the pool of black liquid, which let go its grip with an ugly squelching sound. All three stumbled out of the room, and Harry slammed the door behind them.

Sarah shuddered. 'What was that awful stuff?'

'Some kind of nutrient, I think. Seemed almost alive, didn't it?' The Doctor had held on to the wire which was now running under the door. For want of a knife, he bit through the wire with his teeth and began peeling back the protective plastic coating, revealing the gleaming metal underneath. Then he peeled off another length of wire, bared both ends and looked round for a power-source. A wall-light glowed dimly nearby. In a moment the Doctor had dismantled it, and fixed one end of his wire to its inner workings, sucking his fingers as blue sparks shot out. Holding the wire from the light in one hand, the wire from under the door in the other, the Doctor said, 'All I have to do is touch *this* wire to this one, and the explosives will go off.'

Sarah spoke impatiently, 'Then what are you waiting for?'

'Do I have the right?' said the Doctor simply.

Sarah was astonished. 'To destroy the Daleks? How can you possibly doubt it? You know what they'll become.'

In an agonised voice the Doctor tried to explain, 'It isn't so simple, Sarah. The evil of the Daleks produced counter-reactions of good. Many future worlds will stop warring among themselves, join in alliance to fight the Daleks.' Sarah looked at him, unable to believe that the Doctor was held up by ethical scruples at a time like this. But the Doctor was perfectly serious. To him the moral issue was real and vital. 'Suppose somebody who knew the future told you a certain child would grow up to be an evil dictator—could you then destroy that child?'

Sarah made a last attempt to talk sense into him. 'We're not talking about some imaginary child, Doctor, we're talking about the Daleks. The most evil creatures ever created. Complete your mission and destroy them. You must!'

The Doctor stared at the gleaming wires as though mesmerised. 'I simply have to touch *this* to *this* and generations of people might live without fear, never even hearing the word "Dalek".'

'Then do it,' urged Sarah. 'Suppose it was a question of wiping out the bacteria that caused some terrible disease. You wouldn't hesitate then, would you?'

The Doctor looked at her solemnly. 'But if I wipe out a whole intelligent life-form, I'll be no better than the Daleks myself.' In an agony of indecision, the Doctor repeated his question. 'I could destroy the Daleks, here and now. But do I have the right?'

11

TRIUMPH OF THE DALEKS

They were never to know how the Doctor would have resolved his moral dilemma. A shout from the other end of the corridor interrupted them. They turned to see Gharman running towards them his face alight with triumph. 'Doctor, I've been looking for you. We've won! Davros has submitted to all our terms!'

'Davros surrendered? Just like that?'

Gharman waved a dismissive hand. 'He is trying to save face, of course. He asked to be allowed to speak to a full meeting of the Elite. But that's no more than a formality. The voting will be a landslide against him.'

The Doctor took the wire projecting beneath the door and gave a sudden heave. Somewhere inside the room the wire snapped. The Doctor reeled it in until the broken end came from under the door. 'Gharman, I'm more grateful than you'll ever know. You've saved me from the most terrible decision of my life.'

Gharman was too excited to listen to him. 'The meeting is just about to begin, Doctor. I wanted you to be there. Will you come?' Taking the Doctor's assent for granted, he led the way back down the corridor.

'With the greatest of pleasure.'

The Doctor followed the eager Gharman, and Sarah and Harry hurried after them. At the back of her mind, Sarah was wishing Gharman had arrived a moment later. The Doctor might have decided to set off those explosives after all ...

The big central laboratory was an impressive sight. Every scientist and security man in the Bunker had somehow managed to squeeze inside. They were all tightly packed on one side of the room. On the other Davros sat alone in his chair, Nyder by his side. The Doctor, Harry and Sarah watched from a position by one of the doors. Gharman stood at the front of the crowd, opposite Davros. 'Everyone is here, Davros,' he said. 'We are waiting to hear whatever you have to say.'

Davros began to speak. He described his years of struggle to develop the travel machine that would protect the creatures into which their race must evolve, of his desire that when the war was over, his own race should stand supreme. The assembled crowd listened in courteous silence, but it was clear that his words had no appeal for them. At long last the Kaleds were sickened of war and slaughter. They wanted no part of Davros's dreams of conquest.

Satisfied that the vote against Davros would indeed be a landslide, the Doctor whispered to Sarah and Harry, 'Let's get the Time Ring while they're all occupied.'

They began working their way round the edge of the crowd towards the corner desk that had once been Ronson's. Progress was slow, since the crowd was densely packed. All the while they heard Davros droning on. By now the crowd was shuffling restlessly, impatient for him to end. 'At this very moment,' Davros was saying, 'the production lines stand ready in the workshops, on the lower levels. They are totally automated, fully programmed. The Daleks no longer depend on us— they are a power in their own right. Would you end everything we have achieved together?'

The Doctor and his friends reached Ronson's desk at last. The Doctor's possessions were still strewn on top of it, and he began stuffing them back in his pocket. But there was no sign of the Time Ring! Frantically they began to search.

Davros had wheeled his chair over to a control panel set into one wall, the crowd falling back before him. He pointed his withered hand at a large red button. 'This is a destruct button. Press it and you will destroy everything in the Bunker, outside of this room. You will destroy the Daleks, and with them the future of our race. Which of you will do it?' The crowd shuffled uneasily. Such was the dominance of Davros's personality that no one dared step forward. 'You are men without courage,' Davros spoke scornfully. 'You have lost the right to survive.'

Stung by the contempt in his voice, Gharman stepped forward to address the crowd. 'You have heard Davros's case. What he does not tell you is that there is another way—to destroy his conditioned, conscienceless creatures and allow our mutation to follow its natural course. Our race will survive—survive with all the strengths and weaknesses we have ourselves, not as an unfeeling and heartless monstrosity. That is our choice. Now it is time to decide.'

Most of this debate was lost on the Doctor and his friends, since they were frantically searching the area round the desk. It was Sarah who spotted the Time Ring at last. It had fallen from the desk and had been kicked by some careless foot until it was almost out of sight beneath a work-bench. Sarah wriggled underneath, scooped out the bracelet and handed it to the Doctor, who slipped it back on his arm with a sigh of relief. 'Bless you, Sarah. Now if we can only manage to find that tape-recording and destroy it—we can all go home!'

Over the heads of the crowd they heard once more the voice of Davros. 'You have heard my case, and you have heard Gharman's. I will give you a few more minutes to decide. Then you must answer, not only to me, but to your future.'

Outside the blockhouse that led to the Bunker a small army of Daleks was grouped, silently waiting. Hidden in a trench nearby, Bettan, Sevrin and their little band looked on, wondering what was happening.

(In the centre of the laboratory, isolated amidst a largely-hostile crowd, Davros was also waiting. He glanced at a digital clock set in one wall. As the figures clicked up to record the passing of another time-unit, his finger stabbed down on one of the buttons on his console.)

The metal gates of the blockhouse slid smoothly open.

Bettan and Sevrin watched as the army of Daleks glided through. The inner gates opened, and the Daleks disappeared down the tunnel that led to the Bunker. No sooner were they out of sight than Bettan and her ragged band of commandos ran through the gates after them.

Bettan gave swift orders. 'Right. Set charges there ... there, and more there. Go as deep inside the tunnel as you can without being seen.' She turned to Sevrin. 'This is the only way into the Bunker?'

'It is now,' Sevrin said grimly. 'There was once a way in from the Kaled City, but your rocket buried that for ever.'

Bettan nodded satisfied. 'Then if we do the same to *this* entrance, we can bury the Daleks with those who created them.' There was no pity in her voice. The slaughter and destruction she had seen in her own city were too fresh in her mind.

'But surely you will give the Doctor and his friends time to get clear?'

Bettan shook her head. 'I can't. I *must* blow the tunnel as soon as the charges are prepared. If anyone sees what we're doing, we're too few to fight them off.'

'How long?' asked Sevrin.

'Thirty minutes. Possibly less.'

'Then I must go inside and warn the Doctor.'

'That's very brave of you,' said Bettan. She hesitated. 'You understand, I *can't* delay things? If you're not back by the time we're ready ...'

'I understand,' said Sevrin. 'But I must try.'

Bettan nodded. 'Good luck. I hope you make it.' It was clear that she never expected to see him again. Swiftly and silently, Sevrin ran down the tunnel into the Bunker.

Sarah, Harry and the Doctor were waiting impatiently. 'How much longer?' asked Sarah.

'Not long,' whispered the Doctor. 'It's nearly time for the grand finale.' As yet he didn't realise the ghastly truth of his words.

Davros wheeled his chair to face the crowd. 'You have had ample time to decide. Let all those who are loyal to me and to the future of our race move forward to stand at my side.' The gap between Davros and the crowd seemed very large now. At first no one moved to cross it. At last one man moved. Then another. A handful more, and that was all. Davros looked round. 'No more?' he asked ironically. 'Kravos, will you betray me? Fenatin—my science saved your life. Do *you* turn against me?' The named men shuffled uneasily. But they did not move to join him.

The Doctor watched, almost with pity, as Davros appealed in vain to first one man then another. It was somehow degrading to see him plead. Why didn't he just accept defeat?

Harry noticed that Nyder had edged away from Davros and was slipping out of the laboratory. He nudged the Doctor. 'Where do you think old Nyder's off to?'

The Doctor gave him a thoughtful look. A strong feeling of unease was creeping over him. Something about Davros's behaviour just didn't ring true, and Nyder's disappearing act made the feeling stronger. 'Let's find out,' he suggested. They slipped out of the laboratory after Nyder.

They followed him down one of the perimeter corridors that ran round the laboratory and up some steps, catching up with him along an upper corridor. At the sight of his unwelcome followers Nyder reached for a gun, but Harry tackled him hard, and sent him crashing half-stunned to the ground.

Nyder scrambled to his feet and started to run, but the Doctor reached out a long arm to grab him. Harry joined in and there was a wild three-cornered fight which ended with Nyder disarmed and subdued. 'Now, where were you off to in such a hurry?' panted the Doctor.

Nyder shrugged. 'I was getting out while I could. Davros is finished—that means I'm finished too.'

The Doctor shook his head. 'That doesn't ring quite true. Let's try something else. Where's Davros's office? I want the tape-recording you took away.'

Nyder said nothing. Harry grabbed him by the throat and shook him till he choked. 'Just along there ...' Nyder nodded to a heavy steel door along the corridor. They moved to the door. It was locked. Nyder produced a key to open it and they all went inside.

Davros's office was small and functional, the walls covered with blueprints of early Dalek designs. The main feature was a small inner window which looked down on to the main laboratory below. They could see Davros haranguing the crowd, still with only one or two supporters beside him. The Doctor looked at Nyder. 'Where is it?' he snapped. Nyder said nothing, but instinctively his eyes flickered to a safe set in the wall. There was a combination-dial in the door. 'Be a good chap and open it for us,' urged the Doctor.

'Only Davros knows the combination.'

The Doctor looked at the safe. It was set fairly high in the wall. He pushed a chair underneath and sat down. 'I doubt that. Davros has the use of only one arm.' The Doctor raised his own right arm. From a sitting position the safe dial was well out of reach. 'You must have to open the safe for him. So open it for us, Nyder, or I'll let Harry throttle you. We're desperate men, remember.' Harry did his best to look ferocious. He must have done pretty well. Nyder went to the safe and spun the dials. The door swung open, revealing the tape-spool on a shelf in plain sight. The Doctor took it out and dropped it into a metal waste-bin. 'Now, we need some way to destroy it.'

'How about this, Doctor?' Harry had picked up a Dalek gun from the desk. Evidently an experimental model it was plugged into a portable power pack.

'A Dalek gun,' said the Doctor, pleased. 'How *very* fitting!' With an appropriately ceremonial air, he raised the gun and fired it. The spool exploded into flames. They stood and watched it burn. Unfortunately they forgot to watch Nyder at the same time. Seizing his chance, he sprinted through the door, slamming and locking it behind him. Harry rattled the door furiously but it was no use. The Doctor was quite unconcerned. 'Let him go, Harry, he's not important. Our job here's over now anyway. The power of Davros has been broken. Old Gharman will see that the Daleks of the future are, well, humanised, you might say.'

'What about the ones Davros already has operational, Doctor?' Sarah asked. 'The ones you saw attacking the Thal City.'

'Gharman will have them recalled and destroyed,' said the Doctor reassuringly.

Harry thumped the door. 'Well, we're still locked in.'

The Doctor smiled. 'Doesn't matter in the least, old chap. We'll simply leave from here. All we have to do is stand in a circle and touch the Time Ring …' The Doctor touched his wrist. 'Oh no!' The Time Ring wasn't there.

They stared wildly at each other. 'It's outside,' said Sarah suddenly. 'It's got to be. It must have come off in that fight with Nyder.'

Suddenly getting the door open became a matter of vital importance. Harry and the Doctor kicked at it to no avail. They tried the Dalek gun on it, but the power-pack must have been nearly exhausted. After charring the steel quite promisingly, the gun suddenly went dead. The Doctor produced a piece of wire and tried to pick the lock. 'It's no good,' he said disgustedly. 'He's left the key in the lock on the other side. Oh well, never mind. When the dethroning of Davros is over I expect someone will turn up to let us out.' The Doctor wandered over and looked at the scene in the laboratory below them. 'You know,' he said slowly. 'I *still* can't help feeling it's unlike Davros to give in so easily.'

The Doctor noticed a switch near a speaker-grille beside the window. He flicked it idly. Immediately they could hear the voice of Davros in the laboratory below. Isolated and alone, he was still talking as if *he* was the one who held power. 'This is your last chance. Join me, or suffer the consequences!' No one moved.

Pityingly Gharman said, 'Accept defeat. It is over for you, Davros!'

'No!' shouted Davros suddenly. 'It is over for *you*! I allowed this charade for only one reason. I wanted to know who was truly loyal to me.' He gestured at the small group around him. 'With these few faithful helpers, I shall continue my great work.'

From his viewpoint above the laboratory, the Doctor saw Gharman's shake of the head. 'You are insane to talk like this, you must see that you are totally outnumbered.'

'No,' said Davros again, this time his voice low and menacing. 'It is *you* who are outnumbered, Gharman, you and your traitor friends.' With an elaborate gesture, Davros pressed a control. Every one of the many doors around the laboratory slid open. Framed in each stood a Dalek.

The crowd fell back in terror as the Daleks glided into the room.

12

A KIND OF VICTORY

Davros and his supporters retreated into one corner of the room. The rest, the vast majority, were herded into a tightly packed circle, surrounded by a ring of Daleks. Tighter and tighter the circle was drawn until men were jammed one against the other. For a long, terrible moment Davros regarded his enemies. Then he said, 'Exterminate them!' Fire blazed from the Dalek guns.

The Doctor and his horrified friends had grandstand seats at a massacre. Bodies fell in swathes as the Daleks fired into the tightly packed crowd, and the room was full of screaming. Nyder entered from a door by Davros's side, and stood looking on with evident satisfaction. Not all of Davros's supporters were so lacking in feeling. One of them, an officer of the Security Elite, recoiled in horror from the carnage. 'Stop them, Davros,' he screamed, 'you've *got* to stop them.' He grabbed Davros by the shoulder, but Nyder pulled him back, shoving him out into the crowd. Away from the charmed group around Davros, he was immediately shot down by Dalek guns.

Sarah turned sickened from the slaughter below and hammered hysterically on the door. 'Let us out. Please someone let us out!' she screamed.

Harry tried to calm her. 'It's no use, Sarah ...'

The Doctor tapped him on the shoulder. 'Don't be so sure, Harry!' He pointed. The handle of the door was moving, turned from the outside. They heard the key in the lock. The door began opening slowly, and a gun-muzzle appeared. The Doctor and Harry backed away—and Sevrin's hooded face appeared round the door.

Sarah ran to him and hugged him, but he cut short her thanks. 'I was looking for you when I heard your voice. We have very little time.

93

The Thals have set explosive charges at the entrance. They'll detonate as soon as they're ready.'

'Thank you, Sevrin,' said the Doctor. 'Now if I can just find that Time Ring ...'

They found the Time Ring easily enough, in the corridor outside. Just as the Doctor snatched it up, a Dalek appeared at the end of the corridor. They set off at a run, only to find a second Dalek facing them at the other end. Skidding round they hurled themselves down a side corridor, relieved to see no more Daleks. They ran frantically down endless corridors, not pausing till the Daleks were far behind. The Doctor stopped in a wide corridor, buttressed by huge pillars. 'We are near the entrance now,' gasped Sevrin. 'If we can make it through the next section we'll be safe.'

The Doctor slipped the Time Ring from his wrist and passed it to Sarah. 'Look after this for me, will you? Sevrin—I'm relying on you to get my friends out of here.'

Sarah stared at him. 'What are you going to do?'

'I'm going back to the Incubator Room. The charges are still laid. This time I'll blow the place up as I should have done before. Now, you three get out of here.'

Before anyone could argue the Doctor was sprinting down one of the side corridors. 'Come,' Sevrin spoke urgently. 'Time is short now.' Quickly he led them on their way.

Davros regarded the bodies of his fallen enemies. 'Now the traitors have been disposed of, the Daleks will take over security of the Bunker. The rest of us will go on, working to improve every aspect of Dalek design.'

Nyder ran back into the laboratory, stepping casually over the fallen bodies. 'Davros, the alien prisoners I locked in your office have escaped.' Davros could not bear that anything should mar his triumph.

'Then they must be found. Seek them out and exterminate them.'

Immediately there came a chorus of Dalek voices, 'We obey!' Daleks glided from the laboratory.

*

Bettan stood waiting in the blockhouse, looking nervously down the tunnel. A Thal soldier came running out of the tunnel, playing out flex behind him. He ran up to Bettan. 'That's the last charge in position.'

'Very well, prepare to detonate.'

The soldier began wiring the flex to a big portable field-detonator. Bettan stood watching him, spinning round as she heard footsteps running out of the tunnel. It was Sevrin with Harry and Sarah. 'I'd given you up,' she said, amazed. 'Better move back, we're almost ready to detonate.'

Sarah clutched her arm. 'You *can't*, not yet. The Doctor's still inside…'

Harry added his plea. 'Give him a few minutes more at least.'

Bettan hesitated. 'Very well, just a few minutes. But if the Daleks start coming up that tunnel—then I detonate!'

The Doctor crouched in the Incubator Room, rewiring the charges with nimble fingers, ignoring once more the horrors gibbering all around him. His work concluded, he backed out into the corridor, trailing the wire behind him. The wire from the wall power-source was still stretched from the other side of the corridor. The Doctor grabbed it and was just about to bring the two wires together when a Dalek appeared at the end of the corridor. It fired, charring the wall by the Doctor's head. The Doctor leaped back, letting go of both wires as he did so. He sheltered behind the wall buttress and peered out. The Dalek hadn't moved. The Doctor could see the ends of the two wires, tantalisingly close together. If he could only manage to join them … He stretched out a long arm, grabbed the nearest wire, and started edging it towards the other. The Dalek spotted the movement and fired again. The edge of its blast caught the tip of the Doctor's fingers and he snatched his hand back in pain.

A wild thought struck the Doctor. He looked at the end of the two wires, so very near each other … It might work, he thought. Suddenly the Doctor leaped from cover and zig-zagged down the corridor in full view of the Dalek. It fired, missed, fired again. The second blast missed too, and the Doctor leaped into a side-corridor out of sight. Angrily the Dalek started in pursuit. As it glided down the corridor the metal of its body casing, vibrant with static electricity, passed over the two wires and completed the circuit … There was a huge detonation and the wall of the Incubator Room exploded outwards, burying the Dalek in rubble. The Doctor popped his head round the corner, took a quick look at the wreckage. He gave a satisfied nod and started sprinting for the main exit.

In the blockhouse checkpoint, the anxious group looked down the empty tunnel. Nervously one of the soldiers began fiddling with the scanning equipment. Suddenly he shouted, 'Look, I'm getting a picture on one of these scanners.' Sure enough, one of the screens was showing a blurred picture of the main laboratory. They could even hear a faint murmur of sound.

'Try for more volume,' ordered Bettan. 'We may be able to find out what's happening down there.'

Obediently the soldier adjusted controls. The picture improved, and sound came through clearly. Sarah shivered as she heard the voice of Davros. 'Send a patrol of Daleks to secure the main entrance.'

'I obey.'

'That is it,' snapped Bettan. 'I *must* detonate right away.'

'Give it one minute more,' begged Harry, 'Please!'

Bettan said, 'I'm sorry. I daren't wait any longer.' She turned to the soldier. 'Get those tunnel doors closed and we'll detonate from in here.'

The Doctor was haring down a corridor, running for his life. A patrol of Daleks appeared behind him. Their guns blazed and their metallic voices filled the air. 'Exterminate! Exterminate! Exterminate!'

Safe in his laboratory, surrounded by a guard of Daleks, Davros was preparing to resume work. His eye was caught by flashing lights on an indicator panel. He wheeled his chair round angrily. 'The Dalek production line has been started. I gave no such order. Who is responsible?'

Davros looked angrily at the handful of surviving scientists scattered about the room. None of them spoke. A Dalek glided forward. 'I gave the order,' said the metallic voice.

Davros looked at his creation angrily. Some minor malfunction, no doubt. It could be corrected, perhaps even by a simple verbal re-programming. He glided his chair up to the Dalek and spoke slowly and clearly. 'You will perform no function unless directly ordered by *me*. You will obey only *my* commands. The Dalek production line will be halted immediately.'

The Dalek did not move.

Davros was enraged. 'You heard my order. Obey! Obey!'

Still the Dalek did not move. Nyder sighed. He moved towards the control panel. 'All right, I'll do it …' He reached for the control. Almost casually, the nearest Dalek swivelled round and blasted him down. Davros looked on unbelievingly as Nyder's smoking body twisted and fell.

The Dalek spoke again, 'Production will continue.' Davros backed his chair slowly away …

Harry and Sarah watched helplessly as the iron doors of the tunnel began to slide slowly closed. Bettan stood watching too, beside her a soldier with his hand on the plunger of an old-fashioned field detonator. Bettan said, 'Fire!'

The soldier heaved up the plunger handle. He was about to force it down, when Sarah screamed, 'Wait, please wait. The Doctor's coming!'

The soldier hesitated. Harry and Sarah ran to the doors and held them back by force. The Doctor came tearing along the tunnel, a patrol of Daleks close behind him. Just as their strength failed, the Doctor reached the fast-narrowing gap and squeezed through.

The Daleks glided in pursuit, gun-sticks blazing, then were hidden from view by the closing door …

Bettan tapped the soldier on the arm. He pushed the plunger down with all his force. A thunderous explosion on the other side of the doors shook the checkpoint, sending them all flying.

Sarah picked herself up, and staggered over to the scanner screen. Incredibly, it was still working. On it they could see Daleks in a menacing circle around Davros. Davros was desperately trying to regain control of his creations but they could hear the fear in his voice. 'You must obey me,' he was saying. 'I created you. I am your master!'

One of the Daleks seemed to be speaking for the others, as if already they had evolved their own leaders. 'Our programming does not permit us to acknowledge any creature superior to the Daleks.'

'Without me you cannot exist,' insisted Davros. 'You cannot progress.'

There was total arrogance in the Dalek voice, the arrogance that Davros himself had given it. 'We are programmed to survive. We have the ability to evolve in any way necessary for that survival.'

Another Dalek glided in. Ignoring Davros, it reported to its leader. 'Main exit blocked by explosion to length of one thousand units.'

The Dalek began issuing orders to deal with the problem. Other Daleks glided to obey.

Sarah nudged the Doctor. 'Did you manage to do anything in the Incubator Room?'

'Quite a bit—with a little help from a Dalek. The damage I did will set them back a thousand years.'

'That's pretty good then, isn't it?'

The Doctor smiled ruefully. 'In the totality of Time, it's no more than—that!' and he snapped his fingers.

Harry drew their attention to the screen. 'Look, something's happening.'

Fascinated they gathered round to watch the inevitable end of the clash between Davros and the monsters he had created. The terrified handful of scientists who had elected to support Davros were being herded into a corner. The Dalek leader spoke. 'All inferior creatures are the enemy of the Daleks. They must be destroyed.'

Davros began pleading for the few men who had been loyal to him. 'Wait. These men are scientists. They can help you. Let them live. Have you no pity?'

'Pi-ty?' The word sounded strange in the Dalek voice. 'I have no understanding of the word. It is not registered in my vocabulary bank.' It wheeled to face the other Daleks. 'Exterminate them!' Once again the Dalek gun-sticks roared, and the handful of humans crumpled and fell.

In the centre of the laboratory, Davros confronted the Dalek leader. 'For the last time … I am your creator. You must … you will … obey me!'

'We obey no one. We are the Daleks!'

The watchers saw Davros spin his chair and speed it towards the destructor button on the wall. As his withered hand reached up, they heard the voice of the Dalek leader. 'Exterminate him!' All the Daleks seemed to fire at once, and Davros and his chair exploded in flame, the destructor button still untouched.

The Dalek leader glided forward to address its fellows. The action brought it closer to the scanner screen so that it seemed almost to be talking to the small group watching in the checkpoint. 'We are entombed here, but we still live on. This is only the beginning. We will prepare. We will grow stronger. When the time is right, we will emerge. We shall build our own City. We shall rule Skaro. The Daleks will be the supreme power in the Universe …!' Suddenly the screen went blank.

'Thank goodness,' said Sarah. '*Please*—can we go now?'

Sevrin, Bettan and the others were already leaving, assuming the Doctor and his friends would follow them out of the blockhouse.

The Doctor said, 'The Time Ring please, Sarah.'

As Sarah gave him the Ring she said, 'We've failed, haven't we, Doctor?'

'Not entirely. We've given the Daleks a nasty setback, perhaps that's all we were intended to do … it's a kind of victory.'

He smiled at Sarah who said, '*You* don't seem too disappointed anyway.'

'Hand on the ring, please,' said the Doctor briskly. He held it up, and Harry and Sarah obeyed. Their fingers touched the metal and after a moment Sarah felt a strange disembodied sensation sweeping over her.

Sevrin, who had come back into the checkpoint to see what was delaying his friends, was astonished to see them simply fading away into nothingness. Sarah waved, called 'Goodbye, Sevrin …' and vanished.

Sarah felt everything dissolve into spinning blackness. But somehow she could still hear the Doctor's voice echoing hollowly. 'Disappointed, Sarah? No, not really. You see, although I know that Daleks will create havoc and destruction for untold thousands of years … I also know that out of their great evil … some … great … good … must come.'

DOCTOR WHO AND THE PYRAMIDS OF MARS

PROLOGUE

THE LEGEND OF THE OSIRIANS

In a galaxy unimaginably distant from ours, on a planet called Phaester Osiris, there arose a race so powerful that they became like gods.

As well as mastering technology and science, the Osirians developed powers of pure thought, bending the physical world to their will by the strength of their minds alone.

As they grew in power, so they grew in wisdom—all but one. His name was Sutekh and he was great among the Osirians. But greater still was his brother Horus, whom all Osirians called leader. All but Sutekh, who hated Horus and was jealous of him.

The Osirians spread throughout the galaxies of the cosmos. They ruled many worlds, and were often worshipped as gods. But Sutekh stayed on Phaester Osiris, their home planet, working to develop his powers so that he might one day overthrow his brother Horus.

The Osirians were a long-lived race. Sutekh worked and studied for thousands of years, until his powers were truly awe-inspiring. But his mind was full of jealousy and hatred, and in time this turned to madness. Over-mastered by his own fears, Sutekh became convinced that not only the other Osirians, but *all* sentient life was his mortal enemy. Not just the more intelligent life-forms, but animals, reptiles, insects, plants … Sutekh hated them all. He feared that someday, somewhere there might evolve a life-form powerful enough to destroy him.

An insane ambition formed in Sutekh's twisted mind. He would range through the galaxies and destroy *all* life, until only he remained as unchallenged ruler. He became Sutekh the Destroyer—and he began by destroying his own planet.

Leaving the shattered desolation of Phaester Osiris behind him, Sutekh blazed a trail of havoc across the cosmos, wrecking and smashing world after world with his titanic powers. Soon news of his madness reached fellow Osirians. Led by Horus, they began the search for Sutekh, determined to destroy him.

Tracking him by his trail of destruction, they hunted him across the cosmos. At last Sutekh took refuge on an obscure planet called Earth, and here, finally, his fellow Osirians found him.

The battle was long and fierce, for Sutekh was a formidable opponent. Seven hundred and forty Osirians came to Earth to combine against him, before he was finally defeated and made captive, in a land called Egypt.

They brought him before his brother Horus for judgement. Many urged that all the Osirians should link their minds and blast Sutekh from existence. But Horus would not agree. To kill Sutekh would mean that they too were destroyers. Horus decreed that Sutekh should not die but should be made eternally captive. A pyramid was built to become his prison. And since more than walls of stone were needed to imprison such a being as Sutekh, he was locked in the grip of a mighty forcefield, paralysed and utterly helpless.

For even greater safety, the control-point of this forcefield was placed not on Earth, but on one of the other planets circling its sun. On Earth, a secret cult of Egyptian priests was set up, to guard the Pyramid.

Satisfied that Sutekh was for ever bound, Horus and the other Osirians went on their way. What became of the Osirians no one can say. They vanished from our cosmos and were seen no more. On Earth they left behind them legends of the all-powerful gods who fought wars among themselves.

Deep inside the Pyramid, Sutekh lived on. For thousands upon thousands of years he endured his long captivity. Bound by the forcefield of Horus, scarcely able to move a muscle, only his twisted brain was active. It planned and plotted without cease, waiting for the day of his escape. For Horus would not leave even Sutekh quite without hope. He had told him that escape *was* possible, though the difficulties and obstacles were so great as to be almost insurmountable.

The mighty civilisation of Egypt rose and fell. Other civilisations and Empires took its place. Sutekh and Horus and the Osirians were remembered only as a legend. Still Sutekh waited in his hidden Pyramid. Until one day …

1

THE TERROR IS
UNLEASHED

In a hidden valley, shimmering in the blazing heat of the Egyptian sun, two men stood gazing at the squat black shape of a Pyramid. One was an Egyptian in tattered, striped robes and red fez. The other was tall and thin, with a keen, scholarly face. Despite the heat, he wore a white tropical suit, with stiff collar and public school tie. The year was 1911, and Englishmen abroad were expected to maintain certain standards.

The Englishman was Professor Marcus Scarman and he was a dedicated Egyptologist. At this moment, his eyes were blazing with controlled excitement as he gazed on the greatest discovery of his career. A secret Pyramid of unfamiliar design, tucked away in a valley still unvisited by other Egyptologists. Here was a find to make him the envy of all his rivals. Rumours of the existence of a hidden Black Pyramid, centre of some secret native cult, had long been circulating in archaeological circles. Many had scoffed at them. But Marcus Scarman had passed long years tracking them down, spending many English sovereigns to buy information in the bazaars of Cairo. At long last he had found Ahmed, whose love of gold had finally overcome his fear. They had journeyed together into the desert for many days, and now they had arrived.

Near by, a gang of half-naked Egyptian labourers squatted patiently by the tethered camels. Marcus made a brief examination of the exterior of the Pyramid, then beckoned them over. 'There's a sealed entrance—here. Shouldn't take you long to get it open. Ahmed, go and fetch two lanterns.' The labourers began swinging their picks, and Marcus watched impatiently as they chipped away mortar and started lifting aside the heavy stone blocks. As soon as the space was big enough, he pushed them aside. 'All right, that'll do. Ahmed, tell them to wait here. You come with me.' Eagerly Marcus climbed through the gap, Ahmed following cautiously behind him.

They found themselves in a long stone-walled tunnel, going deep into the heart of the Pyramid. Marcus pressed eagerly ahead. The tunnel led into a huge echoing burial chamber. Marcus held up his lantern and looked around. The light flickered eerily off jewelled caskets and ornately decorated golden urns. 'Perfect,' he breathed. 'Absolutely perfect and quite untouched. The reliquaries are still sealed. Great Heavens, what a find! This tomb must date back to the first dynasty of the Pharaohs.'

Ahmed looked about nervously, sharing none of the. Englishman's enthusiasm. In the dank, echoing darkness of the burial chamber, surrounded by mysterious shapes, he was overcome by the fear that he was blaspheming the ancient gods of his people. Surely there would be punishment ...

Too absorbed to notice his companion's lack of enthusiasm, Marcus moved through the chamber, till he reached the wall at its far end. The wall was hung with a jewel-encrusted tapestry of enormous value. Marcus stretched out a trembling hand and touched it reverently. 'How many thousands of years since the priests sealed the inner chamber, and draped this tapestry over the entrance?' he whispered to himself. It was obvious from the rich furnishings of the burial chamber that this had been the tomb of some great one of ancient times. But whose? Impatient to know the answer, Marcus reached out and carefully drew back the tapestry. Behind it was a wall built from blocks of stone. The mortar between them was old and crumbling—the wall would be easy to move away. As he studied it, Marcus became aware of something strange. In the centre of the wall a glowing red light had appeared. It actually seemed to come from deep *inside* the stone ... Marcus turned to the Egyptian. 'Ahmed! Your lantern, man. Quickly!'

Reluctantly Ahmed came forward, holding up his lantern. In the light of the two lanterns, the ruby-red glow burned even brighter.

Ahmed backed away. 'It is the Eye—the Eye of Horus!' he muttered in his own language. 'It is a warning. Do not cross the threshold of the gods or you will die!' Dropping his crowbar with a clatter, Ahmed turned and ran, back down the stone passage towards the daylight.

Marcus Scarman called after him angrily. 'Come back here, I need your help!'

All, he heard in reply was the wailing voice of the Egyptian, echoing down the tunnel. 'If you cross the threshold of the gods you will die ...'

'Superstitious savage,' muttered Marcus. He looked back at the wall. The eerie red glow had faded. Determinedly he picked up Ahmed's crowbar. 'I've come too far to turn back now ...' He jammed the crowbar into a crevice and began to heave. Mortar crumbled away beneath his onslaught. Marcus jammed the crowbar deeper. Groaning with effort he heaved again ...

There came a deep, hollow grinding sound, and a whole section of the wall swung away. Marcus stepped forward into the gap, and was immediately transfixed by a blaze of green light. He looked upwards. Above him there hovered an indescribably malignant face, a mask of pure evil. Marcus tried to scream but the sound was locked in his throat. Then came a sudden huge blast of sound, like a discord from some enormous organ. The wave of sound seemed to lift Marcus's body and hurl it to the ground. He lay sprawled out, limp and motionless, eyes closed and face a deathly grey.

Through the swirling chaos of the Space/Time Vortex, that strange continuum where Space and Time are one, there sped the incongruous shape of a square blue police box, light flashing on the top. Inside the police box, which was not a police box at all, was a vast ultra-modern control room, dominated by a many-sided centre console of complex instruments. A tall man was staring intently into the console's glowing central column. He had a mobile intelligent face crowned with a mop of curly brown hair. A battered, broad-brimmed hat was jammed on the back of his head, an extraordinarily long scarf trailed around his neck. His usually cheerful features were set in a frown of brooding intensity.

An inner door opened, and a slender, dark-haired girl came into the control room. She wore an attractive, old-fashioned dress. 'Look what I've found, Doctor.'

The Doctor glanced at her absentmindedly. 'Hello, Victoria.'

The girl, whose name was Sarah Jane Smith, looked at him indignantly. 'Hello *who*?'

The Doctor looked up, emerging from his abstraction. 'Oh, it's you, Sarah. Where did you get that dress?'

'I found it in the wardrobe. Why, don't you like it?'

The Doctor nodded vaguely. 'Oh yes, I always did. It belonged to Victoria. She travelled with me for a time.'

The Doctor smiled at the memory of Victoria, always so frightened, always trying so hard to be brave. Finally the strain had been too much for her and she'd left the TARDIS to return to Earth, though in a period much later than her own Victorian age.

Sarah looked at the Doctor thoughtfully. There was no doubt about it, the Doctor in his fourth incarnation was a distinctly more elusive character. Sarah suddenly realised how little she really knew about him. She knew he was a Time Lord, with the ability to travel through Space and Time in the strange craft he called the TARDIS—initials which stood for Time and Relative Dimensions in Space. She knew, because she'd seen it happen, that he had the power to transform his appearance, replacing a damaged body with what seemed to be a completely new one.

Sarah had first met the Doctor in his capacity of Scientific Adviser to UNIT, the United Nations Intelligence Taskforce, that special organisation set up to protect Earth from attack from outer space. Brigadier Lethbridge-Stewart, head of UNIT's British Section, had known the Doctor for a very long time, and looked upon him as a valued colleague. Sarah had been the Doctor's companion on many adventures, both before and after his change of appearance. But she realised that the Doctor had had many lives and many companions, and that she had been involved in only a small proportion of his adventures.

The Doctor's usual mood was one of infectious high spirits. But very occasionally he would lapse into a kind of brooding thoughtfulness, when it was very difficult to get through to him. She tried to cheer him up. 'So the dress was Victoria's? Well, as long as it wasn't Albert's, I'll wear it.' The Doctor went on staring at the control column. 'Oh come on, Doctor,' said Sarah. 'That was worth a smile, surely? What's wrong? Aren't you glad to be going home?'

The Doctor looked up. 'Earth isn't my home, Sarah,' he said sadly. 'I'm a Time Lord, remember, not a human being ... I walk in eternity.'

'And what's that supposed to mean?'

'It means I've lived for something like—oh, seven hundred and fifty years, in your terms.'

'Soon be getting middle-aged,' said Sarah lightly.

Once again the Doctor ignored her little joke. 'What's more,' he went on, 'it's high time I found something better to do than run round after the Brigadier.'

Sarah smiled. So that was it. The Doctor still resented being summoned back to Earth by the Brigadier to deal with the Zygon invasion.* Sarah sympathised but she was determined not to encourage him in his sulk. 'If you're getting tired of being UNIT's Scientific Adviser, you can always ...'

A sudden terrific jolt shook the TARDIS, and Sarah was flung across the console. '... resign,' she gasped, completing her sentence. 'Doctor, what was that? What's happened?'

The Doctor was too busy to answer her. His hands flickered rapidly over the console as he fought to bring the TARDIS back under control. The TARDIS rocked and spun, and a deep thrumming noise filled the air, like a discord from some giant organ. Sarah lost her hold on the console and staggered across the control room. She fell in a heap in a corner and gazed muzzily upwards. There seemed to be a cloud of smoke. Was the TARDIS on fire?

A hideous face, malignant and somehow bestial, had formed in the smoke cloud and was glaring down at her. It seemed half human, half wolf or jackal. Sarah screamed ...

The apparition vanished, the organ noise stopped, the TARDIS settled down. Everything was back to normal. Sarah picked, herself up and ran across to the Doctor. She grabbed his arm. 'Doctor, what *was* it?'

The Doctor was absorbed in his instruments. 'The relative continuum stabiliser failed. Odd—that's never happened before.'

'No, not the upset. I mean that *thing!*—and that noise?'

He gave her a puzzled look. 'What thing? What noise?'

---

*See 'Doctor Who and the Loch Ness Monster'

Sarah shuddered. 'It was like an organ ... and I saw this horrible face ... Just for a second, then it was gone.'

The Doctor looked at her. Indignantly, Sarah said, 'You don't believe me, do you?'

'My dear Sarah, nothing hostile can possibly enter the TARDIS. Unless ...' The Doctor broke off suddenly and returned to the console. 'Mental projection?' he muttered to himself. 'Mental projection of that force is beyond belief ... and yet—it could explain the stabiliser failure! Now let me see, it was at this end of the spectrum ...' The Doctor's hands once again began moving over the controls.

Sarah tugged him away from the console. 'No, Doctor. Please don't try and bring it back. Whatever that thing was, it was totally evil ...'

There was another, smaller jolt, and the central column stopped moving. 'We've arrived, Sarah. UNIT H.Q.!' The Doctor checked the instruments, operated the door control.

'Hang on a minute,' said Sarah hurriedly. 'I know we've landed somewhere. But are you sure ...'

She was too late. The Doctor was already outside. Sarah sighed and followed him.

They found themselves in a large, well-proportioned ground-floor room, with windows facing on to a garden. The TARDIS was in a corner surrounded by huge packing cases. The room looked like a miniature museum. All around stood various forms of Egyptiana— mummy cases, funeral urns, painted wooden chests.

Many were already on display and others simply scattered about. It was as though someone had brought home an enormous collection of Egyptian relics, but hadn't yet finished unpacking all of them. Sarah threw the Doctor an accusing look. 'UNIT H.Q.?'

The Doctor cleared his throat. 'Ah, well ... you see, we've arrived at the correct point in Space, but obviously not in Time. We've had a temporal reverse. Some vast energy-impulse has drawn the TARDIS off course.' The Doctor smiled, evidently quite satisfied by his own explanation.

Sarah looked around. 'Are you telling me this is UNIT H.Q., years before I knew it?'

The Doctor nodded. 'That's right.'

'But it's all so different. This isn't even the same house.'

'No, it isn't …' Suddenly the Doctor smiled. 'Of course, this must be the Old Priory. The UNIT house was built on the same site.'

'So it was. The Old Priory burnt down, didn't it?'

The Doctor held up his hand for silence.

'What is it?'

'Atmosphere,' said the Doctor mysteriously. 'I sense alien vibrations. There's something very wrong here, Sarah …'

A deep, discordant organ-note shattered the silence. Sarah looked fearfully at the Doctor. 'That's the noise I heard before. That thing that came into the TARDIS—it must be here, somewhere in this house …'

2

THE MUMMY AWAKES

In the organ room on the other side of the house, an immaculately dressed Egyptian called Ibrahim Namin sat at the keyboard. His thin brown fingers swept across the keys, filling the room with a crescendo of discordant sound. The room quivered and shook with the deep throbbing chords. They created an atmosphere of madness, of chaos in which all normal laws were suspended. The room was thick with a sense of ancient evil.

As he played, Namin glanced from time to time at an alcove just beyond the organ. In it stood an upright Mummy casket, richly decorated, flanked by four ceremonial urns. Namin's music was a kind of prayer, a tribute to his gods. He was the High Priest of the Cult of the Black Pyramid.

Namin had served the Cult all his life, like his ancestors before him. For thousands upon thousands of years the priests had served the high ones who built the Pyramid, carrying out the proper ceremonies, ensuring that the Black Pyramid in its secret valley remained: inviolate. Then scholars from the West had come with their expeditions, prying into the ancient secrets. One day Namin heard the news he had always dreaded—an archaeological expedition was on its way to the Black Pyramid.

Namin and his fellow-priests had sped there at once. The fleeing Ahmed and the terrified labourers had all been captured and killed instantly, their bodies buried in the desert. Then, in fear and trembling, Namin had entered the desecrated Pyramid, prepared to die for having failed his trust. To his terror and delight, one of the Great Ones had spoken to him. All was well. The Great Ones were not displeased— the opening of the Pyramid was a part of their plan. Namin had been given his orders. Now, in a strange land wearing strange clothes, he served the Great Ones as before. At first Namin had been very puzzled by these orders. In the Secret Writings of his cult it was laid down that the Pyramid must *never* be broken into, or the most terrible disaster would overwhelm the world.

But Sutekh, the Great One within the Pyramid, had told him the writings were mistaken. The Pyramid was a prison in, which he had been cast by treachery, thousands of years ago. Now the time was approaching for his release. Soon Sutekh would return to rule the world. Ibrahim Namin and his fellow-priests would be exalted as they had been in ancient times, rulers of the people, and servants of the Great Ones.

Many and complicated were the tasks that had been laid upon Ibrahim Namin. He had to go to a hotel in Cairo, posing as the servant of Professor Scarman, and obtain the Professor's luggage. He had to hire workmen to make wooden crates, and porters to carry them to the Pyramid.

Inside the Pyramid, many sacred objects were packed by the hands of Ibrahim and his fellow priests. All these crates had first to be taken to Cairo, then shipped to England. Strangest of all, Ibrahim Namin was ordered to accompany them to this house in England, guarding them most strictly all the while. Once in the house, he was to install himself and wait, allowing no one to enter or to touch the sacred relics.

All this Namin had done. But he was not too happy in England. Although Collins, the servant of the house, had accepted his letter of authority, it was clear that he was puzzled and suspicious. The brother of Professor Scarman had also been a source of trouble, protesting vigorously when barred from the house. A certain Doctor Warlock in the village had written a letter inquiring about Professor Scarman. Namin had ignored it. On his rare visits to the village, he was aware of a climate of hostility and suspicion. Surrounded by infidels and strangers, Namin pined for the burning deserts of his own country. He began to dream of the day when he would return as a great man, no longer priest of an obscure sect but king, a ruler of the world on behalf of the Great One. He hoped the time would not be long in coming ... Something disturbed his reverie. He looked up angrily. Through the clamour of his own playing, he could hear a knocking at the door.

In the corridor outside, an elderly man in the formal black clothes of an upper servant was hammering on the heavy wooden door. He had little hope that Namin would hear him over the noise of the organ, or would bother to answer if he did. But Collins had been in service all his life. Even though things at the Old Priory had changed so drastically, he still knew the proper way to behave in a gentleman's household.

Salvaging his conscience with another barrage of knocks, Collins flung open the door. Namin looked up angrily from the keyboard, still crashing out great discords on the organ.

Collins called, 'Excuse me, sir ...' but his quavery old voice was swallowed up by the noise.

Namin shouted, 'Get out. Get out of here!' He rose from the organ, and as the thundering discords died away, Namin stalked angrily towards the old servant. 'How dare you disturb me! Get out at once.'

Collins stood his ground. 'I'm sorry, sir. But the gentleman insisted.'

'Gentleman? What gentleman?'

'An old friend of Professor Scarman's, sir.'

Namin's black eyes blazed with fury. 'I ordered that no one was to be admitted, Collins. I told you no callers.'

A burly figure in country tweeds shouldered his way past Collins and into the room. 'Don't blame Collins, sir. I'm afraid it's a case of forced entry. Since you didn't answer my letter ...'

Namin glared angrily at the intruder. 'This is an outrage ...'

'Call it what you like. I've a few questions to put to you, and I'm not leaving till I've asked them.'

Namin looked thoughtfully at the ruddy-faced, balding figure in front of him. A typical English country gentleman, with all the unthinking arrogance of his kind. Clearly he wouldn't give up easily. Controlling, his anger Namin said, 'All right, Collins, you may go.' Thankfully Collins scuttled away. Namin turned to his visitor. 'So! You have questions, have you? May I ask who you are?'

'My name's Warlock. Doctor Warlock. Live in the village. Marcus Scarman happens to be my oldest friend.'

Namin gave a curt nod. 'I am Ibrahim Namin. I—'

'I know your name,' interrupted Warlock brusquely. 'It's your business I'm concerned with. Called at the Lodge on my way up, had a word with Laurence. He tells me you've had the infernal impudence to bar him from this house.'

'I am acting on the direct orders of Professor Scarman.'

'Marcus Scarman ordered you to shut out his own brother? I don't believe it.'

Namin made a mighty effort to control himself. 'I have Professor Scarman's letter of authority. I have brought from Egypt all the relics discovered by the Professor on his recent expedition. My orders are to store them safely, and to allow no one admittance to the house until the Professor himself returns.' Namin's voice rose to an angry shout. 'And that is the end of the matter, Doctor Warlock!'

Warlock was quite unimpressed. 'Oh no it isn't, sir. Not by a long chalk!'

In the corridor outside, Collins listened to the angry voices, shaking his head in dismay. He was confused and frightened by all that had happened since Namin's arrival, but had thought it best to accept the orders in the letter. Now Warlock's visit was making him wonder if he'd done the right thing after all.

He turned to go, looking worriedly around the hall. Something caught his eye. The handle of a door on the far side of the hall was *moving*. Collins saw it turn, first one way and then the other, as someone tried to open the locked door ...

On the other side, the Doctor took his hand away from the door-knob. 'Why bother to lock all these internal doors?' he asked aggrievedly.

Sarah shrugged. 'Obviously this wing of the house isn't in use. It smells awfully musty.'

'More Mummy than musty,' said the Doctor cheerfully. The challenge of a new adventure had restored his usual good spirits. He produced a wire contraption from his pocket. 'French picklock. Never fails. Belonged to Marie Antoinette, charming lady, pity she lost her head poor thing ...'

Sarah grinned at the Doctor's flow of cheerful nonsense. Suddenly she tensed. From the other side of the door came the sound of a key turning in a lock. The Doctor took Sarah's arm and led her away.

Collins opened the door into the passage. It was empty. Puzzled he moved along to the Egyptian Room.

When Collins came in, the Doctor was leaning against a packing case, hands in his pocket, chatting to Sarah. 'A house like this would make an ideal headquarters for some semi-military organisation,' he was saying. 'This room could easily be converted into a laboratory ...'

Collins looked at the two intruders in astonishment. 'Who are you? How did you get in here?'

'We popped in through the window,' said the Doctor airily. 'I understood the property was for sale. I wanted to take a look.'

Collins was shaking his head shrewdly. 'You're not fooling me, sir. You came with Doctor Warlock, didn't you?'

'Did we?'

Collins gave a knowing nod. 'Asked you to scout round, didn't he, while he kept his nibs busy?' The old man's face became suddenly grave. 'Listen, sir, if you *are* a friend of Doctor Warlock's—tell him to watch out!'

'Watch out for what?' asked Sarah.

Collins turned to her. 'That Egyptian gentleman's got the temper of the devil, miss. No telling what he might do if he knew you'd been here, in the Egyptian room.'

The Doctor glanced round the cluttered room. 'A live Egyptian, eh? I suppose this is where he keeps his relatives?' The old man looked blankly at him. 'Relatives ... *Mummies* ...' said the Doctor hopefully. 'Oh, never mind.'

'It's no joke, sir,' said Collins sternly. 'Mr Namin's only been here a short while, but I can tell you, I wouldn't be staying myself only ... well I've worked for the Scarmans for a very long time. I keep hoping Mr Marcus will come back.'

As he talked the old man kept looking nervously over his shoulder.

'You're frightened,' said the Doctor suddenly. 'What are you afraid of?'

Collins lowered his voice. '*He* locked this wing. Ordered it all sealed off. He'd go stark, staring mad if he caught *me* in the Egyptian room, and as for you two ... Please go now, sir, for my sake.'

The Doctor looked thoughtfully at him. 'I see ... Well, if it's like that, perhaps we had better leave.'

He moved towards the door, but the old man caught his sleeve. 'Not that way, sir, he might see you. Go the way you came—through the window.'

Trapped by his own story, the Doctor glanced at Sarah, then turned back to the old man. 'As you wish,' he said gently.

They moved to the window. The Doctor opened it and started to climb out. Collins leaned closer to him and whispered, 'Remember to tell Doctor Warlock what I said, sir.'

'I'll remember, don't worry.' The Doctor helped Sarah through the window and Collins closed it behind them.

Old Collins watched the disappearance of the Doctor and Sarah with great relief. They'd seemed pleasant enough, but there would be the devil to pay if that Egyptian discovered they'd been in the house. Particularly in the Egyptian room, which was his particular obsession.

Collins looked round the room sadly, remembering the long hours Mr Marcus used to spend here, sorting through all his Egyptian stuff. Nasty old rubbish, Collins called it. But Mr Marcus was mad on it, had been ever since he was a child. From the very beginning he'd turned this room into a kind of museum, with all his treasures proudly displayed.

Collins looked gloomily at the pile of packing cases. Now there was a fresh batch of the stuff, cluttering up the house. No doubt Mr Marcus would want it all unpacked, the minute he got home.

Collins frowned at the sight of a tall blue box in the corner. He didn't remember seeing that one before. It had probably been delivered while he was in the village … Crates had been arriving from Egypt for days now. Heaven knows how much more junk would turn up before Mr Marcus arrived to deal with it.

Muttering and grumbling to himself, Collins began shuffling around the room. He fished out an old rag and did a bit of defiant dusting. Whatever that Egyptian gentleman said, he wasn't going to neglect his duties. He dusted one of the newly-arrived Mummy cases, glaring at it disapprovingly. It wasn't the first Mummy they'd had in the house, of course. Mr Marcus had explained all about Mummies, but Collins still didn't care for them. As far as he was concerned, a dead body was a dead body and its place was in a cemetery, not in a gentleman's house.

Absorbed in his dusting and his grievances, old Collins didn't notice when the lid of one of the Mummy cases started to open. It opened further, then further, swinging fully back with a crash. Collins looked up in horror as a huge bandage-wrapped figure began stalking towards him ...

The Doctor and Sarah were moving through a dense shrubbery, which ran close to the side of the house. All around them was the beauty of an English country garden in summertime. The smooth green lawn, broken up with hedges and flower-beds, stretched away to the woods which surrounded the house. There was the hum of bees around a white-painted hive, the occasional chirrup of a bird. It was hard to reconcile this peaceful scene with the atmosphere of exotic horror in the room they had just left.

Sarah caught up with the Doctor and whispered, 'Where are we going?'

'I'm rather interested to see what this fearsome Egyptian looks like, aren't you?'

Sarah wasn't, but before she could say so, they heard angry voices from a near-by ground-floor window. One voice was gruff and very English, the other smooth and sibilant, with a marked foreign accent.

'Humbug!' roared the English voice. 'Utter humbug! That letter is a fabrication if ever I saw one.'

'You allege that it is forged?' hissed the foreign voice angrily.

'I do, sir, and I intend to prove it.'

'I warn you, Doctor Warlock, do not interfere!'

'Are you threatening me, sir?'

Intrigued by this very promising quarrel, the Doctor and Sarah edged closer to the window.

Inside the organ room, Warlock and Namin stood glaring at each other. Warlock was bristling like an angry bulldog, and Namin was quivering with rage. 'It is not *I* who threaten,' he whispered. 'There are ancient forces gathering in this place. Powers of ancient purpose, beyond the comprehension of mere unbelievers.'

'Powers of ancient balderdash!' said Warlock contemptuously. 'Let me warn you, Namin, unless you give me some honest answers, I'm going straight to the police.'

'To tell them what? That some suspicious foreigner is actually daring to live in Professor Scarman's house?'

Warlock's voice was calm and determined. 'To tell them that Professor Scarman has not been seen for weeks. To tell them that he left Cairo quite some time ago, and no one has seen him since. Oh yes, I've had inquiries made in Egypt ...'

A quavering scream, suddenly cut off, echoed through the room. 'What the devil ...' said Warlock. He ran from the room, heading in the direction of the sound. The Egyptian hesitated, then followed.

The window slid cautiously open, and the Doctor arid Sarah started to climb in.

Doctor Warlock rushed into the Egyptian room, then stopped abruptly. The dead body of Collins lay on the floor, bulging eyes staring sightlessly at the ceiling. Horrified, Warlock knelt by the body, not noticing that a near-by Mummy case was quietly closing ...

Warlock looked up as Namin hurried into the room. 'The poor fellow's been strangled.'

There was no shock or horror on Namin's face, only a look of exaltation. His voice was triumphant. 'The gods have returned! I, Ibrahim Namin, servant of the true faith, rejoice in their power!'

'Fellow's cracked,' thought Warlock to himself. He stood up. 'We'd better get the police, the murderer can't have got far.'

Namin rounded on him. 'You blind pathetic fool! The servants of the all-powerful have arisen. When the temple is cleansed of all unbelievers, the high ones themselves will come among us. Thus it was written.'

More than ever convinced that he was dealing with a madman, Warlock spoke soothingly. 'Yes, I see, old chap. Still, I think the police ...' His voice tailed off. A small black automatic had appeared in Namin's hand.

Menacingly the Egyptian said, 'You should have listened when I told you to leave, Doctor Warlock. Now you have seen too much. You shall be the second unbeliever to die!' He levelled the gun at Warlock's heart.

The Doctor appeared silently in the doorway behind Namin. Just as the Egyptian pulled the trigger, the Doctor's scarf looped out over his head and shoulders, jerking backwards. The gun exploded, and Warlock staggered, clutching his shoulder.

The Doctor tried to get hold of the gun, but Namin was lithe and active, and seemed incredibly strong. He twisted the barrel of the automatic towards the Doctor's head, just as the Doctor gave him a shove that sent him flying across the room. Namin landed in the corner, the gun dropping from his hand. Quickly the Doctor and Sarah bustled the reeling Warlock from the room, slamming the door behind them.

Namin scrambled cat-like to his feet, picking up the gun. He seemed about to set off in pursuit, then suddenly stopped himself. The gun disappeared inside his coat, and Namin straightened his clothing and smoothed his hair. He moved to a near-by Mummy case and flung it open. Inside stood the huge bandage-wrapped figure of a Mummy. Namin raised his hand, and the ornate ruby ring on his finger glowed bright red. 'Arise!' he chanted. 'In the name of the High Ones, I command thee—arise!'

Slowly, the Mummy stepped from the case.

In the hall Sarah supported the wounded Warlock, while the Doctor dragged a heavy chest across the floor and jammed it against the door to the East Wing. 'That should hold him for a while. Right, come on!' They ran out of the house by the front door. Behind them the barricade began to shake under the impact of a powerful shove.

On the other side, Namin found the weight of the chest too much for him and stepped aside. He spoke to the towering form beside him. 'Open it,' he commanded. The Mummy stalked forward. It smashed open the barricaded door with ease, sending the heavy chest flying across the hall to crash against a distant wall.

Namin ran into the hall, the Mummy close behind him. 'This way!' ordered the Egyptian. Followed by his ghastly servant, he hurried across the hall and through the open front door.

The Doctor and Sarah were deep in the woods surrounding the house. They could have escaped with ease by now, but their pace was slowed by the wounded Warlock. The spreading bloodstain on his shoulder was widening steadily, despite Sarah's attempts to staunch it with a handkerchief, and his face was white. Suddenly he slid to the ground. 'No good,' he muttered, 'can't go further.'

The Doctor looked back. They were still quite close to the house. 'I'm afraid you must,' he said urgently. 'We're sitting ducks out here in the open.'

Warlock shook his head. 'I … can't … Get to the Lodge … just by main gates. Tell Laurence … Scarman's brother. He lives there …'

Warlock's head rolled back. He was unconscious.

The Doctor straightened up. 'He needs help badly. Sarah, you go on and find this Laurence.'

'What about you?'

'I'll manage,' said the Doctor cheerfully. 'Now go, we'll only slow you down.'

Sarah knew it was no time to argue. She nodded and ran off, slipping quickly through the trees. The Doctor grabbed the inert form of Warlock and hoisted it over his shoulder. In the process he dislodged his hat, which dropped softly to the leaves underfoot. Not bothering to pick it up, the Doctor set off after Sarah at a stumbling run.

Minutes later, Namin came through the trees, the Mummy just behind him. The Egyptian's eyes gleamed in triumph at the sight of the battered broad-brimmed hat on the ground. He turned to the Mummy, and made a sweeping gesture. 'Circle around the edge of the wood and get ahead of them.'

Moving swiftly despite its huge bulk, the Mummy stalked away. Namin drew his gun, and set off on the trail of the Doctor.

Stumbling and gasping for breath, Sarah ran on through the woods. Through the trees she saw a high brick wall, a pair of heavy iron gates and a low cottage-like building just inside them. Sarah gave a gasp of relief and started to run faster. Suddenly she heard a thunderous crashing sound coming towards her. She dived for the cover of a clump of bushes, wriggling deep inside them. From her hiding place she saw with amazement the giant form of an Egyptian Mummy stalking along. Somehow it had got ahead of her. Now it was moving back through the woods—towards the Doctor and Warlock. Instinctively Sarah moved to warn them—then stopped. There was nothing she could do. Better to obey the Doctor's original instructions and get help from the Lodge. She ran towards the little building.

In the heart of the wood, the Doctor stumbled on. Warlock was a big heavy man, and with such a burden even the Doctor couldn't move very fast. Nor could he watch his footing. He stepped on a dry branch, and it cracked with a noise like a pistol-shot. The Doctor paused, listening. In the woods behind him Namin, gun in hand, stood listening too. He smiled in satisfaction, and went on, following the direction of the noise.

Suddenly the Doctor heard the sounds of close pursuit. Wearily he lowered Warlock to the ground. What was he to do now? There was no real cover near by, and unless he abandoned the wounded Warlock, no hope of running.

The Doctor stood quite still, listening keenly. For a moment the noises stopped too, then they began again. The Doctor was as motionless as any Indian warrior, trying to sort out the meaning of the sounds.

There were two pursuers, he decided. The smaller one was behind him moving quickly and fairly quietly. The larger was somewhere ahead, crashing through the bushes with no attempt at concealment. The Doctor guessed the smaller one was Namin. But the larger ... he had no idea. Clearly Namin had called on some huge and powerful ally.

The Doctor went on listening. The two pursuers were moving through the woods in a regular search pattern, trying to trap him in a kind of pincer movement. Alone he could have slipped between them with ease. But with the weight of a very heavy wounded man on his back, flight was out of the question.

The only remaining chance was concealment. There was a clump of particularly thick bushes not far away. Shouldering Warlock, who was moaning and breathing stertorously, the Doctor moved towards them. The thick branches and leaves made a kind of cave, and the Doctor crawled inside dragging Warlock after him. He settled down to wait.

Gun in hand Namin ran through the woods. He knew the fugitives wouldn't travel very fast, burdened as they were with a wounded man. Namin's plan was simple. He hoped to drive the Doctor and his friends into the arms of the Mummy. If it caught them, it would dispose of them soon enough. And if he himself got a clear sight of them, he would simply shoot them down.

In his hiding place, the Doctor lay quietly waiting. Beside him Warlock moaned, and the Doctor put a gentle hand over his lips to quiet him.

From outside, the Doctor heard the sound of approaching movement. As if guided by some uncanny instinct, *both* his pursuers seemed to be making straight for his hiding place. He was trapped.

3

THE SERVANTS OF SUTEKH

A deep, booming sound echoed through the woods, like crashing discords from some enormous organ. In their different parts of the wood, Namin and the Mummy stopped dead. Namin turned to face the house, his face exultant. 'The all-powerful one descends. Oh noble god, your servant hears your voice.' He started running towards the house. At the same moment, the Mummy began stalking in the same direction.

The Doctor listened, puzzled, as the sound of Namin's movements suddenly moved *away* from him. The second pursuer, the larger one, was moving too. The sound came closer, then died away, as it moved past him somewhere just out of sight.

The Doctor was about to pick up Warlock when he heard someone else coming towards him. He grabbed a fallen branch for a club and stood ready to defend himself. He tossed it aside with relief as Sarah and a small round-faced man appeared through the trees. Sarah performed breathless introductions. 'Doctor, this is Laurence Scarman. Mr Scarman, this is the Doctor.'

Laurence gave the Doctor a puzzled look, then moved straight to his old friend. 'Oh the poor chap,' he said fussily. 'Is he badly hurt? What should we do?'

'Get him somewhere safe and stop the bleeding,' suggested the Doctor practically.

Laurence nodded. 'Yes, of course. We'll take him back to the Lodge.'

The Doctor and Laurence raised Warlock between them, and began half-carrying, half-dragging him away. Sarah moved close to the Doctor. 'Listen,' she whispered, 'I saw a Mummy. A walking Mummy!'

'Nonsense, Sarah. Mummies are eviscerated, embalmed corpses. They do not walk.'

'But I tell you I *saw* one.'

'Never mind that now,' said the Doctor impatiently. 'Give Mr Scarman a hand, Sarah. I've just remembered, I lost my hat! Be with you in a moment.' The Doctor strode away.

Sarah glared furiously after him, opened her mouth, shut it again, and helped Laurence carry Warlock towards the Lodge.

Distantly from the house they heard the deep rolling notes of the organ.

Inside the sitting room of the Lodge, Laurence fussed round with towels, bandages and hot water, while the Doctor, now returned with his recovered hat, swiftly and efficiently dressed Warlock's wound.

When Warlock was comfortably settled on an enormous sofa, his shoulder bandaged and his arm in a sling, Sarah had time to look around her. It was evident that if his brother was obsessed with Egypt's past, Laurence Scarman's interests were all turned towards the future, and particularly the future of Science. The sitting room was cluttered with a variety of scientific devices, most of them obviously rigged-up by Laurence himself. The heavy old-fashioned equipment, with its brass and mahogany fittings, was the kind of thing Sarah remembered seeing on childhood visits to the Science Museum.

Warlock's eyes flickered open, and Sarah leaned over him.

'How do you feel? Is there anything I can get you?'

Warlock looked vaguely at her. Sarah guessed he was suffering from delayed shock. 'No … no …' he muttered. 'I'm all right now … must rest.' His head nodded and his eyes closed.

'That's right, have a good sleep,' said Sarah gently. She settled him comfortably on the pile of sofa cushions.

The Doctor, meanwhile, was prowling interestedly round the room, peering at the various pieces of equipment. He looked up as he saw Laurence Scarman heading for the door. 'Where are you off to, old chap?'

'To fetch the police, of course. I mean, in view of what you've been telling me ...'

The Doctor shook his head reprovingly. 'No, no, no, Mr Scarman, this is much too grave a matter for the police.'

Laurence gaped at him. 'Too grave for the police?'

The Doctor nodded solemnly. 'I'm afraid they would only hinder my investigations.'

Once again Laurence could only repeat the Doctor's words unbelievingly. '*Your* investigations?'

'That's right. Why do you think I'm here? Someone is interfering with Time, Mr Scarman—and Time is my business.'

Laurence moved away from the door, staring at the Doctor in total bafflement. 'Look here,' he demanded a little peevishly, 'who *are* you?'

Absorbed in a piece of equipment, the Doctor didn't seem to hear him. Sarah felt politeness demanded some sort of reply.

'I'm Sarah Jane Smith,' she said brightly, 'I'm a journalist.'

Laurence looked at her sceptically. 'A journalist—I see! And your companion?'

'Oh he's—well he's just the Doctor. We travel in time, you see—I'm from the future.'

Laurence sighed and scratched his head. 'This is all utterly preposterous, Miss Smith.'

'Yes it is, isn't it,' agreed Sarah sympathetically. 'I'm sorry.'

The Doctor had moved to yet another piece of equipment. 'This is a most interesting contraption,' he said affably. He was looking at a glass dome which covered a number of complicated-looking valves, and a paper-roll on which rested an ink-stylus.

Laurence bustled over to him. 'Kindly leave that alone,' he said severely. 'It is a delicate piece of apparatus, the purpose of which you do not understand. Furthermore, it contains a highly dangerous electrical charge!'

'So I perceive,' said the Doctor. 'What year is this?'

Laurence stared at him. 'Year?'

'Simple enough question surely?'

'Are you telling me you don't even know the year?'

'If I knew I wouldn't ask, would I? Don't be obtuse, man!'

Laurence controlled himself with an obvious effort. 'The year is nineteen-eleven,' he said stiffly.

The Doctor beamed at him. 'Oh splendid, an excellent year, I really must congratulate you, Mr Scarman. You've invented the radio telescope about forty years too early!'

'That sir,' said Laurence with dignity, 'happens to be a Marconiscope. Its purpose is—'

'—to record emissions from the stars,' completed the Doctor.

Laurence gave him a wondering look. 'Now how could you possibly know that?'

The Doctor smiled. 'Well, you see, Mr Scarman, I have the advantage of being a little ahead of you. Sometimes behind you, but normally ahead of you.'

'I see.'

'No you don't, but it's nice of you to try. Now, suppose you show me how this gadget of yours works?'

Laurence's scientific pride overcame his bewilderment. 'You'd like me to demonstrate?'

'If you please.'

Laurence bent over the glass dome and flicked a number of brass switches. Immediately the Marconiscope began to hum with power, and the valves glowed brightly. The roll of paper started to revolve, and the stylus traced out a jerky pattern. 'Amazing!' said the Doctor softly.

Laurence smiled shyly. 'You're very kind, Doctor.' He flicked more switches and then looked up in alarm. 'I can't switch it off!'

The valves glowed more fiercely, the power-hum rose in pitch, and the cylinder of paper began to revolve faster and faster. Suddenly a valve burst with a sharp crack, and the Marconiscope juddered to a halt, giving out clouds of smoke. The Doctor fanned away the fumes with his hat. Sarah coughed and said, 'Very impressive.'

Laurence shook his head. 'Extraordinary. It's never done that before.'

The Doctor lifted off the glass dome and carefully removed the paper cylinder. 'Fascinating,' he muttered. 'A regular pattern, repeated over and over again.'

Sarah was puzzled. 'Like an SOS, you mean?'

The Doctor looked thoughtfully at her. 'I wonder ... Where was your apparatus trained, Mr Scarman? Would it have been on Mars?' When Laurence nodded, the Doctor produced a small device from his pocket. He touched an inset control, and a long aerial extended itself. The Doctor adjusted more controls. 'I just want to verify the signal. No harm in double checking.' He touched a switch and the instrument began to give out a rapid regular beep, beep, beep.

Laurence looked on in fascination. 'What *is* that thing, Doctor?'

'In principle, exactly the same device that you've invented, my dear fellow. Perhaps a little less ... cumbersome.' The Doctor listened to the beeping for a few minutes, then nodded, satisfied. 'Yes, it's the same signal all right.' He switched off the device, retracted the aerial and stowed the whole thing away in his pocket. 'Now then, pencil and paper if you please.'

Laurence hurried to provide them. 'What are you going to do?'

'Decipher the message. It shouldn't take long. They'd try to make it easy.'

'Who would?'

Absorbed in his calculations, the Doctor didn't seem to hear him. 'Now let me see ... *this* pattern recurs three times in one line, so we'll call that "E" ...'

Sarah answered Laurence's question. 'Whoever transmitted the message, I suppose.'

The Doctor's pencil sped across the paper, filling page after page with rapid calculations. Laurence and Sarah looked on, not daring to speak. At last the Doctor threw down his pencil. His face was grim. 'Got it. It says *"Beware Sutekh!"* '

'Who's Sutekh?' asked Sarah.

The Doctor was pacing about the room, his eyes staring into some unimaginable distance. 'He may be better known to you as Set,' he said absently.

Sarah struggled to summon up her knowledge of Egyptology. Long ago she'd researched an article on Egyptian mythology for some educational magazine ... 'Wasn't Set one of the Egyptian gods? He was defeated in a great battle with Horus, the god of light.'

The Doctor nodded. 'That's right. If my theories are correct, your world may be facing the greatest peril in its history.' He strode briskly towards the door.

'Hey, wait for me,' called Sarah.

The Doctor paused in the doorway. His voice was grave. 'No, Sarah. The forces that are being summoned into corporal existence in that house are more powerful and more dangerous than anything we've ever encountered. Stay here.'

'I've got a hunting rifle,' offered Laurence. 'It might come in useful.'

'Certainly not,' said the Doctor severely. 'I *never* carry firearms.' And with that he was gone.

Laurence turned to Sarah. I think we *ought* to go with him. And I should feel better if I brought a rifle.'

'So should I,' said Sarah grimly. 'Bring it! '

She waited impatiently while Laurence fished the rifle from a cluttered cupboard, which held several other guns. There was a further wait while he found the ammunition and loaded the rifle. When at last all was ready, they hurried off after the Doctor.

Night was falling as the Doctor hurried through the shadowy woods. As he neared the house, the deep throbbing notes of the organ grew louder. The hideous, discordant sounds shattered the peace of the night. Still the noise had its use, thought the Doctor. It would at least cover his approach. He went boldly up to the front door, only to find it locked. A few minutes work with his picklock took care of that. The door creaked open and the Doctor slipped into the darkened house, moving along the gloomy passages.

All was dark until he came to the organ room. An eerie green glow was shining from beneath its door. The noise of the organ was terrifying. It seemed as if the old house might be shaken to pieces by the vibration. The Doctor moved to the door, opened it a crack and peered inside.

Namin sat at the organ, hammering at the keys in an exalted trance. Three of the giant Mummies stood around the alcove in a half-circle. Their bandaged arms were raised as though invoking some mystic power. The fierce unearthly green glow came from the ornate urn-flanked Casket, in its special alcove. It filled the room with an eerie flickering light. Suddenly the lid of the Casket seemed to shimmer and

130

dissolve. It was replaced by a spinning Vortex, a kind of whirlpool in space. The Doctor thought to himself that it was like staring down an immensely long tunnel into the eye of a typhoon. The tremendous energy from the Casket dominated the room. It seemed impossible to look anywhere else.

Namin stopped playing and knelt before the swirling Casket. Now, as if in reply, the deep throbbing discords seemed to come from the Casket itself. Namin raised his arms in prayer. 'All-high, all-powerful, most noble Master,' he chanted. 'Thy humble servant welcomes thee.'

Far away at the end of the tunnel a figure appeared. It wore black robes, a shining globe covered its head, and its feet were bare. It rushed closer and closer until it filled the entrance to the Casket …

As the Doctor looked on in fascination, he heard a whisper beside him. 'Doctor …' It was Sarah. Beside her was Laurence Scarman. Totally absorbed, the Doctor waved them to silence. They crouched beside him, peering through the crack. The black-robed figure stepped from the Casket. With a thrill of horror, Sarah saw that its bare feet left charred, smoking footprints on the carpet.

Namin knelt before the figure, his face to the grounds. 'Master, at last you are here. I, Ibrahim Namin, and my forebears have served you faithfully through all the years that you have slept. We have guarded the secret of your tomb …'

The figure spoke. Its voice was cold and dead. 'Stand. Look upon my face.'

Namin's voice trembled. 'Oh Great One, Lord Sutekh … I dare not.'

'Look,' the cold voice commanded again. 'Is this the face of Sutekh?'

Shuddering, Namin looked up. As the figure advanced towards him, he cringed back in sudden fear. 'Oh Master, spare me,' he shrieked. 'Spare me! I am a true servant of the great Sutekh.'

The figure's hands clamped down on Namin's shaking shoulders. Immediately Namin's whole body twisted. He let out a shuddering scream and struggled to break free. His clothing began to smoulder beneath the figure's hands.

'I am the servant of Sutekh,' the dead voice said. 'He needs no other.'

Namin struggled wildly, but the fiery grip was strong as steel. 'Die!' said the voice. 'I bring Sutekh's gift of death to all humanity.'

4

THE RETURN OF MARCUS SCARMAN

The hands released their grip, and the still-smoking body dropped to the floor. Death was Ibrahim Namin's reward for a lifetime of faithful service. The black-robed figure glowed and *changed*. Its new form was that of a tall, thin man, with a scholarly face. He wore a white suit, stiff collar and public-school tie. His face was ghastly, with greyish skin, bloodless lips and red-rimmed eyes that burned like fiery coals. It was a face that meant nothing to the Doctor and Sarah. But Laurence Scarman recognised it instantly. 'It's *Marcus,*' he whispered. 'That's my brother Marcus—' The Doctor grabbed Laurence's arm in a painful grip, and touched a warning finger to his lips. Laurence fell silent.

For a moment it seemed as if Marcus Scarman might have heard the whisper from outside the door. The burning eyes swept swiftly round the room. Then, apparently satisfied, he turned to the waiting Mummies. 'Take the generator loops. Place them in position at the compass points. Activate at ground strength.' Each of the three Mummies picked up one of the urns flanking the Casket. Scarman himself picked up the fourth.

As the strange procession headed for the door the Doctor whispered, 'Quick, everybody. Hide!'

When Marcus flung open the organ-room doors, the passage was empty. He led the Mummies along it, into the hall and out of the front door. In the passage, the Doctor slid his long body from a cramped position behind a grandfather clock, and opened the lid of a large oak chest. Laurence climbed out, followed by Sarah. She looked round. 'Where have they gone?'

'To set up a deflection shield around the house. It'll take them a while. Obviously he's planned every step.'

Laurence said unbelievingly, 'Who has? Marcus?'

The Doctor shook his head. 'No. Sutekh.' He led them into the organ room. 'Sutekh is breaking free his ancient bonds. If he succeeds, he'll destroy the world.'

'So Sutekh wasn't destroyed by Horus?' asked Sarah. 'He's still—alive?'

The Doctor went over to the Casket, and knelt to examine it more closely. 'He destroyed his own planet, Phaester Osiris, and left a trail of havoc across half the galaxy. Horus and the other Osirians must have cornered him on Earth.'

'In Egypt,' said Sarah, still struggling to understand. 'What you're saying is that Horus and Set and all the other Egyptian gods were really immensely powerful aliens from some other planet. When they came to Earth, the Egyptians worshipped them as gods.'

The Doctor nodded, running his sonic screwdriver along the side of the Casket. 'The war of the gods entered into Egyptian mythology. In fact their whole Egyptian culture was founded on the Osirian pattern.'

Laurence Scarman had been listening uncomprehendingly. 'I'm afraid all this is beyond me.'

'Don't worry,' said Sarah consolingly. 'Most of it's beyond me too.'

There was a triumphant exclamation from the Doctor. 'Ah, found it.' He removed a concealed panel on the side of the Casket, exposing a maze of complex circuitry. 'This is the lodestone that drew the TARDIS off course.'

Laurence peered fascinatedly at the circuits. 'What is it?'

'The entrance to a Space/Time tunnel,' replied the Doctor solemnly.

Sarah came over to look. 'Leading where?'

'To Sutekh,' said the Doctor, cautiously adjusting a circuit. Suddenly his fiddling produced dramatic results. The spinning Vortex reactivated, the organ-noise boomed out, and the Doctor was dragged closer and closer to the mouth of the Space/Time tunnel.

'Stay back,' he yelled. Sarah and Laurence looked on helplessly. Struggling desperately, the Doctor was sucked closer and closer to the Vortex. Clinging to the edge of the Casket with one hand, he used the other to whip the TARDIS key from its chain around his neck and swing it across the Casket's mouth. There was a bang, a brilliant flash and the Vortex died away. The force of the explosion flung the Doctor backwards across the room.

Sarah and Laurence ran across to the body. The Doctor was quite unconscious. Sarah knelt down, trying to revive him. 'Doctor, come on. Wake up, please!' The Doctor didn't stir.

Laurence shook his head. 'It's no use. He took the full force of the blast.'

Sarah looked round anxiously. 'They're bound to come back soon.'

'We could try carrying him to the lodge,' suggested Laurence.

Sarah shook her head. 'We'd be too slow. We'd probably meet those Mummy things just outside the house. We've got to find somewhere to hide him.'

Laurence's face lit up. 'Wait—there is a place. If I can still find it …' He crossed to one wall and began running his fingers over the moulding of the oak panelling.

Sarah watched, puzzled. 'In here?'

'Somewhere here. Marcus and I discovered it as boys. We called it the priest's hole.' Suddenly a section of wall slid back, revealing a small black opening. 'There it is. There's a kind of room inside. It's not very large I'm afraid.'

Sarah looked dubiously down at the Doctor. 'And he is! Help me get him inside.' They started to drag the Doctor's inert body towards the panelling.

At dawn the following day, Ernie Clements was slipping quietly through the woods around the Old Priory. The deep pockets of his coat concealed traps, snares and a sack, and he carried a folding shotgun. Ernie was a poacher, who took an almost professional pride in his work. He had long regarded the Old Priory estate as his own personal preserve. With Mr Laurence all wrapped up in his newfangled experiments, and Mr Marcus away in Egypt half the time, there was no one to take care of the game on the estate.

Who would look after the partridges and pheasants, and keep the rabbits under control, if Ernie didn't see to it? He regarded himself as the Scarmans' unpaid gamekeeper. Now, whistling silently, Ernie was moving through the woods, giving his traps a final check before going back to his cottage for a well-earned rest.

Suddenly he heard the snap of a trap, and a low inhuman snarl. One of his traps had caught something —and the something sounded very much larger than a rabbit. Ernie slipped through the trees in the direction of the noise. Peering round a thick tree-trunk he froze in unbelieving horror. A giant bandage-wrapped figure was thrashing about and roaring, its huge foot caught in one of Ernie's traps.

Ernie stared at it in amazement. One of them Egyptian mummy things, wasn't it? He'd seen pictures of them on occasional visits to the house. But those things were supposed to be dead. This one was very much alive and very angry.

After struggling furiously for a few minutes, the creature wrenched the stake chain from the ground and prised open the jaws of the trap. Releasing its foot, it hurled the trap crashing against a tree. Then it turned and stalked back towards the house.

Shaken and trembling Ernie watched it go. He picked up the trap. The metal was mangled and twisted. Dropping it quickly, Ernie turned and ran for his life, vowing that he'd never poach again.

Ernie had reached the edge of the wood around the estate when he ran into his second shock of the morning. He ran into it quite literally—it was an invisible wall. There was a crackle of static power and *something* threw him back. He slowly picked himself up, recovered his gun and moved cautiously forward, hands outstretched. At the same point he felt a shock as his hands touched an invisible wall of energy. Hurriedly he drew them back. He picked up a pebble, tossed it. The pebble bounced back—off nothing. Scratching his head, Ernie turned back the way he had come. Frowning thoughtfully he made his way across through the woods, keeping well out of sight of the house. He was moving east, planning to take refuge in his old hut, just on the borders of the estate. Well, it wasn't *his* hut, exactly. He'd found it abandoned and half ruined, so he'd patched it up and taken it over.

But Ernie wasn't able to reach his hut. On the eastern edge of the estate he ran into the same invisible wall, with the same painful results. This time he made the mistake of taking a run at it. He finished up on his back several yards away, winded and shocked. Ernie picked himself up disgustedly. But he wasn't going to give up. This time he worked his way *along* the wall. He came to one of those Egyptian urn things—someone must have carried it out from the house. The urn seemed to hum, and was warm to the touch. Ernie decided to leave it alone. But he made an interesting discovery. At the urn, the invisible wall made a right hand turn—he was on the inside of an invisible corner. Doggedly Ernie traced the course of the wall. It took him a long time because the wall enclosed the entire estate. And there was an urn standing at each invisible corner ...

Realising at last that there was no escape, north, south, east *or* west, Ernie decided there was only one thing for it. He'd go down to the Lodge and have a word with Mr Laurence. For all the fact that his head was full of this scientific mumbo-jumbo, Mr Laurence was a good sort. Ernie had often taken both brothers poaching their own game when they were boys. If Mr Laurence *had* invented an invisible wall, he'd just have to turn it off so Ernie could go home. And he certainly ought to be told about that Mummy thing. Rampaging round the place, smashing a man's traps. Having convinced himself of a legitimate grievance, Ernie set off boldly for the Lodge.

Doctor Warlock woke from an uneasy, feverish sleep. He seemed to have heard someone coming into his room. His eyes opened, and it took him a while to realise where he was. Why wasn't he at his home in the village? What was he doing on a sofa in the Lodge? He tried to sit up. His shoulder ached fiercely and one arm was strapped up. Suddenly the events of the previous day came flooding back. Warlock sat up painfully. The curtains were still drawn, the room in semi-darkness. He turned up the wick of the oil lamp that burned on a table beside his couch. Then he started back. The yellow light showed a white-clad figure standing over him.

Doctor Warlock blinked and rubbed his eyes. It was Marcus. Marcus Scarman! Poor fellow looked shockingly ill, though. Skin a terrible greyish colour, eyes sunken and red-rimmed. Maybe he'd picked up one of those filthy tropical diseases out in Egypt. 'Marcus, my dear fellow,' said Doctor Warlock heartily. 'At last you're back!'

Marcus Scarman spoke coldly. 'Why are you here?'

Doctor Warlock knew at once that something was terribly wrong. The face was Marcus's, though shockingly changed, but the voice was not. It was cold, dead, utterly inhuman. Doctor Warlock had the fleeting thought that *something* was speaking through Marcus's lips. He looked at the expressionless face. 'What's the matter?' he asked gently. 'For goodness sakes, old fellow, don't you recognise me?' Perhaps the illness had affected Marcus's brain.

The burning eyes in the grey face stared at him for a long moment. Then the bloodless lips said stiffly, 'Warlock?'

'That's right,' said Doctor Warlock, encouragingly. 'Marcus, we've all been most dreadfully worried about you ...'

The dead voice interrupted him. 'I came to find the other Scarman.'

'The other—you mean Laurence, your brother?'

'The other Scarman. The human. Where is he?'

Warlock said, 'Look here, old chap, if this is some kind of macabre joke ...'

There was a definite threat in the cold voice now. 'The other Scarman, Warlock. Where is he?'

Convinced that his old friend was deranged, Doctor Warlock decided to humour him. 'Laurence went up to the house. It may interest you to know that your Egyptian servant went berserk and took a pot-shot at me. Laurence and the Doctor went off to deal with him. There was a girl with them. Plucky young thing.' Warlock fished out his pocket watch. 'They've been gone a devil of a time. Hope nothing's amiss.'

'Who is this Doctor?'

Warlock shook his head. 'No idea. One of Laurence's friends, I imagine. Scientist chappie. I'd just been shot when I met him, so my memory's a bit hazy.'

'Why did this Doctor interfere?'

'Interfere? He probably saved my life, Marcus. Now you see here ...'

Astonishingly Marcus said, 'He should not have interfered. *All* humans within the deflection barrier are to be destroyed.'

Warlock was totally baffled. 'Great heavens, Marcus, what's wrong with you?'

Marcus Scarman turned away dismissively. 'Destroy this human.' He spoke not to Warlock, but to a giant figure that loomed out of the shadows. Warlock backed away in terror as the Mummy lumbered forward. He screamed as two great hands reached out for him. 'Marcus, no ...'

From just outside the Lodge, Ernie Clements heard the scream. The terrifying sound made him pause and dart back from the door. He flattened himself against the wall just around the corner. He watched in amazement as the Mummy came out of the Lodge and moved away. And there was a man with it. Ducking back into hiding, Ernie caught just a glimpse of someone in a white suit. Cautiously, he slipped inside the Lodge. Sprawled on the sitting-room floor he found the body of Doctor Warlock.

Ernie knelt beside it. 'Murdering swine,' he muttered. Doctor Warlock had been a good friend. He'd bought many a rabbit or partridge with no questions asked.

Confused as he was by all that had happened, one thing was clear to Ernie. The white-suited man had obviously been controlling the Mummy. Therefore *he* was responsible for Doctor Warlock's death. Angrily, Ernie loaded his shotgun and left the Lodge, determined to track down the murderer of his friend. Someone was going to pay for Warlock's death.

5

THE WORLD
DESTROYED ...

Ernie Clements had no very clear idea what he was going to do as he tracked the white-suited man and his monstrous companion back to the Priory. He was just in time to see the two strange figures enter the house by the front door. 'Just as if they ruddy well owned it,' muttered Ernie.

He was still hoping to find Mr Laurence. *He* was the one who'd know what to do about all this. They were dealing with murder now after all, and Ernie's instinct was to hand over to someone equipped to deal with such things.

But he couldn't just walk into the Priory, not with this white-suited bloke and his pet monster around it. Maybe they'd taken the place over. And where was Mr Laurence, anyway? A prisoner in the house perhaps ...

Ernie began to work his way closer to the Priory. If he could get to the shrubbery unseen, he might be able to take a look through the ground-floor windows, find out what was going on that way.

Moving with all the skill of a born poacher, Ernie slipped quietly into the shrubbery. He looked in several windows without success. All the rooms were silent and empty. He didn't even catch sight of old Collins prowling about.

When he came to the Egyptian room, Ernie had better luck. There were lots of those Mummy things in there, taking stuff out of crates. He caught a glance of the white-suited man too. He was just going out of the door, some of the Mummies following behind him. Ernie

139

moved along the outside of the house paralleling their course. He looked through the window of the organ room, and there they were.

He had another quick glimpse of the white-suited man, though a Mummy was blocking his view of the man's face. Then he saw one of the Mummies drag away a body. Another body! Convinced by now that he was dealing with a dangerous murderer, Ernie raised his gun to his shoulder—awaiting his chance for a clear shot at the man in white...

Inside the priest hole, Sarah, Laurence and the still-unconscious Doctor were crammed into the tiny room. The remainder of the night had passed very slowly. The only light came from a solitary flickering candle, last of a batch, left behind from one of the Scarmans' boyhood adventures. Sarah woke suddenly from a nightmare-ridden doze. Laurence was asleep in a corner, mouth open and snoring quietly. His eyelids fluttered, and he began to stir.

Sarah shook Laurence awake. 'Look! I think the Doctor's coming round.'

'What?' Laurence woke with a start, rubbing his hand across his eyes.

The Doctor's eyes flicked open. 'A parallax coil! ' he said suddenly. 'I never expected that. A simple trap. Blew up in my face. Clever.'

Laurence shook his head. 'Delirious, poor chap.'

Sarah shushed him. 'Mustn't underestimate Sutekh.' continued the Doctor, still to himself. 'Thinks of everything.' He sat up and looked round. 'Where are we?'

'Hiding.'

'I can see that! Where?'

Laurence answered for Sarah. 'In a priest's hole.'

'In a Victorian Gothic folly?' said the Doctor severely. 'Nonsense.'

'Well we're here, aren't we?' said Sarah crossly. 'Don't be so pedantic, Doctor. If the Victorians copied the architecture, they could copy the priest's hole too. Anyway, does it matter?' Her cramped and uncomfortable night had left her tired and cross.

The Doctor wasn't listening. He stared abstractedly at the flickering candle flame. 'If only we knew Sutekh's exact physical location.' He turned to Laurence. 'Where was your brother's expedition bound for?'

'Somewhere called Sekkara, I believe. He wrote to say he'd discovered a hidden pyramid in that region. He believed it concealed what he called a mastaba, a burial chamber.'

The Doctor frowned. 'Somewhere near Sekkara ... that's pretty vague. There might be one chance ...'

'To do what?' asked Sarah.

'Stop Sutekh. With the equipment at the Lodge I could set up a jamming signal. And as Sutekh is controlling operations by mental force ...'

'You could block his power?'

'Possibly. But only if the etheric impulse was projected along precisely the right axis. Otherwise it'd be no good ...' Suddenly his face cleared. 'The Egyptian's ring! '

'What about it?'

'It's a slave relay. Calculating the reverse polarisation will be child's play. Why didn't I think of it before?' The Doctor scrambled to his feet, ready to set off at once.

Sarah heard sounds from the other side of the thin panel. She raised her hand. 'Sssh! Listen ...'

Peering through a crack in the panelling, Sarah saw Marcus and three Mummies re-enter the organ room. Marcus paused and pointed at the body of Ibrahim Namin. 'Remove this carcass!' One of the Mummies grabbed the body by an arm and began dragging it out. Marcus turned to the others. 'There are other humans still within these walls. Find and kill them!' The Mummies turned and marched away.

Marcus Scarman stood alone in the centre of the room. The burning red-rimmed eyes in the grey face swept around the walls. Clearly something was troubling him. Some long-buried memory was making him walk towards the secret panel ...

'He's coming over,' breathed Sarah. Marcus was just the other side of the panel now, fingers groping for the hidden catch in the wainscoting. Sarah cowered back ...

Ernie Clements crouched in the shrubbery outside the organ room. He watched the man in the white suit give his orders to the Mummies. Now the man was alone, his back to the window, apparently searching for something along the wall. In a sudden surge of furious rage, Ernie raised his shotgun and smashed the window with the barrel. The man whirled round to face him, and Ernie fired ...

From her hiding place Sarah heard the crash of broken glass, and the roar of the gun. She felt the thump as Marcus Scarman was blown back against the panelling.

'What's happened?' whispered Laurence. He struggled to get up, but the Doctor stretched out a long arm and held him down.

Outside the window, Ernie saw the blast from both barrels strike the man in the chest, hurling him against the wall. He was suddenly appalled by what he had done. Shot at such close range, the man must be dead, or at least badly wounded. Then, to his horror, the man he had just killed straightened up and started moving towards him. It was Professor Scarman! Ernie *saw* the holes in Scarman's chest—then he saw them close up and disappear. His nerve broke. Dropping his gun, he turned and ran for the woods.

Scarman stood at the window, staring after him. His lips framed a silent command. 'Seek and destroy!' Almost at once, a Mummy appeared round the corner of the house and set off after the fleeing Ernie. It stumbled over the shotgun, picked it up, snapped it in two, then resumed the pursuit. Scarman turned away from the window.

From her crack, Sarah saw him look round the room once more. She was astonished to see that despite having been shot he was apparently unharmed. The incident seemed to have driven the secret panel from his mind. Marcus glanced round the room, frowned like someone trying to remember something, then turned and left the room.

Sarah waited a minute or two, and slid open the panel. She climbed stiffly out, followed by Laurence and the Doctor.

The Doctor said, 'Seems to be all clear.' He headed for the door.

Laurence scuttled after him. 'Where are we going, Doctor?'

'To find that Egyptian.' The Doctor was already out of the room, and moving along the passage.

Sarah caught up with him. 'One of those Mummy things took the body off somewhere. We can't search the whole Priory.'

'We won't have to—look.' The Doctor pointed. The dragging heels of the dead Namin had left a clear track along the floor.

The Doctor set off, his nose to the trail like an eager bloodhound, and Sarah and Laurence followed.

The trail led them along a familiar route through the corridors of the old house and towards the Egyptian room in which the TARDIS had first arrived. As they neared a corner the Doctor paused, holding up his hand. They heard a door open, and dragging footsteps. He looked cautiously round the corner. Marcus Scarman was leaving the Egyptian room, two Mummies following behind him. The Mummies were laden with strange objects. The Doctor watched the procession turn in the other direction and disappear down the corridor. When they were out of sight, he beckoned his companions on.'

In the Egyptian room the piles of crates were scattered, and many had been unpacked. The body of Ibrahim Namin lay sprawled in an empty crate. The Doctor crossed over to it and removed the ornate ruby-red ring from the finger.

Sarah looked round the room, 'What do you think they're doing?'

The Doctor was examining the ring. 'I'm not really sure yet.'

Laurence peered into an open, half-empty crate. 'This is interesting, Doctor. It appears to be some kind of machinery.'

The Doctor and Sarah went over to the crate. Inside was a pile of strangely shaped metal objects. Sarah had never seen anything similar before, but the Doctor seemed to recognise them at once. 'Part of an Osirian anti-gravity drive. They must be building a rocket!'

'Egyptian Mummies building a rocket?' said Sarah sceptically. 'That's *really* crazy, Doctor.'

The Doctor smiled. 'Not really. Those aren't Mummies at all. They're service robots.'

'Robots? Then why do they look like Mummies?'

'The Osirians made them that way to keep the Egyptians in order, back in the days when they ruled as gods.'

'All right then,' persisted Sarah. 'Why are these robots building a rocket?'

'So that Sutekh can break free of the power of Horus.'

'Where's Sutekh now?'

'Exactly where Horus left him, seven thousand years ago. Trapped beneath a pyramid, powerless to move ... Listen!'

The dragging footsteps were coming back along the corridor. Instinctively the Doctor and Sarah ran for the shelter of the TARDIS, leaving Laurence looking after them in amazement. As the footsteps came nearer, the Doctor reached out a long arm and pulled him inside, closing the TARDIS door behind them both.

When Scarman and the Mummies re-entered the room it was empty, the TARDIS in its corner. Since the TARDIS had been there when he arrived, Marcus, or rather the being that now controlled him, had no curiosity about it, accepting it as part of the furniture.

Inside the TARDIS, Laurence Scarman was showing a great deal of curiosity. He stared round the brightly-lit control room with an air of bemused astonishment.

The Doctor smiled down at him. 'You're going to say it transcends the normal laws of physics?' he suggested kindly.

'I am, yes. I mean—it does,' spluttered Laurence. 'It's preposterous!'

'Yes it is, isn't it,' agreed the Doctor cheerfully. 'I often think dimensional transcendentalism is quite preposterous, but it works. Would you care to take a look around?'

'May I? May I really?'

'Please do ... but I wouldn't touch anything.'

Laurence scampered round the TARDIS like a child on its first visit to the Science Museum, uncertain where to begin. Sarah moved closer to the Doctor. 'Now we're here ... why don't you just—leave, take me back to my own time?'

'I can't.'

'Why can't you?'

'Unless Sutekh is stopped, Sarah, he'll destroy your world.'

Sarah stared at him. 'But he *didn't*, did he? I mean, we knew the world didn't end in nineteen eleven.'

The Doctor looked strangely at her. 'Do we?'

'Of course we do!'

The Doctor sighed. 'All right, Sarah. Let's see what the world looks like in your time.' His hands flickered over the controls, there was a hum of power, and the central column began rising and falling.

'I say,' said Laurence excitedly. 'This is just like one of those scientific romances by that Wells chappie!'

Their journey was a brief one. Soon the Doctor adjusted controls again, and the TARDIS came to a stop. 'Here we are, Sarah, if you want to get off.' His voice was grave.

Sarah looked doubtfully at him. But she wasn't going to back down now—not until she'd seen what was out there. She moved over to the doors, and the Doctor touched a control on his console. The doors slid open, and Sarah looked out on to a landscape of hell.

6

THE MUMMIES ATTACK

Sarah saw a huge bleak, barren plain, stretching endlessly away, devastated by a perpetually howling dust-storm. Here and there were a few shattered ruins. That was all. No plants, no trees, no animals, no people, no life of any kind. A dead world.

Shuddering, Sarah stepped back, and the Doctor closed the doors. Angrily she said, 'That wasn't Earth. It's all some horrible trick.'

The Doctor shook his head sadly. 'No, Sarah. That's your world as Sutekh would leave it. A desolate planet circling a dead sun.'

'But I don't understand. Earth *isn't* like that.'

'Every point in time has its alternative, Sarah. You've just seen into alternative time.'

Laurence had been listening in fascination. 'Extraordinary. Are you saying that the future can be *chosen*, Doctor?'

'Not chosen but ... *shaped*. The actions of the present fashion the future.'

'So a man can change the course of history?'

'To a small extent. After all, the actions of many men *are* history. But it takes a being of Sutekh's limitless powers to *destroy* the future.' He turned to Sarah. 'Well?'

Sarah's face was bleak. She hated the thought of returning to face the horrors they had just left. But she was willing to do anything to prevent the Earth she knew turning into the desolate horror outside the TARDIS doors. 'We've got to go back, haven't we?'

'Yes,' said the Doctor quietly. 'We've got to go back.' His fingers moved once more over the controls.

Sarah and Laurence waited while the Doctor returned the TARDIS to nineteen eleven. He switched on the scanner—the Egyptian room was empty again. He opened the doors, and they left the TARDIS.

146

The Doctor led them straight towards the window and flung it open. 'Out we go—and keep down. We're heading back to the Lodge.' Sarah and Laurence climbed out and the Doctor followed, closing the window behind him. Crouching low, they ran for the cover of the woods.

Marcus Scarman was too occupied to be concerned about them. He was standing before Sutekh's Casket in the alcove. From inside the Casket came an eerie green glow. Marcus was talking to his Master. 'Several humans within the deflection barrier have been killed, but others remain.'

Sutekh's voice was soft and ferocious at the same time, like that of some great beast. 'Eliminate them!'

'The Servicers are searching for them, but this delays the assembly of the rocket.'

The voice became angry. 'Destruction of the humans must not be allowed to delay the construction of my rocket. That is of paramount importance.'

'Your orders will be obeyed, Sutekh. I shall recall two of the Servicers to the rocket assembly.'

The green glow died away. Knowing he was dismissed, Marcus Scarman turned and left the room.

Rather to their surprise, the Doctor and his friends reached the Lodge quite safely. Inside, Sarah drew back the dining-room curtains, revealing the stiffened corpse of Doctor Warlock. They lifted him on to the sofa, and Laurence spread a sheet over the body. He shook his head in horror and disbelief. 'I can't believe my brother was responsible for this. He and Warlock were the closest of friends.'

The Doctor was already at work on the Marconi scope. 'If you can manage to stop thinking of him as your brother, it will be a great deal easier for you,' he said gently. 'By the way, do you have any spare valves?'

Laurence brought some over to him. 'But Marcus is my brother!' he said miserably.

'Not any longer. The moment he entered Sutekh's tomb, he became totally subject to Sutekh's will. As a human being, Marcus Scarman no longer exists. He is simply a walking embodiment of Sutekh's powers.

He has given the paralysed Sutekh arms and legs, a body to use as a means of escape.'

As he talked the Doctor was replacing the burnt-out valve in Laurence's Marconiscope. He began attaching leads from the tuner to the slave relay ring he had taken from Namin's body.

Sarah looked on as he worked absorbedly. 'If Sutekh is so totally evil, why didn't Horus and the other Osirians destroy him when they had the chance?'

'Against their code,' said the Doctor. 'To kill Sutekh would have made them no better than he was. So they simply imprisoned him.'

'How?'

'Some kind of forcefield, I imagine. Controlled by a power source on Mars.'

'On *Mars*?' repeated Laurence incredulously.

The Doctor looked up. 'Of course. Remember that message we picked up? When your brother blundered into Sutekh's tomb, he triggered off the monitoring system on Mars. It sent out an automatic alarm signal.'

Sarah was beginning to work it out. 'So that rocket the Servicer Robots are building ...'

'Will be aimed at the forcefield control point on Mars. Exactly, Sarah. If that warhead hits its target, Sutekh will have succeeded in releasing himself.'

'To destroy the world,' said Laurence in a horrified tone.

'Not only this world. Anywhere that life is found ... Do you happen to have a magneto, old chap?'

Laurence stared blankly at him. 'A magneto? Yes, of course.' He went to a cupboard and started rummaging inside.

Ernie Clements was tearing through the woods at a stumbling run too frightened and too exhausted now to worry about moving quietly. He'd thought at first it would be easy to slip away from his pursuers. But the Mummies were too many and too determined.

They were quartering the woods with a methodical machine-like persistence. Since they were not flesh and blood, they didn't tire— unlike Ernie who by now was panting and exhausted. He felt like the fox at the end of a very long chase. For the first time in his life he felt some sympathy for the animals he hunted and trapped.

He leaned against a tree, his chest heaving. For one blissful moment he thought he had shaken off his pursuers. Then he heard the steady crashing through trees and bushes. They had him surrounded now, and were driving him forwards as a beater drives game on to the guns.

Just one thing gave Ernie a vestige of hope. They seemed to be chasing him in the direction of the Lodge, and that was the very place he wanted to be. He still had hopes that Mr Laurence would turn up to help and advise him. And even if he didn't the Lodge was a sturdy old building. Maybe he could barricade himself inside. Ernie remembered something else. There were guns in the Lodge too. They'd belonged to the Scarman boys' father, a big-game hunter in his day. Give him a nice heavy hunting rifle, Ernie thought grimly, and he'd soon show those Egyptian horrors a thing or two. They'd *need* bandages by the time he was done with them.

Fortified by this resolve, and with at least some of his breath back, Ernie set off on a last desperate dash for safety. Only one thing worried him. The trees didn't go right up to the Lodge. For the final dash he'd be in open country and in plain sight.

Ernie's luck held good till almost the last minute. He reached the edge of the woods and set off on his final run. But just as he left cover, two Mummies emerged from the woods, one to each side of him. Snarling angrily, they set off after him. They were very close, but Ernie reckoned he could just about make it …

Sarah looked on as the Doctor finished connecting the Marconiscope to the ring. 'What are you going to do with that thing?'

'Block the mental beam that transmits Sutekh's power. He'll be helpless then.'

Sarah was struck by a thought. 'What will happen to Marcus Scarman?'

'He'll simply collapse.'

'You mean—die?'

The Doctor nodded, testing the connection on one of the leads. 'He's not alive now, in any real sense. Only the will of Sutekh animates him. And deprived of his outside contact, Sutekh will be as powerless as the day Horus imprisoned him.' The Doctor looked round. 'The main power switch is over beside the door, Sarah—I'll stay by the Marconiscope to calibrate, you throw the switch when I give the word.'

Over by the cupboard, Laurence Scarman stood listening to the low voices. He found the magneto at last and took it over to the Doctor, who looked up. 'Did you find one, old chap?'

Laurence nodded slowly. 'Here you are, Doctor.' Almost reluctantly, he handed it over.

The Doctor began wiring it in. 'Splendid.' He looked up at Laurence. 'Is there anything—'

A terrified scream came from just outside the Lodge, and grabbing his rifle, Laurence tore out of the room, through the hall and to the front door. He saw Ernie Clements running from the woods, two pursuing Mummies converging on him. Even as Laurence watched, the little poacher stumbled and fell. Ernie picked himself up and went on running, but the delay was fatal. The two giant Mummies slammed together, Ernie Clements jammed between them. His final scream of terror was cut off abruptly, and he dropped to the ground, all life crushed from his body.

Laurence Scarman threw his hunting rifle to his shoulder, and fired. One of the Mummies staggered and turned back towards the Lodge, growling with rage. The other followed. As the two horrible shapes stalked closer, Laurence fired again and again. The Mummies staggered a little as the bullets struck, but still lurched remorselessly forwards. They were almost upon Laurence when the Doctor appeared in the doorway.

'Come on, man, inside,' he yelled. He grabbed hold of Laurence and heaved him back into the house, slamming and barring the door. Ignoring Laurence's protests, he bustled him into the sitting room, shutting and locking that door too. Releasing the little man abruptly, the Doctor made a final check of the rejigged Marconiscope. There came a shattering crash as the front door gave way to the Mummies' onslaught. The Doctor made a final delicate adjustment. 'Switch on the power, Sarah.' he yelled. Already the Mummies were battering at the sitting-room door.

Just as Sarah was about to switch on, Laurence Scarman threw himself upon her, pulling her away. 'No, don't,' he cried. 'I heard what you said. You'll kill my brother!'

The door began to splinter and the Doctor rammed a heavy armchair against it. 'Sarah, switch on!' he shouted.

Sarah struggled desperately to break away from the frenzied Laurence, while the Doctor fought to keep the Mummies out of the room. Once the switch was thrown and Sutekh's mental beam blocked, the Mummies, like Marcus Scarman, would simply collapse ...

Just as Sarah tore free from Laurence, there was a splintering crash and the first of the Mummies forced its way into the room. The Doctor closed with it immediately, and actually managed to hold it for a moment. Then the Mummy threw him across the room, and lurched forward. It stumbled over the chair and into the Marconiscope—just as Sarah pulled the switch.

There was a crackle of electricity, a bang and a flash. Blue sparks arced across the Mummy's body and it dropped to the floor. But by now the second Mummy was in the room. Laurence Scarman made a brave but futile attempt to hold it. It smashed him to one side and bore down on Sarah ...

7

THE DOCTOR FIGHTS BACK

Sarah cowered away as the Mummy loomed threateningly over her. On the far side of the room, the Doctor was struggling to his feet. Sarah heard his voice, 'The ring, Sarah! Find the ring!'

She looked round frantically. There was a red gleam among the ruins of the shattered Marconiscope. Snatching the ring she held it up before the advancing Mummy and shouted, 'Stop!' To her astonished relief, the Mummy stopped.

'Tell it to return to Control,' called the Doctor.

'Return to Control,' ordered Sarah nervously. The Mummy turned and lumbered from the room. Sarah collapsed into a chair.

The Doctor was on his feet, helping the half-stunned Laurence to get up. 'Are you all right?'

Laurence rubbed his head. 'I think so ...'

'Then you don't deserve to be,' said the Doctor angrily. 'You nearly got us all killed! What's worse, you've wrecked my only chance of stopping Sutekh.'

'Forgive me, Doctor. I just couldn't face the thought of killing my own brother.'

The Doctor crossed over to Laurence and put a hand on his shoulder. 'Now listen to me,' he said firmly. 'That thing walking about out there is no longer your brother. It is simply a human cadaver, animated by the power of Sutekh. Do you understand that?'

Laurence nodded, unable to speak. Sarah couldn't help feeling sorry for him. Whatever the Doctor said, it couldn't be easy for Laurence to accept that what looked like his brother was really the puppet of some alien power.

The Doctor moved towards the door. 'If Sutekh succeeds in freeing himself,' he warned, 'the consequences will be incalculable. Somehow we've *got* to stop him …'

As the Doctor strode from the room, Laurence looked at Sarah. 'Where's he going?'

'To see what Sutekh's up to, I suppose. I'd better go with him.' Sarah hurried after the Doctor. Laurence collapsed into a chair, his face in his hands.

Sutekh, at that particular moment, was once again in conference with his servant Marcus Scarman. 'I detected electro-magnetic radiation,' Sutekh snarled. 'There was a deliberate attempt to block my cytronic control.'

Marcus Scarman bowed his head before the green glow from the Casket. 'I know nothing of this, Sutekh.'

'The source of power was *within* the deflection barrier.'

Marcus frowned in thought. 'There are still some humans alive within the barrier. Warlock spoke of one called the Doctor—and a girl. There is still the other Scarman, Laurence. I can order the Servicers to hunt them down and destroy them, but that will delay work on the missile.'

Sutekh's response was immediate. 'No! The missile must be fired at the appointed time. Immediately after, you will find and kill these humans.'

Marcus bowed his head. 'As you order, Sutekh, so shall it be.' The green glow faded.

Sarah and the Doctor worked their way cautiously through the woods, back towards the Priory. As they came nearer, the Doctor spotted huge figures moving to and fro in the yard behind the house, 'There they are,' he whispered. 'Let's take a closer look.' Wriggling forwards on their stomachs, they worked their way as near to the yard as they dared, stopping behind the cover of a dense clump of bushes. Sarah raised her head and peered through the leaves. She saw an opaque

Pyramid made from some material that looked like heavy plastic. One side had an entrance hatch, with a ramp leading to the ground. As they watched, a Mummy came out of the hatch, walked down the ramp and moved back towards the house. Another Mummy appeared from the house, cradling in its arms a heavy metal object. It climbed the ramp and disappeared inside the Pyramid.

Sarah whispered in the Doctor's ear. 'That Pyramid thing—what is it?'

'An Osirian war missile. Almost completed by the look of it.'

'You mean that thing *flies*?'

'It transposes the power of Sutekh's will. You might call it Pyramid power.'

Marcus came round the corner of the house and stopped just by the Pyramid. Sarah had a nasty feeling he was staring straight at their hiding place. After a moment he climbed the Pyramid ramp and disappeared inside. Sarah and the Doctor slipped away, retracing their tracks to the Lodge.

They found Laurence staring sadly at an old family photograph, two solemn-faced little boys in wing collars and knickerbocker suits. He put the photograph down and looked up eagerly. 'Did you learn anything?'

'Only that time is short,' said the Doctor. He crossed to the electrocuted Mummy, sprawled face-down on the floor, and studied the pyramid shape on its back. 'Cytronic induction,' he said thoughtfully.

Sarah said, 'Come on, Doctor. Explain.'

'The Servicer robots are drawing their energy from a cytronic particle accelerator—which must be in Sutekh's tomb. After all, he's had seven thousand years to build one.'

'So?'

'So—put that out of action and he'd have no work-force, and no missile.'

Laurence broke in, 'But Sutekh's tomb is some where in Egypt. How could you possibly ...'

The Doctor was striding about the room. 'Marcus came from Egypt, didn't he? Through the Space/Time tunnel. And it must be a two-way mechanism.'

Her worst fears confirmed, Sarah said, 'If you go through that tunnel, Doctor, Sutekh will kill you.'

The Doctor didn't reply—mainly because he knew there was a very good chance that Sarah was right. But if there was no alternative …

Timidly Laurence said, 'Wouldn't it be better—'

'No it wouldn't,' snapped the Doctor, and made for the door. Then he paused. He didn't really want to go through that Time tunnel. Not if, there really was some other way … He came back into the room and sat down. 'Well,' he said grumpily. 'Wouldn't *what* be better?'

Laurence took a deep breath. 'Wouldn't it be less risky just to blow up the missile?'

'Of course it would,' said the Doctor crossly. 'But what with?'

Sarah could see that Laurence was anxious to redeem himself. 'What about blasting gelignite?' he suggested eagerly.

The Doctor looked at him in surprise. 'I suppose you just happen to have some about the place?'

'Well, no. But I do know poor Ernie Clements kept a supply in his hut. I'm afraid he used it for fishing?'

Sarah looked puzzled. 'How do you fish with gelignite?'

'You set it off and chuck it in the water,' said the Doctor. 'The underwater explosion kills the fish and they float up to the surface. It's a deplorable method, but very effective.'

Laurence nodded. 'That's right,' he confirmed, 'I heard poor Ernie "fishing" just a few nights ago.'

The Doctor rubbed his chin. 'And where did he keep this gelignite?'

'I'm not absolutely sure. But he had an old hut on the east side of the woods. That would be the obvious place.'

The Doctor made up his mind and stood up. 'Come on, Sarah.'

'I'll come with you, shall I?' offered Laurence. 'I could show you the way.'

The Doctor said quickly, 'It's all right, we'll find it.'

Laurence stopped. 'You think I'll let you down again, don't you?'

Since this was precisely what the Doctor *did* think, he was somewhat at a loss for an answer. After a moment he said gently, 'Mr Scarman, if you really want to help, you might start getting the binding off that Servicer robot.'

The Doctor left. Sarah gave Laurence a quick smile of sympathy, and followed him out.

Laurence watched them go, a worried frown on his face. He fished an old clasp-knife from a drawer, and knelt by the collapsed robot. Cautiously, he started to saw away at its bandaging.

Sarah and the Doctor were moving eastwards through the woods when suddenly the Doctor stopped. He picked up a long branch and started waving it about in front of him. Sarah stared. 'What are you doing, Doctor?'

'Being careful. Walking into a deflection barrier is like walking into an invisible wall. Painful.'

'I'd forgotten about the barrier. You mean it's between us and the hut?' The Doctor nodded, still waving his stick about. 'Can we get through it?'

The Doctor stopped as the end of his branch brushed against the invisible forcefield. 'Ah, here we are! Now all we have to do is find the door.' Using his branch as a guide, the Doctor moved along parallel with the deflection barrier, accompanied by a mystified Sarah. He followed the invisible wall until he came to an ornately decorated urn, standing incongruously beneath a tree. 'There you are,' said the Doctor happily. 'Door.' He produced his sonic screwdriver and held it up. 'Key!'

Sarah looked at him sceptically. 'As simple as that, is it?'

Regretfully the Doctor said, 'Well, no, not quite.'

Sarah groaned. 'I didn't think it could be!'

The Doctor started prodding the area round the urn with his branch. 'No obvious booby-traps, anyway.' He knelt to examine the urn more closely. After a moment, he turned and looked up at Sarah. 'Well, are you going to help, or just stand there admiring the scenery?'

'Actually I wasn't looking at the scenery,' said Sarah with dignity. She pointed down at the Doctor's boot-soles, one of which was developing a hole. 'Your shoes need repairing! Well, what do you want me to do?'

'Come and hold the base of this urn for me. And be careful—if it falls over we're done for.'

Sarah knelt on the other side of the urn, steadying it with her hands. At this close range she could hear a kind of low electronic hum. The urn vibrated slightly beneath her hands. 'Is it dangerous?' she asked nervously.

'Of course it's dangerous,' said the Doctor impatiently. He began making short, delicate sweeps across the face of the urn with his sonic screwdriver. Nothing happened. He adjusted the screwdriver and tried again. The note from the urn started to rise. It shot up to a high-pitched electronic scream ...

The Doctor made another hasty adjustment, and the sound returned to its former level. The Doctor sat back on his heels, mopping his face with his scarf. 'Deactivating a generator loop without the correct key is like repairing a watch with a hammer and chisel. One false move and you'll never know the time again.'

'Any more comforting thoughts?' asked Sarah shakily.

'Just keep that urn steady. Oh, let me know if it starts to feel warm.'

'Don't worry, you'll know. You'll hear me breaking the sound barrier.'

The Doctor grinned and went on with his delicate task.

Far away in Egypt, in a dark cell beneath the Pyramid of Sutekh, a monitor screen occupied one wall. On the screen, four lines of light formed the pattern of a pyramid. One of these lines began flashing on and off, and a low alarm signal filled the air. From his throne, the robed, masked figure of Sutekh was looking into the monitor. 'Interference,' he snarled. 'There is interference!'

In the woods, the Doctor made a final adjustment. The sound from the urn stopped completely. Gently the Doctor unscrewed the lid of the urn, and drew out a metal cylinder. Dropping it to the ground, he stamped on it hard. 'Just to make sure,' he said cheerfully. 'Come along, Sarah.'

A thought-impulse from Sutekh triggered off the organ-like signal. Marcus came running to stand before the Casket in the Egyptian room. In Sutekh's cell, his face appeared as a flickering distorted image on the monitor. Marcus listened as Sutekh told him of the interference. 'Sutekh, I do not understand how this can be,' he protested.

'I tell you the barrier to the east has been deactivated.'

'That just isn't possible.'

'It has been deactivated,' Sutekh repeated angrily. 'The power line has gone from my monitor.'

'But the humans do not have the knowledge to shut down a deflection barrier.'

'Then it is clear that an extra-terrestial intelligence is operating against us.'

Marcus found it difficult to accept the thought. 'An extra-terrestial—an alien? Here?'

A note of insane rage came into Sutekh's voice. 'I have endured an eternity of impotent darkness. I will not be denied now. Hear my commands. You will look for the humans. But the missile is to be constantly guarded. The Servicers must maintain total vigilance.'

'All shall be as you say, Sutekh. The Servicers shall guard the missile while I check the barrier and search for your enemies.'

Sutekh's voice rose to a maddened howl. 'Once the missile is projected, I shall seek out and destroy *all* my enemies. This alien who dares to intrude … All the humans … birds, fish, reptiles, plants … *all* life is my enemy. All life shall perish under the reign of Sutekh the Destroyer!'

Marcus Scarman echoed the hideous chant. 'All life shall perish. Only Sutekh shall live!'

8

'I AM SUTEKH!'

Once through the deflection barrier, the Doctor and Sarah soon found Ernie Clements' hideaway. The ruined hut had never been his home. He had a comfortable cottage in the village. But the hut made a useful hiding place for guns, traps, ferrets, dead birds and rabbits, and all the other things Ernie had preferred not to keep in the cottage. Including the gelignite, used in his drastic but efficient method of fishing ...

The Doctor and Sarah came into the hut and looked around. It held an assortment of odds and ends. Crates, boxes, cages, rolls of wire, bits of traps, ricketty chairs and sagging cupboards ... It was hard to know where to start looking. They began a methodical search.

As they worked, Sarah asked, 'How powerful is Sutekh, Doctor?'

The Doctor was rummaging in an old battered chest. 'All-powerful,' he said shortly. 'If he gets free, there isn't a life-form in the galaxy able to stand against him.'

'Not even your lot—the Time Lords?'

'Not even my lot. Sutekh was only defeated in the end by the combined efforts of over seven hundred of his fellow Osirians, led by Horus.'

Sarah racked her brains to remember the article on Egyptian mythology she'd researched so long ago. 'The seven hundred and forty gods whose names are recorded in the tomb of Thutmose III, I suppose?' she said airily.

The Doctor chuckled at this display of one-upmanship. 'That's right,' he agreed. 'I'd be careful of that cage, Sarah. I think there's a ferret in it!'

Sarah opened the cage. A slim grey shape leaped out and flashed across the floor of the hut, disappearing under the door.

Sarah turned her attention to a cupboard that leaned crazily out from the wall. She groped on the top shelf and encountered what felt like soggy cardboard. She took the box down. It held cakes of some clammy substance. 'Could this be it, Doctor?' she asked, handing him the box.

The Doctor took the box without really looking. Then he straightened up, glanced inside the box and froze like a statue.

'What's the matter?' asked Sarah. 'Isn't there enough of it? It seems to have gone all soggy!' She poked the clammy stuff with one finger.

The Doctor's voice was almost unnaturally calm. 'Sarah—take your hand out of that box, very, very carefully.'

'All right,' said Sarah obligingly. 'What's the matter?'

The Doctor drew a deep breath. 'That stuff is gelignite. It's soggy because it's old and in poor condition. They call it "sweating". Sweaty gelignite is highly unstable. One good sneeze would be enough to set it off.'

Sarah stepped back hastily. 'Sorry!' she said rather inadequately.

The Doctor set the box down on the table. 'Any sign of detonators or fuses?'

Sarah rooted through the cupboard and shook her head. 'No, nothing else.' She looked back at the Doctor. 'Maybe he just used to sneeze on it?'

The Doctor scowled fiercely at her, but made no reply. Picking up the cardboard box with loving care, he led the way out of the hut.

Marcus Scarman's check of the deflector shield eventually led him to the dismantled urn. He stood looking at it for a long time. His burning gaze swept the woods around him. Then he turned and hurried away, towards the Lodge. A little later, the Doctor and Sarah appeared, following the same route to the same destination. But they were slowed by the need to move cautiously with the gelignite. They didn't see Marcus. By now he was well ahead of them.

Obeying the Doctor's rather mysterious instructions, Laurence Scarman was removing the last of the wrappings from the disabled Mummy. As they came away they revealed a kind of metallic skeleton with cross-braced metallic strips replacing pelvis and rib structure. The circular frame for the head appeared to be empty, apart from a lateral bar which was connected to the central mechanism—a pyramid of some red vitreous material.

Laurence took off the last of the wrapping and looked at the thing distastefully. Absorbed in his task, he didn't notice someone come silently into the room and stand over him.

Suddenly, warned by some instinct, he looked up. 'Marcus!' he said joyfully.

Marcus Scarman looked impassively down at him. Laurence rose to his feet. 'Marcus, old chap, don't you know me? I'm your brother!'

'Brother ...' Marcus spoke the word as if it had no meaning.

'That's it, I'm your brother Laurence.'

Marcus seemed to consider this for a moment. Then he said, 'As Horus was brother to Sutekh!'

Laurence's voice was low and appealing. 'Marcus, you're ill. You must let me help you.' He stretched out a hand. Marcus knocked it away with a bestial snarl.

'Trust me,' urged Laurence. 'I won't harm you.'

'Trust?' Obviously this word too was meaningless.

Laurence looked desperately round the room, seeking some way to reach his brother. He snatched up the photograph and held it out. 'Don't you remember *anything*, Marcus? Look, that's us when we were boys.'

Marcus stared down at the two young faces. Something seemed to get through to him. When he spoke again his voice held a more human note. 'Marcus ... Laurence ...' he said slowly.

'That's right. You do remember.'

'I was—Marcus.'

'And you still are,' said Laurence reassuringly. 'Now, let me help you.'

Marcus's face twisted as if in pain. 'I *was* Marcus. Now I am Sutekh!'

'No, Marcus, no. You went to Egypt, remember? You must have fallen under some kind of mesmeric influence ...'

Marcus's voice rose to a hoarse chant. 'Sutekh the great destroyer. Sutekh the lord of death. I am his instrument ...'

Laurence spoke in a voice of desperate urgency. 'Now you listen to me, Marcus, that's all nonsense. You are *Marcus Scarman*, Professor of Archaeology, Fellow of All Souls—'

Marcus's arm swept out, knocking the picture from Laurence's hand. 'You!' he snarled contemptuously. 'What do you know of Sutekh! Where are the others?'

Laurence backed away, frightened by the sudden violence. 'What others?'

'You are being helped. The mind of Sutekh has detected an alien intelligence at work.'

'I suppose you must mean the Doctor ...'

'Doctor,' repeated Marcus in a tone of savage satisfaction. His hands shot out and seized Laurence by the shoulders. With horror Laurence saw that his brother's hands were black and charred. Their touch seemed to burn, he smelt smoke rising from his jacket. 'Marcus,' he choked, 'your hands ...'

Marcus shook him savagely. 'This Doctor ... where is he? *What is he?*' He shifted his grip to Laurence's throat.

The Doctor and Sarah crouched near the pyramid-shaped Osirian missile. Two Mummies stood guarding it like sentries. Carefully the Doctor hid the box of gelignite under a bush. 'We'll leave it there for the moment. Should he safe enough.'

Sarah gave him a sceptical look. 'You know this just isn't going to work, Doctor? No detonators, no fuses ... so even if you get near enough to place the charge without being spotted, how are we going to explode it?'

'Do stop asking silly questions,' snapped the Doctor. 'I've already thought of all that—and that's where you come in.'

Before Sarah could ask more questions, he set off for the Lodge.

When they came into the living room, Laurence Scarman was slumped in a chair, head drooping on his chest. Thinking how dejected he looked, the Doctor tried to cheer him up. He waved towards the unwrapped Mummy framework. 'Well done, Mr Scarman. An excellent job.'

Laurence didn't respond. Sarah tapped him on the shoulder. 'Mr Scarman?'

Laurence keeled over and slumped to the floor. Sarah jumped back with a cry of shock. The Doctor knelt beside the body, then rose, shaking his head. 'Strangled, poor chap.'

'The Mummies must have come back.'

'Not this time, Sarah. There are—marks on the neck. His late brother must have called.'

'That's horrible,' said Sarah. 'He was so concerned about his brother ...'

Already the Doctor had moved away from Laurence, and was examining the exposed Mummy frame. 'Told him not to,' he said absently. 'Told him it was already too late.'

Sarah looked indignantly at him. 'Sometimes I don't understand you, Doctor. Sometimes you don't seem—'

Sarah checked herself, and the Doctor completed her sentence for her. 'Human? You're forgetting, Sarah— I'm not.' He returned to his study of the robot mechanism. 'Splendid workmanship, this. Typical Osirian simplicity.'

Sarah could have shaken him. 'A man's just been murdered and—'

'*Five* men,' interrupted the Doctor. 'Six if you count Marcus Scarman himself. But there's no time for mourning, Sarah. Those deaths will be the first of untold millions, unless Sutekh is stopped.' He looked down at the body. 'Know thine enemy. Admirable advice. I did try to warn him, you know.'

Sarah heard the pain in his voice and realised that the Doctor was hiding his feelings under a mask of flippancy. 'All right, Doctor,' she said gently. 'What do we do now?'

'If we're going to do anything about that missile, we'll have to move quickly. I'll need your help, Sarah.'

'What do you want me to do?'

The Doctor was sorting through a pile of Mummy bindings. 'Clever chaps, the Osirians,' he said conversationally. 'These wrappings are chemically impregnated to protect the robots against damage and corrosion.' He began to wrap a binding around one leg. 'An impenetrable disguise, wouldn't you say?'

Sarah looked at him in alarm.

The Doctor smiled. 'Now then, what sort of a shot are you?'

While Sarah helped the Doctor to swathe himself in Mummy bindings, Marcus Scarman was supervising the other Servicer robots in their work. Two of them were lifting a heavy cylinder from one of the crates. Marcus called, 'Stop!' The Mummies stopped. Marcus examined the hieroglyphics on the side of the cylinder. 'This is the Warhead trigger charge, Phase One. It must be placed directly under the detonation head. Signify your understanding.' Both Mummies lowered their heads. Satis-fied Scarman said, 'Continue.' The Mummies moved out of the room.

Sarah fixed the last of the wrappings around the Doctor's feet. A muffled voice said, 'Hurry up.'

'I am hurrying,' she replied indignantly. 'Don't want to come unwrapped, do you?' She fixed the wrapping in place. 'There.'

Swathed in bindings from head to foot, the Doctor made an impressively Mummy-like figure. 'That'll do,' he said. 'It doesn't have to be perfect, you know. I may have to mingle with the Mummies, but I definitely shan't linger. How do I look?'

Sarah shook her head sadly. 'It must have been a terrible accident.'

'Don't provoke me,' said the muffled voice. Lurching a little, the disguised Doctor picked up his coat, scarf and hat and moved towards the door. 'Come along, Sarah. And don't forget that rifle.'

Marcus Scarman stood before the glowing Casket, his hands raised in supplication. 'The work on the missile is almost complete, Sutekh. We need only the target co-ordinates.'

The voice of Sutekh said, 'I shall now release them.'

The glowing Casket blurred and faded, to be replaced by the spinning Vortex of the Space/Time tunnel. Tumbling end over end, a white cylinder appeared, speeding closer and closer to Marcus until it shot from the tunnel like a projectile and rolled across the floor to his feet. Marcus bent and picked it up.

The cylinder glowed with the fire of Sutekh and there was a horrible sizzling sound as Marcus touched it. But he felt no pain. Only the living feel pain.

Sutekh ordered, 'Engage the co-ordinates in the projection dome monitor.'

'Immediately, Sutekh.' The still-smoking cylinder in his hands, Marcus turned and left the room.

Moving awkwardly because of his bindings, the Doctor took the box of gelignite from its hiding-place. Beside him, Sarah was settling into position, prone on the ground with the rifle, like someone at a firing-range. The Doctor looked down at her. 'You know what to do?'

'Give you time to get clear and—pow!'

'And be sure to shoot straight. You won't get a second shot.'

'Don't worry, Doctor. I know what I'm doing. Good luck!'

The Doctor lumbered away. Sarah saw him move across the yard and up to the missile. The Mummy on guard paid no attention. Sarah guessed the intelligence of the Mummies was limited and strictly functional. They would do what they were ordered, no less, but no more. And since no one had actually told them to look out for another Mummy with a box of gelignite ... Sarah watched tensely as the Doctor made his way to the ramp. He climbed stiffly up it, and put the box just beside the open hatch. Sarah began lining up her rifle-sights. Now the Doctor was descending the ramp. He reached the bottom and started back towards her. Sarah cuddled the rifle-butt into her shoulder. Just let him get a little further from the missile and ... To her horror, she saw Marcus Scarman appear from the house and make straight for the Doctor.

Through a tiny gap in the wrappings the Doctor saw Scarman coming towards him, a white cylinder in his hands. He heard Scarman's voice. 'Stop!'

The Doctor went on walking. The voice came again. 'Stop! Turn about.'

The Doctor stopped, turned. Marcus came up to him. 'Is your relay defective?'

The Doctor stood motionless. Scarman frowned for a moment then held out the metal cylinder. 'This is the co-ordinate-selector. It is to be placed in the projection-dome monitor. Indicate your understanding.' The Doctor managed a Mummy-like nod.

'Then obey my order,' said Scarman sharply.

Stiffly the Doctor turned and reascended the ramp. Marcus moved back towards the house. Inside the rocket, the Doctor dumped the cylinder at random, and hurried back down the ramp.

Sarah watched impatiently as for the second time the Doctor began walking across the yard towards her. This time there was no interruption. The Doctor maintained his stiff Mummy-like gait until the sentinel robot turned away from him, then he broke into a shambling run.

When he was near the edge of the trees, Sarah lined up her sights on the cardboard box. Slowly and carefully she squeezed the trigger ...

9

IN THE POWER OF SUTEKH

The rifle cracked, arid the butt recoiled against her shoulder. Sarah saw the cardboard box jerk. There was a sheet of flame then—nothing. No sound, and no explosion.

Sarah looked up as the disguised Doctor threw himself down beside her. 'I hit it, Doctor,' she said helplessly. 'I *know* I hit it!'

'You hit it all right,' agreed the Doctor grimly. 'Sutekh must be containing the explosion by sheer mental power. There's only one hope left, I've got to get to him. Somehow I've got to break his concentration.' Swiftly the Doctor began stripping off his Mummy disguise.

'Come on, Sarah,' he said urgently. 'Give me a hand.'

Sarah helped him to strip off the bindings. They rolled them into a ball and stuffed them under a bush. From beneath another bush the Doctor produced his hat, coat and scarf.

'He'll get himself killed over that silly hat and scarf one day,' thought Sarah, remembering how he'd gone back for his hat earlier.

Restored to his old self again, the Doctor stood up and stretched with evident relief. 'Somehow I don't think I was meant to be a Mummy,' he said solemnly. 'Anyway, I need to look my best to meet someone as distinguished as old Sutekh …'

Sarah was appalled. 'As distinguished as who? Doctor, you're not going down that Space/Time tunnel thing!'

'Oh yes I am, Sarah. If I can distract Sutekh for just one second, his concentration will break and the balloon, or rather the missile, will go up. Sutekh will be imprisoned again for ever. We'll have won!'

'Oh will we? We'll have won, and you'll be in Sutekh's den. How do you think he'll feel when he realises he's got you to thank for blowing up his missile and spoiling his plans for a comeback?'

'Well, he may be a bit put out,' the Doctor admitted, 'but I'm sure I'll manage to smooth him over.'

'And if you don't?'

'Then I'll just have to escape. After all, I've walked into many a tight spot before.'

'As tight as this?'

'Well, perhaps not quite as tight as this. Good-bye, Sarah.' He touched her cheek gently with his hand, turned and ran towards the front of the house.

Sarah called after him. 'Doctor, he'll kill you ...' But she was too late. The Doctor was gone. Dejected she turned back towards the Lodge for a hiding place. Her anxiety for the Doctor made her careless. Within minutes she ran straight into the arms of a Mummy. Seizing her arm in an iron grip, ignoring her cries and struggles, the Mummy started dragging her towards the Priory.

The organ note boomed out from the Casket. Marcus Scarman ran to stand before it.

'I hear you, Master,' he called.

'On the missile loading-ramp ... a crude detonation device. Another human attempt to delay my return. They must be found and punished— but first attend to the device. I cannot hold back the exothermic reaction for many minutes. It is taking an intense toll of ... available energy.' There was the sound of hideous strain in Sutekh's voice.

'It will be done immediately, Master.' Scarman bowed, and ran from the room.

The window opened and the Doctor clambered through. He moved cautiously over to the Casket, examined it for a moment, then touched a control inside it.

The Space/Time tunnel appeared. The Doctor stepped into it and was whirled away, spinning off into the depths of infinity. His senses blurred and he lost consciousness ...

*

So small and inconspicuous was the cardboard box that it took Marcus a moment or two to find it. He saw it at last, and ordered one of the Servicer robots forward. Stiffly it began walking up the ramp.

The Doctor recovered consciousness with a jolt, and found himself standing in the antechamber of an Egyptian tomb. A tapestry-covered doorway lay just before him. The Doctor reached out and moved the tapestry aside. It smouldered as he touched it, and he snatched back his hand. He paused for a moment, then bracing himself, stepped through the doorway.

He found himself in a dark, cave-like chamber. The Doctor had a quick impression of monitor screens and some kind of advanced computer. Dominating the chamber was the figure of Sutekh himself. He sat on a raised throne, a robed, masked figure, staring intently into a monitor. The screen showed a wavering picture of the pyramid-shaped missile, far away in England.

The Doctor drew a deep breath. Then he spoke, his voice deliberately loud and resonant. 'Greetings, Sutekh, last of the Osiriaris!'

Slowly Sutekh turned his head, his concentration momentarily broken ...

On the missile ramp the Mummy bent to pick up the box ... There was the sudden roar of an explosion. Mummy and missile disappeared in a sheet of flame.

Sutekh's head swung back to the monitor screen. Appalled, he watched the destruction of the missile that represented his only chance of freedom. The masked head turned slowly to the Doctor and a blaze of fierce green light burned from its eyes. As the light struck him, the Doctor was transfixed, helpless, writhing in agony ...

For a long moment Sutekh watched the Doctor's suffering. Then the glow faded from his eyes, and he spoke in a voice of restrained fury. 'No ... you shall not die yet. Death would be too easy. Identify yourself.'

The Doctor's voice was scarcely more than a painful whisper. 'Destroy me, Sutekh. Enjoy your revenge. Nothing else is left within your power.'

'Identify yourself!' Sutekh's eyes glowed once more, and again the Doctor writhed in agony. 'It is in my power to choose the manner of your death,' said the hateful voice. 'I can if I choose, keep you alive for centuries, wracked by the most excruciating pain. Since it is your interference that has condemned me to remain for ever prisoner of the Eye of Horus, that would be a fitting end for you. You might make an amusing diversion.' The green light died down. 'Identify yourself— plaything of Sutekh,' said the voice contemptuously.

The Doctor gasped weakly. 'I am a … traveller …'

'From where?'

'Gallifrey, in the Constellation of Kasteroborous.'

'These names mean nothing to me,' snarled Sutekh. 'What is the binary location from galactic zero centre?'

Now that he was free of the incessant pain, some of the Doctor's strength was returning to him. His voice was firmer as he replied. 'Ten, zero eleven … zero … zero … by zero two.'

Sutekh considered. 'It seems to me that I know this planet.' He looked towards the computer and ordered, 'Data retrieval.' On a screen numbers and hieroglyphics appeared, changing swiftly, fixing at last on a single line of complex symbols. There was a ring of triumph in Sutekh's voice. 'So! You are a Time Lord!'

The Doctor shook his head. 'Not in the sense that you mean; I come of the Time Lord race, but I renounced their society. Now I am simply a traveller.'

'A traveller in Time and Space?' asked Sutekh eagerly.

The Doctor did not reply.

'In Time and Space?' Sutekh insisted.

Reluctantly the Doctor nodded. Sutekh's voice dropped almost to a whisper. 'Approach closer.' Reluctantly the Doctor moved nearer the throne. 'What are you called, Time Lord?'

'I am called the Doctor.'

'I offer you an alliance, Doctor. Serve me truly and an empire can be yours.'

The Doctor drew back. 'Serve *you*, Sutekh? Your name is abomination in every civilised world. Whether that name be Set, Satan, Sadok …'

The voice of Sutekh hardened. 'You *shall* serve me, Doctor …'

'Never.' The Doctor's voice was utterly determined.

The green glow blazed out from the eye-slits of Sutekh's mask. Caught in its beam, the Doctor twisted in agony.

Sutekh laughed. 'You dare to pit your puny will against mine? Kneel ! Kneel before the might of Sutekh.'

Slowly, fighting the power of Sutekh's mind every inch of the way, the Doctor was forced to his knees. Sutekh's voice boomed out. 'In my presence you are an ant, a worm, a termite. Abase yourself, you grovelling insect.'

The booming note of the organ-signal interrupted Sutekh's sport. The face of Marcus Scarman appeared on a monitor screen 'Well?' demanded Sutekh. 'Speak!'

'Sutekh, great master, a Servicer has captured one of the humans responsible for the destruction of your missile.'

Sutekh said dismissively. 'The extra-terrestial, their leader, is already my prisoner. I have no interest in the other humans.'

Scarman waved the Mummy forward. 'Then this prisoner can be destroyed?' To his horror, the Doctor saw Sarah struggling in the Mummy's grip.

Sutekh nodded indifferently. 'Let it be killed at once.'

The Doctor struggled to his feet. 'No, Sutekh!'

On the monitor he saw the Mummy holding Sarah grasp her more firmly, while another raised its great hand for the death blow ...

'No!' he shouted again.

Suddenly Sutekh intervened. 'Wait! Keep the human alive, Scarman. It may yet have some use.'

'As you command, Great One.' Marcus raised his hand in a signal and the Mummies became motionless once more.

Sutekh turned to the Doctor. 'You are a Time Lord. What interest have you in humans?'

The Doctor knew what would happen if he admitted that Sarah's fate was important to him. 'I have long taken an interest in Earth and human beings,' he said calmly. 'All sapient life-forms are our kin, Sutekh.'

Angrily Sutekh hissed. 'Horus held that view—but I refute it. All life is my enemy.'

'And I know why,' said the Doctor boldly. 'Because you fear them. You fear that some other intelligent life-form will arise, and grow to rival you in power. So you destroy all life, wherever you find it.'

By deliberately provoking Sutekh, the Doctor hoped to divert his attention away from Sarah. Sutekh's next words made him realise that the attempt had failed.

'Your words are a cloud,' said Sutekh slowly. 'But I see through them, and into your mind.' The green eyes behind the mask-slits burned into the Doctor's own. 'The human girl ... ah, I see. She travels with you, Doctor, does she not, in this—TARDIS?'

Sutekh looked towards his monitor screen. Slowly an image of the TARDIS began to form. The Doctor's shoulders slumped defeatedly. 'If you read *my* mind by mental force, Sutekh, then nothing can be beyond you.'

A note of self-pity crept into Sutekh's voice. 'Nothing. Except to free myself from this prison in which Horus has bound me.'

'Your imprisonment was well deserved,' said the Doctor sternly. 'You chose to use your great powers for evil.'

Again Sutekh gave his chilling laugh. 'Your evil is my good, Doctor. I am Sutekh the Destroyer, Where I tread I leave nothing but dust and darkness. *That* I find good.'

The Doctor straightened up. 'Then I curse you in the name of all nature, Sutekh. You are a twisted abhorrence.'

The eye-slits in Sutekh's mask blazed green. A cry of pain was torn from the Doctor's lips as the ray caught him with all its agonising force. Through a roaring in his ears he heard the cold voice of Sutekh. 'Any further insolence, Doctor, and I shall shred your nervous system into a million fibres. Is it understood?'

The green light faded and the Doctor dropped to the ground, almost unconscious. For a moment Sutekh sat considering the crumpled figure. The key of the TARDIS rose on its chain around the Doctor's neck. The loop of the chain pulled itself over his head and floated in the air, propelled by the power of Sutekh's will.

The recovering Doctor looked on helplessly as the key floated before Sutekh's mask. Then Sutekh called, 'Scarman!'

Immediately Marcus's face appeared on the monitor. 'I hear you, Master.'

'See,' said Sutekh exultantly. 'My enemies have brought me my deliverance. The Doctor's TARDIS will be the means of my escape!'

10

A JOURNEY TO MARS

Gripped firmly by the Mummy, Sarah saw a tiny object appear, far down the Space/Time tunnel. It grew larger and larger until it shot out of the Casket, and dropped into Marcus Scarman's hands.

Sarah gasped in horror. 'The TARDIS key!' Now she knew that the Doctor was a helpless prisoner in Sutekh's hands. He would never otherwise have parted with the TARDIS key.

Sarah heard the voice of Sutekh boom out from the glowing green casket. 'This allows you entry to the Time Lord's Time/Space machine. Take one Servicer, and travel to the Pyramids of Mars.'

In Sutekh's cell, the Doctor was struggling to his feet. Despite all he had undergone, a little of his old jauntiness was returning. 'I'm afraid Scarman won't find it possible to obey your order, Sutekh.'

The masked figure glared down at him. 'Marcus Scarman is my puppet. My mind is in his.'

The Doctor managed a smile. 'Perhaps so. But the controls of the TARDIS are isomorphic.'

'One to one ...' mused Sutekh. 'I see. So they will answer to you alone?'

'Correct.'

'Then it seems I was wise to spare you, Doctor. Scarman!'

In the Egyptian room, Marcus Scarman, the TARDIS key in his hand, turned back to the Casket. Sutekh's voice rolled out triumphantly. 'I send you my captive. The Time Lord will control the machine. The human girl will accompany you. If the Time Lord attempts treachery, kill her.'

Marcus bowed. 'It is understood, Master.'

Sarah strained her eyes to look into the Space/Time tunnel. Again she saw a tiny shape spinning towards them. As it grew larger, it turned into the Doctor, sitting cross-legged like a Buddhist monk in meditation. The figure grew life-size, straightened up and emerged from the mouth of the Casket. The Doctor stood quite motionless, while the Space/Time tunnel glow faded behind him.

Wrenching free from the grip of the Mummy, Sarah tried to run to him. Marcus thrust out an arm and barred her way. 'Stand back. He is possessed by the Great One.'

Sarah called, 'Doctor, it's me!' The Doctor made no reply. He was staring straight ahead, his face completely blank.

Marcus stepped in front of him. 'Whom do you serve, Time Lord?'

For a moment the Doctor was silent. Then his lips moved and a single word came from his mouth. 'Sutekh.'

'Who holds all life in his hands?'

'Sutekh.'

'Who is the bringer of death?'

'Sutekh.'

Scarman nodded satisfied. 'Venerate his name, and obey him in all things.'

One final sentence seemed forced from the Doctor's lips. 'Sutekh is supreme.'

Sadly Sarah whispered, 'Oh, Doctor …' It was terrible to see the Doctor, always so independent, reduced to a mindless puppet, parroting praise of Sutekh.

Marcus was speaking to the Casket. 'Control is established, Great One.'

'It is well,' said Sutekh's voice. 'But these Time Lords are a cunning and perfidious species. Dispose of him when you reach the Pyramids of Mars.'

'It shall be done, Sutekh.' He turned to the Doctor. 'Come.'

The Doctor followed Scarman out of the room.

Before Sarah could protest, the Mummy dragged her after them.

In the Egyptian room, Scarman handed the key to the Doctor, who opened the TARDIS doors and led the way inside. He went straight to the controls, closed the door and set the TARDIS in motion.

Marcus Scarman and the Mummy stood motionless, showing no reaction as the take-off noise began and the central column began to rise and fall. Sarah managed to move closer to the control column. 'Doctor, it's me, Sarah,' she hissed again. The Doctor ignored her, moving blank-faced around the console.

The nightmare journey was soon over. The Doctor landed the TARDIS, opened the doors and went out. Marcus, Sarah and the Mummy followed. The Doctor closed the door and stood waiting.

Sarah looked around her. She was in a huge stone chamber, which might have been the interior of a pyramid somewhere on Earth. The strangest thing about the place was the fact that it seemed to have no entrance or exit. Every wall was a blank face of solid stone.

Marcus walked across to the nearest wall. The voice of Sutekh, distant but still clear, echoed through the chamber. 'My reading indicates that you are in an antechamber under the main Pyramid. Seek the control centre. Scan for the door.'

Marcus stretched out a hand, and swept it to and fro across the stone. His hands traced the outline of a door—and a door appeared. Marcus was about to step through it, then he turned. 'Sutekh has no further need of the Time Lord. Destroy him.'

Sarah screamed, 'No!' and threw herself in front of the Doctor. The Mummy swept her aside with one savage blow, and she reeled against the far wall. The Mummy locked its huge hands round the Doctor's throat and squeezed. The Doctor stood motionless, making no attempt to defend himself. Its gruesome work done, the Mummy let go and stepped back. The Doctor's body dropped limply to the floor.

'Come,' said Marcus impatiently. He stepped through the door, the Mummy lumbering behind him.

Sarah got to her knees and crawled painfully, across to the Doctor. She wondered why they hadn't killed her too. Perhaps she just wasn't important enough … She'd die here anyway in time. Or perhaps Sutekh himself would blast her once he was free. Such was Sarah's misery that her own fate hardly interested her. She fell across the Doctor's body, sobbing bitterly, thinking only of the way he'd been savagely murdered before her eyes …

A hand tapped her on the shoulder and a muffled voice said reprovingly, 'Sarah, you're soaking my shirt!'

Incredulously, she realised that both hand and voice belonged to the Doctor. She sat up and looked at him. 'Doctor, you're alive.'

The Doctor sat up too, rubbing his neck and wincing. 'Well, of course I'm alive. Respiratory bypass system. Very useful in a tight squeeze. Mind you, I'll have a bit of a stiff neck for a while.'

'I thought you'd been turned into another zombie, like Scarman.'

The Doctor rose, helping Sarah to her feet. 'Well, I suppose I must have been for a while. But once Sutekh didn't need me any more he stopped thinking about me. His mind relaxed its grip.' He looked round interestedly. 'Now then, where are we?'

'Sutekh ordered you to take us to the Pyramids of Mars. Marcus and one of the Mummies came with us.'

'Yes, of course. Sutekh will have sent Marcus here to deactivate the forcefield control in the Pyramid. Which way did he go?'

'Through that door,' gasped Sarah. 'Well, there *was* a door. It seems to have vanished.' The stone wall was blank and smooth again.

The Doctor studied the area of wall. 'A door can't vanish,' he said severely. 'That simply isn't logical. It's just that the door isn't visible.'

Sarah shrugged. 'Same difference, surely.'

The Doctor was examining the wall with feverish intensity. 'I've got to find Marcus … Somehow I've got to stop him.'

Marcus Scarman, the Servicer robot behind him, was patiently walking along an endless stone passage. He halted only when a blank metal wall barred his way. Just to one side of it was a switch. Marcus reached out to touch it, but the voice of Sutekh warned, 'Stop. I sense danger. That relay switch is a power conductor terminal. The true bulkhead release will be concealed. Scan!'

Again Marcus stretched out his hand and moved it over the surface of the metal bulkhead. 'There—now!' said Sutekh exultantly. Marcus touched the indicated point and a small panel swung open to reveal a switch. He operated it, the bulkhead slid back and Marcus went on his way, the Mummy following behind.

The Doctor was tracing his fingers over the chamber wall, just as Marcus had done before him. He found the right area at last, and the door reappeared beneath his hand. 'Triobyphysics,' said the Doctor in a pleased tone, and led the way through.

They followed the stone passage and came to the same métal wall that had blocked Marcus's progress. The Doctor reached for the switch, then drew back his hand.

'What's the matter?' asked Sarah.

'Too obvious—and too easy.'

'A door handle usually is obvious, surely?'

'Not in a jail,' said the Doctor. 'Horus would have left traps for the unwary intruder.'

'I thought Horus was one of the good guys?'

'He was an Osirian—with all their guile and ingenuity.' The Doctor was studying the metal door as he spoke. 'They had dome-shaped heads and cerebrums like spiral staircases. They just couldn't help being devious!'

The Doctor's searching fingers found the hidden panel. It sprung open to reveal the second switch. The Doctor operated it and the wall slid back. He turned to Sarah and grinned, childishly, pleased with his own cleverness. They went on their way, the wall sliding back behind them.

There followed a long journey through more and more passages. Frustratingly it ended before yet another bulkhead, exactly like the previous one.

'Maybe we've come in a circle?' suggested Sarah.

The Doctor shook his head. 'This one is similar—but not the same.' He looked at the wall switch, then opened the hidden panel. As he was reaching for the panel switch he drew back his hand. 'Now, Horus wouldn't set exactly the same trap a second time—or would he?' The Doctor stood brooding. 'I wonder. Double or triple bluff.'

Sarah pointed to the wall switch. 'You mean Horus might expect a visitor to work out that the panel switch would be booby-trapped—and still booby-trap this one?'

The Doctor rubbed his chin. 'Or if Horus expected an intruder to work that out, he might booby-trap the panel switch anyway!'

'So what do we do?'

'We apply scientific method, Sarah. We test our suspicions.' The Doctor produced an extendable electronic probe and swept its end across the panel switch. There was a bang and a flash. The probe flew from his hand as the panel switch exploded in sparks and smoke. The Doctor sucked his fingers, recovered the probe and operated the wall switch. The barrier slid back. 'Triple bluff,' said the Doctor happily, and they went on their way.

Some way ahead of them Marcus Scarman was confronting yet another metal wall, this one studded with several rows of switches.

'Stand back and scan,' ordered Sutekh. Marcus stood back, sweeping his hand backwards and forwards across the wall.

On Earth, in Sutekh's Egyptian cell, the wall appeared on a monitor screen as a pattern of dots joined by radiating lines, with rows of binary numbers superimposed. Sutekh laughed. 'Horus, do you think to confound Sutekh with these childish stratagems?'

On Mars, Marcus heard the familiar voice. 'The floor is charged with explosive. Count to the fifth row up—now, the extreme right switch.'

The bulkhead slid back, and Marcus went through. The Mummy followed him. It paused for a moment, looking back suspiciously. Then it followed Marcus and the bulkhead slid closed behind it.

Seconds later, the Doctor's and Sarah's heads popped round the corner. 'That was a near one,' whispered Sarah. 'I thought it had seen us.' She looked at the wall. 'Oh Doctor, there are dozens of switches.'

The Doctor pointed to an immensely complicated graph on the wall to one side of the bulkhead. 'Horus has very kindly provided a key, though.'

'Some key,' muttered Sarah. 'What does it mean?'

The Doctor had fished out a grubby scrap of paper and a stub of pencil. 'Well, obviously the length of the lines provides a scale of measurements.'

Sarah studied the graph, shaking her head. 'Didn't you run into something like this in the City of the Exxilons?'

The Doctor was in no mood to discuss his past adventures, particularly those which had taken place in earlier incarnations. He was muttering busily to himself. He looked up as Sarah stretched out a tentative hand to one of the switches, half inclined to choose by good old feminine intuition.

'Don't touch anything,' he said sharply.

Sarah snatched back her hand. 'I wasn't going to.'

'Well, don't. One false move and you'll probably set off an explosive charge!'

The Doctor returned to his calculations. 'Now let me see. Twenty point three centimetres multiplied by the binary figure ten zero zero ... that's a pretty simple calculation ...'

'Show off!' muttered Sarah rather sulkily.

The Doctor ignored her. He whipped off his scarf and held it before him like a tape-measure. 'Now then, feet and inches one side, metres and centimetres the other. One hundred and sixty-two point four— that should be about three stitches.'

The Doctor made a few measurements, then slung his scarf back round his neck. He muttered more calculations, all totally incomprehensible to Sarah, and stretched out his hand. 'Now I *think* this is the right switch ...'

Nervously Sarah asked, 'What happens if you're wrong?'

'I imagine we'll all be blown to blazes,' said the Doctor cheerfully. He reached out and flicked the switch.

11

THE GUARDIANS OF HORUS

Instinctively Sarah drew back from the bulkhead. For a moment after the Doctor pressed the switch—the extreme right-hand switch on the fifth row up—nothing happened. Then the bulkhead drew slowly back. The Doctor gave Sarah a self-satisfied smile and walked through. Sarah followed and the door closed behind them. They found themselves in a dark chamber, lit only by strangely-glowing walls. They moved forward cautiously, almost feeling their way. Sarah stopped and looked up at the Doctor. 'Which way do we go now?'

'I'm not too sure. Stay here, while I look around.' The Doctor moved on a few paces. There came a sudden scream from Sarah, just as suddenly cut off by a hollow, ringing, sound. The Doctor whirled round. Sarah was trapped inside a transparent glass bell. She hammered frantically at the glass, her lips moving soundlessly.

The Doctor moved round the bell, studying it. 'A Decatron crucible,' he muttered to himself. There was no way to break into it—it would have to be removed by the agency which had placed it there. Unless it *was* removed, and quickly, Sarah was going to die of suffocation. 'All right, Sarah, keep calm,' called the Doctor, although he knew she couldn't hear him.

Inside the bell, Sarah was shouting frantically. The Doctor sighed. 'Oh, Sarah, I should never have brought you here.' Then he lip-read her words.

'Look out. Behind you.'

The Doctor spun round. Two Mummies had materialised in the darkness. They were similar to the robot servants of Sutekh, but larger, and the golden ornamentation of their bindings seemed to suggest some kind of rank.

A voice spoke out of the darkness. It was like and yet unlike that of Sutekh, its tones holding wisdom and power rather than Sutekh's cruelty and hatred. 'Intruders,' the great voice boomed, 'you face the twin guardians of Horus. One is programmed to deceive, the other points truly. These two switches control your fate—instant freedom, or instant death.'

A section of wall with two switches set into it was suddenly illuminated.

The Doctor walked over to the switches and stood before them.

The voice said, 'Before you choose you can ask *one* guardian *one* question. This is the riddle of the Osirians. Which is the guardian of life?'

The Doctor's mind was racing frantically. He glanced across at Sarah, already showing signs of distress inside the glass bell. Unless he solved the riddle soon she was doomed. He looked again at the two impassive figures of the Mummies. 'Which indeed,' he thought. 'Now if they're contra-programmed, so one *must* always give a false indication ...'

The Doctor smiled. He turned to the nearest guardian. 'One question, eh? Now, if I were to ask your chum there, your fellow guardian, which was the switch that meant life—which one would he indicate?'

The guardian swung round and pointed to the switch on the Doctor's right. The Doctor nodded. 'I see. So if you're the true guardian, that must be the death switch. And if you're the automatic liar, you're trying to deceive me. So that must still be the death switch.' Hoping his logic was water-tight, the Doctor pulled the switch on his left. The two guardians disappeared—and so did the glass bell surrounding Sarah. Gasping for breath she staggered out into the Doctor's arms. He steadied her on her feet. 'Are you all right?' She nodded weakly. 'Then come on. We've got no time to lose.'

In his cell on Earth, an impatient Sutekh was following the progress of his servants through the Martian Pyramid. On the monitor Sutekh could see a squat, tomb-like shape. 'The inner chamber,' he hissed.

'The control centre of the Pyramids! The sign of the Eye, Scarman. Make the sign of the Eye!'

On Mars, standing before the door of the tomb, Scarman sketched the sign of the Eye with one hand. There was a high-pitched electronic sound and the door swung open. Behind it was blackness. Marcus Scarman moved slowly inside.

He found himself in a chamber of light, lit by a flickering eerie glow from walls and floor. In the centre of the chamber cradled in a silver tulip-shaped cup was what appeared to be a giant ruby, bigger than a man's head. Four silver rods projected from it, like the rays of a stylised sun, and it pulsated regularly with a fierce red glow.

Scarman heard the exultant voice of Sutekh. 'It is the Eye. The Eye of Horus. Destroy! Destroy! Destroy!'

Scarman moved towards the Eye. A huge Mummy stepped from the darkness, wearing the gold ornamented bands that denoted the guardians of Horus. Marcus said sharply, 'Stop. Deactivate!' The guardian came on.

From the air a voice spoke. 'The servants of Horus obey only the voice of Horus.' Its tone changed. 'Drive out these intruders.'

Marcus dropped back, and waved his own Mummy forward. 'Attack!'

The two giant figures lumbered towards each other, colliding with a mighty impact in the centre of the chamber. They began to attack each other with great swinging blows. As the two giants battled on, Marcus Scarman was able to move closer to the Eye. He stretched out his hands, hearing the voice of Sutekh. 'Destroy! Destroy! Destroy!'

Marcus Scarman's whole body seemed to blaze with energy, as he became the channel for Sutekh's powers. The Doctor and Sarah ran through the open door and skidded to a halt. The figure before the Eye had the body of Marcus Scarman. But its head was that of Sutekh. Not the savage mask that the Doctor had already seen, but Sutekh's true visage, the snarling, bestial, jackal face that had appeared to Sarah in the TARDIS.

For a moment they stood frozen in horror, and that moment was all Sutekh needed. Mental energy poured through Marcus Scarman, and the Eye of Horus exploded in a shattering blast.

Sutekh's head faded and Marcus, once again in his own form, swung round to face the Doctor. But it was still the exultant voice of Sutekh that came from his lips. 'Free! I am free at last!'

The body of Marcus Scarman collapsed, disintegrating before their eyes into a heap of smoking ashes.

In an awe-stricken voice Sarah whispered, 'He's won. Sutekh's won!'

The Doctor stood quite still. The Chamber was silent.

The two Mummies had battered each other into mutual destruction. Still locked together in conflict, they lay motionless on the floor.

Suddenly the Doctor's face lit up. 'Not yet, he hasn't,' he shouted. 'He's forgotten the Time Factor. Come on, Sarah—*run!*'

Exultantly Sutekh looked round his cell for the last time. 'I have won my freedom, Horus,' he roared. 'Now begins the reign of Sutekh the Destroyer. I shall crush this miserable planet Earth and hurl it into the outer most depths of space. My vengeance starts here!'

12

THE WEAPON OF THE TIME LORDS

The Doctor and Sarah covered the distance from the Chamber of the Eye back to the TARDIS in a single mad dash. Doors opened and closed before them as though the Pyramid of Horus itself was co-operating with their flight. The Doctor's speed was such that Sarah could scarcely keep up with him. By the time she reached the TARDIS, the Doctor was already inside. The control column was moving up and down, the dematerialisation noise filling the air.

With a shriek of 'Wait for me!' Sarah leaped through the TARDIS doors just as they closed.

The Doctor was working feverishly as the TARDIS made the journey back to the Earth of nineteen eleven. He had already removed a side panel from the TARDIS console by the time they landed. The instant the centre column stopped moving the Doctor began to dismantle part of the TARDIS's control console. He extracted a complex piece of equipment and ran out of the TARDIS at top speed, wires trailing behind him. Sarah followed, wondering what was happening but not daring to ask. It was clear from the Doctor's manner that even a second's delay could be fatal.

Stiffly, Sutekh rose from his throne and took a step forward. 'The paralysis has left me,' he said exultantly. 'I can move again, I can move!'

He threw both arms wide in a gesture of triumph. 'Now, Horus, we shall see who rules the cosmos!'

In the organ room, the Doctor knelt by the Casket, working at frantic speed. He was attaching the trailing wires from the piece of TARDIS machinery to the Casket's control panel. His fingers moved in a blur of activity.

As he made the last connection, he looked up and smiled, seeming to notice Sarah for the first time. 'According to my estimate, we've got about twenty seconds,' he said calmly.

'Twenty seconds to what?' wondered Sarah. Suddenly the Space/Time tunnel effect began building up in the mouth of the Casket. The Doctor smiled. 'Well, here he comes,' he said. 'Right on time!' He might have been talking about an Inter-City Express.

A tiny speck had appeared in the depths of the endless tunnel. It came closer and closer, then turned into the terrifying figure of Sutekh. His mask was gone, and the jackal head snarled savagely at them.

When the figure reached the mouth of the Casket it seemed to pause and hover. 'Who is here?' demanded Sutekh hoarsely. 'Who dares to interfere with my vengeance?'

The Doctor stepped boldly forward. 'I do, Sutekh. You forgot that Time is the weapon of the Time Lords. I have used Time to defeat you. You are caught in a Temporal trap.'

Sutekh gave a scream of rage. 'Time Lord, I shall destroy you. I shall destroy you …'

His voice faded and diminished, as the Doctor spun one of the controls on his TARDIS equipment. At once Sutekh dwindled, retreating down the tunnel, his voice fading away. The Doctor spun more dials, and Sutekh moved forward, hovering, trapped at the mouth of the Casket.

The Doctor looked dispassionately at him. 'How long do Osirians live, Sutekh?'

The Doctor adjusted more dials, and once again the figure of Sutekh retreated slowly down the endless Space/Time tunnel. 'Release me,' he screamed.

'Never! You're trapped again, Sutekh, trapped in the corridor of eternity.'

The voice of the dwindling figure floated back down the tunnel. 'Release me, insect, or I shall destroy the cosmos.'

The Doctor shook his head. 'You're a thousand years past the twentieth century, Sutekh. Go on for another ten thousand.' His face set and remorseless, the Doctor spun another dial.

Faintly the voice called, 'Release me and I will spare the planet Earth. I'll give it to you for a plaything. Release me! Release me … Release me …'

The Doctor shouted, 'No, Sutekh, the time of the Osirians is long past. Go *on*!' The Doctor gave the dial a final turn and stepped back. From far down the tunnel came the death scream of Sutekh, fading away into eternal nothingness.

The Doctor heaved a great sigh of relief. 'That's it, Sarah. All over. He lived about another seven thousand years.'

Sarah could hardly believe it. 'He's dead? Sutekh is really dead?'

'At last.' The Doctor began unclipping the leads joining the section of the console to the Casket.

Sarah perched on a chair and watched him. 'I know that's the Time Control Unit from the TARDIS. But what did you actually do with it?'

'I moved the threshold of the Space/Time tunnel into the far future, so Sutekh could never reach the end.'

'But Sutekh was free! How were you able to—'

The Doctor beamed. 'Elementary, my dear Sarah. After the Eye of Horus was destroyed, I realised we still had just over two minutes to get back here and deal with Sutekh—the time it takes radio waves to pass from Mars to Earth.'

Suddenly Sarah understood. 'So the Eye of Horus was *still* holding Sutekh—for two minutes after it was broken?'

Unclipping the last of his leads, the Doctor got wearily to his feet. He stared for a moment down the endless Space/Time tunnel, as if still seeing the dwindling figure of Sutekh. 'The Egyptians called him the Typhonian Beast, you know,' he said absently.

Before Sarah could reply, there was an explosion inside the Casket. Smoke and flames began belching out from its mouth.

The Doctor gave a contrite tut-tut. 'Now that, *was* careless of me. I should have realised the thermal balance would equalize …'

The Casket had turned into a furnace, lashing out sheets of flame. Interestedly the Doctor moved over to investigate, but Sarah pulled him back. 'Doctor, you remember the Old Priory was burned to the ground?'

The Doctor looked thoughtful. 'Yes, maybe it *is* time we were getting out of here. Don't want to get the blame for starting a fire, do we?'

Sarah had a nightmare vision of trying to explain recent happenings at the Priory to some heavily-moustached village policeman of the year nineteen eleven. 'Oh no,' she said fervently, 'we don't want that.'

They ran out of the organ room, along the corridors and back towards the Egyptian room. The fire was spreading with amazing rapidity and they had to make a desperate dash for the TARDIS through smoke and flames.

Once they were inside, the Doctor closed the door, shutting off the roar of the flames. Working quickly he wired the Time Control Unit back into the centre console and closed the panel. He touched controls and the dematerialisation noise began.

Outside the TARDIS, the Egyptian room was an inferno. The blazing roof collapsed in flames, just as the TARDIS disappeared.

The fire spread rapidly through the old house. Walls began to collapse and the roof fell in. The woods around the house caught, and the fire even spread to the Lodge. Soon most of the Scarman estate was an inferno of flame.

Safe inside the TARDIS, Sarah waited for it to return her to her own time. The Doctor was quietly checking over the instrument console, showing little sign of his recent ordeal. Sarah, weary and exhausted, wanted only to return to familiar twentieth century surroundings. She was still haunted by the death of Sutekh—and all the other deaths that had gone before. There had been so many … The old servant, Collins. Ibrahim Namin, the servant of Sutekh, discarded when he was no longer needed. The bluff and hearty Doctor Warlock. Poor little Ernie Clements, the poacher. Laurence Scarman—she could remember him looking round the TARDIS with bright-eyed eagerness. And most tragic of all, Marcus Scarman, taken over and burnt out by Sutekh's horrible alien power. She remembered Sutekh free only briefly after his long captivity, screaming with powerless rage as he died in the Doctor's temporal trap.

'Doctor,' she asked, 'Won't all this business get out? I mean, *didn't* it get out, back in nineteen eleven? Everything that happened at the Old Priory?'

The Doctor looked up from the console. 'I very much doubt it, Sarah. Time has a way of taking care of these things. Anyway, when we get back home, you can look it up and see!'

EPILOGUE

Later, much later, when she finally arrived safely back on Earth after many adventures, Sarah remembered the Doctor's words. She went to the offices of the local paper in the little country town near UNIT H.Q. and persuaded them to let her see the files for nineteen eleven. Before long she found the item she wanted.

> BROTHERS DIE IN TRAGIC FIRE
> HOLOCAUST SWEEPS COUNTRY ESTATE
> *Many others feared killed.*
>
> *The whole countryside was shocked and saddened today by the news of the tragic fire at the Old Priory in which a number of well-known local figures perished. Fire broke out suddenly during the night and swept the Priory, the Lodge and much of the heavily wooded estate at great speed.*
>
> *Among the victims of the blaze is believed to be Professor Marcus Scarman, the well-known Egyptologist, who had just returned from a successful archaeological expedition to Egypt. His brother Laurence, the distinguished amateur scientist, also died in the flames. Further victims include Josiah Collins, who had been in the service of the Scarmans all his life, a Mr Ibrahim Namin, believed to have been a guest of Professor Scarman, and a family friend, Doctor War lock who was visiting the Priory. In the grounds, the remains were discovered of Ernest Clements, a*

local villager with a history of poaching. It is feared that this unfortunate man was trapped by the blaze while engaged in his nefarious pursuits.

An element of mystery still surrounds the death of Professor Scarman himself. He had not been home for some time, and was thought to be on his way back from Cairo. However, investigations in Cairo revealed that Professor Scarman had left some time ago. It is believed that the unfortunate Professor, by an unlucky coincidence, must have returned to his ancestral home on the very night of the fire, though as yet no trace of his remains have been discovered.

The cause of the blaze is still unknown, but there is speculation in the village that one of the many advanced scientific devices which Mr Laurence Scarman had installed in the Lodge may somehow have been responsible ...

Sarah skimmed through the rest of the report. So that was what the Doctor had meant. The terrible events surrounding the return of Sutekh had found a natural explanation, a deplorable but soon forgotten tragedy in an English country village.

Sarah looked through the window, out into the bustling high street of the little country town. She shivered at the memory of the desolate world she had seen through the doors of the TARDIS—the world Sutekh would have made if he had not been defeated. The sacrifice of all those lives had not been in vain. The pity was that no one would ever know.

Sarah closed the heavy old volume and went into the summer sunshine of her own, unchanged, twentieth century.

DOCTOR WHO AND THE TALONS OF WENG-CHIANG

1

TERROR IN THE FOG

They were having a good night at the Palace. Even though it was only the first performance of the evening the theatre was packed. In the boxes and the front stalls sat the toffs, men immaculate in evening dress, ladies in fine evening gowns, all down in the East End for a night at the Music Hall. The body of the theatre and the Grand Circle above were filled with local people, tradesmen and their wives and families, bank clerks and shop assistants. High above in the top most balcony, known as the 'Gods', the poorer people were crowded on to hard wooden benches. Labourers, dock workers, soldiers and sailors, even some of the half-starved unemployed—they'd all managed to scrape together a few coppers for the big night of the week. They were a tough crowd up in the 'Gods', ready to show their feelings with boos, catcalls and rotten fruit if an act wasn't to their liking. But now, like everyone else in the theatre, they were staring entranced at the gorgeously robed figure on stage, the famous Chinese magician Li H'sen Chang.

It was a tough, savage place, this London of the eighteen-nineties; a place of contrasts. Victoria was on the throne, and the British Empire covered much of the globe. England was powerful and prosperous, and London was the trading capital of the world. There were those in the theatre who shared their country's prosperity, spending gold sovereigns with a free hand, living comfortable lives, with servants to look after them. Yet there were many more who were short of the money to pay for their next meal, or even for a roof over their heads. However, tonight they were united in a common aim, to forget their troubles and have a thoroughly good time.

The audience watched spellbound as Chang ushered a smiling chorus girl into a metal cabinet in the centre of the stage. He closed the door, and slid sword after sword through the slots in the cabinet's sides. He waved his hands, withdrew the swords. There was a bang and a flash, and he threw open the door, to reveal the chorus girl, smiling and unharmed. There was a roar of applause. Chang folded his hands in his sleeves and bowed low, and the curtain came down.

Immediately stage hands rushed on, clearing away the props from Chang's act, setting things up for the first act of the second house. Chang went over to a chair, where Mr Sin sat waiting for him.

Mr Sin was a ventriloquist's dummy. He was larger than most, as big as a child or a dwarf. He wore silk trousers and jacket and a little round cap, and his little face was a wooden parody of Chang's handsome oriental features. The little dummy was one of the most popular features of Chang's act. Most magicians performed in mysterious silence, but for much of the time Chang worked with the dummy on his arm. Throughout the act Mr Sin kept up a running fire of disrespectful comment.

Carrying Mr Sin, Chang was making for his dressing-room when Jago, the manager and proprietor of the theatre, intercepted him in the wings. A stout, red-faced figure resplendent in evening dress with diamond studs, Jago was positively glowing with happiness. 'Mr Chang! Wonderful, sir, wonderful. Words fail me!'

Chang bowed. 'Most unusual,' he said ironically.

'Never, in my thirty years on the halls, have I seen such a dazzling display of lustrous legerdemain, so many feats of superlative, supernatural skill.'

It was Mr Sin who answered the flood of compliments. 'Honorable Master,' he piped eerily. 'You are most kind to bestow praise on miserable, unworthy head of humble Chang.'

Jago grinned appreciatively. 'Dashed clever, the way you work the little fellow. Wires in the sleeves, eh?' He held up a hand, interrupting himself. 'Oh, but I'll not pry, Mr Chang. The secrets of the artiste are sacred to me.'

There was a sudden scuffle by the stage door at the far end of the corridor. Casey, the skinny little Irish door-keeper, was trying to prevent a burly tough-looking character from forcing his way into the theatre. As they watched the man broke free, and he came running up to them. Jago was outraged. Members of the public were never allowed backstage. 'What the deuce? You've no right to burst in here like this. Who are you?'

'Name's Buller, sir. Cab driver. I've no quarrel with you, Mr Jago, it's *him* I want.' He shook a massive fist at Chang. 'My Emma came in here last night, and nobody ain't seen her since. Now I'm asking you, mister, what's happened to her?'

Jago grabbed him by the arm. 'Don't trouble yourself, Mr Chang, the fellow's drunk, or mad! I'll have him ejected.'

Buller wrenched himself free. 'You do and I go straight to the police.'

'It is all right, Mr Jago,' said Chang smoothly. 'Do not trouble yourself. I'm sure we can settle, this misunderstanding peacefully. If you will come to my dressing-room, Mr Buller?'

There was something almost hypnotic about Chang's soothing voice, and with surprising meekness, Buller allowed himself to be led away.

Jago shrugged at Casey who'd come up to help. 'Courteous coves, these Chinese. I'd have propelled him on to the pavement with a punt up the posterior!' Casey grinned, and went back to the stage door.

Setting Mr Sin on a stool, Chang turned to face his angry visitor. 'Now then, Mr Buller, this missing lady. She was your wife?'

'That's right. Emma Buller. Don't deny she was here, because 1 saw her with my own eyes.'

'Many ladies come to the theatre ...'

'Not round the stage door they don't. Look, mister, I was passing in my cab, and I saw her as plain as plain.'

'What makes you think it was me she was calling on?'

'She's been acting queer ever since you put the 'fluence on her last week.'

Chang smiled. 'Ah, now I see. She came up on the stage, for one of my demonstrations of hypnotism?'

'That's right—last week. Levitated her, you did. Had her floating up in the air as stiff as a board. She's not been the same since. Affected her reason, I shouldn't wonder. She's been talking about you ever since. And last night she came back to this theatre.'

'Perhaps. But not to see me.'

'Don't come the innocent,' said Buller furiously. 'She's *disappeared*. Nobody's seen her since she came here. I want to know where she is, or I'm calling the law, clear?'

Chang looked at him impassively. 'We have a saying in my country, Mr Buller. The man who goes too fast may step in bear trap.'

Buller stared at him in baffled anger, then turned to the door. 'You've had your chance. I'm going straight to the peelers.'

As the door slammed behind him, Chang turned to Mr Sin. A very strange thing happened. Although it was on the other side of the room, the dummy turned its head towards him—and smiled malevolently.

Outside the theatre, thick fog swirled through grimy deserted streets that sloped down towards dockland. Gas lamps flared dimly through the fog, and occasionally there came a burst of laughter from some street corner pub. There was no one about. These little streets had an evil reputation of late. There was fear in the air, almost as thick as the swirling mist.

In a cobbled alley close by the river there was a wheezing, groaning sound, and a square blue shape materialised out of the fog. It was a London police box, of a type that would not come into use for many years. Out of this anachronism stepped a tall brown-haired girl, and an even taller man. The girl was wearing a kind of tweed knickerbocker suit with matching cap, and she seemed obviously uncomfortable in the thick, bulky garments. 'These clothes are ridiculous. Why must I wear them?'

Her companion, that mysterious traveller in Space and Time known only as 'The Doctor', was dressed for the period too, in checked cape and deerstalker cap. He smiled indulgently at her. It was natural enough that Leela should find Victorian clothes constricting. She had been born on a distent tropical planet, one of a colony of settlers from Earth who had degenerated to a near Stone Age level. Leela had grown up as a warrior of the Sevateem, and she usually dressed, and acted, rather like a female Tarzan.

'Be reasonable, Leela,' said the Doctor soothingly. 'You can't walk, round Victorian London dressed in skins. Don't want to be conspicuous, do we?' The Doctor turned up the collar of his cape, and adjusted his deerstalker to a jaunty angle.

There came a low, booming roar, and Leela dropped into a fighting crouch, reaching for the knife that no longer hung at her waist. 'A swamp creature. That was its attack cry!'

'On the contrary, that was a boat on the river. Excellent. It means we can't be far away.'

'Far away from where?'

'From where we're going!' said the Doctor provokingly.

Leela gave an unladylike snort. 'You make me wear strange clothes, you bring me to this evil place and you tell me nothing—' she began.

'I'm trying to re-educate you, Leela, to broaden your mind. You want to see how your ancestors from Earth enjoyed themselves, don't you?' Ignoring Leela's shrug of indifference the Doctor continued, 'Of course you do. I'm taking you to the theatre.' A garish poster on a nearby wall caught his eye. 'Here we are.' The poster bore a Chinese face and the words, 'LI H'SEN CHANG. MASTER OF MAGIC AND MESMERISM'. 'Li H'sen Chang, eh? I'd rather hoped it would be Little Tich. Still never mind. Come on, Leela, we'll just be in time for the second house.'

The Doctor strode off into the fog, and Leela followed. For all the Doctor's protestations, she was sure this was more for his enjoyment than her education.

Jago closed his handsome gold watch and returned it to his pocket. Anxiously he surveyed the bustle of backstage activity. The first-house crowd had gone, the second-house audience was filing in, and soon it would be time for curtain-up again. A belated chorus girl scurried by on the way to her dressing-room, and Jago gave her a friendly slap on the rump. 'Prance along there, Della, it's time you had your tail pinned on!' The girl giggled and hurried past. Jago's eyes widened as he saw the skinny figure of Casey staggering along the corridor towards him. Casey was doorman, caretaker and general odd job man. He was reliable enough as a rule, though with a weakness for the bottle. Just now he had eyes like saucers, his straggly grey hair was all on end and his grimy collar wildly askew. Jago stared at him. 'What's the matter with you, Casey, got the oopizootics coming on?'

'Mr Jago, I seen it, I seen it again ...'

Glancing round worriedly, Jago dragged the little Irishman to a quiet corner. 'Quiet, will you? I've told you before ...'

Casey was beyond all reason. 'It was horrible, Mr Jago, horrible! A great glowing skull coming at me out of the dark ...'

Jago clapped a hand over the doorman's mouth. 'Do you want to bankrupt me? Keep your voice down. I'll be threadbare in Carey Street if people get the notion the place is haunted.'

Casey's muffled voice emerged from beneath Jago's palm. 'Nine foot tall it was, chains clanking …'

'You've been drinking, Casey!'

'Not a drop, sir, I swear it.'

'Then it's time you started.' Jago produced a silver hip-flask. 'Take a drop of this to steady your nerves.'

Casey swigged gratefully at the brandy. 'I ain't never going down that cellar again, Mr Jago. I was just fixing the trapdoor when this apparition rose out of the ground … hideous, it was.'

He took another swig at the flask and Jago snatched it back. 'That's enough. It's just your imagination.'

'Never, Mr Jago. Never.'

'Tell you what, I'll come down there with you tonight, soon as the house is clear, and we'll have a good look round. Probably find it's a stray cat …'

'It's no cat, sir, it's a horrible phantom. I've *seen* it I tell you.'

'All right, Casey, mum's the word. Get back to your work, it's almost time to ring the bell for curtain-up.'

Casey hurried away, and Jago looked worriedly after him. Several times recently the little man had come to him with these tales of a ghost in the cellar. Jago had put it down to a mixture of gin and imagination, but now he wasn't so sure. Whatever it was, he'd get to the bottom of it when the theatre closed. No phantom was going to disturb the smooth running of *his* theatre.

Collar turned up against the cold, hat pulled down over his eyes, Alf Buller hurried through the empty streets towards the local police station. In his mind he was going over and over his story. Probably they wouldn't believe him at first, but he wouldn't go away until he got satisfaction. An English bobby would know how to deal with that smooth-talking foreigner.

Something dropped from a wall, landing just in front of him. Buller looked down unbelievingly. It was Mr Sin, Chang's evil-looking dummy, and in its hand glinted a long-bladed knife.

Buller stood frozen in terror as the little figure stalked towards him.

2

THE HORROR IN THE RIVER

The Doctor and Leela were nearing the end of the long alleyway. Leela looked up at the tall buildings all around them. 'A big village, this. What is the name of the tribe that lives here?'

The Doctor grinned. 'Cockneys,' he said briefly.

A hoarse scream pierced the fog—and suddenly cut off. Leela froze. 'The sound of death!'

'Wait here,' snapped the Doctor, and disappeared into the fog. Ignoring his command, Leela hurried after him.

The Doctor turned the corner and came upon a bizarre and terrifying scene. Four black-clad Chinese were dragging a dead body along the pavement.

'Can I help you?' asked the Doctor politely. The nearest man flew at him, knife in hand, and the Doctor promptly knocked him down. Dropping the body, the other three hurled themselves on the Doctor, and he went down beneath a pile of bodies. Leela sprinted round the corner and hurled herself joyfully into the struggle.

There was a wild and confused mêlée, arms and legs whirling wildly in the tumbled heap of bodies. Somewhere on the bottom of the pile the Doctor was clubbed behind the ear with a blackjack, and fell to the ground semi-conscious. The attackers concentrated their attention on Leela. She fought like a wildcat, wishing desperately that she had ignored the Doctor's ridiculous ban on carrying weapons. But she was considerably outnumbered and soon things were going badly for her. Her arms and legs held fast, she saw the glint of a knife coming nearer and nearer to her throat. Suddenly the shrill blast of a police whistle cut through the fog.

Immediately the gripping hands released her as the Chinese ran off. They snatched up the dead body, which had been left sprawled in the gutter, and carried it away with them.

Leela made a desperate grab at the last attacker to flee but he wriggled free of her grip and dashed away—only to be tripped by the Doctor's outstretched foot. He pitched headlong into the road, and Leela pounced like a great cat, grabbing the man's long pigtail and winding it round his throat.

The Doctor staggered to his feet, and set off after the fleeing Chinese with their grisly burden. Through the fog he saw them turn a nearby corner and disappear into a side street. He hurried after them, turned the corner and stopped in amazement. The long straight street stretched away empty before him. The Chinese and their burden had vanished.

The Doctor stood for a moment, rubbing his chin. He had been only minutes behind the Chinese, so they should still have been in sight. There were no side turnings, no alleyways, and they had been hampered by the weight of a dead body. How could they have disappeared so quickly?

The Doctor moved a few paces forward and paused by a round metal shape in the middle of the road. A man hole cover. He knelt and touched the rim with a finger. Blood.

Aware of angry voices behind him in the fog, he reluctantly straightened up and went back the way he had come.

The Doctor turned the corner to see two burly oil-skinned and helmetted figures dominating the scene.

The police had arrived. One held the remaining Chinaman in a powerful grip, the other was steadily advancing upon Leela, with the traditional cry of the British bobby in times of crisis. 'Now then, now then, what's going on?'

Leela backed away. 'Touch me and I'll break your arm.'

The policeman smiled tolerantly. 'Come along now, miss, don't be foolish …'

Well aware that Leela was more than capable of carrying out her threat, the Doctor hurried to intervene. 'Good evening, officer,' he said cheerily.

'Keep back, Doctor,' shouted Leela. 'Blue guards! They may be hostile.'

The Doctor ignored her. 'Can I be of assistance, constable?'

'Do you know this young lady, sir?'

'She's my ward. We were on our way to the theatre when we were attacked by this man—and several others.'

The constable nodded ponderously. 'They'd cleared off by the time we got here. All except for this one—the young lady was strangling him with his own pigtail.'

'Girlish enthusiasm,' suggested the Doctor hopefully.

'You can call it that if you like, sir. I call it making an affray: I must ask you to come down to the station with me.'

Puffing contentedly at his cigar, Jago stood watching in the wings, as Chang moved towards the climax of his act. Mr Sin on his arm, the magician stood beside three gilt chairs lined up across the centre of the stage. Lying across the chairs was the same scantily dressed chorus girl who had survived the Cabinet of Death at the end of the first house. She lay stiff and motionless, her eyes closed.

Chang gestured to the audience. 'Please to see, ladies and gentlemen, my subject is now in a state of deep hypnosis.'

Mr Sin's piping, sceptical voice cut through the spattering of applause. 'She has fallen asleep!'

The crowd roared, and Chang looked down at the dummy on his arm. 'No, Mr Sin! She is not asleep.'

'She sleeps! She has been smoking pipe of poppy!'

Again the crowd laughed, this time at the reference to the habit of opium smoking, undoubtedly widespread among the Chinese population of Limehouse.

'Be quiet,' said Chang sternly. 'I will prove young lady not asleep.' He waved to his assistant Lee, who took away the central chair. The girl's body remained rigid, supported only at head and heels.

There was a gasp of astonishment from the crowd, and more applause, interrupted once again by Mr Sin. 'She is lying on metal bar!'

'She is *not* lying on metal bar!' Chang nodded to Lee, who took away the two remaining chairs, leaving the girl floating in mid-air.

Even this wasn't enough to convince Mr Sin. 'You can't fool me. She is held up by wires!'

'Enough!' roared Chang. He dumped the dummy on to one of the gilt chairs, and drew the ceremonial sword at his waist.

The dummy let out a shrill squeak of fear. 'Don't touch me. Help! Police! Murder!'

Chang swished the sword through the air, above the floating girl. 'You see,' he said triumphantly. 'No wires, Mr Sin!'

Jago looked on appreciatively as the act moved towards its climax. No doubt about it, he was a real wonder, this Li H'sen Chang. He congratulated himself on his shrewdness in booking the Chinese magician.

Jago had first heard of Li H'sen Chang through the theatrical grapevine of fellow theatre managers. Previously unknown in the profession, the magician had appeared from nowhere. Perhaps he really was from China as he claimed. After all he really was Chinese, unlike most Oriental magicians who were usually English enough once the make-up was off.

Whatever his origins, Chang's act was brilliant enough to pack any theatre. He was completely professional, never argued about money and never performed for more than a few weeks at any one theatre. He seemed to prefer the smaller halls on the outskirts of London. Jago knew for a fact that Chang had refused several lucrative offers to appear in the West End.

Perhaps he was perfecting his act, thought Jago, planning to take London by storm when he was ready. Not that the act needed perfecting. Jago had watched it night after night, and still had no idea how much of it was done. Take that dummy for instance—sinister-looking thing. But it was wonderful how Chang used it to give variety to his act, lightning the mysterious effect of his magic with Mr Sin's disrespectful jokes.

'I will now demonstrate art of levitation,' Chang was saying. 'I shall raise most beautiful young lady high above own topknot!'

He raised his hand and the stiff body of the girl rose slowly in the air.

This time the storm of applause was uninterrupted by Mr Sin. Jago glanced at the little dummy, slumped on its chair. His eyes narrowed and he looked again. There was a tiny pool of some dark liquid beneath the chair, and as Jago looked another drop splashed from the dummy's hand. It looked exactly like blood ...

Leela looked round the room disparagingly. If this was the home of the ruler, she didn't think much of it. A small white walled chamber, furnished with a desk, chairs and a table, all in plain battered wood. More of the blue guards, and behind the desk an older one with strange markings on his sleeve. He was writing in an enormous book, using a metal pen which he dipped into thick blue fluid in a metal pot.

Sergeant Kyle finished his entry, blotted it and looked up at the strange pair before him. He had seen pretty well everything during his service in London's East End, and it was going to take more than a couple of vagabonds to worry him. Routine was routine, and everything had to be dealt with in the proper order.

He stroked his heavy moustache and addressed the Doctor. 'Now then, sir, a few preliminary details if you please. Name?'

'Just call me the Doctor. The young lady's name is Leela.'

Sergeant Kyle gave him a sceptical look, but made an entry in his ledger. 'Place of residence?'

'We've only just arrived here.'

'Your home address will do for the moment,' said Kyle patiently. He looked hard at the Doctor. 'You do have a permanent address *somewhere*, sir?'

'No, Sergeant. We're travellers.'

'I see. Persons of no fixed abode.'

'Oh, we have an abode all right, but it isn't fixed. It's called the TARDIS.'

Kyle put down his pen. 'I could give you and the young lady a fixed abode, sir. Quite easily.' He glanced meaningfully at the heavy iron door that led to the cells.

The Doctor turned to Leela. 'Flat-footed peeler,' he muttered.

'What was that sir?' asked Kyle sharply.

'Nothing complimentary, Sergeant.'

Kyle sighed wearily, and decided to try again. 'Now look, sir, we've got our hands full here at the moment. I don't know if you know it, but there's quite a few girls gone missing from this area. If you'll just co-operate by answering my questions, we'll get on a lot quicker.'

The Doctor was fast losing patience. 'See here, Sergeant, all this nonsense about who we are and where we come from is completely irrelevant. I came here to lay information about a serious crime ...'

'We'll come to that in good time, sir ...'

'We'll come to it *now*. We stumbled across a kidnapping, perhaps even a murder, and my friend here caught one of the criminals for you.'

The captured Chinaman was sitting at the wooden table, guarded by a constable. He was staring straight ahead, apparently oblivious to his surroundings.

Kyle gave the man a puzzled look. 'Well, he isn't saying much, sir. And we've only your word about all this.'

'And mine,' said Leela angrily. 'This man and the others were carrying the body of one who had been stabbed through the heart.'

'Indeed, miss? And how can you be so sure of that?'

'I am a warrior of the Sevateem. I know the different sounds of death.' Leela pointed to the motionless Chinaman. 'Now, put our prisoner to the torture and get the truth from him!'

'Well if that don't take the biscuit,' said Kyle wonderingly. 'This ain't the dark ages, you know, miss. Torture, indeed!'

'Make him talk!'

'He happens to be a Chinee, miss, if you hadn't noticed. We get a lot of 'em round here, Limehouse being so close. So we shouldn't understand him if he *did* talk.'

Sergeant Kyle came out from behind his desk and leaned over the prisoner. 'You jaw-jaw-plenty by'n by eh Johnny?'

The man ignored him.

'You see?' said Sergeant Kyle. 'I've sent for an interpreter. We'll get a statement from him soon.'

'Quite unnecessary,' snapped the Doctor. 'I speak Mandarin, Cantonese and most of the dialects.'

'Very remarkable, Doctor. Still, you being a party to the case, it wouldn't really be proper ...'

*

From somewhere nearby there came the sound of police whistles. Kyle went to the door and looked out into the fog. 'Came from down by the river, that did. They've probably found another floater ...'

The police constable shone his torch out over the river. Beside him a raggedly-dressed man jumped up and down with impatience. 'I tell you I saw it, Guv. Look, there it is, see?' He pointed to a dark shape bobbing on the water.

The policeman looked over his shoulder. 'Where's that boat-hook, then? Hurry, or we'll have to get a boat.'

A second policeman appeared and thrust a boat-hook into his hand. The constable leaned out over the rushing water and made a desperate lunge, hooking the floating shape.

'You got him, Guv,' shrieked the ragged man. 'Don't forget I spotted him first, I gets the reward.'

But as the policeman drew in his catch, even the ragged man's greed was silenced. The policeman looked down in horror. He had taken many a corpse from the river, but never one like this. Beside him, the ragged man echoed his thoughts. 'Oh my oath. Never seen anything like that in all my puff!'

United in their horror, they stared down at the body. It was savagely mutilated, torn almost to pieces, by giant fangs ...

3

DEATH OF A PRISONER

Stage make-up removed, dressed in everyday clothing, Li H'sen Chang came into the police station and nodded to Sergeant Kyle.

'You sent for me, Sergeant?'

Kyle bustled forward. 'That's right, sir. Good of you to come so prompt.'

Chang spread his hands. 'Not at all. I am finished at the theatre—and I'm always pleased to be of service to London's wonderful police. What can I do for you?'

'Complaint against one of your fellow countrymen, sir, I'm afraid. Lady and gentleman here swear they saw him, together with others not in custody, carrying what appeared to be a dead body. A European body, as I understand it, sir.'

'Indeed.' Chang stared thoughtfully at the Doctor and Leela, who returned the look with equal interest. 'What happened to the others involved in this strange incident?'

It was Leela who answered. 'They escaped. I caught only this one?'

'*You* caught him?' Chang seemed both incredulous and amused. 'How very remarkable!'

The Doctor was studying Chang's face with absorbed interest. 'Don't I know you from somewhere?'

Chang turned away and said abruptly, 'I think not.'

'I'm sure I've seen you somewhere before ...'

'I understand that to you European gentlemen, we humble Chinese all look alike.'

The Doctor shook his head. 'It's funny, I could have sworn ... Mind you, I haven't been in China for at least four hundred years ...'

Chang looked significantly at the Sergeant. 'You are taking this gentleman's statement seriously?'

'We have to look into it, sir. Will you be good enough to question this man for me?'

'Of course.' Chang went over to the table and sat down opposite the prisoner. 'Perhaps you could provide me with pen and paper?'

'Of course, sir.'

Kyle went over to his desk, and Chang moved so that his body screened the prisoner from view. He touched the ornate dragon-seal ring on his finger, and a small black pill dropped from the hidden compartment, rolled across the table and landed before the prisoner's folded hands. The prisoner's eyes widened, then he bowed his head submissively. As Kyle brought pen and paper to the table, the man snatched up the pill and slipped it into his mouth.

'Li H'sen Chang!' said the Doctor suddenly. 'I saw your face on the poster. Master of Magic and Mesmerism, eh? Show us a trick!'

The prisoner gave a sudden choking cry, rose to his feet, then slumped dead across the table.

'Very good,' said the Doctor appreciatively. 'How did you do that?'

'I did nothing,' said Chang in a shocked voice. 'Clearly the man has killed himself.'

The Doctor gave him a thoughtful look and went to examine the body, feeling in vain for any sign of a pulse. 'Concentrated poison of some kind. Could be scorpion venom.' He turned over the dead man's hand, displaying the inside of the forearm. 'Do you know what this is, Sergeant?'

Kyle looked at the scorpion tattoo. 'It's a Tong sign, isn't it, sir?'

'The Tong of the Black Scorpion. Probably one of the most dangerous criminal organisations in the world—wouldn't you agree, Li H'sen Chang?'

Chang rose from the table. 'If it is a Tong sign, Sergeant, your mystery is solved. Many of my misguided countrymen belong to these organisations—they have frequent wars among themselves. I imagine you stumbled upon an incident in such a war. Your prisoner committed suicide, rather than be forced to speak—the other killers and their victim will never be found. A truly regrettable incident, but one that is now closed.' Chang moved towards the door, pausing a moment in front of Leela. 'Perhaps we shall meet again in more pleasant circumstances?' There was an undertone of menace in the remark that made it sound almost like a challenge.

'Perhaps we shall,' said Leela flatly. Chang nodded coolly to the Doctor, and disappeared into the night.

Sergeant Kyle scratched his head, looking at the body of his late prisoner, then back to the Doctor and Leela. 'Blowed if I know what to do about all this, and that's a fact.'

'Then I'll tell you,' said the Doctor crisply. 'You can start by getting this body to the nearest mortuary and arranging for an immediate post mortem. I need to know whether my theory about scorpion venom is correct.'

'*You* need to know, sir?'

'My dear Sergeant, if the Tong of the Black Scorpion is active here in London, you're going to need my help. Now cut along and do as I ask.'

Such was the authority in the Doctor's voice that Kyle found himself obeying without question. 'Constable,' he called. 'Get out the ambulance-cart and wheel this body round to the mortuary. Ask Professor Litefoot to perform an immediate post mortem.'

In the Palace Theatre all was dark and still. The audience had gone, the performers and stage staff had gone, and Casey the caretaker was alone backstage—alone, that is, except for Jago who appeared suddenly in the backstage corridor and said reproachfully, 'Twinkle, twinkle out in front, Casey. The gallery lights are still burning.'

'Just going to see to them, Mr Jago.'

'Everyone else gone?'

'That they have, Mr Jago. I've just locked the stage door.'

'I hope those girls have the sense to go straight home to their digs.'

'That they will, sir, with all these disappearances in the papers.' He lowered his voice to a ghoulish whisper. 'There's nine of 'em now, sir. Nine girls missing, vanished off the streets—and all in this area too.'

Jago shrugged. 'They were probably stony broke. Scarpered because they couldn't pay the rent. You cut along and turn those gallery lights out. I'll wait for you here.'

Casey headed for the stairs and Jago paused for a moment, lost in thought. Slowly, almost unwillingly, he began walking towards Chang's dressing-room.

He opened the door cautiously and looked inside. Everything was quiet. He went to the wicker hamper that lay beside Chang's make-up and opened the lid. Mr Sin lay staring lifelessly up at him.

Jago reached into the basket and lifted the wooden hand—and the dummy's eyes flew open. Letting go the hand, Jago jumped back in alarm. Then he grinned ruefully. Moving the arm must have operated the eye mechanism. He gave the dummy a cautious shake and the eyes clicked shut.

He lifted the arm again, and rubbed the wooden hand with his handkerchief. There was a faint red stain on the white silk. 'It *was* blood,' muttered Jago. 'Blood all over the hand. Now how did that get there?'

Behind him the door creaked slowly open. For a moment Jago stayed where he was, frozen with terror. He dropped the lid of the hamper and turned—to see Casey in the doorway. 'Ready, Mr Jago?'

'Casey! Don't ever do that to me again. If Chang caught me prying into his secrets ...'

'What were you after doing, sir?'

Jago decided to say nothing about the blood. Casey was panicky enough already. 'I had some idea the dummy might be a midget dressed up. But it's just an ordinary ventriloquist's doll.'

'Are we going to take a look down the cellar, Mr Jago—like you said?'

'Of course, Casey, of course. When I promise to do something, it gets done. Determination, Casey. Character. That's the secret of my success. We'll go and hunt for your ghost.' Outside Chang's dressing-room, Jago paused. There was something rather unattractive about the thought of poking about in the cellar. 'Tell you what, Casey, we'll go to my office and have a little drink before we start, eh? Maybe one kind of spirit will help us to deal with the other!'

The Doctor strode confidently through the swirling fog, Leela hurrying to keep up with him. 'Where are we going now, Doctor?'

'To the mortuary, the place where they keep the dead bodies. A doctor is going to examine the body of that prisoner.'

'Why? He is dead.'

'We may still be able to learn something more about *how* he died.'

Leela shook her head, baffled. There was no point in worrying about the body of a dead enemy. Live ones were far more important. 'What is this Tong of the Black Scorpion, Doctor?'

'A Chinese secret society, fanatical followers of an ancient Chinese god called Weng-Chiang. They believe that one day he will return to rule the world.'

Leela paused, and looked over her shoulder. She had a kind of tingling sensation between her shoulder-blades—usually a sure sign she was being hunted. But the long dark street behind them seemed completely empty. She hurried after the Doctor.

(Behind her, a black-clad figure, almost invisible in the darkness, slipped out of an alleyway and followed soundlessly.)

Catching up with the Doctor, Leela asked, 'What is he like, this Weng-Chiang?'

'Not very pleasant company. They say he blew poisonous fumes from his mouth, and killed men with a great light that shone from his eyes.'

Leela was impressed. 'Magic?'

'Superstitious rubbish,' said the Doctor briefly. 'Ah, this looks like the place.' They had reached a long, low building, set back a little from the cobbled street, yellow light shining from its windows. A couple of steps led up to a central door. The Doctor flung it open, and ushered Leela inside.

(As the door closed behind them, a black-clad figure slipped out of the darkness, and peered cautiously through the window.)

Leela found herself in a place not unlike the police station they had just left. Whitewashed walls, a desk, wooden benches. This time there was something different, a pervading smell of disinfectant that hung on the air like a gas, and one end of the long bare room was concealed by screens.

The Doctor was talking to another of the blue guards. 'You mean nothing's been done? Surely you got the Sergeant's message? He sent a note round with the body of the man.'

'We got the message right enough, sir!' said the policeman patiently. 'But Professor Litefoot is already doing a post mortem examination. A body was taken from the river, not half an hour ago.'

'Well, our case is far more urgent.' Brushing the attendant aside, the Doctor marched behind the screens. A body was laid out on a mortuary slab and a tall, grey-haired man with a beaky nose was holding a test tube up to the light, and frowning fiercely at it. 'Professor Litefoot, I presume?' said the Doctor cheerfully.

Litefoot glared at him. 'Who the devil are you, sir?'

'I'm the Doctor. I've come to help you.'

'When I need anyone's help in pathology, Doctor, I'll ask for it.' Ignoring the Doctor, Litefoot went on with his examination.

Professor Litefoot was a well-known local character. A member of a wealthy upper-class family, he could, if he wished, have had a fashionable practice in Harley Street. But after a spell in the Army, he had deliberately chosen to come and work at a hospital in London's East End. Here he could do real and useful work, instead of, as he put it himself, 'dosing a lot of silly women suffering from the vapours'. Worse still, he had taken the post of police pathologist, deliberately involving himself in the crime so common in the area. His aristocratic relations had long ago given up trying to make him see reason. Litefoot went his own way, and he always would.

Deliberately ignoring the Doctor's presence, Litefoot went on with his examination. He was frequently plagued by visiting dignitaries from Scotland Yard, the Home Office and various government Committees, and assumed the Doctor was another of their number. In Litefoot's experience, if you ignored these people they eventually went away. To his annoyance, the Doctor refused to go away, and began studying the body with almost professional interest. 'I thought the constable said this was a drowning case?'

'Body was fished from the river. Not drowned, though.'

'Attacked by some kind of animal too—*after* death.'

Litefoot looked at his visitor with new respect. 'That was my theory, too. But what kind of animal leaves marks like that?'

The Doctor studied the terrible wounds. 'Something with chisel-like incisor teeth. In other words, a rodent.'

'A rodent? Look at the *size* of those marks!'

'What was the actual cause of death?'

'That's another thing. *Not* drowning, and not these bites, either.' Litefoot pointed. 'The man was killed by a knife-blow to the heart.'

The Doctor glanced at Leela, who had followed him round the screen. 'It seems you were right after all.'

'About what?'

'The different sounds of death.' He turned to the policeman. 'Where are the man's clothes?'

'Here, sir.' The policeman indicated a shabby bundle on a table in the corner. 'No documents on the body, but we found this.' He picked up a big metal disc with a number stamped on it. 'Means he was a licensed cab driver. We'll be able to identify the poor chap by the number easy enough.'

'The body those men were carrying wore clothing much like this,' whispered Leela.

The Doctor picked up the shabby coat and held it up to the light. He plucked something from the coat between finger and thumb.

'What have you found, Doctor?' asked Litefoot curiously.

The Doctor held out his hand, a few coarse grey hairs in the palm. 'Rat's hairs.'

Litefoot stared. 'Do you know what you're saying?'

'I always know what I'm saying, Professor Litefoot. Others are sometimes a little slow to understand.'

'But the hairs on a rat must measure less than a quarter of an inch. These are nearly three inches long!'

The Doctor nodded. 'Interesting, isn't it?' He looked thoughtfully at Leela. 'You know, I've just remembered something else about Weng-Chiang.'

'What, Doctor?'

'He was the god of abundance,' said the Doctor slowly. 'When he wanted to, he could make things grow very big.' He took a policeman's lantern from a shelf on the wall. 'I'll borrow this if I may,' he said, and made for the door.

Leela followed him. 'Where are we going, Doctor?'

The Doctor waved her back. 'You're not going anywhere, Leela. I want you to stay here. *I'm* going out to look for a giant rat!'

4

THE MONSTER IN THE TUNNEL

Closing the mortuary door behind him, the Doctor strode rapidly along the deserted street. A black-clad figure slid round the corner of the building and set off in pursuit.

As he padded silently after the Doctor, the Tong assassin slipped a hatchet from beneath his tunic. Truly Weng-Chiang was smiling upon him this night. He had been ordered to kill the two strangers, quietly without fuss. When they had entered the place where there were more accursed police he thought he had missed his chance. Now the tall man had come out—alone and unprotected. When the man was dead, he would return and wait for the girl.

The tall Doctor paused by a lamp-post before a row of terraced houses. There would never be a better chance. Drawing back his arm, the assassin hurled the deadly hatchet with all his force ... just as the Doctor took a step forward. The hatchet whizzed past his ear and thudded into a doorpost beside his head.

The Doctor whirled round. The assassin was standing motionless on the pavement some way behind him. He was quite still, as if paralysed by the failure of his attack. The Doctor wrenched the hatchet from the doorpost and strode grimly towards his attacker. 'I take it you were trying to attract my attention?'

The assassin did not move or speak. He stared bulging-eyed at the Doctor for a moment, then pitched forward, falling face down on to the cobbles. Leela stepped from the doorway behind him, tucking a pointed object back into the waist-band of her suit.

'Leela, what is that?' demanded the Doctor sternly.

'A Janis thorn.'

The Janis thorn was a product of Leela's native planet. It produced instant paralysis, followed by inevitable death. 'I thought I told you never to use those things again.'

'He was trying to *kill* you, Doctor.'

The Doctor considered. He was against killing of course. But he was also against being killed. 'All right,' he said ungraciously. 'Since you're here, you'd better come along.'

Leela grinned, and followed him down the street.

He led her to a road junction, close to the spot where they had first seen the four Chinese with the body. Kneeling on the cobbles, he shone his lantern on to the round manhole cover.

Leela looked down at it. 'What is it, Doctor?'

'This is where they took the body when they disappeared so suddenly.'

'Where does it lead?'

'Into the Thames, eventually. All the sewers must be connected.' The Doctor was busily prising up the manhole cover. It landed on the cobbles with an echoing clang, revealing a dark opening with a ladder bolted to the side. Swinging nimbly on to the ladder, the Doctor disappeared into the darkness, and a moment later, Leela followed him.

They climbed down into a dank and echoing tunnel, through the centre of which flowed an evil-smelling stream. Lantern held high, the Doctor moved ahead, Leela close behind him. She felt she had never been in a more unpleasant place. 'What are we looking for, Doctor?'

'Anything we can find.' The Doctor shone the lantern down the tunnel, and Leela caught a glimpse of bright-eyed, grey shapes scurrying away into the darkness.

'What are those creatures?'

'Rats.'

'They don't look too dangerous.'

'Not singly, perhaps. But they hunt in packs, and they're very cunning. Besides if my theory is correct, we may well run into something rather—'

The Doctor broke off. From the darkness ahead came a high squealing sound, and the patter of hundreds of scampering feet. The beam of the lantern showed a flood of grey shapes rushing towards them.

Leela grasped the Doctor's arm. 'We must flee. The rat creatures are massing to attack us.'

The Doctor stood his ground. 'I don't think so. They're running *from* something.' Sure enough, the stream of grey shapes flowed by ignoring them. There was a moment of silence and then another sound, like the squealing of rats magnified a hundred times.

The Doctor raised his lantern. Scurrying down the tunnel towards them was a enormous rat.

Leela gasped. The creature was huge and savage, at least twice as big as a man. It paused, red eyes blinking in the light, then with a trumpeting scream it charged them, the yellow fangs bared in fury.

'Run!' yelled the Doctor. They turned and fled, back down the sewer tunnel. When they reached the ladder, Leela clambered up with frantic speed. The Doctor paused and hurled his lantern at the huge grey shape rushing out of the darkness. As the Doctor scrambled up the ladder, the lantern smashed on the stone pavings and burst into a sheet of flame. The monster retreated with a scream of pain.

The Doctor shot out of the manhole like a jack-in-the-box, slammed the cover back in place and sat on it gasping for breath. From below came a muffled roar, as a vast bulk hurled itself against the ladder.

Leela looked disapprovingly at the Doctor. 'That was foolishness. We might have been killed.'

'Well, at least we know I was on the right track,' said the Doctor defensively. 'What a whopper, eh? Ten feet, from whiskers to tail!'

'We should have taken weapons.'

'What kind of weapons? You'd need a cannon to stop that brute.'

'Shall we tell the blue guards?'

'The police? They'd never believe us. At most they'd send a sanitary inspector—and he might get a nasty shock!'

The roaring below had died away. The Doctor got cautiously to his feet. 'You know, Leela, I think that thing was a kind of guard, to keep people like us away. So there must be something worth guarding down there, eh? Come on!'

'*Now* where are we going?'

'Back to the police station. I want to see if they've got a plan of the sewers.'

When they reached the station, Sergeant Kyle listened to the Doctor's request with his usual air of weary patience. 'A plan of the sewers, Doctor? We don't keep one here, I'm afraid. Why do you ask? If you've any information—'

'At the moment, Sergeant, we're looking for information ourselves.'

Kyle stroked his moustache. 'I see,' he said heavily, though he didn't see at all. 'I do have a message for you though, sir. From Professor Litefoot. He'd like to see you at the mortuary as soon as possible.'

'Still there, is he?'

'Oh yes, sir, he's still there. Apparently they found another body, soon after you left. Another Chinese. He was in the street, not far away.'

'Very convenient,' said the Doctor blandly.

'Very mysterious, sir. Don't suppose you know anything about it?'

'Of course we do,' said Leela helpfully. 'As a matter of fact, I—'

'Thank you for the message, Sergeant,' interrupted the Doctor hastily. 'We'll go and see Professor Litefoot at once.'

It took quite a few little drinks before Jago and Casey were ready to go looking down the dark cellar. But they screwed up their courage at last, and pleasantly aglow with brandy, they made their way down to the huge cellar that ran underneath the stage. 'Black as Newgate's knocker down here, Mr Jago,' said Casey, as they came down the cellar stairs.

Jago shone his lantern. The cellar was piled high with all kinds of junk, accumulated during the long life of the theatre. There were boxes, crates, baskets, coils of rope, abandoned stage props. Jago decided he really must get it cleared out some day.

Casey pointed to an arched recess in the wall. 'That's where I saw it, Mr Jago.'

'Flickering shadows,' said Jago, trying to convince himself he wasn't frightened. 'Just a trick of the light.'

'Shadows don't groan,' whispered Casey sinisterly. 'Shadows don't clank chains and moan, like all the tormented souls in hell.'

Jago held up his lantern and advanced determinedly towards the recess. He jumped back as a demoniacally grinning face jumped

214

out of the darkness. 'There's your ghost.' He held the lantern up to a carved Indian totem pole leaning against the wall. 'Six-gun Sadie and her Wild West Troupe left it behind. Lombard Street to a china orange that's what frightened you.'

Casey said stubbornly, 'Weren't that old thing. I saw a ghost—and heard it too, I tell you.'

'Look,' said Jago patiently, 'the old Fleet River runs under here. Running water makes all kinds of noises ...' He paused and picked up something from the floor. 'What's this, Casey, you been bringing a lady friend down here? Lady's glove, monogrammed "E.B.".' He slipped the glove into his pocket. 'Come on, Casey, we've wasted enough time on your spook.' He led the way upstairs, and ushered the still-grumbling Casey to the stage door. 'Now, straight home with you, Casey, and no lingering on the way. Someone might mistake you for a pretty girl. Doubtless I shall descry your lugubrious lineaments at the crepuscular hour.'

'What's that, sir?'

Jago gave him a friendly shove. 'See you in the morning!'

'You're a card, Mr Jago. A card and a half, you are.' Still chuckling, Casey went off down the alley.

Locking the stage door Jago turned—to find Chang looming over him. His heart gave a great leap, and he caught his breath. 'By Jiminy, you gave me a shock, Mr Chang. I thought you'd gone.'

'I had, Mr Jago. But I have returned to see you.'

'Nothing wrong, I hope?'

'Be so kind as to step into my dressing-room.'

Jago put on his most jovial manner as he entered the little dressing-room. 'If it's about your contract, Mr Chang, let me say right away that I plan to offer you better terms. We've been attracting such good houses, it's the least I can do.'

Chang made no reply. He stared at Jago, eyes glittering hypnotically. Jago stumbled on. 'I venture to say no management in London could offer an artiste better terms. What would you say to an extra two percent of the gross, Mr Chang? I think that's fair ... that's fair ...' Jago's voice faltered and died away.

'Hear me, Jago,' said Chang softly. 'You will forget everything about Buller, the cab driver who came here earlier. You did not see him.'

'I did not see him.'

'You will go to your office, and remember only that you have just said good night to Casey.'

'I have just said good night to Casey.'

'Good. Now go.'

Jago turned at once and walked from the room. A few minutes later he found himself sitting down at his desk, going through the accounts for the evening. He rubbed his hand over his eyes. He'd felt a bit queer for a moment. Must have been old Casey, with all that nonsense about ghosts in the cellar. Lighting a fresh cigar, Jago went on with his work.

Chang made his way through the darkened theatre and down the cellar steps. He went to the recess where Casey had seen his 'ghost', took an iron bar from its hiding place in the corner, and knocked three times on the stone flags. There was a grinding sound, and a flagstone slid back revealing a wooden ladder that led down into darkness. Chang started to descend.

The ladder ended in a vaulted chamber deep below the theatre. It was furnished with a strange mixture of Chinese-style drapes and hangings, and ultra-modern scientific equipment. A shallow culvert ran along the far side of the room. It ended in a barred arch, through which could be heard the sound of running water.

Waiting at the foot of the ladder was a strange and terrifying figure. It was tall and thin, dressed in close-fitting black garments and an all-enveloping black cloak. A soft black-leather mask covered the face, which was overshadowed by a broad-brimmed black hat. Chang dropped from the ladder, and bowed low before the sinister apparition. This was his lord and master Greel, living embodiment of the god Weng-Chiang.

Greel spoke in a dry rasping voice, each word forced out with painful effort. 'You are late.'

'I am sorry, Lord. I was delayed.'

Suddenly Greel staggered, supporting himself against the wall with a long-taloned hand. Chang looked up in concern. 'You should not go out tonight, Lord.'

Greel hobbled painfully across the chamber, and sank wearily on to a stool. 'I must. Tonight, *every* night, until the Time Cabinet is found.'

'You are ill.'

216

'I am *dying*, Chang. You must bring another linnet to my cage.' Greel waved towards a sinister-looking complex of machinery that stood against the far wall. Its dominant feature was a transparent cabinet from the top of which were suspended two golden metal balls.

'Already, Lord?' whispered Chang. There was fear in his voice. 'But only yesterday ...'

'My disease grows worse,' rasped Greel. 'Each distillation has less effect than the one before.'

'But Lord, each missing girl increases the panic, and the suspicion. Even tonight, there was danger.' Hurriedly Chang told his master of Buller's suspicions, of the murder on the way to the police station, and his hypnotising of Jago.

Greel showed little appreciation of the many efforts of his servant. 'I have given you mental powers undreamed of in this primitive century, Chang. What have you to fear from these savages?'

'True, Lord: I read their minds with ease. But tonight there was a stranger, one whose thoughts were hidden from me.'

'Describe him.'

'He calls himself the Doctor. Tall with wide, pale eyes, and hair that curls close like the ram. He asks questions, many questions.'

Greel made a dismissive gesture. 'A Time Agent would not ask questions, Chang. A Time Agent would *know*.'

Chang was not convinced. 'I sensed danger from him and from his companion. I have ordered your servants to slay them.'

'Opium-addicted scum of the Tongs! They are all bunglers. You should have seen to it yourself.'

'I will do so, Lord, should he trouble us further.'

Greel wrapped his cloak about him, and made for the ladder. 'We are wasting time. Come, we must begin our task.'

Outside the theatre a carriage was waiting, a black-clad, pigtailed driver at the reins. Soon Greel and his servant Chang were rattling through the cobbled streets on their terrifying errand.

5

THE QUEST OF GREEL

Professor Litefoot rolled down his sleeves and slipped into the coat held for him by a respectful constable. 'I must confess, Doctor, this thing has me beaten. One of those Chinese was poisoned orally, the other pricked by some poisoned instrument. Different poisons in each case. Understand you suggested scorpion venom, for the first chap?'

The Doctor passed Litefoot his overcoat. 'It's a possibility. Highly concentrated of course.'

'And the second?'

The Doctor coughed and shot Leela a warning glance. 'I really couldn't say.'

Litefoot seemed positively stimulated by the dramatic events of the evening. 'What a night, eh?' he said gleefully. 'Most of the corpses around here are very dull. Now I've got a couple of mysteriously dead Chinese and a poor perisher who was bitten by a giant rat after being stabbed by a midget!'

Leela stared at him. 'A midget?'

Litefoot made an upward stabbing gesture. 'Angle of the wound—sorry, my dear.'

'What for?'

Litefoot looked embarrassed. 'For mentioning such indelicate topics in the presence of a lady.'

Leela gave the Doctor a baffled look. 'Does he mean me?'

'I think so,' said the Doctor solemnly.

Leela turned back to Litefoot. 'You can tell the height of the attacker by the way the blade was thrust?'

'Quite so, my dear. But you mustn't bother your pretty head …'

'We were always taught to strike upwards under the breast-bone when aiming for the heart.'

'Well, upon my soul, young lady ...'

The Doctor took Litefoot aside. 'Raised by savages,' he whispered. 'Found floating down the Amazon in a hatbox!'

'A hatbox?'

Before the Doctor had a chance to elaborate on his story, they were interrupted by the return of the police constable who had been on duty earlier. He was strangely bright and cheerful, despite the foggy night. 'Still here then, Professor? I've just traced your cab driver for you.' He produced his notebook with a flourish. 'Name of Alfred Buller, of Fourteen, Fish Lane, this parish.'

'Splendid work, Constable Quick,' said Litefoot heartily. 'The Coroner will want the details for his report. Did someone identify the clothing?'

P.C. Quick produced his notebook. 'Mother-in-law, Mrs Nellie Gossett, of the same address. Deceased had lived with her since his marriage six months ago.'

The Doctor's nostrils twitched. A familiar odour had come into the room with P.C. Quick—a faint but unmistakable whiff of gin. 'You stayed for a drink with Mrs Gossett, I think, Constable. What else did she have to say?'

Guiltily Quick wiped his moustache with the back of his hand. 'Well as the bearer of sad tidings, sir, I did share a glass or two, just to help the poor old dear get over the shock.' He consulted his notebook. 'She said the deceased had been in a state all day, owing to the fact that his wife, Emma Buller, didn't come home last night. Deceased had several drinks then went off to the Palace Theatre where he believed his wife was to be found. Mrs Gossett said he went off making horrible threats.'

The Doctor rubbed his chin. 'Thank you, that's very interesting.'

Professor Litefoot didn't seem to think so. 'Just put the relevant information in your report, Constable. Clearly the man got stupidly drunk, then got into a fight with a dwarf!'

'Yessir, very good sir,' said Quick woodenly, and disappeared to make out his report.

Litefoot turned to the Doctor and Leela. 'A busy night does wonders for my appetite, I'd be honoured if you'd both come home and share a spot of supper with me.'

The Doctor stood lost in thought, and didn't seem to hear the Professor's invitation. Leela nudged him in the ribs, and he looked up. 'What's that Professor, supper? I'd be delighted.'

Litefoot had a hackney-cab waiting outside, and soon they were rattling over the cobbles. It was very late now. The pubs and theatres had closed, the last revellers had made their way home and the foggy streets were dark and empty.

Litefoot produced a huge curved pipe, and began trying to light it with a succession of matches. 'Normally the police would have these cases cleared up in no time. But with these Chinese involved— different kettle of fish, what?'

Leela had been watching Litefoot's efforts with fascination. 'Why are you making a fire in your mouth?'

"Pon my soul, girl, haven't you ever seen a pipe before?'

The Doctor smiled. 'People don't smoke where Leela comes from. In any case, it's a most unhealthy habit.'

'Quite agree,' said Litefoot, taking another puff at his pipe. 'Yes, as I was saying, they're a mysterious lot, the Chinese. I never came anywhere near understanding 'em, and I grew up in China.'

'How did that come about?' asked the Doctor curiously.

'Father was an army man. Brigadier, actually. Went out with the punitive expedition in 1860. Stayed on in Peking, as a palace attaché. Poor old buffer died out there in the end. Fireworks at the funeral, I remember.' Litefoot puffed meditatively at his pipe. 'Odd custom. Odd sort of people altogether.'

The Doctor reached up and rapped sharply on the roof of the cab, to signal to the driver to stop. He swung his long legs out of the carriage and stood beside it looking thoughtfully up at them. 'Evil spirits,' he said suddenly. 'They use fireworks to frighten off evil spirits.'

'I know that,' spluttered Litefoot. 'What's the matter, Doctor?'

The Doctor ignored him. 'You go on with the Professor, Leela. I'll join you later.'

'Where are you going?'

'To the Palace Theatre. All right, Cabbie, drive on!'

The Doctor slapped the side of the carriage, and before Leela could protest further, the carriage was jolting on its way, leaving the Doctor behind.

Litefoot shook his head. 'Extraordinary feller. How can he join us later? He doesn't know my address.'

'Four, Ranskill Gardens,' said Leela promptly. 'He heard you tell the driver.'

Litefoot stared admiringly at her. 'Gad! That's amazing. You're as sharp as a trout'

'Trout?'

'It's a kind of fish, my dear ...'

The hackney-carriage rattled on its way.

Jago had just finished totting up the night's takings when he heard a persistent banging. He climbed wearily to his feet, went along the corridor and opened the stage door. A very tall man slipped nimbly through the gap, and stood beaming at him. 'Thank you very much. Terrible fog tonight.' Calmly the stranger closed the stage door behind him. 'Are you the manager?'

'Manager and owner, sir. Henry Gordon Jago, at the end of a long, hard day. So if you will kindly state your business—'

The Doctor seized Jago's hand and shook it warmly. 'A very great pleasure, Mr Jago. I'm the Doctor. How do you do?'

'The Doctor?'

'Exactly.'

Jago nodded understandingly. 'Aha! Now I've rumbled your game. I admire your brass, sir, but it won't do. Call back on Saturday. Auditions commence at ten sharp, supporting acts booked for one week only.'

Suddenly the Doctor realised that Jago had taken him for a music-hall performer trying to get a booking. He smiled delightedly. 'Just one moment, Mr Jago.' The Doctor snatched the white handkerchief from Jago's breast-pocket and flourished it. Immediately the handkerchief turned into a string of flags of all nations. Still beaming, the Doctor crumpled the flags into a ball, and they turned into a live dove, which fluttered away down the corridor.

Jago shook his head. 'I'm sorry, Doctor, we've already got a very good magician.'

The Doctor gave a disappointed sigh. 'Dramatic recitations? Tap dancing?' he said hopefully. I can play the Trumpet Voluntary in a tank of live goldfish!'

Jago waved him towards the door. 'Don't bother about coming back on Saturday ...'

The Doctor grinned, and abandoned his masquerade. 'As a matter of fact, Mr Jago, I didn't come here for a job. I came to ask you a few questions—about a cab driver by the name of Buller.'

Immediately Jago's face went blank. 'Never heard of him.'

The Doctor looked hard at Jago. It was as if a shutter had suddenly slammed down behind Jago's eyes. 'I'm also a master hypnotist,' said the Doctor sternly. 'How long since *you* were under the influence?'

Jago was indignant. 'Me, sir? I am a man of character and determination. The Rock of Gibraltar would be more easily ... more easily ...' Jago's voice faltered. The wide staring eyes of the stranger held him trans-fixed.

'As I thought,' said the Doctor gently. 'Now, what was your last order?'

'To remember nothing since I said good night to Casey,' said Jago tonelessly.

The Doctor spoke in a low, compelling voice. 'Henry Gordon Jago, I want you to tell me everything you were ordered to forget. You will remember everything when I count to three. One ... two ... three!'

Jago blinked. 'I tell you sir, I have a will of iron ... What the blazes were we talking about? Oh yes, that fellow Buller. Burst in and accosted Mr Chang between houses. Something to do with a lady called Emma.'

'His wife, Emma Buller. She disappeared last night. What's the matter?'

Jago was staring blankly at him. 'Emma Buller.' He fished a crumpled glove, from his pocket, and handed it to the Doctor.

The Doctor read the monogrammed initials. 'E.B. Where did you find this?'

'In the cellar. I say, are you from the police?'

'I'm helping them. Now, Mr Jago, I want to take a look at this cellar of yours.'

While Litefoot's carriage carried the Professor and Leela back towards his neat suburban villa, another carriage was rattling through the deserted streets not far away. Inside were Greel, Li H'sen Chang—and Mr Sin. Greel was holding a saucer-shaped crystal pendant in his hands. He stared hard at the pendant, and sighed with disappointment. 'You are certain these are *different* streets?'

'The driver knows his orders, Lord. Every night we search a new area.'

'Yes! And for how much longer? How many more nights must I spend in this endless quest?'

'Patience, Lord. The city is large. But we know that the Time Cabinet is here, in the house of some infidel. We *shall* recover it.'

'I grow weary, Chang. Weary!' Greel slumped disconsolately back in his seat.

Chang looked worriedly at the black-masked visage of his master. It is no small responsibility to be the servant of a dying god. He made his voice encouraging. 'Tomorrow I will bring you two new donors. Young and vigorous girls. The distillation of their life-essences will quickly restore your powers.'

Greel nodded wearily. Chang looked sadly at his master. Greel was weakening fast. Unless the Time Cabinet was found soon, it would be too late to save him—however many young girls were sacrificed.

Jago held up his lantern. 'The glove was lying just here, Doctor. I came down to reassure Casey, my caretaker. He's taken to seeing ghosts lately.' Jago jumped back. Disturbed by the light of his lantern, a huge round black shape had scuttled away into a dark corner. 'What a spider, eh? That must be the granddad of them all.'

It's a money spider,' said the Doctor absently. He shone his lantern around the cellar.

Jago laughed nervously. 'Money spider, eh? Don't kill it, Doctor, it'll bring us luck. Why's it so big though?'

'Genetic disruption,' said the Doctor to himself. 'Affecting the size of the local fauna—like that rat. Emanations of some kind ... but where are they coming from, eh?' He swung round on Jago. 'Is there anything under us here, Mr Jago?'

'Under here? Where we're standing you mean? Well, this theatre was built on the site of a much older building. And they say the course of the old Fleet River lies right under these foundations.'

The Doctor nodded happily. 'Splendid. Now we're getting somewhere!' He knelt down and examined the flagstones, rapping hard at different points, and listening to the resulting sound. 'If there is an entrance here, it's expertly hidden …'

Jago looked nervously round the gloomy cellar. The abandoned theatre-props seemed to form strange shapes in the darkness. Suddenly a glowing point of light appeared in the arched recess. It grew and grew until there was a flouting shape inside the arch, a horrible glowing figure with a skull-like face. 'Look out, Doctor,' yelled Jago. 'It's the ghost!'

Slowly, the hideously glowing figure floated towards them.

6

THE TONG ATTACKS

The Doctor studied the approaching phantom with scientific detachment. 'Interesting,' he murmured. 'Extremely interesting.'

Jago couldn't quite manage the Doctor's calm. His nerve broke and he turned and ran. Unfortunately his foot became tangled in a trailing rope. Convinced the ghost had caught him, Jago gave a yell of terror, wrenched himself free and crashed head-first into a stone pillar, knocking himself senseless.

The Doctor knelt at his side. Jago lay unconscious, a bruised forehead. Glancing over his shoulder, the Doctor saw the phantom hover, fade and vanish. He looked down at the unconscious Jago. 'Come on, Rock of Gibraltar,' he murmured. Hoisting Jago on to his shoulder, he carried him out of the cellar.

Litefoot ushered Leela into his dining-room. He was a little dubious about the propriety of being with an unchaperoned young female so late at night. But he'd already seen enough of Leela to realise that ideas of polite behaviour meant little to her.

Leela looked curiously round the sitting-room. To her it seemed cluttered, overcrowded with heavy furniture and a variety of fussy ornaments. She knew too little of Earth's culture to realise that two distinct styles were mingled in the room. The mahogany dining table, the ornately carved chairs, the overstuffed armchairs and divans were all the standard furnishings of a prosperous Victorian home. But the ornate tapestries, the lacquer-work cabinets and the strangely-carved jade ornaments came from a far older culture. They were all souvenirs of China, brought home from Peking. The pride of the collection stood in a corner of the room. It was a huge black cabinet, decorated with ornate golden scrolls. It was roughly the size and shape of the Doctor's TARDIS.

Litefoot was lifting covers from a side table. 'Mrs Hudson, my housekeeper, always leaves me a cold collation when I'm working late. Now, let's see what we have here. Ham, roast beef, chicken, tongue … and those look like quail, unless I'm much mistaken.' Litefoot rubbed his hands. He had a handsome private income, and was accustomed to doing himself well. 'Perhaps we needn't wait for your friend the Doctor, my dear. Just help yourself, will you? Plates at the end of the table. I'll put a knob or two on the fire.'

While Litefoot busied himself with coal scuttle and tongs, Leela tore off a chunk of beef with her fingers, tasted it and nodded appreciatively. Litefoot straightened up in time to see her seize the joint in both hands and tear at it with strong white teeth. He gulped. 'Er, would you care for a knife and fork?'

Leela saw a carving knife on one of the platters. She snatched it up and ran a thumb appreciatively along the edge … 'Ah … it's a good knife.' She started sawing chunks from the joint and stuffing them into her mouth. She looked at Litefoot in surprise. 'Aren't you hungry?'

A Victorian gentleman to the core, Litefoot was well aware of the first rule of true hospitality. A guest must never be made to feel awkward or uncomfortable. Manfully, he snatched up a whole boiled ham and began biting into it. Leela smiled happily, and went on with, her meal. From somewhere nearby came the sound of a passing carriage …

Greel's eyes were half closed, his head slumped forward, as the carriage jolted through the night streets on its endless journey. He was beginning to lose hope, to feel he must die here in this barbaric century. Would he never be able to return to his own place and time? Not until the Time Cabinet was found …

Suddenly his eyes snapped open, and he sat bolt upright. The crystal pendant, dangling unregarded from his hands, was beginning to *glow* … 'Stop!' he called. 'Our search is over. The Time Cabinet is *here*—somewhere among these dwellings …'

The carriage clattered to a halt, and Chang jumped down, assisting Greel to climb painfully after him. They stood in a tree-lined suburban street. Greel swung round in a circle, and when the pendant began to glow more brightly, he moved slowly forwards.

The pendant led them straight towards a solid Victorian villa, set well back from the road, behind a front garden filled with dense shrubbery. 'It is here,' croaked Greel. 'The Time Cabinet is *here*, in this house!' Relief left him suddenly weak and he staggered and almost fell.

Chang caught his Master by the arm and steadied him. 'You grow weak, Lord. Leave the rest to your servants and go back to your abode.'

The eyes behind the mask glowed with an obsessive passion. 'The cabinet … Chang. I must have the cabinet.'

'Rest, Lord, and I will bring the cabinet to you …'

Greel's bony claw gripped his arm. 'Very well. But do not fail me, now, Chang. *Do not fail me!*'

Greel climbed into the carriage. At a sign from Chang, the Chinese driver cracked the whip and drove away. Mr Sin on his arm, Chang moved cautiously towards the house.

The Doctor held a glass of water to Jago's lips. 'Here, sit up and drink this. You'll soon feel better.'

Fearfully Jago opened his eyes and found to his relief that he was out of the cellar, propped up against the wall in the corridor backstage. He swigged gratefully at the water, and looked up at the Doctor. 'The ghost! I saw it. Oh, Casey forgive me, I saw it.'

The Doctor helped him to sit up. 'What you saw, Mr Jago, was a hologram.'

'A grinning skull,' gasped Jago. 'A monster ten foot high. I always knew there was something, unnatural about that cellar.'

'There's nothing unnatural about the holograph technique,' said the Doctor severely. 'Simply a way of using a laser-beam to project a three-dimensional image. What *is* unnatural is the use of the technique in this century. It hasn't been discovered yet!'

Jago struggled to his feet. 'Oh, I see,' he said blankly. Suddenly he caught a glimpse of a dark shape, moving into the wings.

'Someone's moving! Over there on the stage.'

'Stay there. I'll go and take a look.' The Doctor disappeared into the wings.

Behind the lowered curtain, the stage was in utter darkness. The Doctor saw a black shape dodge in front of the curtains. He followed, and found himself on the narrow strip of stage on the other side. In front of him were the footlights, the darkness of the orchestra pit and the rows and rows of empty seats. Everything was dark and silent.

The Doctor stood listening. He heard a faint scuffling from the orchestra pit, and immediately jumped down. A fleeting glimpse of a black-cloaked figure—and an orchestra chair smashed down, knocking him off his feet.

The chair was spindly, and the Doctor got his arms up in time to protect his head. Struggling to his feet, he saw his attacker disappear behind the curtain, and staggered in pursuit.

Once again his attacker had vanished. The Doctor listened, and heard a scrabbling sound from the other side of the stage. He crossed over. An iron ladder, bolted to the wall, led upward into darkness. Guessing his attacker was somewhere above him, the Doctor started to climb. Something heavy hurtled out of the darkness, knocking him clean off the ladder. An open costume-basket broke his fall, and disentangling himself from a pile of draperies, the Doctor saw that the missile had been a stuffed tiger's head. He climbed out of the basket and started climbing again.

The ladder took him up to a kind of catwalk, high above the stage. All around were the various ropes and counterweights by means of which the backdrops to the acts were raised and lowered. The Doctor was edging his way along the narrow walk-way when a huge black shape, swinging on one of the dangling ropes, hurtled out of the darkness like a giant bat, aimed a kick that missed by inches and disappeared into the darkness on the other side of the stage. The Doctor ran in pursuit. The figure landed on the catwalk and disappeared into the dark area behind it.

By the time he reached the other side of the catwalk, his attacker was nowhere to be seen. The Doctor wondered if his quarry was already climbing the ladder. A black shape appeared behind him, and thrust him over the edge of the catwalk with a savage heave.

The Doctor hurtled downwards, frantically reaching out for something to hold on to. He managed to grasp the edge of the velvet side-curtain, and hung on desperately. The curtain began to tear beneath his weight … As he struggled to improve his grip, the Doctor saw his enemy slide down a dangling rope to the stage below, and run towards the cellar steps. The curtain gave way, and the Doctor tumbled downwards in a tangle of red velvet.

Jago meanwhile had got to his feet and was staggering gallantly to the Doctor's aid. He reached the stage just in time to be knocked down by the black-cloaked figure. By the time he had picked himself up, it had disappeared down the cellar steps. Struggling free of the torn curtain the Doctor followed it, and Jago hurried after him.

He found the Doctor at the bottom of the steps, looking thoughtfully round the empty cellar. 'What happened?' panted Jago. 'Who was that?'

'I haven't the faintest idea. He didn't introduce himself. Anyway, he seems to have gone back to his rats.'

Jago stared at the cellar floor. 'I'll get the police down here with picks and shovels,' he said fiercely.

'Our reclusive phantom would vanish straight away, I'm afraid.' The Doctor laid a hand on Jago's shoulder. 'We shall tackle this together, Mr Jago.'

Jago winced, but tried to sound enthusiastic. 'Yes, indeed, Doctor. What *are* you going to do next?'

'Think!' said the Doctor solemnly. 'Now if you'll excuse me, I have a supper engagement!'

Leela tossed aside a well-gnawed bone, and wiped her greasy hands on her suit. 'Napkin?' suggested Litefoot tactfully. He passed one to Leela, and took one himself. Dabbing at his moustache, Litefoot wandered over to the window. 'Doctor's a long time. I hope he did note the address.' He opened the long velvet curtains and peered out. 'Great Scott!'

'What is it?'

'There's someone watching the house.' He pointed. 'Look, over there in the shrubbery.'

Leela looked out, but saw only the thick bushes in the dark front garden. 'Are you sure, Professor?'

'Saw him duck back into the shrubbery, just as I looked out. Chinese, I think.' Litefoot went to a bureau drawer and took out a heavy revolver. 'Well, whoever he is, I'll give him more than he bargained for. Wait here, my dear.'

Revolver in hand, Litefoot marched determinedly down the hall and out of the front door. He had seen service on the North-West Frontier in his Army days. No Chinese bandit was going to rob him without a fight.

He paused on the front steps and looked round. There was no one in sight. Revolver in hand, he made for the place where he'd seen the lurking figure. No one there. 'Sneaked round the back to look for an open window,' thought Litefoot. 'With any luck, I'll catch him in the act.' Revolver levelled, he crept cautiously round the side of the house.

In the dining-room, Leela waited. Had Litefoot really seen something, or was it all imagination? She was about to go out and look for him when she heard the front door open. 'Is that you, Professor?' she called.

Litefoot's cheerful voice came back. 'It's all right, my dear, nobody out there now. I've been all round the house. Fellow must have seen me coming and—'

There was a thud and a muffled groan. Then silence.

'Professor?' called Leela. There was no reply. The dining-room door swung silently open. A strange little figure stood in the doorway. It wore silk jacket and trousers and a little round cap, and its Oriental face stared impassively at her. In its hand gleamed a long pointed knife, held point-upwards. Leela backed cautiously away. Her instinct told her that despite its lack of size, the thing was deadly dangerous.

The hand with the knife came up, and the manikin stalked slowly towards her.

7

THE LAIR OF
WENG-CHIANG

Leela covered the distance to the dining table in a single backwards leap. Snatching up a carving knife she turned to the attack.

The manikin was still moving forward. Leela hefted the knife to judge the balance, shifted her grip to the blade then threw with all her strength. The knife spun in the air and thudded into the manikin's throat.

The manikin stopped for a moment, then shuffled forward again. Leela felt a chill of superstitious terror. She feared no living enemy— but now she was being hunted by something that could not be killed.'

Knife in hand, the sinister little figure shuffled forward.

Just inside the open doorway of the house, Chang stood waiting for Mr Sin to complete his work. In his hand he held Litefoot's revolver, and the Professor's unconscious body lay at his feet. Suddenly Chang heard the crunch of footsteps on the gravel path. He ducked back into the doorway and peered out. The Doctor was strolling up the front path towards the house. Chang raised the revolver ...

Step by step the manikin backed Leela into a corner. She could retreat no further. One more step and it would be close enough to use the knife.

Tensing her muscles, Leela took a flying leap forward, clean over the manikin's head. It slashed up at her, but missed. She rolled on to the dining table and jumped to her feet. The manikin had swung round to resume its remorseless pursuit.

*

Leela ran the length of the dining table and dived head-first for the curtained window ...

Leela exploded through the window with a crash of shattered glass. The Doctor swung round and Chang fired—and missed.

The Doctor ran to Leela, and yanked her into the cover of the shrubbery. The revolver boomed again, and a shot whistled over their heads. The Doctor and Leela instinctively dropped to the ground, and wriggled backwards into deeper cover.

Revolver raised, Chang crouched by the door. He peered into the darkness, but there was nothing to be seen. 'Sin,' he called, and the manikin stalked out of the dining-room towards him.

'Where's Litefoot?' whispered the Doctor.

'In the hall, I think. He went out to look for an enemy outside the window. They must have ambushed him when he got back.'

'And then you jumped through the window?'

'I *had* to. There was this—*thing* ...'

Before Leela could explain, the Doctor whispered, 'Stay here.' He slipped away through the shrubbery.

As soon as Mr Sin was near enough, Chang snatched him up and began backing away from the house.

The Doctor forced the kitchen window and climbed swiftly through.

Crouching in the shrubbery, Leela heard the clatter of hooves in the road. A carriage came tearing along and stopped outside the house. Chang ran down the front path, Mr Sin in his arms. He jumped into the carriage and it sped away.

Unable to bear the thought of their enemy escaping, Leela acted purely by instinct. She dashed after the carriage and leaped for the back step, clinging on as the carriage rattled away. It vanished from sight just as the Doctor ran through the house and out on to the front step. He looked round in astonishment. Chang had gone, and there was no sign of Leela. Only Litefoot was left, groaning feebly just inside the door.

Reflecting that this seemed to be his night for lugging bodies about, the Doctor picked Litefoot up and carried him into the dining-room. He put him on the couch, fetched water and a towel from the back kitchen, and bathed the Professor's forehead until he recovered consciousness. Litefoot came round with an indignant groan. 'The sheer criminal effrontery of it! Things have come to a pretty pass when ruffians attack a man in his own home.'

'*Chinese* ruffians, by any chance, Professor?'

'That's right. I wonder what they intended.'

The Doctor looked round the cluttered room. 'Robbery, perhaps?'

'It's very probable. I've quite a few valuable things here. That K'ang-hsi vase, for instance. Family brought that back from Peking. Or that Chinese cabinet.'

The Doctor went over to the cabinet and examined it. He tried the door, but it refused to move.

'I'm afraid it doesn't open. I spent ages looking for a secret spring, but it's no use.'

'Fused molecules, Professor.'

'No, no, Doctor. Lacquered bronze.'

The cabinet seemed to fascinate the Doctor. 'You're *sure* this is from *this* planet?'

'Of course it is. It comes from Peking—a gift from the Emperor himself.'

The Doctor was staring into space. 'Then what was a piece of technology as advanced as this doing in nineteenth-century China?' He stared intensely at Litefoot. 'Of course! That must be the answer ...'

Litefoot dabbed the bruise on his forehead. 'What *are* you babbling about, Doctor?'

'Weng-Chiang!'

Litefoot groaned. 'Not him again.'

'As soon as it's light, Professor, we must try to find Leela. I think she followed our Chinese friends—and by now she could be in serious trouble.'

Chang rapped three times on the cellar flagstones, the trapdoor opened and he climbed down into the darkness. Leela watched, fascinated, from her hiding place near the cellar door. She felt her impulse to jump on to the cab had been justified, since she had been able to track the enemy to his lair. Blissfully unaware that the Doctor already knew about the cellar hideout, Leela settled down to wait, with all the patience of a hunter outside the den of some dangerous wild beast.

In the secret chamber, Chang was bowing his head beneath the fury of his lord. Greel was occupied in hacking the carcase of a sheep into bloody chunks of raw meat. Chang winced as the cleaver thudded down. Such was Greel's fury that Chang felt his own neck might be the cleaver's next target. 'I will not tolerate failure,' roared Greel.

'There has been no failure, Lord.'

'Then where is the cabinet?'

Chang did not dare to confess that he had tried to obtain the Time Cabinet, and failed. Instead he told Greel that he had deliberately chosen to wait for a better opportunity, 'The house is marked and watched, Lord. When night returns, your servants of the Tong will descend and take the cabinet.'

'I put no trust in your opium-ridden scum,' snarled Greel. He gathered the chunks of raw meat into a pile and carried them across the chamber, dropping them in a heap by the far wall. Greel pulled a lever and a section of wall drew back to reveal a barred gap, beyond which was the dank blackness of a sewer tunnel. One by one Greel tossed the chunks of meat through the bars. He struck the gong that hung nearby, and a low booming note echoed through the cellar. Chang made another attempt to placate his Master. 'I promise, Lord, you shall have the Cabinet of Weng-Chiang before the next sunset!'

Greel thrust a last chunk of meat between the bars. 'Do not fail me, Li H'sen Chang. I grow weary of this hole in the ground.'

'You are safe, here, Lord.'

'Safe?' The word only increased Greel's fury. 'This place is a trap, Chang. I was seen tonight as I returned.' He told Chang of his encounter with the Doctor.

There came a trumpeting squeal and a giant grey shape thudded against the bars. Huge teeth snapped down on the chunks of meat, dragging them away one by one. Greel gave a gloating laugh. 'My little pets, Li H'sen. My offerings have made them larger and more savage than any lion. None may attack us through the sewers while my pets stand guard!'

From the blackness behind the bars came savage grunts as the giant rat devoured the meat. Greel listened with satisfaction. It had amused him to feed the rats on the specially treated meat, irradiated in a way that caused them to grow to enormous size. He had little enough amusement, living like a rat himself in this hole in the ground.

Turning away from the bars, Greel returned to his grievance. 'Yes, Chang, the Doctor almost captured me. And he was led here by *your* blundering!'

Chang's eyes glittered with rage and resentment. 'He shall die, Lord!'

'The list of your failures is growing,' hissed Greel malevolently. He brooded for a moment. 'When you do succeed in obtaining the Time Cabinet, I must be ready to move quickly. I shall need strength.'

'I will bring a girl, Lord.'

'Two girls, Chang. I need *two* strong young donors, and I need them *now*.'

Chang remembered his earlier promise. But then he had had the whole night before him. It was too difficult to snatch up any girl unwary enough to be out so late. Now it was morning, and the streets would be full of the City's peasants whose work started early. Dock workers, factory girls, cleaning women … There would be people everywhere—and the accursed police for ever on the watch. It was the nature of his god to be demanding. But no servant, however faithful, could achieve the impossible. 'It will be dangerous, Lord. The streets at this hour are busy …'

Greel's long-taloned hands seized him by the throat in a choking grip, shook him savagely and hurled him across the cellar to the foot of the ladder. 'No excuse. Get them!'

Chang picked himself up, his heart filled with resentment that he dared not show. 'Yes, Lord,' he said submissively, and turned to climb the ladder.

Leela ducked back into hiding as the trapdoor opened and Chang climbed through the gap. The door closed behind him, and he went up the cellar stairs. Leela slipped silently after him.

Still in pyjamas and dressing-gown, Professor Litefoot came yawning and stretching into the dining-room, and found the Doctor sitting at the dining-room table, drawing a map on the cloth with a silver pencil.

Litefoot looked at his strange guest in astonishment. 'Haven't you even slept, Doctor?'

'Sleep is for tortoises,' said the Doctor severely, and went on drawing his map.

'Miss Leela hasn't returned then?'

'Not yet.'

'Perhaps we should inform the police?'

'With nine missing girls on their list already, they won't have much time to spare for a tenth. But tell them by all means—and ask them to put a police guard on the house.'

'Surely those other poor girls disappeared in different circumstances?'

'Unless I manage to rescue her, Leela may well suffer exactly the same fate. I think I know why those girls were taken.' The Doctor leaped to his feet and paced angrily about the room. 'Some slavering, gangrenous vampire comes out of the sewers and stalks this city at night. I shall attack him in his lair!'

Litefoot peered at the map on the table-cloth. 'What's all this about?'

'I've been trying to work out an approach through the sewers.' The Doctor pointed to the map. 'Here's the Thames. This is the course of the River Fleet. And this is the Palace Theatre.'

'How do you know the course of the Fleet? It's been covered for centuries.'

The Doctor smiled reminiscently. 'I caught a salmon there once that would have hung over the sides of this table. Shared it with the Venerable Bede. He loved fish.'

Litefoot gave him a worried look, wondering if the events of the night had affected the Doctor's brain. 'Do you need the map any more?'

The Doctor shook his head and Litefoot bundled up the cloth. 'I'd better dispose of this before my housekeeper sees it!' He took the cloth out of the room, dropping it into the laundry basket on the porch. When he returned, the Doctor was putting on his cape, and adjusting his deerstalker to a jaunty angle. 'Time we were off, Professor. Do you happen to have an elephant gun by any chance?'

'I've a Chinese fowling piece, if that's any good. Used for duck mainly. It's somewhere in the cellar.' Litefoot left the room for a few minutes and returned carrying a canvas bag, and a fearsome looking weapon, which he handed to the Doctor. It was an ancient long-barrelled muzzle-loader, a cross between a rifle and blunderbuss. 'I've even got the powder and shot for it here.' Litefoot tapped the canvas bag.

The Doctor took the heavy weapon and examined it. 'Splendid, Professor. Made in Birmingham, I see!' Opening the bag he started to load the weapon. 'Do you know where we can hire a small boat?'

'I imagine so.' Litefoot was beginning to wonder what extraordinary request the Doctor would come up with next. 'May I ask the purpose of these preparations?'

'First we shall find the confluence of the Thames and the Fleet, Professor. Then I shall follow the Fleet upstream to a point close to the villain's lair!' The Doctor aimed the enormous gun through the window and looked menacingly along the barrel. 'And then, Professor, we shall see what we shall see!'

8

THE SACRIFICE

Leela trailed Chang through the maze of little back streets around the theatre. For quite some time, she followed him at a safe distance, constantly ducking out of sight round corners or behind garden walls. Luckily for her Chang seemed to have no suspicion that he might be followed. He wandered about almost aimlessly, with an air of worried preoccupation.

In fact, Chang was obsessed with carrying out his master's almost impossible command. Conditions could scarcely have been worse. At this hour the streets were almost deserted. Very soon they would be all too busy. Chang's usual hunting time was the hours after midnight, when there was a chance of picking up some solitary girl whose absence would go unnoticed, at least for a time. Where was he to find *two* suitable girls, so soon after dawn?

He was lurking at the mouth of a secluded cul-de-sac when a hansom-cab drove along the street and stopped outside one of the little houses. A girl in cloak and bonnet got out and paid off the driver, and the cab rattled away. Purposefully Chang stalked onward, unaware that Leela was close behind him.

Teresa Hart was a waitress in a gambling club, in Mayfair on the other side of London. Play usually went on until the small hours of the morning, and she often got home to bed at a time when others were getting up. She was fumbling for her key when a shadow fell over her doorway, and a voice said, 'Pleasant are the dreams of morning.'

She whirled round to find Chang bowing, at her. 'You gave me a turn, dearie!'

'Fresh as dew and bright with promise,' said Chang with another bow.

Teresa sighed. She was quite used to being approached by strange gentlemen, particularly those who'd been out for a night on the town. She smiled and shook her head. 'All I want is a pair of kippers, a cup of tea and a bit of kip.'

'Budding lotus of the dawn, Chang has other plans for you.'

'Well, I can tell you what to do with them,' began Teresa spiritedly. Then she broke off. The stranger's eyes seemed to be burning, turning into glowing points of light.

'You will come with me,' said Chang. Teresa followed him.

Leela followed them both back to the theatre, and saw Chang take Teresa into his dressing-room. 'Await my return,' he ordered and went out into the corridor.

From her hiding place, Leela saw Chang pause irresolutely. A burst of laughter came from the auditorium—*female* laughter. As Chang made his way on to the stage, Leela slipped into the dressing-room.

The girl was sitting on a chair staring blankly into space. When Leela passed a hand in front of her face she didn't even blink. Clearly she was under an evil spell. Leela looked round the room, and saw the tall Wardrobe cupboard where Chang kept his costumes. She opened it, and looked back at the hypnotised girl. A plan was forming in her mind ...

Chang peered through a gap in the stage curtain, and saw a band of chattering cleaning women working busily in the otherwise empty theatre, sweeping and dusting between the rows of seats. Most were middle-aged, but a younger one was sweeping the orchestra pit below him. Swiftly Chang dropped down into the pit. The girl looked up opening her mouth to scream. But Chang's eyes burned into hers, and she shut her mouth and stood still. 'Come,' whispered Chang, and the girl followed him out of the pit.

Exultant with success, Chang hurried into his dressing-room. A female figure, head bowed and face obscured by a bonnet, sat waiting in the chair.

Leela waited breathlessly, wondering if her masquerade would be discovered. As she'd hoped, Chang scarcely bothered to look at her. Then to her horror she saw that the wardrobe door was swinging open, revealing Teresa in her petticoat propped inside. But Chang was too impatient to notice. Seizing Leela by the wrist he dragged her into the corridor, where the cleaning girl stood waiting.

Chang bustled the two girls towards the cellar steps. 'Hurry,' he hissed. 'My master must be fed!'

Early morning mist drifted over the river, and a cargo steamer gave a mournful hoot as it prepared to cast off. The old boatman sculled his boat along the bank of the river, wondering about his two strange passengers. The taller of them had an enormous fowling piece balanced across his knees. Where did he think he was, the Norfolk marshes? Someone should tell him London docks was no place for duck shooting. The waterman chewed meditatively on his quid of tobacco, and spat over the side into the Thames. After all, it was none of his business. He'd been handsomely paid, that was all he was worried about.

The Doctor smiled quietly to himself, guessing at the thoughts in the old man's mind. He wondered what the man would think if he knew what they were really hunting.

As they rowed along, the Doctor's keen eyes were constantly scanning the river bank. Suddenly he stood up, making the boat rock dangerously. 'There it is—that creek inlet over there!'

'Do sit down, Doctor,' said Litefoot peevishly. 'I assure you the boatman knows his business.'

The Doctor sat down. 'I always enjoyed messing about in boats!' As usual, the approach of danger found him in tremendous spirits. Litefoot frowned disapprovingly. 'I must say, Doctor, I think this entire enterprise is extremely rash.'

'My dear Litefoot, thanks to your invaluable help, I have a lantern, an excellent pair of waders and probably the most fearsome piece of hand artillery in England. What can possibly go wrong?'

Litefoot looked dubiously at the ancient fowling piece. 'That thing can, for a start. With the amount of buckshot you crammed in there, it'll probably explode in your face.'

'Unthinkable,' said the Doctor solemnly. 'You forget, it was made in England.'

Stolidly the boatman rowed towards the inlet.

*

Greel was busy at the controls of the machine that filled one corner of his underground chamber. There was a hum of power, and the central cabinet began to glow with life. Greel turned from his instruments and studied the waiting victims. 'Where did you get these girls?' he croaked irritably. He pinched Leela's arm, then moved to the second girl.

'Are they unsuitable, Lord?'

Greel examined the cleaning girl's arm. 'This one has muscles like a horse.' he grumbled. 'Oh, I suppose they'll do. At least they're young, their life essence is still strong.'

'They are but peasant wenches, Lord. I took what I could find. It was not easy ...'

Irritably Greel waved him aside. 'Why must you always whine and complain so, Chang? I have given you knowledge that makes you a ruler among your fellows. And what do I ask in return? A few pitiful slatterns who will never be missed.'

'But they *are* missed, Lord,' said Chang. Greel seemed to have no understanding of the terrible risks he was taking. 'Because of your urgent need I was forced to act rashly. One of these girls I took from the theatre above us. Nobody saw. But when she is missed, it will bring the police ever nearer.'

Greel turned away. 'It is of no consequence. Once I have the Time Cabinet I shall leave here.' He thrust the cleaning girl towards Chang. 'Put this one in the dilation chamber, then go. Leave me to my work.'

As Chang led the girl to the machine, Greel glanced at Leela. 'Stay here. I shall not keep you waiting long.' He turned back to his instruments.

The Doctor climbed out of the boat and into the tunnel-like opening of the sewer outlet. Litefoot passed him the gun and the lantern. 'All right, Doctor?'

'All right, Professor.' The Doctor produced a match, and lit his lantern.

Litefoot hesitated. 'I'll wait for you here then?'

'That's right,' said the Doctor cheerfully. 'If I'm still in here at high tide—don't bother to wait any longer.'

'Good luck, then, Doctor.'

'Thank you,' said the Doctor. Gun in one hand. lantern in the other, he disappeared into the darkness of the tunnel.

Leela stood in the corner of Greel's chamber considering her next move. For the moment she was forgotten. Chang had left the cellar, and the strange black-masked being was busy with the victim now in the machine. Leela knew she must act soon if she was to rescue her fellow captive.

Greel fixed the girl in the cabinet, adjusting the two metal spheres so that they rested one each side of her head. He stepped back and looked at her, nodding in satisfaction. 'A few minor readjustments and all will be ready,' he muttered. Once more he bent over the controls.

Leela slipped quietly out of Teresa's dress. The garments hampered her movements, and soon she would be fighting for her life. Stepping out of the dress she stood in camisole and long Victorian pantaloons. Not so practical as the animal-skin costume she wore on her native planet, but it would have to do. She saw that Greel had completed his adjustments, and was standing back for a final check. Leela crept silently towards him and as Greel reached for the master-lever, she sprang.

She was a fraction late, and Greel had time to wrench back the lever before he went down under her attack. There was a fierce hum of power, the machine vibrated and lightning arced between the two metal spheres, passing through the head of the unfortunate cleaning girl. She went rigid, her mouth opening in a silent scream. Gradually her skin began to wither.

Leela and Greel rolled over and over, fighting furiously, and dropped into the culvert that ran down the side of the chamber. Leela landed on top, and gripping Greel by the throat she began throttling him with all her strength. Greel's body went suddenly limp. Leela let go of the scrawny neck, climbed out of the culvert and ran over to the machine. To her horror she saw the body of the cleaning girl had turned into a mummified husk. Leela tried frantically to switch off the machine, but could make nothing of the maze of controls in front of her. The machine gave a final surge of power and the cleaning girl's body disappeared. The vibrating died down, and the machine seemed to switch itself off, the grisly process complete. A retort-like container connected to the machine glowed brightly, as it filled with some luminous fluid.

Leela realised that all she could do now was to save herself. She climbed the ladder, but the opening to the cellar was closed. Clinging to the top of the ladder Leela began heaving desperately at the trapdoor.

Below her, Greel stirred, and crept feebly from the culvert. He crawled painfully across the floor and pulled himself upright, snatching a laser-pistol from a bench.

Leela felt a blast of heat and a chunk of stonework beside her head exploded into dust. She dropped catlike from the ladder and rolled over between the benches for shelter, dropping into the culvert where she had fought with Greel.

There was another blast, and a piece of the wall beside her was blown away. Leela could see only one chance of escape. Hurling the nearest container at Greel's head to distract his aim, she squeezed through the gap below the bars at the end of the culvert. Wriggling through she dropped into the darkness of the sewer tunnel, just as another shot blasted the stonework. She scrambled to her feet and flattened herself into a niche in the tunnel wall, and waited panting.

In the chamber, Greel moved to follow her through the culvert, then drew back. The girl had been terrifyingly strong, and even with the laser-pistol he would be at a disadvantage in the darkness. An evil smile twisted the distorted lips beneath Greel's leather mask. There was a better way.

He hobbled to the lever that controlled his feeding-hatch and pulled it. The hatch slid open. Snatching up his hammer Greel beat again and again on the gong. The booming notes echoed away down the tunnel. The sound would bring the giant rats scuttling for their meat. But this time there would be no meat. Only Leela.

Greel gave a maniacal laugh. 'When my beauties find her,' he snarled, 'she will wish she had died here in my machine.'

From somewhere in the sewer tunnel came the hungry squeal of a giant rat.

9

IN THE JAWS OF THE RAT

Leela stood waiting silently for a moment, the sound of the gong ringing in her ears. As it faded she heard an angry squealing. She hurried along the sewer tunnel away from the terrifying sound.

Lantern held high, the Doctor splashed through the murky stream that flowed down the centre of the sewer. He came to a T-junction and paused to review his mental picture of the map he had drawn on Lite foot's table-cloth. Taking the left turn he splashed steadily on his way. If his calculations were correct, the cellar hideout was very near.

Sitting in the rowing boat just outside the sewer outlet, Professor Litefoot looked at his watch for the tenth time. The tide would be rising soon. The Doctor's time was almost up. Litefoot sighed, and put another match to his pipe. He tossed the spent match into the river, and watched it float away. Hunched over his oars, the boatman spat impassively into the water.

Meanwhile a brightly painted horse-drawn cart was drawing up outside Professor Litefoot's door. A policeman stepped suspiciously out of the shrubbery. 'Here, what's all this?'

The pig-tailed Chinese driver appeared to speak no English. He chatted incomprehensibly, and pointed to the side of the cart, on which was written, 'LIMEHOUSE LAUNDRY CO.' He pointed to the porch where there stood a wicker hamper, the same words written on the label on its side. He opened the back of his cart, and pointed to an identical hamper, making crossover gestures with his hands.

The constable grinned. 'I get you, Johnny. Clean laundry come, dirty washing go away!'

The Chinese bowed and smiled. He took the basket from his van, and put it on the porch, lifted the basket on the porch into the back of his van. Jumping into the driving seat, he cracked his whip and drove away.

Wondering vaguely why the Chinese had such an affinity with laundries, the constable resumed his patrol around the house. As he moved away, the lid of the wicker basket moved slightly, and then became still. Now there was a tiny gap between basket and lid—just big enough for someone to look out.

Arriving at the theatre to start his day's work, Casey was scandalised to see a half-dressed female run out of Chang's dressing-room. 'Hey, you,' he called. 'What do you think you're doing?'

The girl stared blankly at him. 'Where am I? What happened to me last night? I can't remember.'

Casey grabbed her by the arm. 'I'll remember *you* all right if anything's missing.'

Indignantly Teresa pulled away. 'You keep your hands off me, I'm a lady,' she screamed.

Jago came on the scene, to find a fine old shouting match going on; 'Now then, Casey, what's the trouble?'

'No trouble, Mr Jago, sir. Just seeing this lady off the premises.'

Jago turned sternly to Teresa, but she ignored him. She was staring in terror as a poster on the wall—the poster that bare Chang's face. 'It was him,' she gasped. 'Oh my lord, it was him! Let me out of this place!' She turned and ran out of the still-open stage door.

Jago said thoughtfully 'Remember this incident, Casey. It may have some relevance to the investigation.'

'What's that, sir?'

'The investigation, Casey,' whispered Jago mysteriously. 'Last night I made the acquaintance of a very high-up gentleman, an amateur investigator called in by Scotland Yard.' Jago's chest swelled with pride. '*I* am assisting him, Casey!'

Casey's eyes widened. 'No!'

'I am. He has asked me to watch, Casey. And I am watching—everywhere!' Jago disappeared into his office. Casey shrugged wonderingly, and disappeared backstage. After a moment Chang stepped from the doorway where he had been watching and hurried towards the cellar steps.

The moment he entered Greel's chamber a storm of rage broke over his head. 'Fool,' screamed Greel. 'Stupid incompetent fool!' Angrily he told of Leela's attack on him, and of her escape into the sewers. 'She was a tigress. Had I not feigned death, she would have killed me!'

'I can explain, Lord,' pleaded Chang. 'She substituted herself for the girl I had chosen. And I recognise your description of her. She was with the Doctor.'

Greel hobbled to a metal chair close to his attraction machine, and fastened electrodes to his wasted body. He operated controls and the retort glowed brightly and then faded again. There was a rushing sound as the life essence of the sacrificed girl flooded into Greel's body. Greel waited for a moment, then stood up. As he removed the electrodes he could feel the strength returning to his body. But he knew all too well that the effect was only temporary. Soon he would weaken again, and it would need more donors, and yet more, to keep him from wasting away. The knowledge added to his anger, and he turned once more on the unhappy Chang.

'You have failed me, Li H'sen. You know that until I have the Time Cabinet I can never be whole, never be cured of this wasting sickness ...'

'Lord, hear me,' pleaded Chang. 'I would lay down my life in your service. You shall have the Time Cabinet tonight, the plans are already made ...'

'Fail me once more and I shall dismiss you, Chang. I cannot leave my fate in such blundering hands.'

Chang fell to his knees. 'Great One, I shall find this Doctor. I shall strike him down for the harm he has done you!'

Greel waved him away. 'Do not beg, unworthy one. Go!'

Leela ran frantically through the sewers. From somewhere behind her came the savage squealing of the giant rats. Summoned by the gong, they had come rushing to Greel's feeding hatch. Leela had managed to dodge them, hiding in an alcove as the great grey shapes came rushing by. Finding no meat at the grating the monsters had begun casting about the tunnels.

Leela ran blindly on. Since she had no idea where she was or where she was heading she was as likely to run into one of the creatures as to escape from them. Her only hope was to keep on the move.

Suddenly she heard a fierce trumpeting squeal close behind her. One of the monsters had picked up her scent.

Not far away, the Doctor heard the squeal, He paused to check his fowling piece, then moved towards the sound.

Leela sped on through the darkness. She could hear scurrying footsteps behind her, and the angry screams of the giant rat. She tripped and fell, and struggled desperately to her feet again. Wet and filthy now, she staggered on. A tiny point of light appeared in the tunnel far ahead. With the last of her failing strength, she reeled towards it.

The Doctor heard the terrifying roar of the giant rat. Calmly he placed his lantern on a ledge and raised the gun to his shoulder.

A shape loomed up, the Doctor sighted along the barrel of the gun … and realised that the shape was Leela!

Hastily lowering the gun, he called, 'Leela, it's me!'

Leela paused for a moment, gasping with relief—and the giant rat sprang out of the darkness and seized her leg. She gave a despairing scream, as the rat began dragging her back along the tunnel.

10

A PLAN TO KILL THE DOCTOR

For an agonised moment the Doctor hesitated. To shoot with the rat and Leela so close together meant taking a terrible risk. But there was no alternative. He dropped to one knee, threw the gun to his shoulder, aimed and fired.

There was a great boom of an explosion, and the recoil of the heavy weapon made him stagger back. Clouds of black smoke poured from the barrel of the gun, and peering through the haze, the Doctor saw Leela crawling towards him. Behind her the giant rat lay on its side, a gaping hole in its chest, lips drawn back from the yellow fangs in a dying snarl.

The Doctor helped Leela to rise. 'Are you all right?'

Leela rubbed her leg. 'I think so—the teeth just bruised me. Some use in these stupid clothes after all.'

'You were lucky.'

'I deserve to die, Doctor. I had the chance to kill our enemy, and I failed.'

The Doctor took off his cape and wrapped it round Leela's shoulders. 'What chance? Where?'

A distant roar came echoing down the tunnel. The Doctor picked up his gun. 'The trouble with this thing is it takes about half an hour to load. Come on, Leela. You can tell me what you've been up to on the way back.'

With preparations for the evening meal well under way, Jago decided to slip out to the pub across the street for a little liquid refreshment.

248

He was just leaving the theatre by the stage door when he met Li H'sen Chang, who was just arriving. 'Here already, Mr Chang?' said Jago jovially. 'I shall have to start charging you rent for that dressing-room.'

Chang smiled coldly. 'There is much to prepare before the performance, Mr Jago.'

'Yes, of course, of course. The art that conceals art, eh? Tell me, Mr Chang ...' Jago paused awkwardly. 'About last night ...'

'Yes?'

'Think I must be working too hard, overcrowding the old brainbox. I know I spoke to you about your contract, but I've forgotten how we left matters ...'

'I am considering your new offer.'

'Ah, I see. A generous offer, was it, Mr Chang?'

'Merely—reasonable.' Chang turned to go to his dressing-room, then paused. 'Incidentally, I shall be appearing tonight without Mr Sin. He is—indisposed.'

Jago chuckled. 'Very droll. I shall treasure that witticism, Mr Chang. Indisposed, eh? I suppose the poor little fellow's got a touch of woodworm, eh?'

Ignoring Jago's little joke, Chang turned and headed for the dressing-room. Jago mopped his brow and plunged through the stage door. Somehow after his meeting with Chang, he needed a drink more than ever.

The Doctor was sitting wrong way round on one of Litefoot's dining-room chairs, folded arms resting on the high back, chin resting on his arms. He was staring fixedly at the Time Cabinet, as if hoping to fathom its secrets by sheer will power. Leela was warming her hands at the blazing fire, still swathed in the Doctor's cape. She was telling him about the girl who had been sacrificed in Greel's machine.

'She aged and withered, Doctor. Her skin went dry, like old leaves. The machine did it to her. Then she vanished ...'

'Dry, like old leaves,' repeated the Doctor thoughtfully. 'It sounds like organic distillation. Her life-essence was drained away.'

'Why? What is our enemy doing?'

The Doctor jumped up. 'He doesn't *know* what he's doing,' he shouted in sudden anger. 'He's a madman. A monstrously deranged sociopath!'

The door opened and Litefoot staggered in. He was loaded down with parcels, which he passed over to Leela with a sigh of relief. 'There's your new outfit, my dear. I hope it's suitable. If you'd like to take these things upstairs Mrs Hudson will help you change.'

Leela went out with the parcels, and Litefoot sank into a chair, mopping his brow. 'Dashed embarrassing business, that, choosing togs for a young lady. You have to be jolly careful it's the right fashion. Clothes matter to women.'

'They do?' said the Doctor abstractedly. He resumed his study of the Time Cabinet, running his hands over the surface. There was a saucer-shaped depression in the middle of what was presumably the door. 'A keyhole,' muttered the Doctor. 'But where's the key?'

'Still trying to get that thing open, Doctor?'

'I'm trying to place the exact period. It can only be opened by a key of the correct molecular combination.'

'Heard you shouting as I opened the front door. Something about a madman ...'

'Yes. Weng-Chiang. He's probably got the key.'

'Weng-Chiang? He was one of the ancient Chinese gods.'

'This Weng-Chiang's no god. He must have arrived in your Time Zone in this contraption.' The Doctor tapped the cabinet. 'What do you know of its history?'

'It was a gift to Mama from His Highness, T'ungchi. Been in the family for years.'

'You're lucky he hasn't traced it before now,' said the Doctor broodingly.

Leela came back resplendent in a new gown.

'Charming,' said Litefoot immediately. 'Don't you think so, Doctor?'

The Doctor focused his attention on Leela. 'What? Oh yes, quite delightful. I shall be proud to escort you to the Palace Theatre tonight.'

Leela was pleased in spite of herself. The clothes of this century were ridiculous and impractical—but they were rather becoming in their way. 'Then we're going to the theatre after all, Doctor?'

'That's right. We've an appointment with the great Li H'sen Chang.' The Doctor beamed, cheered up as always by the prospect of action. 'Tell you what, Leela. If you're a very good girl—I might even buy you an orange!'

Jago stood backstage, watching the bustle of activity all around him. The first house had gone off well, and now it was almost time for the second to begin. As always, once the performance got under way, the evening seemed to flash by at an incredible pace.

He went on to the stage itself, and peered through the gap in the curtains. The house was filling up nicely—though disappointingly there was still no sign of the one person he'd most hoped to see.

'Looking for someone, Mr Jago?' said a familiar voice behind him.

Jago turned. 'The Doctor, Casey. My collaborator and fellow-sleuth. No sign of him yet. Oh well, he'll be here, Casey. I'll lay a guinea to a gooseberry on it!'

Behind them, in the centre of the stage, Chang was checking the operation of a trap-door that was used in his act. He straightened up at Jago's words, and went to his dressing-room. He took a shining nickel-plated revolver from a drawer and began to load it. If the Doctor did come tonight, Chang would be waiting.

There was the sound of horses' hooves in the road outside, and Litefoot went to the window. 'There you are, Doctor, your cab's arrived.'

The Doctor was putting on his cape, and Litefoot turned to help Leela with her cloak. 'You'll need to wrap up. Fog's getting thick again.'

The Doctor paused at the door. 'I know there's a policeman outside, Professor, but don't just rely on him. Lock and bar your doors, as soon as we've gone—and keep your revolver handy.'

Litefoot saw them into the hall. 'You really think those scoundrels may return?'

'That Cabinet is vitally important to their master. They'll stop at nothing to get their hands on it. So be on your guard, Professor.'

'Don't worry, Doctor, I'll be ready for them. They won't catch George Litefoot napping a second time!'

Litefoot opened the front door and watched Leela and the Doctor get into the waiting cab. The driver cracked his whip, the cab rattled away and the patrolling policeman touched his helmet in salute, as it disappeared into the fog.

Litefoot noticed the laundry basket on the porch and thought vaguely that the laundry had delivered a day early. He dragged the hamper through the front door and left it in the hall. Mrs Hudson would see to it in the morning. Returning to the sitting-room, Litefoot put some more coal on the fire and poured himself a large whisky and soda. Glass in one hand, revolver in the other, he settled down for his night's vigil.

Greel was busy dismantling his distillation machine. He paid no attention to Chang, who stood bowing low before him.

Unable to believe that his god would really desert him, Chang said, 'Lord, if this infidel Doctor does come here tonight, then I swear I shall kill him.'

Greel gave a mirthless laugh. 'It is far more likely that he will kill you.'

'No, Lord, I have made a plan to kill the Doctor in public, as a sacrifice to appease your wrath. To prove that I, above all others, am your true servant.'

Greel waved him away. 'You are unworthy to serve me, Li H'sen Chang. I shall lead the Tong myself, and take my own measures to recover the Time Cabinet. Now go!'

Chang bowed low, and turned to the ladder, more determined than ever to carry out his plan. Surely his god would forgive him ... once the Doctor was dead.

The second house was just about to start, and Jago was still scanning the audience. 'There he is, Casey. Look!'

Jago pointed upwards. Leela and the Doctor were just entering the 'Royal' box, the one just beside the stage. 'Trust him to take the best seats in the house,' said Jago admiringly.

Casey stared at the Doctor's tall figure. 'Doesn't look much like a detective to me.'

'Well, he's not going to wear a bowler hat and big boots, is he? High-up secret investigator, he is, a man of a thousand faces.'

'Who's the girl?'

'Window-dressing. Part of his disguise.' Jago turned away from the curtain. 'Think I'll just pop along and let him know we're standing by down here.' Jago's mind returned abruptly to the business of everyday life. 'Now then Casey, have you got that trap-door ready?'

'Not yet, Mr Jago, sir.'

'Then you'd better see to it, my lad—unless you want Mr Chang after you, for ruining his act.' Jago hurried away.

Casey called after him. 'The thing is, Mr Jago, it means going down into that cellar ...'

But Jago was gone. Casey sighed, and moved slowly towards the cellar steps.

The Doctor and Leela were installed in their comfortable box. Leela gazed round the fast-filling theatre with keen interest. Although she didn't really know what was going on, her keen senses were already picking up vibrations of pleasure and excitement in the air. It reminded her of the tribal festivals of her own people.

The Doctor was glancing through the programme when he heard a low 'Psst!' from somewhere near the floor. He looked down and saw Jago crawling into the box on his hands and knees. The Doctor smiled. 'Good evening, Mr Jago.'

'A pleasure to welcome you to my theatre, Doctor—and your charming companion.'

'Thank you. Are you quite comfortable down there?'

'I know the value of discretion, Doctor. May I ask if you've made any further deductions?'

'Quite a few, Mr Jago, quite a few.'

'I thought as much. No doubt you're on the point of solving the mystery of the missing maidens?'

'I expect further developments shortly,' said the Doctor mysteriously.

Jago was thrilled with the romance and excitement of it all. 'Well, if you need any help, I hope I know where my duty lies.'

The Doctor reached down and patted him on the shoulder. 'You're a brave man, Mr Jago. I knew I could count on you.'

'Still, I don't suppose you'll actually be needing me,' added Jago hastily. 'I expect you've got the place surrounded, eh? Armed men scattered in the audience?'

The Doctor shook his head.

Jago paled. 'You mean there's nobody?'

'Nobody,' said the Doctor solemnly. 'When the moments of danger comes, Mr Jago, you and I will face our destiny, shoulder to shoulder.'

'Oh, corks,' said Jago faintly, and backed slowly out of the box.

In fear and trembling, and working as fast as he could, Casey finished preparing the mechanism of the trap-door that formed part of Chang's act. His task completed, he was hurrying from the gloomy cellar when he heard a grinding sound from the corner arch. Terrified, Casey spun round. A black-cloaked figure was climbing up through the trap-door in the floor. It wore a loose-brimmed black hat, its face was entirely covered in a black-leather mask and, incongruously, it was carrying a carpet-bag.

Casey made a terrified dart for the cellar stairs, but the apparition saw him. Dropping the bag it bounded after him with a terrifying snarl. Casey's foot slipped on the bottom stair, he fell and the apparition was upon him. As its skinny hands reached out, Casey heard faint sounds of music from the stage above. Then everything was drowned out by the frightened pounding of his heart …

11

DEATH ON STAGE

The soprano concluded her patriotic song, and exited to enthusiastic applause. The curtains were drawn and Jago appeared in front of them. 'And now, ladies and gentlemen, it is my privilege to introduce to you, in his extended season here at the Palace, in the second of two appearances here this evening, someone whose legendary legerdemain has entertained all the crowned heads of Europe. Here to baffle and bewilder you, the world's foremost magician, straight from the mysterious Orient—ladies and gentlemen, Li H'sen Chang!'

The curtains drew back to reveal a painted backdrop intended to represent an oriental palace. Jago pointed dramatically to the centre of the empty stage and stepped hastily back. There was a brilliant flash, a cloud of smoke, and suddenly Chang was there, bowing low in his Oriental robes. 'Humble Chang is most honoured at this kind reception.' He snapped his fingers and the Chinese assistant Lee carried on a table upon which rested a pack of cards and a nickel-plated revolver. 'First tlick velly simple,' announced Chang. During his act he often spoke in the pidgin English that Englishmen expected from the Chinese. He picked up the cards from the table. 'Will someone take cards please?' Chang walked across to the side of the stage until he stood directly looking up at the Doctor's box. 'You sir? Please catchee cards?'

He tossed the pack into the air and the Doctor caught it. Chang bowed. 'Kindly assist humble magician by finding ace of diamonds and holding up so everyone can see!'

The Doctor found the card and held it up to the audience.

Chang bowed his thanks. 'Ah, so! Now please to put card back in middle of pack, and hold whole pack up with finger and thumb.'

Once more the Doctor obeyed. Chang took the revolver from the table. 'Chang will now shoot magic bullet through ace of diamonds, without hitting other cards. Honourable gentleman will please remain very still.'

Chang levelled the revolver from the stage. The Doctor stood upright in the box, the cards held before his chest like a target.

Leela looked worriedly up at him. 'Doctor, be careful ...'

The Doctor smiled. He knew that Chang intended to try to kill him. But he also knew that the magician wouldn't do it too obviously. This was merely a preliminary challenge, a test of nerve. Deliberately the Doctor moved the pack of cards so it was directly over his left-hand heart.

There was an excited murmur from the crowd, and Chang held up a reproving hand. 'Please to be very still. I shot fifteen peasants trying to learn this trick!'

Slowly Chang raised the revolver and fired. The Doctor stood quite still, and Chang called, 'If most courageous gentleman will now look for ace of diamonds?'

The Doctor found the card and held it up. There was a neat hole drilled through the centre. The crowd gave a round of applause, and the Doctor looked down at Chang. 'Oh, very good! Anything else I can do?'

Chang bowed once more. 'If honourable gentleman will please bring cards down to stage, I have further interesting demonstration, requiring assistant with nerves of steel.'

The Doctor gave Leela a reassuring smile, and left the box. Meanwhile, Lee, Chang's assistant, was wheeling a metal cabinet on stage. Chang flung open the doors and rapped on the sides, demonstrating its solid construction. The Doctor appeared at the side of the stage and Chang beckoned him forward. 'Now I will ask eager volunteer to step into Cabinet of Death.'

Chang smiled as the Doctor moved slowly towards the cabinet. He was banking on the fact that, as with the card trick, the Doctor would be too proud to refuse a public challenge. Once inside the cabinet, the Doctor would be doomed. It was a simple enough trick. The 'victim', usually a chorus-girl, stepped inside the cabinet, which was then closed and locked. Once inside, she pressed a hidden catch and the trick floor of the cabinet slid back. The cabinet was positioned directly over a trap-door in the stage, and at a signal from Chang, Casey would operate the trap-door so that the girl could drop out of the cabinet and under the stage. Chang would then pass swords through the special slits in the side of the empty cabinet. A few minutes later, he would withdraw the swords and give another signal. The girl would come up through the trap-door, there would be a bang and a flash, Chang would open the door and she would step from the cabinet unharmed.

That was the way things *usually* went. This time Chang planned a very different ending. Once the Doctor was inside the cabinet, Chang would thrust the razor sharp swords through the slits—with the Doctor still inside. The Doctor wouldn't know how to find the secret catch—and even if he did, Chang had no intention of giving Casey the signal to open the trap-door. The Doctor would be executed publicly, in full sight of his friends. And no one would be more horrified than Chang at the tragic accident—caused of course by an unfortunate jamming of the equipment.

The Doctor was at the cabinet by now, and at a nod from Chang, Lee attempted to thrust him inside. The Doctor dodged, Lee stumbled, and suddenly found that *he* was inside the cabinet. Instantly the Doctor closed and locked the doors, and turning to the crowd he gave an exaggerated bow. A burst of laughter came from the crowd. Chang glowered, but soon regained control of himself. 'The bird has flown. Alas, it seems that one of us is yellow!'

The crowd greeted Chang's sally with another burst of laughter— and no one laughed louder than the Doctor. Chang realised that the Doctor had outwitted him. All he could do now was go on with the trick.

Chang stretched out his hand and a long sharp sword seemed to appear from thin air. 'Play close attention ladies and gentlemen.' He swished the sword in the air and thudded it point-down into the stage to demonstrate its sharpness. The thud was in reality a signal to Casey down below. It should have been followed by the faint rumble that meant the trap was open. Chang listened, but heard nothing. Anxiously he drew out the sword, and thudded it into the boards once more.

*

257

Below the stage, Greel heard the repeated signal. He had formed a grim plan of his own. He would seal his rejection of Chang by punishing him with a public loss of face—the most humiliating fate that any Chinese can suffer. He readied out and pulled the lever, and Lee tumbled through the trap-door. At the sight of Greel, he prostrated himself on the ground in terror. 'You will serve me, now,' croaked Greel. 'Now listen to my instructions. The sacred things in the secret chamber must be taken to the House of the Dragon, and the Time Cabinet recovered. Summon your brothers of the Tong to help you. Meanwhile I shall deal with our great magician …'

Chang heard the faint vibration of the trap, and sure that the cabinet was empty, he continued with his act. Keeping up a steady stream of comic patter, he began passing sword after sword through the slits in the cabinet. 'In my country,' he hissed, 'this is known as the death of the thousand cuts.' When the last sword was in place, Chang bowed, and spun the cabinet round on its base to reveal that the swords had passed completely through.

He replaced the cabinet and began removing the swords. As he took the last one out he gestured to the Doctor. 'Now, if my new assistant will kindly open the cabinet?'

The Doctor threw open the cabinet door—and Casey fell out on to the stage. There was laughter from the crowd, which turned to uneasy murmuring as the huddled body did not move. A woman screamed …

In the wings Jago grabbed his chief stagehand. 'Get that curtain down—quick!'

As the curtains began to close, Jago ran out in front of them and made a brief, incoherent announcement. 'Ladies and gentlemen … unfortunate accident. No cause for alarm. Performance will continue shortly …' He waved frantically at the conductor and the orchestra struck up a rousing tune.

Jago hurried backstage to find the Doctor kneeling by Casey's body. 'For heaven's sake, what happened, Doctor?'

'He's dead—died of fright. Poor chap must have had a weak heart.'

Leela ran on to the stage. 'What happened, Doctor? Did the magician kill him?'

*

The Doctor shook his head. 'No, Chang was as surprised as anyone.' He looked round. 'Incidentally—where's he got to?'

Despairing, Chang looked round Greel's now-empty secret chamber. The equipment, the distillation chamber, everything was gone. 'The great lord Weng-Chiang has deserted me,' sobbed Chang, and fell to his knees.

He was still kneeling, head bowed, when the Doctor and Leela came down the ladder. He looked up at them apathetically. 'It seems you've been left to carry the can, Chang,' said the Doctor.

Chang raised a hand to his mouth and the Doctor pounced, tugging the dragon-seal ring from his finger. 'No poison for you. There are questions to be answered.'

Chang got to his feet, struggling to recover his dignity. 'I will say nothing. It is time for me to rejoin my ancestors.'

'Tell me about Weng-Chiang,' insisted the Doctor. 'Where's he gone now?'

Chang looked vaguely at him. 'Back to his palace in the sky, perhaps. He was displeased with me ...'

'His mind is broken,' whispered Leela.

The Doctor stared hypnotically into Chang's dazed eyes, willing him to answer. 'You know he's not really a god, don't you? When did you meet?'

Chang's voice became a chant. 'He came like a god, in a glowing cabinet of fire. He came forth and collapsed, weakened by his journey. I was only a humble peasant, but I gave him sanctuary in my hut.'

'What about the Time Cabinet?'

'The soldiers of the Emperor came upon it by chance. They took it away, while my lord was still sick. When he began to recover we searched for it. We learned that it had been given as a gift to a foreign devil-woman who had left the shores of China. Ever since we have searched for the great Cabinet of Weng-Chiang. The god is still sick. He will not be whole until it is found.'

Jago clattered down the ladder and looked round the chamber in astonishment. 'Well, cover me in creosote, I never knew this was here. A cellar under the cellar!'

'Doctor, look out,' called Leela, but it was too late.

Taking advantage of the distraction, Chang ducked into the culvert through which Leela had once made her escape and disappeared into the sewers. Leela started to follow him, but the Doctor restrained her. 'No, Leela.'

'But he'll escape,'

'There's no escape that way. He's gone to join his ancestors.'

From somewhere in the sewers came the scream of a giant rat.

Chang was running frantically through the sewers when he heard the scream. It was somewhere in front of him, very close. He turned and began running towards the hidden chamber, but it was too late. A giant rat sprang out of the darkness, and bore him down. Its teeth closed on his leg, and it began dragging him back towards its lair.

Jago stared around him in fascination. 'So the Celestial Chang really was involved in these Machiavellian machinations?'

'Up to his epicanthic eyelids,' said the Doctor solemnly.

'Well I'll go to Australia!' said Jago. A scream from the sewer cut him short. 'What in the name of heaven ...'

The Doctor turned away. 'You'll need a new top of the bill, I'm afraid.'

'Chang?' whispered Jago.

The Doctor nodded. 'There are giant rats roaming those sewers, Mr Jago. You'd better warn the authorities to seal off this whole section. Cyanide gas will probably settle the brutes ...'

Searching for clues, Leela flung open a corner cabinet. 'Look, Doctor. Women's clothes, lots of them.'

'All that's left of the victims,' said the Doctor grimly.

Jago stared at him. 'The missing girls! So it was Chang?'

'Not Chang. His master—the monstrous crazed maniac who caused all this.'

Leela pointed to the empty corner. 'The death-machine has gone, Doctor.'

'Precisely. He plans to start all over again somewhere else. I've got to find him.'

'But he could be anywhere.' Leela looked at the pathetic bundle of clothes. 'Why did he destroy those girls?'

'He needed their life-essence to survive,' said the Doctor impatiently. 'Unfortunately, the more he absorbs, the more grossly deformed he becomes.'

Leela tried to translate all this into terms she could understand. 'You mean he is like a water-bag with a hole in it—pouring in more water only makes the hole grow bigger?'

The Doctor looked at her in mild surprise. 'That's exactly right—a very good analogy, Leela.'

'What made him like that?'

'An experiment that went wrong,' said the Doctor slowly. 'A dangerous experiment in time travel. It upset the balance of his metabolism. Now he's fighting to restore it by drawing on the life-force of others. Come on, Leela, we'd better get back to that Time Cabinet.' He climbed the ladder and Leela followed him.

Left on his own, Jago was struck by sudden inspiration. 'Got it,' he said. 'I'll run tours of inspection. See the lair of the phantom—a bob a nob!'

Litefoot's head nodded on to his chest, and' he awoke with a sudden start. The coal fire in the grate had burned low. He must have been asleep for quite some time.

He got stiffly to his feet, went over to the window and drew back the curtain. In the circle of light cast by the lamp over the porch, he saw the patrolling policeman, stamping his feet to keep warm. Litefoot felt a pang of sympathy for the poor fellow out in the cold and fog. Reassured, he put some more coal on the fire and poked it into a blaze, then sank back into his comfortable chair.

Outside, the policeman yawned and stretched, and decided to take a turn around the house. Daft idea anyway, all this, he thought. What did old Professor Litefoot need guarding for?

Bored and sleepy, the policeman didn't notice the lithe black-clad figures slipping through the shrubbery and moving ever closer to the house. As he turned to begin his patrol, a hatchet spun out of the darkness and thudded into the back of his neck. He dropped without a sound, and the servants of the Tong began converging on the house.

In the hall, the lid of the laundry basket suddenly flew off. Mr Sin sat upright, eyes wide open, knife in hand.

12

THE HUNT FOR GREEL

The Doctor paid off the cab driver, who raised his whip in salute and drove away. Leela made straight for Litefoot's front door, but the Doctor put a hand on her arm. 'Wait.'

'What's the matter?'

The Doctor pointed. 'Over there.' A booted foot was projecting from a clump of shrubbery. They went over and found the body of the constable, thrust carelessly out of sight.

Leela whirled to face the house. 'Our enemies are here!'

'I doubt it. They've probably been and gone.'

They went to the front door, and found it slightly ajar. The Doctor pointed to the array of locks and bolts on the inside. 'No sign of forced entry. Someone let them in.'

They found Litefoot sprawled on the floor of the sitting-room, blood trickling from an ugly bruise on his forehead.

Leela pointed. 'The Time Cabinet, Doctor. It's gone!'

The pigtailed driver cracked his whip and the black carriage rattled over the cobbles. The Time Cabinet was strapped on the roof. Inside the carriage sat Greel, Mr Sin lolling beside him. Greel's wasted body was shaking with maniacal laughter.

Litefoot could tell them little when he revived. He had been dozing in his chair, the door had been flung open and a horde of black-clad figures had overwhelmed him.

'Chinese Tong-wallahs,' said Litefoot indignantly. 'Funny thing is, I didn't hear 'em breaking in.'

262

The Doctor was standing in the doorway, looking at the laundry basket in the hall. 'Was one of them a midget, by any chance?'

'That's right. How the devil did you know?'

'Elementary, my dear Litefoot. He arrived in your laundry basket, and let the others in.'

Leela went on bathing Litefoot's forehead. 'That creature was here before, Doctor. I fought with it in this room.'

'That's right.' The Doctor sank wearily into an armchair. 'I've worked out what all this is about, now. Everything fits. Chang's Mr Sin is really the Peking Homunculus. It was made in Peking, and presented as a gift to the Commissioner of the Icelandic Alliance, somewhere around the year five thousand.'

'Preposterous!' snorted Litefoot.

Leela waved him to silence. It wasn't often the Doctor was in the mood to explain anything. 'Sssh! Go on, Doctor!'

The Doctor told a horrifying story of war and carnage in the far-distant future. Much of it Leela and the Professor found hard to follow. Somehow it was all tied up with the sinister little manikin. 'It was supposed to be a toy, a plaything for the Commissioner's children. It was operated by a series of magnetic circuits and a small computer, with one organic component—the cerebral cortex of a pig.'

The Doctor paused, remembering the future. 'In reality it was an assassination weapon. It massacred the Commissioner and all his family. That's what set off World War Six. Somehow the thing has been brought from that age to this.'

Litefoot poured himself a large brandy. ''Pon my soul, Doctor, this is a dashed queer story. Time travel, eh?'

'Unsuccessful time travel, Professor. Findecker's discovery of the double nexus particle sent human science of that era into a technological cul-de-sac.'

'Ah,' said Litefoot wisely. To Leela he whispered, 'Are you following any of this?'

'Not a word!'

Unaware that he had left his audience far behind him, the Doctor went on. 'Clearly this pig-thing is still alive. It needs a human operator of course, but the mental feedback is so intense the swinish instinct becomes dominant. It hates humanity, and revels in carnage ...'

Leela decided she'd had all the explanation she could handle. 'So what must we do now?'

'Find the homunculus and destroy it. More important, find its operator, and see he doesn't sacrifice more girls to stay alive.'

'How?'

The Doctor went out into the hall, tore the laundry label from the basket, and carried it back into the room. 'Rundall Buildings,' he read. 'Do you know the place, Professor?'

'I'm afraid I do. It's at the centre of the most notorious part of the East End, a place of vice and squalor, long overdue for clearance.'

'It might be cleared very quickly,' said the Doctor grimly. 'Weng-Chiang, as he calls himself, is like a monkey playing with matches in a gun-powder barrel. A scientific ignoramus who doesn't appreciate the dangers of Zygma energy. If he tampers with that Time Cabinet he'll blow up most of London.'

This was a danger that Litefoot could understand. 'Then we must stop him, Doctor.' He rose to his feet, staggered and sat down again hurriedly.

The Doctor put a hand on his shoulder. 'You're still not fit, Professor. You must stay here and rest. Leela and I will go.'

'You can't take a young woman to that place! At this hour of the night she'll witness the vilest scenes of depravity.'

'She's already encountered Weng-Chiang himself, Professor. And nothing could be viler than that.'

Mr Sin sat on his little throne, following the movements of his master with black glittering eyes. Greel stood beside the Time Cabinet, running his fingers caressingly over its surface. He looked round him in satisfaction. He was in the secret headquarters prepared for him by the Tong, a long low room, ornately furnished in the style of a Chinese temple. At the far end steps led up to a huge Dragon idol on a raised dais, its huge saucer-eyes glaring balefully over the room. Greel's scientific equipment had been reassembled on the waiting laboratory benches, and all around, the black-clad servants of the Tong prostrated themselves before their god, the great Weng-Chiang.

'Liberation, Mr Sin,' said Greel exultantly. 'Freedom! I can become whole again. How I have dreamt of this moment. I can be free of this dying body, refashion myself in some distant time and place. Now that we have the Time Cabinet, we shall not stay long in this barbarous century.' He snapped his fingers: Lee, who had now replaced Chang as Greel's chief servant, hurried forward and bowed. 'The bag,' said Greel impatiently.

'What bag, Lord?'

'I brought it from the chamber beneath the cellar. I ordered you to bring it here, with the other sacred things.'

Lee bowed his head. 'Lord, there was much trouble when the body of the man Casey was found. Many people came to the cellar. I fled. The bag was left behind.'

Greel smashed him to the ground with one savage blow. 'You know the penalty for failing me. Up—and take the sting of the scorpion!'

Greel produced a jewelled box in which lay a small black pill. He stared hynotically at Lee who reached out, took the pill from the box and swallowed it. His body went rigid, he gave a single choked cry and fell dead at Greel's feet.

Greel glared malevolently at the terrified group. 'You have seen the penalty of failure,' he hissed. 'Now, return to the theatre, and *bring me that bag!*'

Jago stood in the theatre cellar looking thoughtfully around him. The evening had ended in disaster as far as the performance was concerned. With the death of poor Casey, and the disappearance of Chang, he had been forced to cancel the performance—*and* refund the audience's money. Before he could open again he had to find a top-ranking act from somewhere to put on the top of the bill. Despite all these problems, Jago was in a cheerful mood. The more he thought about it, the more convinced he became that his latest bright idea was a real winner.

'Shilling a head,' he muttered to himself. 'Guinea a head, more like it! Tours round the lair of the phantom! Personally conducted by yours truly, one of the heroes of the whole affair. The ladies will swoon in my arms! I'll get all this junk cleared out, call in the Electric Light Company ...' Full of plans for a prosperous future, Jago began striding about the cellar—and fell sprawling over some bulky object. Picking himself up, he saw that the obstacle was a bulky carpet-bag. It was incredibly heavy, and it took all Jago's strength to lug it clear of the pile of junk. He opened it and found it full of strange-looking machinery. Resting on top was a saucer-shaped crystal pendant. Jago shook his head wonderingly, and closed the bag again. He stood thinking for a moment. The trap-door to Greel's chamber had been left standing open, and suddenly a dragging sound came from below. Jago looked nervously at the trap-door, grabbed the heavy bag and lugged it up the cellar steps. As he disappeared, the sound of hoarse, painful breathing came from down below. A grimy yellow hand appeared over the edge of the trap, clawing feebly for a hold ...

Professor Litefoot was doing his best to sort out the shambles the band of Tong assassins had made of his living-room. He could well have left the job to the servants, but Litefoot was a tidy soul, and couldn't bear disorder. He took off his coat, rolled up his sleeves, and strapping on one of Mrs Hudson's old aprons, he set about the job of tidying up.

He was sweeping up the remains of a once-valuable porcelain statuette when he heard a knocking on the door.

He looked at the clock, and hesitated for a moment. The police had taken away the body of their unfortunate colleague, accepting Litefoot's assurances that there was no further need for a guard on the door. As the knocking came again, Litefoot wondered if he had been wise to dispense with police protection.

He went slowly into the hall, chose a heavy walking stick from the stand and cautiously opened the door. Facing him was a bulky red-faced figure in full evening dress, carrying, with some difficulty, an enormous carpet-bag.

Litefoot stared at his unexpected visitor in astonishment. 'May I ask who you are, sir?'

Jago saw a tall beaky-nosed old fellow in an apron, with a brush in one hand, and a walking stick in the other, and naturally assumed that he was addressing Litefoot's butler. He strode confidently past him, and set the bag down in the hall. 'Thank you, my man. Tell your master that Mr Jago wishes to see him urgently. Chop, chop, man, hurry up and announce me.'

'Consider yourself announced,' said the Professor acidly. 'I'm Litefoot!'

Jago reeled, but recovered immediately. 'I should have realised—that brow, those hands. England's peerless professor of pathology.' He swept off his top hat with a flourish. 'Henry Gordon Jago, sir, at your service!'

Litefoot decided his visitor was either mad or drunk. 'Just tell me what all this is about, sir,' he demanded.

'It is about the Doctor,' said Jago with impressive dignity. 'The Doctor—and this bag. Shall we go inside?'

Heaving up the bag he marched into the sitting-room, and Litefoot had no alternative but to follow. Jago sat in the best armchair, looked hopefully at the decanter, accepted a large brandy and told the Professor of his association with the Doctor. 'When I found the bag in my cellar,' he concluded, 'I was sure the Doctor would be interested. I inquired for him at the police station, and they told me he had been last seen in your company—so here I am. A great pleasure to be associated with you in this devilish affair.'

Litefoot looked dubiously at the bag. 'I'm sure the Doctor will be very interested. Unforunately he isn't here at present.'

'I know, I know,' said Jago. 'The sleuth who never rests, eh?'

Litefoot smiled. 'He did once remark that sleep was for tortoises.' He opened the bag and peered inside. 'You know, for the life of me, I can't discern what all this strange apparatus might be used for. I gather you think it belongs to this murderous lunatic the Doctor is hunting?'

'Well, it's nothing to do with my theatre, Professor, of that I'm sure.'

Litefoot tugged thoughtfully at his moustache. 'Presumably it was left behind by accident—which means that someone might well return for it.'

Jago nodded shrewdly. 'A good point, Professor. We must mention that to the Doctor.'

'We can do better than that, Mr Jago. We can take a hand ourselves. If we keep a discreet watch on your theatre, we might be able to spot these villains and trail them to their lair.'

Jago got hurriedly to his feet. 'A splendid scheme, Professor. Unfortunately the nocturnal vapours are bad for my chest and …'

Ruthlessly Litefoot over-rode his evasions. 'Don't worry about that, man, I'll lend you a nice heavy cape. Just write a little note for the Doctor, and we can be on our way. You'll find pen and paper on the desk over there.'

Jago saw there was no escape. 'Thank you, Professor,' he said faintly and began to write.

Litefoot picked up his cudgel and waved it fiercely through the air. 'We might just be lucky tonight, Mr Jago. And if we are, I've quite a few lumps to repay!' The Doctor gave a final heave on his burglar's jemmy, and the skylight cracked open. 'Come on, Leela,' he whispered, and dropped down inside. Leela swung her legs through the skylight and dropped down after him.

They had arrived at the laundry building to find it locked, barred and apparently deserted. The Doctor, in no mood to be delayed, had promptly climbed up on to the low roof and broken in. Now they were in a long corridor, piled high with laundry baskets. There was a door at the end, but it proved to be locked. The Doctor peered through the keyhole and saw that the key was in the lock on the other side.

He snatched some wrapping paper from one of the baskets and slid it under the door. Then he took a pencil from his pocket and poked it into the lock, pushing the key out on the other side. The key fell on to the paper, the Doctor drew paper and key back through the gap under the door, picked up the key, opened the door and ushered Leela through.

They entered a long dusty room divided into cubicles by curtains of sacking. Inside each cubicle a rough straw mattress lay on the floor. The Doctor looked round. 'Sleeping quarters for the Tong,' he whispered.

Leela sniffed. 'That smell … what is it?'

'Pipe of poppy—opium! A narcotic.' He looked round the deserted room. 'Apparently the Tong have another warren—which means Weng-Chiang will soon be up to his tricks again.'

'He will sacrifice more girls?'

'He'll need to build up his strength before using the Time Cabinet. He's got to kill again—tonight. But where is he?'

From somewhere nearby a weak voice whispered. 'At the House of the Dragon, Doctor.'

13

THE HOUSE OF THE DRAGON

The Doctor whirled round and ripped the sacking curtain from a nearby cubicle. Stretched out on a straw mattress lay Chang, placidly smoking a long, thin wooden pipe. He was a very different figure from the elegant magician who had dominated the stage of the Palace Theatre. His robes were ragged and filthy now, his face grimy and grey with weariness, and his left leg was a bundle of blood-soaked rags.

'Good evening, Mr Chang,' said the Doctor gently. 'We thought you had already gone to join your ancestors.'

'Not yet, Doctor ... not quite. Though I shall certainly do so before very long.' Chang gestured feebly towards his leg. The Doctor moved to take off the wrappings, wondering if he could still help, but Chang waved him angrily away. 'No, Doctor, it is too late. And thanks to the opium, I feel no pain.'

Leela shuddered, remembering her own encounter with the giant rat. It was easy to imagine what those terrible jaws had done to Chang's leg. 'How did you escape from it?' she asked.

Chang spoke in a quiet placid voice, as if describing events that had happened to someone else, a long time ago. 'When the rat seized my leg, I fainted with fear. I was unconscious when it dragged me away. I awoke in a charnel house of bones and putrefying remains.'

The Doctor nodded. 'The thing couldn't have been hungry. It was saving you for later—rats don't keep a very tidy larder.'

Chang went on calmly. 'I lay in that place of horror and cursed my benefactor Weng-Chiang, who had brought me to such a fate. Hatred gave me the strength to drag myself here. I planned to destroy my

269

false god—the last act of the great Weng-Chiang. But there was no one here. The rats had fled.'

'You should have destroyed him long ago,' said Leela sternly.

'Perhaps. But I believed in him. Just as I believed in myself, the great magician Li H'sen Chang.'

'It was a good act,' said the Doctor gently. 'One of the best I've ever seen.'

Chang smiled bitterly. 'Until Weng-Chiang shamed me. The whole theatre saw my failure. I lost face ...'

Chang's voice faded, and the Doctor leaned forward urgently. 'Tell me about the House of the Dragon.'

Chang's voice was very feeble. 'Soon the Great Chang was to have performed before the Queen Empress ... me, the son of a peasant ...'

'The House of the Dragon, Chang? Where is it?'

Chang struggled to focus his eyes on the Doctor. 'It is his Temple and his fortress, prepared for him by the Tong.' Chang struggled to sit up. 'Beware the Eye of the Dragon, Doctor,' he cried, and slumped back on to the mattress.

The Doctor shook him gently. 'Li H'sen! Where is it?'

Now Chang's voice was a feeble whisper. 'Soon I shall rejoin my ancestors. Already I see them, walking to greet me from the Palace of Jade ... Now I shall cross the golden bridge of the gods.'

'The address, Chang,' shouted the Doctor.

Chang made a last effort to speak, but no words came out. He pitched forward on the mattress, and lay quite still.

'He is dead,' said Leela flatly.

The Doctor sighed. 'And he's left us with a Chinese puzzle. Well there's no point in staying here. Let's get back to the Professor.'

Mr Sin sat, smiling as ever, on his throne beside the dragon stool. Beside him stood Greel, waiting impatiently. Black-clad members of the Tong entered the room and prostrated themselves before him. 'Well?' he snarled. 'Where is it?'

The Tong member who had succeeded Lee as leader of the group was called Ho. He stepped forward, quaking with terror.

'Bag is gone, Lord. We look all places in theatre. Bag not there.'

Greel stormed down the steps of the throne and the terrified men scattered before him. 'You incompetent lice,' he raged. 'You crawling

270

mindless dogs! That bag contains parts for the machine by which I live—*and the key to the Time Cabinet*. I'll find it if I have to take this accused city apart stone by stone …' Greel's pacing about had brought him close to the window. He broke off suddenly, and stared out. When he spoke next, it was in a voice of sinister calm. 'Ho! Were you followed here?'

'Followed, Lord?'

Greel pointed to the window. Nervously Ho came nearer and looked out. Two figures lurked by the gas lamp on the corner, obviously keeping watch on the house. Greel stared hard at the two men. 'One of them is Jago, the man who owns the theatre. They must have followed you here after the search.' Greel was thinking aloud. 'They *expected* you to return to the theatre, and were waiting—*which means they have found the bag!* Bring them to me—alive!'

Jago and Litefoot stood huddled against a wall, looking up at the big detached house on the other side of the road. 'This must be their hideaway right enough,' said Litefoot. 'Damned impudence! This is a thoroughly respectable area.' It was a road of solidly built suburban residences, each set well back from the road in its own grounds— houses that were much like Litefoot's own.

The Professor's plan had worked better than he'd dared hope. They had arrived at the theatre in time to find a band of Tong assassins busily ransacking the place. Restraining the indignant Jago from calling the police, Litefoot had persuaded him to wait outside the theatre until the search was abandoned, and the villains drove away in a waiting carriage. Summoning a passing cab, Litefoot and Jago had followed their quarry across London to this quiet secluded road.

Jago rubbed his hands together to warm them. 'Pity there are too many of 'em to tackle, eh, Professor. I was just itching for a fight!'

Litefoot smiled at his companion's enthusiasm. 'Thing is, Mr Jago, what do we do now?'

'Adjourn for a little liquid refreshment?' suggested Jago hopefully. 'I know a little tavern not far from here.'

Litefoot shook his head. 'I'm afraid not. I think one of us should stay here on watch, while the other returns for the Doctor and the police.'

'Splendid idea,' said Jago promptly. 'I'll be as quick as I can, Professor.'

Litefoot touched his arm and pointed. 'Too late, I'm afraid, Mr Jago.' A ring of black-clad Chinese had appeared out of the darkness, encircling them, creeping steadily closer. 'Oh corks,' said Jago faintly.

Litefoot took a firm grip on his cudgel. 'Backs to the wall, I'm afraid, Mr Jago.'

Jago doubled his fists. 'Keep off you lot, I warn you,' he quavered. 'I'm a tiger when my dander's up!'

The Chinese came forward in a silent rush.

Litefoot and Jago fought valiantly, but they were hopelessly outnumbered. They disappeared beneath a pile of their attackers, and minutes later they were being dragged semi-conscious into the house. The heavy door slammed behind them, and the quiet sub-urban street was peaceful once more.

Battered and bleeding, Litefoot and Jago were thrown at Greel's feet. Jago shuddered, as the sinister figure limped towards them. At a nod from Greel, they were dragged to their feet. He glared malevolently at them. 'So, you choose to spy on the House of the Dragon? That is unwise. You will suffer for it.'

'You'll be the one to suffer once the police arrive,' said Litefoot bravely.

Greel laughed. 'The police. Do you hear that, Mr Sin? They take us for simpletons.'

Mr Sin seemed to smile on his little throne.

Jago tried to back up Litefoot's bluff. 'The police will be here, don't you worry. They're not far behind us.'

'You told them you were coming here?'

'Of course,' said Litefoot. 'We're not fools, you know.'

Greel struck him savagely across the face. 'Lies! You did not *know* where you were going. You followed my men here.' Greel sprang on Jago, and seized him by the throat. 'Why were you waiting at the theatre?'

Jago glanced desperately at his companion. 'Why were we waiting at the theatre, Litefoot?' he croaked.

Litefoot folded his arms. 'I refuse to answer. Do as you please with us.'

'I say, steady on,' gasped Jago. All very well for Litefoot to be so defiant. It wasn't his throat.

Greel tightened his grip. 'Then I will tell you. You were waiting for my men to collect the bag.'

Powerless in Greel's grip, Jago gasped. 'You're choking me … to death …'

'Exactly. Now—where is the bag?'

Jago gave a strangled cry and Litefoot shouted, 'Let him go!'

Greel squeezed harder, and Jago began sagging at the knees. 'The bag is at my house,' shouted Litefoot. 'Now for pity's sake release him.'

Greel let go of Jago, who dropped choking to the floor. 'Very well. You will both die later—and slowly. It will give pleasure to my servants.' Greel gestured to the watching members of the Tong. 'Now put them with the other prisoners—and prepare my carriage! We have work to do.'

The Doctor was reading Jago's note out loud to Leela.

> 'My dear Doctor,
> Contained in this capacious carpet-bag which I discovered inadvertently in the cellar is a collection of sundry items of a baffling nature.
> The Professor and I are keeping observation on the theatre, and shortly hope to report to you the whereabouts of the mysterious Weng-Chiang.
> Your fellow detective,
> H.G.J.'

'What does it mean, Doctor?'

'It means they're in trouble,' said the Doctor ruefully. He opened the bag and rummaged inside. 'Spare parts for an organic distillation set-up by the look of it—aha!'

The Doctor took a saucer-shaped pendant from the bag and held it up exultantly. 'Eureka! Do you know what this is, Leela?'

Leela gave him a look. 'You ask only so that you can tell me.'

'It's the trionic lattice for the Time Cabinet. It's impossible to open it without it.'

'You mean it is a key?'

'Exactly. Our black-masked friend isn't just a scientific fool, he's absent-minded too. First he has the key without the Cabinet. Now he's got the Cabinet without the key!'

'Perhaps he has another Eureka?'

The Doctor grinned. 'Eureka is Greek for "This bath is too hot",' he said obscurely. 'No, there can't be another key of this combination.'

'In that case, he will return to the theatre. We must go.'

The Doctor didn't move, and Leela looked reprovingly at him. 'Our friends are in danger, Doctor. We must help them.'

The Doctor pointed to the ashes in the grate. The coal had burned away to a fine ash. 'Litefoot keeps a good fire—so we know he's been out of the house for some time. We'll do no good rushing all over London looking for Weng-Chiang. Much easier to wait for him to come here.'

Leela stood very still, frowning in concentration. 'When our enemy finds the bag has been taken from the theatre ... he will soon discover that Litefoot and Jago are watching him. He will capture them, force them to tell him where it is—and return here to find it!'

'You're learning to think at last.'

'You thought of all that at once, Doctor?'

'Well, almost at once,' said the Doctor modestly.

Leela looked relieved. 'For a moment I thought you feared to attack our enemy. Where shall we set our ambush?' She went over to the side cabinet and took one of Litefoot's carving knives from a drawer. She found a sharpening stone, and began putting a better edge on the knife. Happily she looked up at the Doctor. 'It is time that we did battle with this underground crab!'

Litefoot and Jago had been thrown into a gas-lit basement kitchen and locked in. Two young women lay unconscious against the wall, and Litefoot was examining them.

Jago looked on gloomily. 'Are they dead, Professor?'

'Drugged, I'd say. He must send those fiends of his to kidnap them off the streets. What unspeakable horror must lie behind that mask he wears.' Litefoot sighed despondently, and began pacing about the room. 'Afraid I don't see any way out of this, Jago. I think we're done for.'

Jago tried to be optimistic. 'You're forgetting the Doctor, Professor. He's a trained investigator, remember. A speck of mud, a fleck of paint … clues like that speak volumes to a great detective. I'll wager he's on our track this very minute.'

Litefoot stopped his pacing. I say, Jago, look at this.' He pointed to a panel in the wall. 'One of those service hatches. Dumb waiters they call 'em.'

'Professor, I don't see how you can think of food at a time like this—'

'My dear man, I'm not thinking of food. We can take the shelves out, squeeze inside and make our escape from this room.'

'By Jiminy, you're right,' said Jago exultantly. 'We'll outwit the blighters yet.'

Hurriedly they pulled out the shelves and with some difficulty squeezed themselves inside the service hatch.

'Those ropes don't look too sound,' said Jago apprehensively.

Litefoot mailed. 'He that is down need fear no fall, Mr Jago. A quotation from Bunyan.'

'Very consoling,' said Jago gloomily.

Litefoot seized a rope and Jago did the same. 'Right, *heave*! And *heave* …'

With much puffing and groaning they hauled the hatch up the chute, until at last they were opposite the hatch on the floor above. They shoved it open and sprang out—to find themselves in what appeared to be a Chinese temple. From the top of a flight of steps a dragon idol leered malevolently down at them.

'This isn't the dining-room,' whispered Jago.

'It isn't the way out either,' said Litefoot sadly. He pointed towards the door. Two enormous Tong hatchet men were advancing menacingly towards them.

Jago sighed. 'Well never mind, Professor. At least we tried.'

Leela studied the layout of the dining-room, considering how to set her ambush. 'We should try to trap them in a crossfire, Doctor …'

To Leela's annoyance the Doctor didn't seem to be taking her combat preparations very seriously. He pointed to a bowl of nuts on a side table. 'A crossfire of what? Hazelnuts? Bread pellets?'

'Surely the Professor must have weapons here? In a place this size, there must be fixed strongpoints to defend the approaches ...'

The Doctor grinned affectionately at her. 'I've brought you to the wrong century. You'd have loved Agincourt. Stay here, I'll see what I can find.'

The Doctor left the room and began rummaging under the stairs, wondering where Litefoot kept the fowling piece that had done so well against the giant rat.

Alone in the dining-room, Leela stood with her back to the curtains, gazing thoughtfully around the room. She didn't see the long-nailed claw-like hand that appeared around the edge of the curtain. It was holding a pad of soft material.

Suddenly Greel sprang out from behind the curtain and clapped the pad over Leela's face. She struggled wildly, but within seconds her head was swimming from the effects of the chloroform. With the last of her strength she wriggled round and clawed desperately at Greel, ripping the black-leather mask from his face.

At the sight of what lay beneath the mask, Leela froze in horror. Greel's face was warped, distorted, *bent*, eyes, nose and mouth jumbled nightmarishly together, like a plasticine face squashed by a fist. Leela had only a moment to take in the terrible sight. The pad came down over her face, and she sank into unconsciousness.

14

THE PRISONERS OF
GREEL

When the Doctor came back into the room some few minutes later, there was no sign of Leela. Greel, his mask now back in place, stood waiting by the curtained window.

The Doctor beamed, apparently unsurprised. 'Ah, good! We've been waiting for you.'

'On the contrary, Doctor, it is we who are waiting for you.' Greel gestured towards the door and the Doctor turned. Mr Sin stalked into the room. Behind him came a little group of Tong hatchet men, one of them supporting the unconscious Leela.

'Life's little surprises,' said the Doctor softly. His voice hardened as he looked at Leela. 'What have you done to her?'

'Nothing—yet.'

'Take my advice—don't,' said the Doctor quietly.

'*Your* advice?' Greel gave a scornful laugh. 'You are an unusual man, Doctor, but in opposing me you have gone far out of your depth. You have something of mine, I believe. I want it back.'

'Something of yours? Now what could it be, I wonder? I borrow so many things and forget where I put them. Terrible habit.'

Greel tapped the carpet bag. 'The Time Key was in this bag. It is not there now. Give it to me.'

The Doctor began a pantomime of patting all his pockets, muttering. 'Time Key, Time Key, now where did I put the wretched thing—ah!'

Greel leaned forward eagerly. The Doctor produced a paper bag and held it out. 'Forgotten I had these. Care for a jelly baby?'

Greel struck his hand aside. 'I will give you three seconds, Doctor, then Mr Sin will kill the girl.'

Knife raised, Mr Sin began stalking towards Leela with jerky eagerness. Greel began counting. 'One ... Two ... Three. Kill her.'

Mr Sin raised his knife—and the Doctor produced the saucer-shaped pendant from his pocket. 'This what you want—the trionic lattice?'

Greel stretched out a claw-like hand. 'Give it to me!'

The Doctor drew back the pendant, holding it just out of reach. 'Careful—you nearly made me drop it.' He studied the pendant thoughtfully. 'Very fragile, this crystalline structure. Probably shatter into a thousand pieces, if I dropped it and trod on it ...' He tossed the pendant carelessly from one hand to the other.

'You arrogant jackanapes,' snarled Greel. 'I will have you killed ...'

The hatchet men surged forward eagerly, and the Doctor held the pendant high. 'Call off your dogs. I get nervous when I'm crowded.'

Greel waved the Chinese back, and the Doctor smiled. 'That's better.'

Greel pointed a skinny finger at Leela. 'Give me the Time Key and I will spare her life.'

The Doctor swung the pendant. 'I never trusted men with long, dirty fingernails.'

Greel was nearing the end of his patience. 'You can trust me to kill you if you do not obey me. Give me the Time Key.'

The Doctor swung the pendant to and fro. 'I'll make a bargain with you. You can have your Time Key back when we reach the House of the Dragon.'

'What trickery is this?'

'I think you're holding two friends of mine prisoner?'

'The two blundering dolts who spied on me? Yes, I have them.'

The Doctor nodded, pleased to learn that Litefoot and Jago were still alive.

'I want them released as well. When we're *all* free, I'll hand over the Time Key—and not before.'

Greel nodded slowly. 'Very well.'

'Right, then. You and your chaps can lead the way.'

Greel picked up Mr Sin, and turned to the Tong hatchet men. 'Bring the bag—and the girl.'

The Doctor said firmly, 'The bag by all means. The girl stays here.'

'You, would be wise not to press me too far, Doctor.'

The Doctor held up the pendant. 'Just lead the way.'

Greel nodded to the Chinese holding Leela. They let her go, and she slumped to the floor. Greel swept out, followed by his hatchet men. The Doctor paused, and looked down at Leela. Her eyes opened and she looked steadily at him for a moment, and then closed them again. The Doctor smiled, and followed the others from the house.

As soon as the front door closed behind them, Leela climbed quickly to her feet and moved quietly out of the room.

Escape attempt thwarted, Jago and Litefoot had been thrown back into their kitchen prison for what seemed hours of waiting.

Litefoot heard a bustle of movement and went to listen at the door. 'Seems to be something happening. Sounds as if a big group of people are coming into the house.'

'More Wongs for the Tong,' said Jago gloomily.

Litefoot looked at his watch. 'It'll soon be dawn.'

Jago looked alarmed. 'I say, that's when these chaps—do things, isn't it? Sacrifice their victims?'

'You're thinking of Druids, old chap.'

Jago seemed unconvinced. 'I've been worrying, rather. Can't seem to stop myself. You see, the trouble with me, Litefoot … I know I talk a lot. But I'm not so jolly brave when it comes to it, old man. Try to be … but I'm not.'

Litefoot nodded understandingly. 'When it comes to it, I don't suppose anyone is.'

'Thought I'd better tell you … in case I let the side down.'

Litefoot clapped him on the shoulder. 'You won't, Henry. I know you won't.'

The Doctor looked admiringly round the Dragon Room, as Greel set Mr Sin on his throne by the Dragon idol. He stared hard into the manikin's unwinking eyes as if transmitting some silent signal, and

Mr Sin's head gave the faintest of nods. Satisfied, Greel turned to Ho. 'Bring the prisoners here.'

The Doctor had wandered over to Greel's reassembled organic distillation set-up, and was studying it thoughtfully. As Greel moved towards him he turned and said cheerfully, 'Very impressive. I'll take the birds'-nest soup. This is where you do the cooking isn't it?'

Greel moved so that his body blocked the Doctor's view of Mr Sin. Behind him the manikin was crawling into a concealed hatchway set into the idol's side.

'You cannot hope to understand its function, Doctor. It is part of a technology far beyond your time.'

'Just simple old-fashioned cannibalism,' said the Doctor scornfully. 'This machine just saves you from having to chew the gristly bits.'

'It contains the secret of life—'

'Rubbish,' interrupted the Doctor. 'Degenerate bunkum! Your superior technology is no more than the twisted lunacy of a scientific Dark Age.' Suddenly the Doctor swung rounds 'Where's your pig-brained Peking Homunculus got to?'

'I have no further need of Mr Sin,' said Greel smoothly. 'I have dismissed him.' To distract the Doctor's attention, Greel moved to a side table on which stood a chessboard set out with ornately carved Chinese chessmen. He made an opening move. Almost automatically, the Doctor moved to the other side of the board and countered it.

Greel moved another piece. 'You know the secret of Mr Sin's construction, Doctor? How can you, in the nineteenth century, know the secrets of the fifty-first?'

Almost without looking at the board, the Doctor moved another piece, 'I was with the Philippino army during the final battle for Reykjavik.'

'You lie!' hissed Greel, as he moved again.

The Doctor studied the board. 'Now listen, what's-your-name—what *did* you call yourself before you started posing as a Chinese god?'

'I am Magnus Greel,' said the black-cloaked figure proudly.

The Doctor stretched his hand towards the board. 'So, you're Greel … the infamous Minister of Justice of the Supreme Alliance. The butcher of Brisbane …'

It was all becoming clear now, thought the Doctor. Greel had created the murderous homunculus with the deliberate intention of triggering off a World War. When the conflict had erupted, Greel and his allies were ready. For a time the Supreme Alliance, a league of ruthless dictators, had ruled most of the Earth. Finally an alliance of their victims had risen against them, crushing them at the terrible battle of Reykjavik...

After the battle Greel had disappeared, taking the homunculus with him. He had been hunted as a War Criminal, but had never been found. Now the mystery of his disappearance had been solved. Fleeing in his newly-developed Time Cabinet he had landed, more or less at random, in nineteenth-century China. Weak and sick from the terrible distorting effects of the Zygma beam, he had sheltered in Li H'sen Chang's hut. Meanwhile the Time Cabinet had been taken by the Emperor's soldiers, given as a present to Litefoot's family, and finished up in Victorian England.

Ever since then Greel must have been striving to recover the Cabinet, handicapped by the recurrent wasting sickness caused by the effects of the Zygma beam. A sickness which could only be held off by the constant supply of young human victims, forced to sacrifice their life essence to keep Magnus Greel alive. Now it appeared that Greel was on the verge of yet another escape, with all his terrible crimes still unpunished...

All these reflections from a history that had yet to happen flashed through the Doctor's mind while he was reaching for his Queen. He moved it forward and said quietly, 'Checkmate, I think.'

Greel's arm flashed out, sweeping the pieces from the board. 'It is *impossible* for you to know these things, Doctor.'

The Doctor looked at him with distaste. 'Is it, Greel? I know you're a war criminal from the future, that a hundred thousand deaths can be laid at your door.'

'Enemies of the state. They were used in the advancement of science.'

'They were slaughtered in filthy machines like that—part of your quest for eternal life!'

Greel felt compelled to defend himself. 'If you are from the future, you are here because of nay work. So, I am remembered only as a war criminal? The winning side writes the history, Doctor. *You* could not be here if it were not for my work.' He waved towards the Time Cabinet. 'I made this possible, I found the resources, the scientists …'

'That abortion?' said the Doctor scornfully. 'Your Zygma beam experiments were a hopeless failure, Greel.'

'I used the cabinet to travel through Time,' screamed Greel. 'I escaped from my enemies.'

'And look what it did to you!'

'There was a temporal distortion of the metabolism. It can be adjusted …' Greel broke off, as Litefoot and Jago were thrust into the room. At the sight of the Doctor, Jago brightened immediately.

'By Jingo, Litefoot, didn't I tell you?' He turned sternly towards Greel. 'The game's up, my friend. We have the place surrounded.'

'I'm afraid we don't, Mr Jago,' said the Doctor. 'All we have at the moment is a rather precarious understanding.'

'I have kept my word, Doctor,' said Greel impatiently. 'Your friends are here. Now give me the Time Key.'

'Not until they're safe out of the house.' The Doctor turned to Jago and Litefoot. 'Off you go—and hurry.'

Jago was already heading for the door, but Litefoot hesitated. 'Doctor, there are two wretched girls downstairs …'

'Take them with you then. Now go!'

Litefoot hurried after Jago, and Greel glared balefully at the Doctor. 'Your demands become too great, Doctor.' Suddenly Greel stepped to one side, leaving the Doctor standing directly in line with the Dragon idol. There was a sudden crackle of power, and a ray of green light stabbed from the Dragon's eyes. Caught by its blast, the Doctor staggered and fell—and Greel snatched the pendant from his hand as he crumpled to the floor.

15

THE FIREBOMB

The Dragon's head swung down, as if to blast the Doctor again, but Greel held up his hand. 'Enough. I want him alive.'

Inside the Dragon, Mr Sin reluctantly removed his hands from the laser-controls, angry because he had not been allowed to kill.

Litefoot had run back into the room, and was kneeling beside the Doctor, whose face was drawn from the effects of the tremendous shock. 'Doctor,' he asked anxiously. 'Are you all right?'

The Doctor opened his eyes with a tremendous effort. 'Beware the Eye of the Dragon,' he whispered and fell back unconscious.

Greel waved to the awe-stricken Tong guards who stood waiting by the door. 'Take them!'

Two guards began dragging the Doctor's body away, while others hustled Litefoot and Jago out of the room. Greel was left alone and triumphant, the Time Key in his hand.

In a corridor at the rear of the building, a Tong guard padded silently towards the back of the house. He had heard faint, suspicious sounds, and was going to investigate.

As he passed a curtained alcove Leela stepped out, took his neck in a choking grip, and dragged him into the alcove. The curtains billowed frantically for a moment, and were still.

Mr Sin sat patiently inside the head of the Dragon. Through the sights of the laser-ray, he could see Greel moving towards the Time Cabinet. Swivelling the sighting-mechanism to keep his master in view, Mr Sin reached out and stroked the firing-controls ...

With loving care, Greel pressed the Time Key into the recess in the front of the Cabinet. There was a hum of power and the door slid open. Most of the inside of the Cabinet was taken up with complicated yet curiously ramshackle equipment. Greel, however, seemed well-satisfied as he checked over the controls. 'Everything exactly as it was … The Parallax synchrons fully charged, the chronos tubes set at maximum …'

With absorbed intensity, Greel began preparing for his departure. 'The Doctor was wrong,' he muttered. 'My Zygma experiment was a success. A complete success! Soon I shall be free once more.'

Thrown back into captivity, Litefoot went on trying to revive the unconscious Doctor. Jago looked on, and the two girls stared dully ahead of them. It was perhaps as well they had no idea of where they were or what was happening to them.

'How is he?' asked Jago worriedly.

Litefoot looked up. 'There's a curious double heart-beat … but there doesn't seem to be any real damage.'

'Struck down from behind by a dastardly device,' said Jago fiercely.

'Sssh! I think he's trying to say something …'

Suddenly, the Doctor spoke. 'There's a one-eyed yellow idol to the North of Katmandu. There's a little marble cross below the town …'

'By jove, he's reciting Kipling,' whispered Jago.

The Doctor opened his eyes. 'Nonsense, it's Harry Champion. Kipling used to get very annoyed about that.' He struggled to his feet. 'How long was I unconscious?'

'Just a few minutes,' said Litefoot. 'A remarkable recovery, Doctor.'

The Doctor stretched and took a few paces around the room. Jago looked on admiringly. 'What an iron constitution!'

The Doctor went over to the bed and examined the two dull-eyed girls. 'The broth of oblivion,' he muttered. Straightening up, he stood looking round the room deep in thought.

'Surely there's something we can do, Doctor?' asked Litefoot.

The Doctor smiled. 'There's always something, Professor. For a start, put those two unfortunate ladies in the corner over there.' Jago and Litefoot moved the unresisting girls, and the Doctor examined the mattress on which they had been sitting. 'Excellent, good thick linen.

It'll do very well.' He saw Jago and Litefoot looking at him expectantly. 'Don't waste time, gentlemen. Help me to wrench that gas pipe away from the wall.'

Greel made a final adjustment, and stepped back from the Time Cabinet. 'All is ready. Time to prepare my two partridges.' With gruesome good humour, Greel called over to the Dragon idol. 'Why don't you come out of there, Mr Sin? Sulking because I wouldn't let you kill the Doctor? You shall kill him soon enough—when I have drained every atom of his knowledge of the Zygma process. Kill them all if you wish, before we leave. As soon as I have re-established my metabolic balance, I shall enter the Zygma beam for the second time. This time there will be no mistake ...'

Engrossed in his plans for escape, Greel failed to see Leela as, knife in hand, she slipped silently into the room and hid behind a laboratory bench.

Suddenly Greel moved away from the Cabinet and went to a gong that hung close to the door. Leela realised her danger too late. Greel was about to summon more of his Tong hatchet men. Well, at least she could kill him before they had time to arrive.

As Greel struck the gong, Leela jumped upon the bench and launched herself across the room in a flying leap. The gong-note was still hanging in the air as she landed on Greel's shoulders, bearing him to the ground. They fought wildly for a moment, but Leela was full of savage anger. Pinning Greel to the ground she brought her knife blade to his throat. 'Die, bent-face!' she hissed.

Greel tried to hold back her arm, but the knife blade came ever-closer. 'No,' pleaded Greel. 'Spare me ...'

As Leela tensed her muscles for the final thrust, the room was suddenly full of black-clad Tong hatchet men. They pulled her from their Master, wrenching the knife from her hand, and held her helplessly captive. Greel staggered to his feet and hobbled towards her, snatching Leela's knife from the hatchet man who had taken it. 'Hold her still,' he commanded. His voice was hoarse with rage, and the memory of his own fear. 'Twice this she-devil has tried to kill me. *Twice!*'

With deliberate slowness, Greel brought the blade to Leela's throat. Then he threw it to the ground. 'No! I have a more fitting fate for you.

You shall be the first morsel to feed my regeneration. Put her in the distillation chamber!'

Tong guards dragged the struggling Leela across to the machine. 'Kill me how you please,' she shouted. 'I do not fear death—unlike you, bent-face!'

Greel flinched at the memory of how he had begged for mercy. He watched with malevolent satisfaction as the guard thrust Leela into the chamber, securing the doors so that only her head was visible, framed between the two metal spheres.

Greel went over to the machine, and stared into Leela's eyes. 'Well, tigress, now it is your turn to beg.'

'I shall not plead,' said Leela scornfully. 'But I swear this to you. When we are both in the great Hereafter, I shall hunt you down and force you through my agony a thousand times.'

Recoiling from the force of her anger, Greel shouted, 'Silence her.'

One of the Chinese thrust a gag into Leela's mouth. 'Bring the other girls here,' ordered Greel, and the guards hurried from the room.

Jago and Litefoot had been working hard under the Doctor's direction. Now they stood back and looked at the results. The Doctor's scheme was simple—and appallingly dangerous. The mattress-cover, now serving as a kind of cloth balloon, was hanging by the door, gas hissing into it from the broken pipe to which it was tied. From the bottom of the mattress dangled a long strip of cloth, the fuse for the Doctor's homemade firebomb.

The bed on which the mattress had once rested was tipped on its side across one corner, the water-soaked mattress propped against it for added protection. Behind the improvised shield the two girls were crouching. By now they were sufficiently revived to understand their danger, and obey the Doctor's instructions.

Jago watched the billowing of the mattress-cover as the gas hissed into it. 'It's leaking,' he said worriedly. 'I can smell it.'

'Bound to be some leakage,' said the Doctor cheerily. 'Not enough to worry about.' He wasn't nearly so optimistic as he tried to sound. Setting off a gas explosion in such a confined space would be almost as dangerous for the prisoners as for their enemies. But a single devastating stroke was needed, to dispose of as many guards as possible before they tackled Greel himself.

'It isn't that I'm *worried*,' said Jago hurriedly, 'but I'd hate to be gassed before we get a chance to see if this stunt works!'

The Doctor gave him a reassuring smile. 'Greel won't keep us waiting long. He needs his nourishment.'

'His what?'

'Greel is dying. His body is constantly wasting away. He is trying to cheat death by feeding upon the life-force of others.' He glanced at the two women in the corner, and then at Litefoot. 'You understand me, Professor?'

'I think so—the principle, at least.'

'The principle is false, in any case. All Greel achieves is a postponement of the inevitable.'

Jago interrupted them. 'Listen, Doctor. I think they're coming.'

'Then you know what to do. Your matches please, Professor.'

Litefoot and Jago joined the two men behind the bed. The Doctor called softly to the two girls. 'Now remember, you two, get out of this house just as soon as you can, and don't stop running till you're a mile away.' Too terrified to speak, both girls nodded.

The footsteps were at the door now. The Doctor lit a match, touched it to the fuse and joined the huddled group in the corner. 'Up troops and at 'em, eh?' whispered Jago excitedly.

They watched the flickering yellow flame run up the strip of linen. Just as the door was flung open, it touched the gas-filled mattress cover.

There was an astonishingly loud explosion and the doorway disappeared in a sheet of flame. Black smoke filled the room, and when it cleared, the guards who had been nearest the door lay stunned on the floor, while the rest ran screaming down the corridor. 'Quick!' shouted the Doctor, and choking in the clouds of smoke the captives dashed into the corridor. The Doctor snatched up a hatchet from a fallen guard as he ran out of the room. Obedient to the Doctor's instructions, the two girls were already running for the back door. The Doctor led Jago and Litefoot towards the main stairs.

Busy at the controls of his organic distillation machine, Greel heard the boom of the explosion, and the screams of his guards. He hesitated, moved towards the door, then returned to the controls looking threateningly at Leela. 'Whatever has happened, there will be no escape for *you*. The talons of Greel will shred your flesh.' He stretched out his skinny hands to the main control—as the door was flung open, and the Doctor ran into the room. 'Greel,' shouted the Doctor, and threw the hatchet with all his force.

Determined on his revenge, Greel snatched at the master-lever. But the Doctor's hatchet was aimed not at Greel himself but at the main power cable of his machine. The hatchet severed the cable in a shower of sparks, and the machine went dead, just as the lever was pulled.

The Doctor ran to the cabinet and threw open the doors. Leela fell into his arms, and he snatched the gag from her mouth.

Greel was scuttling towards the Dragon idol. 'Kill, Sin,' he screamed. 'Kill them all!'

'Down!' shouted the Doctor. He pulled Leela behind the laboratory bench just as the green ray blazed from the Dragon's eyes. There was a fierce crackle of energy, and smoke filled the air as chunks of blazing masonry were blasted from the wall.

Inside the Dragon Mr Sin was hunched over the controls, peering through the sights for a living target. Greel himself was hiding behind the dais on which the idol stood. The Doctor, Leela, Litefoot and Jago were all sheltering behind the heavy laboratory bench which stood by the door. Like two armies on the battlefield, the opposing forces had occupied opposite ends of the long room.

Greel shouted from his hiding place. 'I will spare your lives, all of you, if you will leave now.'

'Very magnanimous, Magnus,' called the Doctor.

'Then go!'

'With your trigger-happy little friend still covering us? No thank you!'

'I'm offering you your freedom, you fools!' screamed Greel.

The Doctor looked at the others. 'We'd be cut down before we reached the door.'

Leela nodded. 'I think so too. There is no truth in him.'

'We're staying put, Magnus,' shouted the Doctor.

'Then you will die here—all of you!'

The Doctor peered over the bench at the huddled figure on the steps. 'You might die first, Greel. You don't sound too healthy—and your food supply is halfway across London by now.'

Hobbling up the steps of the Dragon idol Greel snarled, 'Sin! Burn away that bench!'

The Dragon's eye glowed fiercely and the Doctor and the others ducked down as laser-bolt after laser-bolt sizzled into the bench. With every shot, a chunk of blazing wood was blasted away.

'If only I had a gun,' whispered Litefoot fiercely.

Jago nodded. 'Or even a catapult. I was a dab hand with a catapult as a nipper.'

Another chunk of wood was blasted from the bench, which by now was getting noticeably smaller. 'He is cutting down our cover, Doctor,' said Leela calmly. 'Soon one of us will be hit.'

A spasm of pain wracked Greel's deformed body. 'Hurry, Sin, hurry,' he croaked. 'There is little time left to me.'

Not all the servants of Weng-Chiang had fled after the explosion. A few of the more fanatical had stayed behind, huddling together in the basement. The sound of the laser-battle in the Dragon Room had encouraged them to emerge. The great Weng-Chiang was destroying his enemies with his magic ray. Would he not take a terrible vengeance if his servants deserted him? Gathering all the weapons they could find, the remnant of the Tong hatchet men crept towards the Dragon Room, determined to prove their loyalty while there was still time.

Dodging yet another laser-bolt, the Doctor sensed movement behind him and turned. Tong warriors, armed with hatchets, knives and revolvers were flooding into the room. Now the Doctor and his friends were caught in a crossfire between Tong and Dragon. The petition was hopeless.

Inside the Dragon idol the eyes of Mr Sin blazed with excitement and pleasure. He was weary of shooting at a block of wood. Here were living targets. Gleefully he crouched over the controls and swung the sights.

The laser crackled again, and most of the tightly packed knot of Tong warriors in the doorway died with its first blast. Mr Sin fired again and again, picking off the survivors.

'Stop,' roared Greel. 'Stop, Sin, I command you. I am your master—obey me.'

Sin was deaf to all commands. Crazed with blood-lust, he mowed down the fleeing hatchet men, until the doorway was choked with their bodies.

The last of the guards twisted in the laser blast and dropped to the ground, a heavy revolver falling from his hand. It fell not too far from the bench. Leela nudged Jago and pointed.

Jago looked at the distance he would have to cover and shook his head firmly. 'Not a chance, my dear.'

'He cannot shoot at two targets at once.'

Jago's eyes widened. 'You mean if one of us draws the blighter's fire, the other can get to the gun?'

'Me,' said Leela flatly. 'Because I am quicker.'

With the Tong members all disposed of, Sin returned his attention to the bench. A well-aimed laser-bolt sheared off one leg and the bench lurched dangerously. Litefoot grabbed it. 'Can't hold it for long,' he yelled. 'Another few minutes and we're done for.'

The Doctor snatched up a hatchet. 'Ready then? All together … now!'

Three things happened more or less at once. Jago popped up like a jack-in-the-box, deliberately drawing Sin's fire. The Doctor hurled the hatchet at the Dragon's head. And Leela sprinted to the cover of an iron chest on the other side of the room, scooping up the revolver on the way.

Although it bounced harmlessly off the Dragon's head, the Doctor's hatchet probably saved Jago's life. The sight of it whirling towards him in the sights spoiled Sin's aim, and his laser-bolt crackled over Jago's head, as he dropped flat behind the wobbling barrier of the bench. 'I say, I say,' he gasped, in the comedian's traditional opening phrase. 'A funny-thing nearly happened to me just now. Has she got the gun?'

A bullet whistled over Jago's head, and they all ducked down.

'Hey, who are you shooting at, young lady?' called Litefoot indignantly.

They heard Leela's voice from the other side of the room. 'Sorry! I've never fired one of these before!'

Leela's favourite weapon was the Sevateem crossbow with which she had grown up, though she had used a hand-blaster in an earlier adventure with the Doctor. But she had a natural affinity with weapons, and she soon worked out how to use the big revolver.

Taking careful aim she fired at the glowing eyes in the Dragon idol's head. She missed by inches, the great head swung round, and as the eyes shot out their deadly ray, and the great iron chest glowed red beneath the impact of a laser-bolt, Leela ducked down and waited her chance for another shot.

Jago helped Litefoot to support the weight of the tottering bench. Peering round the edge, the Doctor saw Greel crawling across the room towards the open Time Cabinet. He had suddenly become much feebler, and could only move with agonising slowness.

'It's no good, Greel,' shouted the Doctor. 'You're finished.'

Painfully Greel lifted his head. 'I can still escape you, Doctor, as I escaped my enemies before.' He inched nearer the Time Cabinet.

'Don't try it, Greel.' warned the Doctor. 'If you activate the Zygma beam it will mean certain death for all of us.'

'Lies, Doctor! Lies!' shrieked Greel.

'Listen to me. The Zygma beam is at full stretch. Try to trigger it again and it will collapse. There'll be a huge implosion, and you'll be at the centre of it. The Zygma experiment was a disastrous failure!'

Greel's enormous vanity would not allow him to accept the truth. 'It was a success, Doctor. A total, brilliant success.'

Greel was at the Time Cabinet now, and about to step inside. He saw the Dragon's head swing towards *him*.

'Sin, no!' he screamed. But Sin's blood-lust was totally in control now. To him Greel was just another living target. Greel dropped behind the cabinet as a laser-bolt sizzled past him.

Sin's attempt to kill Greel gave Leela her chance. Leaping to her feet she held the revolver in both hands, took careful aim and squeezed the trigger. The heavy bullet blasted through the focussing crystal that was the Dragon's eye, and the head of the idol exploded in smoke and flame.

Greel leaped to his feet and sprang for the cabinet, but the Doctor was too quick for him. He grappled with Greel, pulling him back from the Time Cabinet. They struggled for a moment, then Greel called up the last of his failing strength. With a frantic lunge he broke free of the Doctor's grip, staggered forward and crashed into the jumble of electronic machinery that filled the centre of the cabinet. There was a blaze of fierce blue sparks, a muffled explosion. Blasted from the cabinet, Greel crashed to the ground.

They all gathered round the huddled black-clad figure. Through the slits of the mask Greel's eyes stared sightlessly up at them.

'Is bent-face dead?' asked Leela.

Litefoot glanced curiously at her. 'Why do you call him bent-face?'

'Becausehe is!'

Curiously Litefoot reached out for the mask, but the Doctor gently restrained him. 'I shouldn't, Professor.'

'Why not?'

'Look!'

Greel's prostrate body was collapsing, crumbling, dwindling away to dust before their eyes. In seconds there was nothing left of him, just a heap of dusty black clothing at their feet.

'Cellular collapse,' said the Doctor softly.

'In all my years as a pathologist I've never seen anything like it,' gasped Litefoot.

'Let's hope you never do again, Professor.'

'But was *was* he?' asked Jago. 'Where was he from?'

The Doctor clapped him on the shoulder. 'A foe from the future, Henry. Let's leave it at that.' Crossing to the Time Cabinet the Doctor closed and locked it—just as a small, malevolent figure leaped from the top of the Dragon idol straight on to Leela's shoulders, a long sharp knife in its hand. Jago and Litefoot ran forward to pull it off. The knife flashed down, and Litefoot staggered back with a cry, blood welling from a wound in his arm. Locking his legs tightly around Leela's neck Mr Sin raised the knife again. The Doctor sprang forward, thrusting Jago out of the way. He wrenched the dummy from Leela's shoulders with one savage heave. Leela staggered back choking, and the Doctor dashed the manikin to the ground with all his strength. He lifted it, slammed it to the floor face-down, groped between, beneath the embroidered tunic and wrenched out a slim metallic tube, flung it to the ground and stamped on it.

'That was what you might call his fuse,' he gasped: 'He's harmless now. As harmless as a ventriloquist's dummy.' The Doctor disentangled the crystal pendant from the pile of black clothes, dropped it beside Sin and ground it to fragments beneath his heel. The anger faded from his face and he smiled wearily at the others. 'There! The Zygma experiment is finally at an end.' He paused. 'Listen!'

They heard a bell ringing in the distance, and a faint muffled cry. 'The muffin man,' said the Doctor happily. 'Come on, I'll treat you all to some muffins!'

They said their farewells over hot tea and buttered muffins in Professor Litefoot's house, then the Doctor insisted politely but firmly that he and Leela must be on their way. He had no wish to become involved in the lengthy investigations that were sure to follow.

Leela was still munching the last of the muffin as they strolled through the night streets back to the TARDIS. Litefoot, his arm in a sling, was doing his best to teach Leela the rudiments of polite behaviour. 'For example, I would say: "One lump or two, Miss Leela?" and you would reply, "One will suffice, thank you."'

'Suppose I want two?'

'No, no, my dear. One lump for ladies.'

'Then why ask me?'

Litefoot scratched his head.

'Do come along, Leela,' called the Doctor. They turned the corner, and there was the TARDIS where they had left it.

'Professor Litefoot has been explaining about tea,' said Leela. 'It is very complicated.'

The Doctor was in a hurry to be off. 'Well, unfortunately we don't have time for any more tea parties. Good-bye, Professor, good-bye, Henry.' He shook hands with them both, unlocked the TARDIS door and ushered Leela inside.

Rather astonished by this abrupt disappearance, Litefoot turned to Jago. 'I thought he said he was leaving. What is that contraption?'

Jago hadn't the slightest idea, but was reluctant to admit it. 'Provided by Scotland Yard.' he said vaguely. 'Look, it says "POLICE" on it. Perhaps it's a small portable Police Station!'

There was a wheezing, groaning sound, and the TARDIS faded away before their astonished eyes.

'Extraordinary,' breathed Litefoot. 'I just don't believe it!'

'I've said it before and I'll say it again,' said Jago. 'Our policemen are wonderful.'

As they turned to go, Litefoot was still spluttering, 'But it's impossible. Quite impossible!'

Jago nodded appreciatively. 'Good trick that, eh?' His eye was caught by a poster for his own theatre. Chang's face looked out at him, and Jago reminded himself that he would have to start looking for a new top-of-the-bill act. 'Yes,' said Jago thoughtfully, 'I venture to say that not even the great Li H'sen Chang himself could have pulled off a better trick than that.' He took Litefoot's arm and led him away. 'Now then Professor, I suggest we round off this extraordinary evening with a celebratory libation. It so happens I know a little tavern not too far from here ...'

Chang's face stared out from the poster as their footsteps faded away into the fog.

DOCTOR WHO AND THE HORROR OF FANG ROCK

PROLOGUE

THE LEGEND OF FANG ROCK

Fang Rock lighthouse, centre of a series of mysterious and terrifying events at the turn of the century, is built on a rocky island a few miles off the Channel coast. So small is the island that wherever you stand its rocks are wet with sea-spray. Everywhere you hear the endless thundering of the waves, as they crash on the jagged coastline that has given Fang Rock its name.

The lighthouse tower is in the centre of the island. A steep flight of steps leads up to the heavy door in its base. This gives entry to the lower floor where the big steam-driven generator throbs steadily away, providing power for the electric lantern. Coal bunkers occupy the rest of this lower area.

Winding stairs lead up to the crew room, where the men eat, sleep and spend most of their leisure time. Next to the crew room is a tiny kitchen.

Above, more store rooms and the head keeper's private cabin, and above them the service rooms, where tools and spare parts are kept, together with rockets, maroons, flares and a variety of other warning devices.

Finally, a short steep iron stairway leads up into the lamp room, a glassed-in circular chamber at the very top of the tower, dominated by the giant carbon-arc lamp with its gleaming glass prisms.

Fang Rock has had an evil reputation from its earliest days. Soon after it was built two men died in mysterious circumstances, and a third went mad with fear. There have been strange rumours, stories of a great glowing beast that comes out of the sea ...

But all that is forgotten now. It is the early 1900s, and the age of science is in full swing. Newly converted from oil to electricity, Fang Rock lighthouse stands tall and strong, the great shining lantern warning ships away from the jagged reefs around the little island.

As night falls one fine autumn evening the lamp is burning steadily. The three men who make up the crew go peacefully about their duties, unaware of the night of horror that lies before them, little knowing that they would soon be caught up in a strange and terrible conflict, with the fate of the Earth itself as the final stake.

1

THE TERROR BEGINS

It began with a light in the sky. It was dusk, and the lamp had just been lit. High up in the lamp room all was calm and peaceful, no sound except for the steady roar of the sea below. Young Vince saw it first. He was polishing the great telescope on the. lamp-room gallery when he saw a fiery streak blazing across the darkness. Through the telescope, he tracked its progress as it curved down through the evening sky and into the sea. For a moment the sea glowed brightly at the point of impact. The glow faded, and everything was normal.

Vince turned away from the telescope. 'Reuben! Come and look—quick now!'

With his usual aggravating deliberation the old man finished filling an oil-lamp. 'What is it now, boy?'

'There was this light, shot across the sky. Went under the sea it did, and the sea was all glowing. Over there.'

Old Reuben rose stiffly, hobbled across to the telescope and peered through the eyepiece. 'Nothing there now.'

'I told you, it went into the sea.'

Reuben grunted. 'Could have been a what d'you call 'em … a meteor …'

He left the telescope and Vince took his place, scanning the area of sea where the fireball had vanished. 'Whatever it was it come down pretty near us …'

'Sight-seeing are we?' asked a sarcastic voice. 'Hoping to spot some of them bathing belles on the beach?'

Guiltily Vince jumped away from the telescope. Ben Travers, senior keeper and engineer of Fang Rock lighthouse, was regarding him sardonically from the doorway. He was a tough, weathered man in his fifties, stern-faced but not without his own dour humour.

Reuben chuckled. 'Young Vince here's been seeing stars.'

Vince reddened under Ben's sceptical stare. 'I saw a light, anyway. Clear across the sky it came, and down into into the sea.'

'Must have been a shooting star, eh?'

'Weren't no shooting star,' said Vince obstinately. 'Seen them before I have. This was—different.'

'Get on with you,' cackled Reuben. 'That were a shooting star, right enough. Bring you luck, boy, that will. Bit of luck coming to you.'

'What, on this old rock? Not till my three months is up!' Keepers worked three months at a stretch, followed by an off-duty month on shore.

Ben went to the telescope. But there was nothing to be seen but the steady swell of the sea. 'Well, whatever it was it's gone now. As long as it's not a hazard to navigation, it's no business of ours.'

That's Ben for you, thought Vince. Duty first, last and all the time. 'I saw it, though,' he persisted. 'It was all glowing …'

'I've heard enough about it, lad. Just you forget it and get on with your work. I'm going down to supper. Coming, Reuben?'

Ben went down the steps, and Reuben followed. Vince returned to polishing the brass mounting of the telescope. He stared out at the dark, rolling sea. 'All the same,' he muttered, 'I know what I saw …'

It surfaced from the depths of the sea and scanned the surrounding area with many-faceted eyes. Just ahead was a small, jagged land mass. Crowning it was a tall slender tower with a light on top that flashed at regular intervals. Clearly there were intelligent life-forms on the island. They must be studied, and eventually disposed of, it thought weakly.

It had been severely shaken by the crash, and its energy-levels were dangerously low. The bright flashing light meant power—and it desperately needed power to restore its failing strength. It had already taken precautionary measures to conceal its presence and isolate the island. Slowly it moved through the sea towards the lighthouse.

In the cosy, familiar warmth of the crew room Ben and Reuben were dealing with plates of stew, and continuing their never-ending argument.

Reuben swallowed a mouthful of dumpling. 'Now in the old days it was all simple enough. You filled her up and trimmed the wick. That old lamp just went on burning away steady as you please.'

'Wasn't only the lamp burned sometimes. How many oil fires were there in those days, eh? Towers gutted, men killed ...'

'Carelessness, that is. Carelessness, or drink. Oil's safe enough if you treat her right.'

'Listen, Reuben, I've been inside a few of those old lighthouses. Like the inside of a chimney. Grease and soot everywhere, floor covered with oil and bits of wick.'

'Never, mate, never!'

Ben was well into his stride by now. 'And as for the light! You couldn't see it inside, let alone out. Clouds of black smoke as soon as the lamp was lit.'

Reuben changed his ground. 'All right, then, if electricity's so good, why are they going back to oil then, tell me that?'

Ben groaned. They'd been over this hundreds of times, but Reuben couldn't—or wouldn't—understand. 'That's an oil-vapour system, different thing altogether. They reckon it's cheaper.'

'Well of course it's cheaper,' grumbled Reuben. 'By the time you've ferried out all that coal for your generators ...'

There was a whistle from the speaking-tube on the wall. Reuben got up, unhooked the receiver and bellowed, 'Ahoy!'

Vince snatched his ear from the receiver and winced. Reuben always bellowed so loud he hardly needed the tube. He put the tube to his lips and said, 'That you, Reuben?'

He held the tube to his ear and grinned at the reply that sizzled from the tube. 'Oh, it's King Edward himself, is it? Well, your majesty, be kind enough to tell the principal keeper as there's a fog coming up like nobody's business.' His voice became more serious. 'Funny looking fog it is too. I never seen anything like it.'

Reuben replaced the speaking-tube. 'Vince says there's a fog coming up.'

'Fog? There was no sign earlier.'

'He reckons it's a thick un, Ben. Something funny about it.'

Ben pushed his plate back. 'Best go and see for myself. Boy's only learning, after all.'

He hurried out of the room. Reuben mopped up the last of his stew with a hunk of bread, stuffed it into his mouth and followed him.

Ben stared out of the gallery, shaking his head. 'Never seen a fog come up so fast—and so thick!'

The fog seemed to be rising straight from the surface of the sea like steam. It surged and billowed round the lighthouse, isolating it in a belt of swirling grey cloud.

Reuben looked out into the grey nothingness. 'Terrible thing, fog,' he said with gloomy relish. 'Worst thing for sailors there ever was.'

Ben shivered. 'And feel that cold. Coming right across from Iceland that, I reckon.'

'It's coming from where I saw that thing go into the sea,' said Vince.

Ben rounded on him irritably. 'Give over, boy. Go and start the siren going.'

Unexpectedly, Reuben came to Vince's support. 'He might be right though, Ben. It do seem unnatural, this fog, coming up so sudden like. I never seen anything like it.'

'Not you too,' said Ben wearily. He nodded to Vince. 'Well, get on with it, boy. Frequent blasts on the foghorn—and I *do* mean frequent.'

Reuben couldn't resist trying to score a point. 'Pity we're not still using oil. Everyone knows an oil-lamp gives better light in fog.'

As always Ben rose to the bait. 'Rubbish, that's just an old wives' tale. Electricity's just as good in fog, and a sight more reliable.'

The lamp went out.

Reuben gave a satisfied cackle. The timing was perfect. 'You was saying something about reliability, Ben,' he said with heavy irony.

Ben grabbed an oil-lamp, lit it and ran from the lamp room.

On the other side of the tiny island there was a wheezing groaning sound and a square blue shape materialised out of the fog. It was a blue London Police Box. Out of it stepped a tall man with wide inquisitive eyes and a tangle of curly hair. He wore loose comfortable clothes, a battered soft hat and a long trailing scarf. He was followed by a dark-eyed, brown-haired girl in Victorian clothes. The man was that mysterious traveller in Space and Time known as the Doctor, and his companion was a girl called Leela.

Leela looked round at the wet rocks and swirling fog. She shivered. 'You said I'd like Brighton. Well, I don't.'

'Does this look like Brighton?' asked the Doctor exasperatedly.

'How do I know? I don't know what Brighton's supposed to look like.'

'It isn't even Hove,' mused the Doctor. 'Could be Worthing, I suppose …'

Leela looked at the Police Box—in reality a-Space Time craft called the TARDIS. 'The machine has failed again?'

'No, not really,' said the Doctor defensively. 'Not *failed*, exactly. It's still the right planet, and I'm pretty sure we're still in the same time-zone—though we may have jumped forward a year or two. We're even in the right general area—assuming this is Worthing, of course.'

'You can't tell!' accused Leela. 'What's gone wrong?'

The Doctor cleared his throat. 'Well, you see, a localised condition of planetary atmospheric condensation caused a malfunction in the visual orientation circuits, or to put it another way, we got lost in the fog!'

He took a few paces around the rocks and paused in surprise. The sea winds had cleared the fog for a second or two, and he caught a glimpse of a tall thin shape towering above them. 'How very strange!'

'What is?'

'A lighthouse—without a light!'

Holding his oil-lamp high above his head, Ben hurried into the big generator room that occupied the whole of the base of the tower. The generator was still chugging busily away. It should have been producing power—but it wasn't. Puzzled, he went to examine the power feed lines. Perhaps a faulty connection … The electric lights came on again.

Ben looked at the throbbing generator. Although he'd never admit it to Reuben, electrical science was still in its infancy, and puzzling things like this still cropped up occasionally. Something in the atmosphere perhaps. Something to do with this strange fog.

With a last puzzled look at the generator, Ben turned and began to climb the stairs. As he left the room, the door to the coal storage bunker opened a fraction. There was a glow, and a faint crackling sound ...

As the light came on again, Vince turned triumphantly to Reuben. 'There, that didn't take long, did it?'

Reuben scowled. A major power failure would have been a big point on his side. 'Working, not working, working again! Never know where you are with it, do you?'

Vince shivered and slapped his arms across his chest. 'Perishing up here. I'll just go down and get my sweater.'

'You do that, boy, and bring mine up as well.'

Vince ran down the stairs, bumping into Ben on the landing. 'Come down for my sweater,' he explained. 'Freezing up there it is.'

Ben followed him into the crew room. 'Same in the generator room, even with the boilers.'

Vince went to his sea-chest, pulled out a heavy fisherman's jersey, and began pulling it over his head. 'Didn't take you long to repair her, though.'

Ben went over to his desk and took the log book from its drawer. 'I did nothing. Came on by herself.' He took pen and ink out of the drawer and opened the log book.

Vince stared at him. 'Came on by herself? What, for no reason?'

'It's got me fair flummoxed, Vince. There's something going on here tonight. Something I don't understand.'

He started writing in the log in his laborious copperplate, then paused and looked up. 'You and Reuben find all the oil-lamps you can get hold of and fill 'em up. I want several in every room— and one left burning. If the power goes again we won't be in the dark.'

The Doctor and Leela were working their way over slippery wet rocks towards the lighthouse. They were very near the coastline and Leela shook herself like a cat as a particularly violent shower of spray drenched her to the skin. She saw a light shining high above them. 'Look, Doctor!'

'Good. We'll just knock on the door and get directions and a date and be on our way. Once I know our exact Time-Space Co-ordinates...'

Leela jumped again, as a low booming note came through the fog. 'What was that? A sea beast?' She felt for her knife, then remembered, the Doctor wouldn't let her wear it with these clothes.

'It's only a foghorn,' said the Doctor reassuringly. 'It's to warn ships to stay away from these rocks. They might not spot the light in this fog.'

Leela stood still, poised, staring intently into the fog.

The Doctor said impatiently, 'Come on, Leela, you know what ships are? You saw some on the Thames, remember?'

The Doctor had first met Leela in the future on a faraway planet. She was a descendant of a planetary survey team that had become marooned. Over the years they had degenerated into the Sevateem, a tribe of extremely warlike savages, and Leela had been one of their fiercest warriors. Her travels with the Doctor had civilised her a little—but she reverted to the primitive immediately when there was any hint of trouble.

Part of Leela's savage inheritance was a kind of sixth sense that alerted her to the presence of danger. It was clear from the expression on her face that this instinct was in operation now. There is something wrong here, Doctor. Something dangerous and evil. I can feel it ...'

Vince filled another oil-lamp, lit it and set it to one side. 'Old Ben's really worried!'

Reuben's head emerged tortoise-like from the neck of his sweater. 'So he should be, boy. Him and his precious electricity. I told him often enough ...'

'Writing it all down in the log he is. Says he can't understand it.'

The electric lights went out again. The two men looked at each other.

Reuben was triumphant. 'Done it again, see?'

Vince shook his head. 'Poor old Ben. He'll be spitting blood, won't he?'

*

Lantern in hand, Ben hurtled down the stairs at a dangerous speed, and arrived panting in the generator room. Once again the generator was chugging merrily away, with nothing to explain the total loss of power. 'Not again,' he muttered. 'I don't believe it! Makes no flaming sense ...' He began checking over the generator.

There was a shattering crash behind him as the door to the coal bunker was flung open with tremendous force. Ben spun round, and his face twisted with horror at the hideous sight before him.

In his terror he dropped his lantern. The generator room was plunged into darkness, illuminated only by the glow of the thing in the doorway.

There was a faint crackling sound as it flowed towards him. Ben screamed with terror ...

2

STRANGE VISITORS

The melancholy boom of the siren drowned the sound of Ben's dying scream.

Vince released the handle and took out his watch. 'She's been off over two minutes this time.'

Reuben nodded gloomily. 'She'll not come back on again so quick this time.'

Vince shrugged. 'Don't make a lot of difference, do it, not in this fog. A ship'd have her bows right on Fang Rock before they'd see our old lamp in this.'

Reuben stared out into the night. There was nothing to be seen but grey swirling fog. 'It's a queer do, this fog. No cause for it.'

Vince tried to remember the scientific principles Ben had taught him. 'Cold air and warm air mixing. That's what causes fog.'

Reuben snorted. 'I've been thirty year in the service, Vince. One look at the sky and I know when fog's coming. And today was clear as clear. It isn't natural ...'

Uneasily Vince said, 'Maybe I'd best go down, see if Ben needs a hand.'

'Aye, you do that, lad.' As Vince moved away the old man repeated softly, 'It isn't natural ...'

The Doctor and Leela reached the lighthouse at last and climbed the steps. The Doctor pounded on the heavy wooden door. 'Keeper! Keeper!' There was no reply. He shoved at the door and it creaked slowly open.

They stood on the threshold of the generator room, peering into semi-darkness. The room was lit only by the faint glow from the boiler fire. The Doctor listened to the steady throbbing of the machinery. The generator seems to be working—so why isn't there any power?'

'I'm not a Tesh—' Leela paused, correcting herself. 'I mean a—Teshnician!'

The Doctor peered at the generator. 'Could be shorting out somewhere I suppose ...'

Leela could see him mentally rolling up his sleeves. 'And I suppose you're going to mend it?'

A little guiltily, the Doctor stepped back. 'What, without permission? Wouldn't dream of it! We'd better find the crew—this way, I think.'

They crossed the room and began climbing the stairs. 'Teshnician, where are you?' called the Doctor. 'Hullo, anybody there?'

A light bobbed down towards them and a scared voice called, 'That you, Ben?'

'No, it isn't.'

They rounded the curve of stairs on to the landing and saw a thin young man in a fisherman's sweater. He was clutching an oil-lamp and was obviously very frightened. He stared at the Doctor and Leela in sheer disbelief. 'Here ... who are you then?'

'I'm the Doctor, and this is Leela. You seem to be having some trouble.'

'How'd you get here?'

'We came in the TARDIS,' explained Leela helpfully.

Before she could go into more detail the Doctor said hurriedly, 'We're mislaid mariners. Our ... craft is moored on the other side of the island.'

Vince nodded, reassured. Funny name, TARDIS, but then, lots of people gave their boats fancy foreign names. 'Got lost in the fog, did you ? You'd best come into the crewroom.'

As he led them inside he asked, 'Where are you making for?'

Leela gave the Doctor a look and said, 'Brighton!'

Vince laughed. 'Well, well, you did get lost then, didn't you?'

He began lighting oil-lamps, filling the room with their warm yellow glow.

The Doctor looked round. Except for its semi-circular shape the room was much like the main cabin of a ship. Bunks lined the walls, there were chests and lockers, and a litter of personal possessions. There was a table in the centre of the room. Against the wall stood an old wooden desk, and a smaller table with a wireless telegraph apparatus.

Vince bustled about, offering them chairs. He was nervous and chatty, obviously glad of company. 'I'll get you some hot food, soon as we're sorted out. You'll not want to put to sea again in this. This TARDIS of yours, small craft is she?'

'Yes,' said the Doctor.

'No,' said Leela.

Vince stared at them.

'Big in some ways, small in others,' the Doctor explained hastily. 'Now then, what's the trouble here?'

'Generator keeps playing up, sir. Lights go off then come on again, for no reason.'

The Doctor nodded thoughtfully. 'Tricky things, some of these early generators.'

'Ours isn't an early one, sir. It's the latest modern design. Driving Ben wild though, all the same.'

'Ben?'

'He's the engineer, sir.'

'Are there just the two of you?'

'Three, sir. Old Reuben's still up in the lamp room. Fit to bust, he is. Fair killing himself.'

Leela was puzzled. 'He is under a spell?'

Vince gave her a look. 'What I mean is, he's one of the old-fashioned sort, see? Hates electricity. Never been happy since they took out the oil.'

The Doctor smiled. 'I know the type. In the early days of oil he'd have been saying there was nothing like a really large candle!'

'That's old Reuben right enough!'

'Where's your engineer now? I should have thought he would have been working on the generator.'

'But he is, sir. You must have seen him when you came in.'

'No, I didn't.'

'He'll have stepped out for a moment then. You missed him in the fog.'

'No,' said Leela definitely. 'If anyone had been near I would have heard them.'

Vince looked utterly baffled. 'Suppose I'd better go and look for him then.' It was clear he didn't have much enthusiasm for the task.

'That's all right,' said the Doctor. 'Tell you what—' he paused. 'What's your name?'

'Vince, sir. Vince Hawkins.'

'I'll go and look for your engineer, Mr Hawkins. As a matter of fact I'm something of an engineer myself. Perhaps I can give him a hand. You look after the young lady.'

There was a note of authority in the Doctor's voice and Vince said meekly, 'Right you are, sir.'

The Doctor went down the stairs and Vince smiled shyly at Leela. 'This is quite a treat for me, miss.'

'Is it?' Leela gave him a puzzled look and wandered over to the telegraph, idly lifting the brass key and letting it fall.

'Don't touch that please, miss,' said Vince apologetically. 'Ben's pride and joy, that is. No one else is allowed to handle it.' Leela moved away from the telegraph and Vince went on. 'It's a lonely life on the lighthouse you see. Sometimes I go out and talk to the seals, just for a change from Reuben and Ben.'

'Seals are animals. Sea creatures?'

'That's right, miss.'

'Then it is stupid to talk to them. You should listen to the old ones of your tribe, it is the only way to learn.'

Vince sighed. 'I'll get you some food and a hot drink, miss.'

Leela tugged ruefully at her wet dress. 'I need some dry clothes more than anything else.'

'I'm afraid we don't have anything suitable for a lady,' began Vince.

'I'm not a lady, Vince,' said Leela calmly. She eyed him thoughtfully. 'We are much of a size. Clothes such as you wear will be quite suitable for me.'

Vince looked down at his fisherman's trousers and sweater. 'But these are men's things, miss, working clothes ...'

He broke off, gasping. Leela had unbuttoned her wet dress and was calmly stepping out of it. 'That's my clothes-chest over there, miss, just you help yourself. I'll get you that hot food.' He turned and almost ran into the kitchen.

As she struggled out of the wet skirt, Leela stared after him in puzzlement. There was no doubt about it, these Earth people were very strange ...

The Doctor gazed into the darkness of the generator room. 'Anyone here?' he called. 'Ben? Ben?'

No answer. The Doctor crossed the room, passing the still-throbbing generator, and opened the outside door. A blast of icy air, mixed with fog, swirled into the room. The Doctor called out into the night. 'Ben? Ben, are you there?' Still no answer. Only the thunder of the waves on the nearby rocks. Puzzled, the Doctor closed the door—and the lights came on.

The Doctor rubbed his chin. 'Curiouser and curiouser!' He began walking round the generator, examining it more closely. The brightness of the electric lamps had dispelled the shadows behind it, and now the Doctor saw a huddled shape lying against the wall. He knelt to examine it, just as Vince came in, and looked round the brightly-lit room in astonishment. 'Well done, sir. You are an engineer and no mistake.' Suddenly Vince realised that the Doctor was nowhere in sight. 'Doctor, where are you?'

The Doctor appeared from behind the generator. 'Over here.'

'You managed to find the trouble, then?'

'I always find trouble,' said the Doctor sombrely.

Vince looked uneasily at him, sensing the strangeness of his manner. 'Ben'll be pleased.'

'I doubt it.'

Leela came into the room. She was wearing Vince's best pair of boots and one of his spare jerseys, and buckling the belt on his best shore-going trousers.

'Oh Ben'll be pleased right enough, sir,' said Vince. 'He couldn't make head nor tail of what was wrong. I wonder where he's got to?'

The Doctor pointed to the shape behind the generator. 'Ben's down here. He's been dead for some time.'

Vince rushed over to the body. 'Ben!' he gasped. 'Oh Ben, no ... no ...' His voice trailed away.

'What killed him, Doctor?' asked Leela practically.

'As far as I can tell, a massive electric shock. He must have died instantly.'

Vince looked up. 'The generator, you mean? But he was always so careful.'

Leela looked at the throbbing machine. 'It was dark ...'

'He had a lantern, though.' Vince rubbed a hand over his eyes. 'I just can't believe this has happened.'

Gently the Doctor helped him to his feet. 'Vince, hadn't you better go and tell Reuben?'

Vince nodded wearily. 'Yes sir.' He stumbled away.

The Doctor looked at the body, and Leela looked at the Doctor. 'You do not believe he was killed by the machine?'

'No.'

'Then what—'

The Doctor put a finger to his lips and crept silently over to the coal store. He picked up a heavy shovel and nodded to Leela. She flung open the door ... but there was nothing there except coal.

The Doctor threw down the shovel. 'I thought perhaps there was something nasty in the coal shed, but apparently not.' He shut the door. 'But there's something very nasty somewhere on this island.'

'A sea creature?'

The Doctor was prowling restlessly about. 'If it is, it's a most unusual one. It opens and shuts doors, comes and goes without so much as a wet footprint, and has a mysterious ability to interfere with electrical power.' He kneeled by Ben's body and examined it once more. He saw that there was something caught beneath it, and dragged it free.

'What have you found, Doctor?'

'Ben's lantern,' said the Doctor slowly. He held it up. The heavy metal frame was melted, warped, twisted, like candle wax in the heat of a furnace. The Doctor handed it to Leela. 'What kind of sea creature could do a thing like that?'

3

SHIPWRECK

Reuben listened to the news of Ben's death in stunned silence. When Vince had finished, the old man said slowly, 'Ben knew every inch of that machine. Don't make sense, boy, him dying like that.'

'That's what happened, according to the Doctor. Massive electric shock, he said.'

'This Doctor—foreigner is he?'

'Don't think so. Young lady speaks a bit strange like, though. Why?'

'Spies!' said Reuben dramatically.

Vince smiled, despite his grief. 'Spies? What'd spies be doing on Fang Rock?'

'There's Frogs,' said Reuben. 'And Ruskies. Germans too. Can't trust none of 'em.'

'These two ain't spies, Reuben.'

'Well, all this trouble started just about the time they got here. Don't forget that!'

'You ain't saying *they* might have done for Ben?'

Pleased with the effect of his words Reuben said solemnly, 'I'm saying there's strange doings here tonight, and for all we know them two strangers are at the bottom of it. Reckon I best go down and keep an eye on 'em.'

Vince didn't know what to think. His instinct was to trust the Doctor, but what Reuben had said was true enough. Another thought struck him. 'Here, Reuben, you'll have to send a message to the shore station. We need a relief engineer—and the boat can take Ben away ...'

'I'll see to it soon as it's light. Where is he?'

'Generator room. I know it don't seem respectful. But it's only till the boat comes ...'

Reuben lowered his voice. 'He won't rest easy, you know, lad!'

'What do you mean?' stammered Vince.

'If he was killed by that machine there'll be anger in his soul. Men who die like that don't never rest easy!'

Reuben stumped off. Vince stood alone in the lamp room. The events of the last few hours suddenly closed in on him and he began shaking with fear.

The Doctor was examining the telegraph apparatus when Reuben came into the crew room.

'Very interesting this, Leela—a fine example of an early Marconi wireless telegraph.'

'Leave that be, sir, if you don't mind,' said Reuben sharply.

The Doctor turned. 'You'll be Reuben I take it. Shouldn't you be using this telegraph to report your engineer's death?'

'Wireless won't bring Ben back. I'll semaphore in the morning, when the fog clears.'

'You do know how to use the telegraph?'

"Course I do, we all does. But Ben was the expert. I'll use the semaphore tomorrow.'

The Doctor nodded understandingly, guessing that the old man had only the vaguest idea how to work the device, but was too obstinate to admit it.

Reuben stripped a blanket from a bunk and folded it over his arm. Leela touched it curiously, but he snatched it away.

'You leave that alone, miss.'

'What is it for?'

'I'm going to make Ben a shroud. We have proper customs here in England. It ain't fitting for a body just to be left.'

Suddenly the Doctor realised the reason for Reuben's hostility. 'You think *we* had something to do with Ben's death?'

'I know what I know. And what I think.'

'Incontrovertible,' said the Doctor politely.

Reuben glowered at him. 'Don't start talking in your own lingo neither, I won't have that.'

'What are you going to do? Clap us in irons?'

'I'm senior on this lighthouse now, and—'

'See here, I'm only trying to help you,' snapped the Doctor.

Reuben backed away. 'Vince and me'll manage. Now I'll just go and tend to poor Ben.'

'Stubborn old mule ...' muttered the Doctor irritably.

Leela was still carrying the twisted remains of the lamp. 'You think the creature that did this will come back?'

'I just don't know.'

As always, Leela was in favour of direct action. 'If it is here on the rock we should take weapons and hunt it!'

The Doctor tapped the lamp with a long finger. 'I don't fancy playing tag in the darkness with something that can do this.' He paused for a moment. 'Young Vince is still pretty shaken. I think I'll go up and have a word with him. You stay here.'

The Doctor went out. As soon as he was gone, Leela slipped a heavy sailor's knife from her boot. She'd found it at the bottom of Vince's chest and appropriated it immediately. Despite the Doctor's prohibitions, Leela never felt properly dressed without a weapon. She hefted the knife thoughtfully, tested point and edge with her thumb, then set off down the stairs.

In the lamp room Reuben sat cross-legged by Ben's body, sewing the corpse into its shroud. Like all old sailors he was handy with needle and thread. He didn't hear Leela as she slipped silently past him and out into the fog.

The Doctor leaned against the lamp-room wall. Vince tended the steadily flashing light and gave regular blasts on the foghorn, while he told the Doctor about the light in the sky. The Doctor listened keenly. 'And what time was all this?'

'Couple of hours ago, just getting dark. It went down into the sea, over there.'

'How far away?'

'About a mile or two, near as I could tell. Dunno how big it was, you see. Soon after that the fog started to come down, and it got cold, all of a sudden like.'

'Yes,' said the Doctor thoughtfully. 'I noticed the cold. Good lad, Vince, you've been very observant.'

'Thank you, sir.' Vince was both flattered and puzzled by the Doctor's interest in his story.

The Doctor stared out at the fog that surrounded the tower. 'A fireball, eh? That might explain a great deal ...'

Knife in hand, body poised for instant attack, Leela crept silently through the darkness. She had already covered most of the tiny island, and so far she had found nothing. She had hoped for some kind of tracks, but nothing showed on the bare rocky surface.

Her foot slipped and she almost tumbled into a shallow rock pool. She drew back, then paused, looking harder at the water. Something was floating on the surface of the pool. Several somethings, in fact. Leela knelt down. Fish! Tiny, dead fish.

There was a faint crackling behind her and she whirled round. She crouched motionless, listening, peering into the fog. But she saw nothing. Just the swirling fog. Stealthily she crept on, moving in the direction of the sound ...

The Doctor was entertaining Vince with accounts of famous lighthouses he had visited during his travels. 'Of course, on Pharos they had terrible trouble keeping the bonfire alight. Mind you, they had plenty of slaves to carry wood ...'

Vince nodded vaguely. 'I suppose it's all done different abroad. Didn't know they still had slaves though.'

(Vince didn't realise that the Doctor's visit to the famous Alexandrian lighthouse had taken place in the third century BC.)

Reuben entered and gave the Doctor a suspicious stare. He nodded to Vince. 'I'll take over here, lad. Time you got some supper.'

'I'm all right,' protested Vince. Somehow he found the Doctor's company reassuring.

'I'll take over,' insisted Reuben. 'Long night ahead of us.' He glared meaningfully at the Doctor. 'I expect you'll be tired, mister? There's bunks in the crew room.'

'Tired?' said the Doctor in surprise. 'No, no, not a bit of it. You carry on, don't mind me.'

Reuben grunted. 'I've stoked the boiler, Vince, and made poor Ben decent.'

Vince nodded silently. He didn't like to think about the corpse down in the generator room.

Reuben glared at the Doctor, who gave him a cheerful smile. He turned back to Vince. 'Well, off you go, lad!'

Vince went.

Reuben gave the Doctor another dirty look, and this time the Doctor replied with a friendly wink.

Reuben turned away in disgust, reaching for his oil-can. Some people just didn't know when they weren't wanted.

Vince was on the landing by the crew room when he heard a dragging sound from down below. He paused, listening. The sound came again, like someone dragging a heavy sack. 'Is someone down there?' he called. There was no answer. Vince bit his lip. 'Ben?' he called fearfully. Still no answer. Just the dragging sound, moving away. Fearfully Vince began to descend the gloomy stairs. The light of his lantern cast wavering shadows on the walls.

Leela stood tensely in the darkness, feeling both frustrated and angry. She'd been close on the track of the crackling sound, then suddenly she had lost it, somewhere near the lighthouse. Now she was waiting, alert for the faintest sound.

Suddenly the crackling began again. It came nearer, nearer—and now it was mixed with a dragging sound …

Leela peered into the darkness. Was there a faint glow there beyond the densely swirling fog?

The crackling moved away. It became fainter, and then suddenly stopped. The creature had gone back into the sea, Leela decided. She headed back towards the lighthouse.

Fearfully, Vince crept into the generator room. It was brightly lit—and empty. The generator was throbbing steadily. Reluctantly he looked at the dark shape by the wall. With sudden horror he realised that the shape wasn't Ben's body after all. It was the ripped-open empty shroud. He ran to the speaking-tube and blew frantically. 'Reuben!' he screamed. 'Reuben, are you there? It's Ben! He's walking ...'

In the lamp room Reuben took the speaker away from his ear and stared at it unbelievingly. 'What's that?' he bellowed. 'Talk sense, boy! Pull yourself together.'

Clutching the speaking-tube Vince babbled, 'It's true I tell you. He's not down here now. He's gone! You said he'd walk. You said—' The outer door burst open with a crash. Vince gave a yell of fear and dropped the speaking-tube.

Leela stood in the doorway. 'Did you see it?' she demanded. 'Did it come here?'

Vince was too terrified to speak.

Reuben blew into the speaking-tube and yelled. 'Vince! What's going on down there?'

The Doctor had been on the outer gallery, staring out into the fog. Now he reappeared, tapping Reuben on the shoulder. 'There's a light out there!'

Confused and angry, the old man whirled round. 'What? What's that?'

'There's a light. Out there at sea. I think it's a ship.'

Leela had managed to shake his story out of Vince. She looked at him disbelievingly. 'The dead do not walk. It is impossible.'

'I heard this dragging noise, I tell you—and when I got down here he'd gone.'

'There was something out there on the rocks just now,' said Leela slowly. 'And I too heard a dragging sound ...'

The speaking-tube gave a shrill blast. Automatically Vince picked it up and listened. 'It's Reuben. He says there's a ship just off the rocks. He says she's going to strike!'

The call to duty overcame Vince's fears and he began dashing up the stairs. With a baffled glance at the empty shroud Leela followed.

*

In the lamp room, everyone was round the great telescope. Reuben was at the eyepiece. 'It's a ship right enough. Steam yacht by the look of her.'

The Doctor took his place. Through the powerful telescope he could see the fog-shrouded shape of the ship, lights blazing as it ploughed recklessly through the waves, heading straight towards them. 'She's going too fast!'

'Fool to be going at all on a night like this,' said Reuben. 'Any skipper worth his ticket—'

The lamp went out.

Luckily the oil lamps were still burning. Reuben was taking no more chances with electricity. He ran to the siren and began sounding it frantically, sending bellow after bellow through the fog. 'Warning devices, Vince,' he shouted.

'I'll get 'em, Reuben.' Vince had already run down the steps to the service room. A moment later he reappeared, his arms full of rockets and maroons.

'Miss, you take over the siren,' shouted Reuben. He grabbed a Verey pistol and loaded it. The Doctor was already mounting a signal rocket on its firing stand.

'They'll strike any minute now,' shouted Reuben. He fired the Verey pistol and a red flare went sizzling out into the fog.

The ship was very close now and they could see frantic figures scurrying about on deck. Reuben was watching in fascinated horror. The Doctor lugged the signal rocket to the gallery rail, but Reuben waved him aside. 'It's no use, they're too late to alter course. She's going to strike!'

With a grinding crash the yacht smashed on to the jagged rocks.

4

THE SURVIVORS

'Too late, she's struck!' shouted Reuben. They caught a brief glimpse of the yacht through a break in the fog. She was well aground on the rocks, her bows thrust unnaturally high into the air. Then the fog closed in, hiding the wreck.

'What will happen now?' asked Leela.

'Sea'll pound her on those rocks till she breaks up, Miss.'

'Then they will all die.'

Leela's prosaic words reminded Reuben of his duty. 'If there are survivors we'll find 'em by East Crag. Tide'll bring 'em in. Mister, you keep that siren going. Vince, bring the rocket-line.'

The Doctor had no intention of missing all the excitement. 'Keep that siren going, Leela,' he ordered and rushed out after Reuben and Vince.

Leela went to the siren and pulled the lever. The deep booming note rang out, like the cry of a love-sick sea monster. Pleased with the effect, Leela pulled the lever again.

Reuben, Vince and the Doctor gathered rescue equipment from the service room, then hurried down the stairs. As they ran through the generator room, Reuben pointed to a coil of rope in the corner. 'Bring that rope, mister,' he ordered.

The Doctor went to obey, amused at the way in which the crisis had restored the old man's confidence. As he bent to pick up the rope, his hand brushed the metal guard-rail around the generator. There was a crackling sound and a flash of blue sparks. The Doctor snatched his hand away. The rail had given him a distinct electric shock.

Puzzled, the Doctor peered at the rail. It was quite separate from the generator. There was no reason for it to be live ...

'You coming with that rope, mister?' shouted Reuben.

The Doctor threw the coil of rope over his shoulder and hurried off after the others.

Reuben led them through the foggy darkness at a run, to a point where a narrow cove cut into the coastline. They clambered down a rocky path on to a little shingle beach, and stared out to sea. 'Tide'll bring 'em here, if they got any boats away,' said Reuben confidently. He re-loaded the Verey pistol and fired, sending a red flare out into the fog. 'Ahoy there,' he called. 'Ahoy!'

Leela gave another blast on the foghorn, then wandered on to the outer gallery, feeling rather indignant the Doctor had managed to trick her into staying out of danger. She leaned over the rail, hoping to be able to see the rescue party. The fog cleared for a few moments and she suddenly caught a brief glimpse of a shapeless glowing mass, moving towards the sea. It slithered across an edge of rock and disappeared.

Leela stared in astonishment—and the lighthouse lamp came on.

Gazing round the little beach, Vince turned and saw the light. 'Reuben, the light is on again,' he called.

Reuben glanced briefly over his shoulder. 'Danged electricity, wouldn't happen with oil.'

'No, I don't think it would,' said the Doctor, almost to himself. 'It seems to need electricity.'

'Listen,' said Reuben, 'I think I heard something.' He fired off another Verey light and shouted again. 'Ahoy, there!'

'Ahoy ...' A faint answering hail came drifting through the fog.

'This way,' bellowed Reuben, in a voice as loud as the foghorn itself. He fired off another Verey light. 'Vince, and you, mister, stand by with those lines.'

They waited tensely, staring out into the fog, while waves crashed on to the tiny beach. Then a shape loomed out of the darkness. It was a ship's lifeboat.

Reuben took the line from the Doctor, uncoiled it and threw with surprising force. The line snaked out and a burly figure in the bows of the lifeboat caught it and made it fast. 'Come on now, haul,' ordered Reuben, and all three men began heaving on the line.

As soon as the lifeboat grated on the shingle, the seaman in the bows jumped out and helped them to haul it in. But before they could bring it much closer to land a second, smaller man took a flying leap from the boat, landing face down in the water.

The Doctor helped the spluttering figure to his feet, passed him along to Vince and turned to the other survivors. There were only two more of them, a tall military-looking man, and a shivering fair-haired girl. He helped them out of the boat and up on to the beach.

Not without difficulty Vince helped the soaking, bedraggled figure of the man who'd jumped, into the crew room. Reuben followed with the tall soldierly-looking man and the girl.

Vince's survivor collapsed gasping on a chair.

He was a stoutly-built man with a spoiled, self-indulgent look about him. Diamonds glinted from his cuff-links and tie-pin, and the rings on his plump fingers. His expensive-looking clothes were drenched with sea-water. Vince couldn't help feeling sorry for him.

He did his best to cheer the man up. 'You'll be all right, sir. Come over by the stove and dry yourself.'

'Needn't have got so wet in the first place,' grumbled Reuben. 'No call to go jumping out like that.'

The soldierly man chuckled. 'His lordship was anxious to get ashore!'

'Brandy!' croaked the stout man faintly. 'Give me brandy.'

'Never you mind him and his brandy,' ordered Reuben. 'See to the young lady first.'

Obediently, Vince transferred his attentions to the shivering girl. 'Here ma'am, let me help you.' He lowered her into a chair and wrapped a blanket round her shoulders.

'I'm all right,' she whispered faintly.

'Well, I ain't,' said the stout man. 'I'm soaked to the skin.'

'Sea water's healthy, Henry,' mocked the tall man.

The other gave him a filthy look. 'I need a drink, I tell you. I'll catch my death like this.' He caught Vince by the sleeve. 'Get me a brandy, young fellow.'

Vince pulled away and began tipping coal on the iron stove. 'You don't need no brandy, sir,' he said cheerily. 'Hot soup's the ticket for you. I'll get you all some in a minute.'

'Don't tell me what I need,' said the other peevishly. 'Dammit, hasn't anybody got a flask?'

Reuben looked disgustedly at him. 'You see to 'em as best you can, Vince. I'd better go up and check on the lamp.'

Vince poked the coals into a blaze and then turned to the girl. 'Come over to the stove and get yourself warm, miss.'

He moved her chair closer to the stove and she hunched over it, warming her hands. 'Thank you, that's very kind of you. What's your name?'

'Vince, miss. Vince Hawkins.'

'Thank you, Hawkins,' said the young lady graciously.

Vince stammered, 'I'd best get on with that soup ...' He hurried off to the kitchen. The stout man glared indignantly after him, and the tall man smiled in sardonic amusement, enjoying the other's discomfiture.

On the lamp-room gallery, the Doctor and Leela were talking in low voices. Leela told the Doctor about the glowing shape she had seen on the rocks.

'What was it like?' asked the Doctor.

'I couldn't see it clearly. But it shone, like a rotten fungus in the forest.'

'Luminous ... Do you think you could take me to the place where you saw it?'

'Yes, I think so.'

'Good. Don't tell the others. We don't want a panic.'

'What do you think be going on here, mister?' asked a voice behind them. Reuben was standing by the door.

'I don't know,' said the Doctor frankly. 'When I find out, I'll tell you.'

'Wouldn't try to find out too much. Some things it ain't wise to meddle with ...'

'What do you mean, old one?' asked Leela.

'I reckon I know what you saw. They always said the Beast of Fang Rock would come back.'

'The Beast of Fang Rock?'

'Aye,' said Reuben. And with gloomy relish, he launched into a long rambling tale of tragedy in the early days of the lighthouse. A three-man crew had, been overtaken by some mysterious and tragic fate. 'When the relief boat come, there was only one left alive, and he was stark staring mad. They found the body of the second cold and dead in the lamp room—and the third was found floating in the sea. Two dead, one mad—that was the work of the Beast! And now it's back.'

In the crew room Vince was still fussing round the blonde young lady. The tall man looked on with quiet amusement, the stout one kept up a constant stream of protest. 'I need some dry clothes, and I need them now,' he said petulantly.

'All in good time, sir! I'll just give the young lady her soup, and then I'll get round to you.'

'But I'll catch my death of cold standing about like this!'

'Shouldn't be so impulsive, Henry,' said the tall man with mock concern. 'Jumping right out of the boat like that!'

'When I want your opinion, I'll ask for it. Now, what about this brandy, young fellow? Surely you keep some in the medical supplies?'

Vince shook his head. 'No liquor allowed on this lighthouse, sir. Against regulations.'

The stout man said angrily, 'To hell with your regulations—' He broke off as the Doctor and Leela came into the room.

The Doctor looked round. 'Where's the other man, your cox'n?'

'Oh, Harker, he stayed to secure the boat, I believe. No doubt he'll be up directly.'

'Good. I'll wait.' The Doctor sat down, and there was a moment of uneasy silence. Leela stood in the doorway, looking round the little group. She could feel the tension in the air.

'Excellent fellow, Harker,' drawled the tall man. 'It was his seamanship got us ashore.'

'Whose seamanship was it that got you on the rocks in the first place?' asked the Doctor blandly.

The tall man looked sharply at him. 'I don't believe we've met, sir. Are you in charge here?'

'No—but I'm full of ideas.'

Vince brought bowls of soup for the two men and said, 'Beg pardon, Doctor, but I think it's time I stoked the boilers.' He looked appealingly at the Doctor, making no attempt to move.

'Off you go then, Vince. Leela, you go with him.'

Vince and Leela left, and the girl looked reprovingly at the Doctor. 'You're a Doctor then?'

'That's right.'

'And you send a woman to stoke boilers?' The young lady was obviously shocked.

'Leela's a rather unusual young lady. Besides, one of the keepers was electrocuted this evening. Since then young Vince doesn't like to go to the generator room alone.'

The soldierly man nodded understanding. 'Disturbing thing for a young fellow, the first sight of death. Remember when I was in India ...'

The other man groaned. 'Oh not one of your army stories, Jimmy. They're even more boring than your House of Commons anecdotes.'

The Doctor looked curiously at the two men. They were travelling companions, and presumably friends, yet they were completely different types, one laconic and soldierly, the other like a spoiled, greedy child. Moreover, they spoke to each other as if they were bitter enemies. He decided that it would help if he had names to attach to all these new faces. He addressed the tall man. 'Shouldn't we introduce ourselves?'

'Yes, of course. The young lady is Miss Adelaide Lesage, Lord Palmerdale's confidential secretary. The wet gentleman is Lord Henry Palmerdale, the well-known financier. And I'm Colonel James Skinsale, Member of Parliament for Thurley. And you are ...'

'I'm the Doctor—my companion's name is Leela. Where were you heading for, when your yacht struck?'

It was Lord Palmerdale who answered. 'Southampton. I've a special train waiting to take me to London. I must be there before the Stock Exchange opens.'

Adelaide sighed theatrically. 'The pressures of business, you know. If we'd been able to stay on in Deauville none of this would have happened.'

'We'd popped across the Channel in the yacht,' explained Palmerdale airily. 'We all had a little flutter in the Casino. Though in Jimmy's case it was more of a plunger—eh Jimmy?'

'You're very cheerful for a man whose yacht has been wrecked,' Skinsale said sourly.

Palmerdale waved a disparaging hand. 'Insured.'

'What about the crew?' asked the Doctor. 'Were any other boats launched?'

Skinsale shrugged. 'I'm afraid we didn't wait to see, Doctor. His Lordship was in rather a hurry to leave the sinking ship!'

Palmerdale shot him a venomous look. 'I've already told you, it's imperative that I reach London before the stock market opens.'

'Oh, was that the reason?' drawled Skinsale.

'I'm afraid you've no chance of getting to London tonight,' said the Doctor firmly. 'Not in this fog.'

Skinsale gave a sudden bark of laughter. 'The wheel of fortune, eh, Henry? Perhaps you didn't win all you thought at the Casino.'

Leela kept watch while Vince shovelled coal into the boiler. As he flung on the last shovel of coal she said, 'Listen!'

'What? I can't hear nothing ...'

'Something is *dragging* over the rocks towards us!'

'Ben?' whispered Vince fearfully. 'He be coming back. Coming back for me!'

Leela grabbed him by the shoulders and shook him. 'Go and tell the Doctor. Call him from the room before you tell him, and don't let the others hear. Give me that!'

Leela took the shovel from Vince's hands and gave him a push. As he fled, she took up her position behind the outer door, shovel raised like an axe.

The dragging sound was very near now. Slowly the door started to open ...

5

RETURN OF THE DEAD

The door creaked slowly open and a massive shape appeared in the doorway. It backed into the room, dragging a heavy burden, wrapped up in an old tarpaulin.

Leela put the cold metal of the shovel against its neck. 'Don't move!'

The figure swung round, revealing itself to be a massive barrel-chested man in a blue seaman's jersey. Leela backed away, shovel raised to strike. 'I said don't move!'

'It's all right, Leela,' said the Doctor's voice behind her. 'This one's a friend—aren't you Harker?'

The big seaman gave a puzzled nod. 'That's right, sir. I was delayed, d'ye see. I found this.' He pulled back the tarpaulin.

The Doctor looked at the mangled shape at Harker's feet. 'Poor wretch.'

Leela came forward. 'What is it, Doctor?'

'All that's left of poor Ben, I'm afraid. Where did you find him, Harker?'

'In the sea, sir. Came drifting in when I moored the boat.' He looked down at the body, then looked hurriedly away. 'Terrible what the sea can do to a man ...'

'It wasn't the sea that did that.' The Doctor paused. 'Harker, there's hot soup waiting in the crew room. It's just up those stairs. The others are already there.'

'Aye, aye, sir,' said Harker obediently, and went off.

The Doctor pulled the body away from the door and closed it. He covered it over again with the tarpaulin.

Leela was no stranger to violent death, but even she was glad to see the body covered up. 'Do you think the Beast attacked him, Doctor?'

327

'What Beast?'

'The Beast of Fang Rock.'

'No such animal—not in the way Reuben means.'

'Reuben said there was.'

'Leela, the people who live in these parts have been fisher folk for generations. They're almost as primitive and superstition-riddled as your lot!'

Leela wasn't convinced. 'Reuben's story about those men ... Two dead, one mad.'

'One man kills the other in a brawl, jumps in the sea in a fit of remorse. Third man spends weeks with a corpse for company and goes out of his mind.'

'All right, then, what about this body? What about those—marks?'

'Post mortem,' said the Doctor briefly. 'Something wanted to make a detailed study of human anatomy. That's why it took Ben's body.'

Vince's voice came down the stairs. 'Doctor? Are you there?'

'Quick,' said the Doctor. They wrapped the body securely in its tarpaulin and thrust it into a corner. Vince came in and looked apprehensively at Leela. 'That noise ... Did you find out what it was?'

'It was only the seaman, returning from the boat,' said the Doctor.

'But the dragging sound?'

Before the Doctor could stop her Leela said, 'He was bringing back Ben's body. He found it floating in the sea.'

Vince gasped. 'So he did walk! It's true what Reuben said ...'

'Stop that, Vince,' said Leela sharply. 'I have told you, the dead don't walk.'

Vince gave the Doctor an agonised look. 'But you said he was dead. How did he get in the sea?'

The Doctor made his voice calm and reassuring. 'Obviously I was too hasty, Vince. Massive electric shock can produce a death-like coma. Poor Ben recovered consciousness, staggered out on to the rocks, fell into the sea and was finally drowned.' Vince stared at him unbelievingly. 'Time you got on with your work,' said the Doctor briskly. 'There's nothing supernatural happening—just a tragic accident.'

'He wasn't breathing when I saw him, that I'll swear.'

'I told you, he was in a coma. Electricity has strange effects, you know.'

Vince nodded slowly. 'Yes, I suppose it must have been the electricity. Sorry, Doctor, I reckon I made a bit of a fool of myself.'

He turned and went slowly away.

When he was out of earshot, Leela whispered, 'Why didn't you tell him the truth?'

The Doctor stared broodingly at the tarpaulin-covered body. 'Because I don't know what the truth is—yet!'

Harker sat silently by the stove, his big hands clasped round a steaming mug of soup. 'You moored the boat securely?' demanded Palmerdale.

Harker looked up at him and nodded, but didn't speak.

'Good. When you're rested we'll make for the mainland.'

Skinsale said, 'Are you mad, Henry?'

'I've made up my mind. It's the only way.'

'But it's out of the question. Good Lord, in a fog like this ...'

'It can't be more than five or six miles,' said Palmerdale impatiently. 'No trouble at all to a seaman like Harker here.'

Skinsale threw up his hands in despair and turned to the girl. 'Reason with him, Adelaide. Perhaps you can make him see sense.'

Before Adelaide could speak Palmerdale shouted, 'You two can come with me, or you can stay here, just as you wish. My mind is made up.'

Harker slammed his mug down on the table. 'And so's mine. I'm not taking a boat out in this.'

Palmerdale stared at him as though a chair or a table had suddenly found a voice. He took it for granted that the lower orders did as they were told. 'What did you say, Harker?'

'I'll take no boat out, not after what I've seen tonight. And that's flat.'

'Damn your insolence,' spluttered Palmerdale. 'You're my employee, and you'll obey my order.'

'Will I?' Harker turned away and spat into the stove.

Skinsale chuckled. 'Hang him from the yard arm, Henry. This is mutiny!'

Abandoning Harker for the moment, Palmerdale turned to a different grievance. 'As I see it, the accident was entirely due to inefficiency on the part of the lighthouse service. So they have the responsibility of seeing I reach the mainland.'

'That won't wash, old chap,' said Skinsale scornfully. 'You can't possibly expect the lighthouse people—'

Adelaide joined in to support her employer. 'His lordship is quite right,' she said primly. 'If the light had been working ...'

'We'd still have struck the rocks, at the speed we were going,' said Skinsale.

Harker looked up from the fire. 'You're right there, sir. We should have been going dead slow in them conditions. And it weren't the Captain's fault, neither.'

Palmerdale went red with anger. 'That's quite enough, Harker. The fact remains that the light wasn't working. There'll be an inquiry, I assure you.'

'The inquiry has already begun,' said another voice. The Doctor was in the doorway, Leela beside him.

Skinsale gaped at him. 'What inquiry? What are you talking about?'

'I just thought I ought to come up and warn you. Keep together, and stay here, in this room. Harker, you ought to get some rest.'

Harker rose obediently, went over to a bunk and stretched out, pulling a blanket over him. The Doctor and Leela went back downstairs, leaving the rest of the castaways gaping after them.

'Amazing air of authority, that chap,' said Skinsale thoughtfully. 'I wonder who he really is?'

Palmerdale slumped into a chair. 'If you ask me, the fellow's not quite all there.' He tapped his forehead meaningfully. 'Those staring eyes ... always a bad sign, that! Girl's probably his nurse.'

Adelaide pursed her lips. 'There's certainly something very strange about her.'

Skinsale grinned. 'Dunno about strange ... but she ain't a bad looker.'

'Positively uncivilised in my view. Perhaps you spent too long in India, Colonel Skinsale!'

'Long enough to learn to appreciate the beauties of nature, my dear.'

Adelaide sniffed disdainfully. 'Since we seem compelled to spend the night in this frightful place, do you think there is a private bedroom where I might get some sleep?'

Skinsale nodded towards the speaking-tube on the wall. 'Well, if this contraption works, I'll see what the proprietors of the establishment have to say.' He picked up the speaking-tube and blew.

The tube whistled shrilly in the lamp room, and Reuben picked it up. 'Ahoy there, what is it?' He listened then said impatiently, 'There's Ben's room, she be welcome to that. He won't be needing it no more.' He hung up the tube. 'Trouble with the gentry, they always wants running after.'

Vince had gone out on to the gallery, and was looking down, 'Reuben, there's someone out there. See them lights?'

Reuben came out on to the gallery. He could just make out the glow of a lantern bobbing about on the rocks. 'It's the Doctor and that girl.'

'They've no cause to be out there,' said Vince uneasily.

Reuben grunted. 'Well, they can't say I didn't warn them. I warned 'em both, right here on this very spot.'

'Warned 'em? What about?'

'The Beast of Fang Rock,' said Reuben solemnly.

Vince gave an uneasy laugh. 'You still on about that old tale?'

'More than a tale, lad. The girl *saw* it tonight. All glowing, like they said ...'

'She couldn't have seen it ...'

Reuben lowered his voice. 'Last time the Beast was seen on Fang Rock was eighty year ago. Two men died that night ...'

Fog swirled dankly round the sea-wet rocks, and the lantern cast only a tiny circle of yellow light.

Leela took a bearing on the nearby lighthouse. 'I'm sure it was somewhere near here I saw it. Close to that flat-topped rock.'

The Doctor fished a compass from his pocket and set it on the rock. The needle spun crazily. 'Aha!' said the Doctor in satisfaction.

Leela looked at the spinning compass needle. 'And what does that tell you?'

'It has a very strong electrical field, strong enough to kill a man on contact ...' The Doctor picked up the compass and moved on. He seemed to be following some kind of trail. It led him to the pool

331

where Leela had found the dead fish. They were still there, floating on the surface of the pool. 'Or kill fish at a distance of several yards,' concluded the Doctor.

'And what do you think it is?'

The Doctor looked round. The fog was closing in and the lighthouse suddenly seemed very far away. 'I don't know what it is—but I think it's desperate, and I think it's cunning and I think we'd better be getting back!'

As they headed back towards the lighthouse, the faintest of crackling sounds came from behind a nearby rock. A glowing shape slid out from its hiding place and flowed across the rocks.

6

ATTACK FROM THE UNKNOWN

When Skinsale came back into the crew room, Harker was sleeping soundly, Palmerdale slumped disconsolately in his chair.

'I think Adelaide will sleep now,' said Skinsale cheerfully.

Palmerdale looked up sardonically. 'Oh, splendid. That's the main thing, isn't it—that my secretary gets a good night's sleep.'

'You'd do well to get some yourself,' said Skinsale amiably. He stretched out on a bunk.

'Sleep? Here, in this hovel?'

Skinsale looked round the crew room. 'Quite a snug little bivouac, this. I've slept in worst places when I was in the Army.'

'Ah, but that was before you retired and went into politics,' sneered Palmerdale. 'Got a taste for good living then, didn't you?'

Palmerdale's rudeness only seemed to increase the other man's good humour. 'Feeling a little frustrated, old chap?'

'Why the hell shouldn't I, when I've been cheated like this?' exploded Palmerdale.

Skinsale's voice hardened. 'I think you'd better watch your tongue. I kept my part of the bargain. I gave you secret advance information about the Government's financial plans. I was a fool and a knave, but I did it. You tore up my gambling IOUs—now we're even!'

'What *use* is your blasted information if I can do nothing with it?'

'Quite. Amusing, isn't it?' Skinsale yawned luxuriously.

'I could still expose you,' threatened Palmerdale.

'Do be reasonable, old chap. If the information is never used, where's the proof I ever gave it? And you're forgetting something else.'

'Am I? What, pray?'

'I'm an officer and a gentleman, Henry. You're a nobody, a jumped-up little moneygrubber for all your bought title. Besmirch my good name and I'll sue you for every penny you've got! So, good night to you.'

Colonel Skinsale closed his eyes and went peacefully to sleep.

The Doctor and Leela came into the generator room. Nothing had changed. The tarpaulin-wrapped body still lay in its corner, the generator was still throbbing away.

Leela looked out into the foggy darkness behind them, and then closed the door. 'You think this creature will return?'

The Doctor nodded. 'I think it was taking Ben's body away for examination when you saw it from the gallery.'

'Into the sea?'

'*Under* the sea … Earlier tonight Vince saw something he called a fireball. It fell into the sea not far away.'

'Another TARDIS?'

'Not a TARDIS—but very possibly some kind of space-craft. An alien, a creature who had never encountered human beings before, might well behave in just this way.'

'Why would it come here? There is nothing on this foggy rock.'

The Doctor pointed to the generator. 'There's power—electricity. Perhaps that attracted it.'

'An alien creature travelling through space—and you said it was desperate, Doctor?'

'Its behaviour pattern is—furtive. It keeps out of sight, spies out the land, weighs up its chances of a successful attack.'

'Then we are not facing a bold enemy?'

'Not bold but cunning, Leela. This fog is no freak of the weather. It was deliberately contrived to isolate us. Now the creature is growing more confident. It's seen this primitive technology, studied the physical limitations of its enemies.' The Doctor sighed, and said gloomily, 'All in all, I've a feeling we're in a lot of trouble!'

'Do not be afraid, Doctor. We shall arm ourselves and post guards. The others will help.'

'We'll have to convince them of the danger first. If we start talking about creatures from space, they'll just think we're mad.'

'We shall explain that we come from space ourselves,' said Leela triumphantly. 'We are not of this Earth, or of this time.'

The Doctor shuddered. 'Don't tell them that, whatever you do.' He remembered something Leela had said a few moments earlier. 'What do you mean, afraid?'

Lord Palmerdale stood looking thoughtfully down at the telegraph. By now Skinsale was fast asleep. Palmerdale crept over to Harker and shook him roughly by the shoulder. 'Wake up, man,' he whispered. 'Wake up!'

Harker awoke in sudden panic, like a man in the middle of a nightmare. 'Look out, look out,' he muttered. 'She's going to strike.'

Palmerdale shook him again. 'That's all over and done with. Wake up, will you?'

Still half-asleep, Harker stared dazedly at him. 'What is it? What d'you want?'

'Do you know how to use a Morse apparatus?'

'Do I what?'

'Can you use a Morse telegraph apparatus, like the one over there?'

'Course I can!'

'Splendid! I want you to send a message for me. It's to be passed on to my brokers in London.'

Sleepily Harker rubbed a hand across his eyes. 'Send a message to London? What about?'

'It's merely an instruction to sell certain shares and buy others. Nothing that need concern you. Just do as I tell you. It's a very important business matter and there's a great deal of money involved.'

'Money?'

'Don't worry, you'll be handsomely rewarded. I had urgent reasons for getting back to London, but this will do just as well.'

'I remember you was mad to get back to England,' said Harker slowly. 'I remember on the bridge, when the fog was coming down. Captain begging for permission to slow down, you telling him full speed ahead and damn the fog.'

'I was the owner,' said Palmerdale angrily. 'It was his duty to obey my orders!'

'He was old and weak, scared he'd never get another ship. You made him do it!'

'Never mind all that, Harker. Just do as I tell you and you'll be well paid.'

Harker rose slowly to his feet, his massive bulk towering over his employer. 'Then, when the ship struck, it was get the owner away, and the owner's fancy woman and the owner's fine friend. Never mind the poor sailor, he can take his chances.'

'I'll have no more of your insolence, Harker. I've offered to pay you …'

Harker grabbed Palmerdale by the collar and lifted him off his feet. 'Pay?' he roared. 'There's good mates of mine feeding the fishes because of you. Will you pay for that?'

He tightened his grip on Palmerdale's collar, shaking him to and fro.

'No,' choked Palmerdale. 'No! Get him off!'

Roused by the noise, Skinsale woke up, realised what was happening and tried to pull Harker away. The big seaman flung him aside, and went on throttling Palmerdale.

The Doctor and Leela arrived just in time. The Doctor flung himself on Harker, and Leela and Skinsale came to help. It took *all* their efforts to pull Harker from his victim.

'Harker, that's enough,' shouted the Doctor. 'Do you want to kill him?'

Harker flung Palmerdale aside, and he dropped choking on to a bunk. Harker glowered down at him. 'There's good seamen dead because of him. He deserves to die.'

'We've got our own lives to worry about now,' said the Doctor grimly. 'I've got news for you, gentlemen. This lighthouse is under attack. Before morning we could all be dead. Is anyone interested?'

It came out of the sea, and slid over the edge of the rocks on to the island. Its many-faceted eyes saw the lighthouse, with its flashing light. It had studied its enemies and made its plans. Now it was time to act. Swiftly and silently the glowing shape moved towards the lighthouse.

*

'Time that boiler was stoked, boy,' said Reuben gruffly.

Vince nodded, but he didn't move. 'Reuben, you don't really believe what happened all those years ago is happening again? The Beast and all that?'

'There's three of us, and there were three of them. Two dead, one mad. Ben's dead, isn't he? And the night's not over yet.'

Vince stood there white and trembling, and Reuben said, 'You're shaking too much to hold a shovel, boy. Stay here, I'll do the boiler.'

'Well if you're sure,' said Vince eagerly. He tried to pull himself together. 'I'll go if you like …'

Reuben shook his head and stumped off,

The Doctor was finishing his speech of warning. The problem was to impress his audience without giving them any real facts. 'No one, no one at all must go outside the lighthouse, for any reason,' he concluded. 'Is that clear?'

Palmerdale had recovered his breath, and his self-assurance. 'No, it's not clear. Lot of ridiculous mumbo-jumbo if you ask me. Just what is this mysterious threat that's supposed to be lurking outside?'

Reuben came on to the landing in time to hear Palmerdale's question. He paused in the doorway and looked at the Doctor. 'You've told 'em you've seen it, have you? Told 'em the Beast is back.'

Skinsale gave an incredulous laugh. 'What Beast?'

'There's always death on the rock when the Beast's about.'

'Preposterous rubbish,' exploded Palmerdale. 'What is the old fool saying?'

Reuben glared malevolently at him. 'I'm saying that what's happened before will happen again.' He disappeared down the stairs.

The Doctor sighed. Reuben's intervention had come at just the wrong time, reducing his warnings of danger to an old wives' tale they could all laugh at.

'Superstitious old idiot,' said Palmerdale dismissively. 'If you expect us to take notice of some drunken fisherman's tale, Doctor …'

Leela decided to apply her own brand of persuasion. She whipped the knife from her boot and thrust it dangerously close to Palmerdale's chest. 'Silence, fat one. You will do as the Doctor instructs, or I will cut out your heart.'

Palmerdale was too terrified to speak.

The Doctor smiled. Perhaps there was something to be said for Leela's methods of persuasion. 'You heard what she said, old chap. And I warn you, she means it—don't you Leela?'

Leela didn't reply. She was staring into space, her whole body tense.

'What is it, Leela?'

'It's getting cold again.'

'You're sure?'

'Yes. The last time it felt cold like this—like a cold wave.'

The Doctor concentrated, testing the atmosphere. 'Yes, I think you're right.'

'Well, I can't feel anything,' said Skinsale.

'Leela's senses are particularly acute,' said the Doctor. 'And if she says it's getting colder—it's getting colder.'

He turned at the sound of movement in the doorway. It was Adelaide. She was wrapped in a blanket, shivering and only half awake. 'What's going on? Something woke me up ... I suddenly felt so cold ...'

'Nothing for you to worry about, Adelaide,' said Skinsale reassuringly.

The electric lights flickered.

They flickered down in the generator room too, where Reuben was stoking the boiler. He paused, looked suspiciously at a pressure gauge. Everything seemed normal. He flung on a few more shovels of coal, exhausting the little pile by the boiler door. With a muttered curse he went over to the door of the coal store and flung it open.

Adelaide looked wildly round the room, wondering why everyone was acting so strangely. 'I don't understand what's wrong with you all. Please, Lord Palmerdale, what's happening?'

Skinsale glared warningly at Palmerdale, who cleared his throat and said, 'Nothing, my dear. There's absolutely nothing wrong ...'

The electric lights went out, and a terrifying scream came echoing up the stairs.

7

THE ENEMY WITHIN

Adelaide's own scream of terror merged with the piercing scream from below, and she flung herself into Skinsale's arms. The Doctor and Leela were already racing towards the sound.

At the door of the generator room, the Doctor held up a warning hand. He stepped cautiously inside. The darkly-shadowed room was empty. The door to the outside was standing ajar, and fog was seeping into the room. 'It's taken Reuben,' said the Doctor. It can't have got far—we may still be in time to save him. Come on, Leela—and don't step on any jellyfish!'

They ran out into the night.

Adelaide was on the verge of hysterics, and Skinsale and Palmerdale tried vainly to calm her down.

'That ghastly scream,' she sobbed. 'What was it? I know something terrible has happened.'

'Control yourself,' said Palmerdale irritably. He was frightened enough himself, and Adelaide was making things worse.

Skinsale patted her soothingly on the back. 'It's all right, my dear,' he said, 'there's no cause for alarm.'

Adelaide refused to be consoled. 'I knew I should never have come on this cruise. My astrologer Miss Nethercott warned me about danger by sea. It was in my stars!'

Skinsale produced a large white handkerchief and handed it to her. 'Come now, that's nonsense. You're overwrought …'

Adelaide sniffed into the handkerchief and her sobs began to subside.

Palmerdale saw that Harker had picked up an oil-lantern and was heading for the door. 'Harker! Where do you think you're going, man?'

'Below. Doctor may need help.' Harker shoved him aside and went on down the stairs.

'Insubordinate ruffian!' said Palmerdale indignantly. 'If there is something dangerous on this rock, we should all stick together!'

Skinsale gave one of his cynical grins. 'That's the ticket, Henry, surround yourself with people! With any luck the Beast will satisfy its appetite before it gets to you!'

This was too much for Adelaide. 'Stop it, stop it,' she screamed. 'Don't say such horrible things.' She collapsed in tears.

Palmerdale looked at Skinsale. 'Now see what you've done, you fool. You've set her off again!'

Harker came into the generator room. 'Doctor?' he called. 'Are you there?' He saw the outside door was still open. The Doctor and Leela must have gone outside. He crossed to the door and stood looking out into the swirling fog, but there was nothing to be seen.

For a moment Harker hesitated, wondering whether to follow the Doctor. Then he heard movement behind him and whirled round.

Reuben stood swaying in the doorway to the coal store, white-faced and glassy-eyed.

Harker stared at him. 'Reuben! Is something wrong, mate?'

Reuben's voice was thick, distorted, scarcely recognisable. 'Leave me be.' He staggered towards the stairs.

Harker looked worriedly after him, wishing desperately that the Doctor was back. He turned and shouted. 'Doctor, ahoy there ...' His voice boomed out into the fog, but there was no reply.

Reuben climbed the stairs with agonising slowness, hauling himself up by the hand-rail. The wail of the foghorn came down from above and he paused, staring upwards with dead, inhuman eyes. He resumed his laborious climb.

Vince gave a final blast on the horn, and with startling suddenness the lamp came on again. Vince shook his head in perplexity. How long would the lights stay on this time? He had a nasty feeling the intervals were getting shorter ...

*

Adelaide was still sobbing. Skinsale gave a sigh of relief as the electric lighting came on again. 'You see, they've repaired the lights again, my dear. It's all right, there's nothing to worry about now.'

Palmerdale was hovering nervously near the door. 'Listen!' he hissed. 'There's someone coming ...'

He looked appealingly at Skinsale who moved quietly over to the door.

'Colonel, please, don't,' whispered Adelaide.

'Sssh!' whispered Palmerdale agitatedly. He wanted to know who was on the stairs, but he didn't want to be the one to go and find out.

Skinsale went on to the gloomy landing. 'Doctor, is that you? Harker?'

Dragging footsteps came up the stairs, and Reuben appeared. His face was deathly white, his eyes fixed and staring. Skinsale stared at him. 'Are you all right? Where are you off to?' Reuben shuffled past without a word.

Skinsale went back into the crew room. 'It's all right, it was only the old chap. He went straight on up the stairs. He looked pretty done in.' He turned to Adelaide. 'The crisis seems to be over, my dear. Why don't you go and lie down?'

Adelaide shuddered. 'Up there alone? Have you taken leave of your senses, Colonel? I shall stay down here!'

Skinsale sighed.

At last there was an answer to Harker's repeated shouts. Suddenly, 'Harker! Is that you?' called a familiar voice.

He saw a lantern bobbing through the fog, and the Doctor and Leela appeared. 'We heard you calling,' said the Doctor. 'There's nothing out there now—nothing we could find, anyway.' They came into the room and the Doctor said, 'Let's get that door shut!' He slammed it behind them, and stood leaning against it, lost in thought. 'You know what I think?'

Leela looked puzzled. 'The creature has killed Reuben?'

'I'm afraid so,' said the Doctor. 'But that's not what I meant. I was wondering if I could work out its size ...'

'Reuben's all right,' interrupted Harker. 'I've just seen him.'

The Doctor didn't seem to hear him. 'It would seem that every time it comes within a certain range of the generator ...'

Leela turned to Harker. 'What did you say?'

'Reuben's all right,' he repeated. 'I just saw him go upstairs.'

The Doctor was lost in a maze of calculations. 'U, by Q, over R,' he said mysteriously.

Leela tugged at his sleeve. 'Doctor, did you hear that?'

'Sssh, Savage,' said the Doctor reprovingly.

'What are you doing?'

'Thinking!' The Doctor touched the metal rail. There was a crackle of blue sparks. He snatched his hand away, sucking his fingers. 'Yes, it's certainly been here. You see, Harker, in the space which surrounds an electrically charged body an electrical potential occurs which is roughly proportional to the charge Q and inversely proportional to the distance R from the centre ...' His voice tailed away as he became aware that Harker and Leela were staring at him with blank incomprehension. Suddenly the Doctor said sharply, 'Well, then, where is he?'

By now Harker was thoroughly confused. 'Who, sir?'

'Reuben. You said you'd seen him.'

'He went upstairs, sir. Looked like he'd seen a ghost.'

'Why didn't you *tell* me?'

'Well I tried, sir. I told the young lady here.'

'Why am I wasting my time trying to work out its size, eh? Why?'

Harker scratched his head. 'I'm sure I don't know, sir.'

'If Reuben's seen it, then obviously he can tell us!'

'That's what I thought,' said Leela. 'But then, I'm only a Savage!'

The Doctor grinned. 'Come on then, Savage, we'll go and find him. Harker, can you secure that door?'

'I reckon wedges'd do it best.'

Then get on with it. I want us sealed in this lighthouse till morning.'

The Doctor and Leela hurried up the stairs.

Adelaide lay dozing on a bunk with a blanket over her. Skinsale too had stretched out again, but Palmerdale was on his feet pacing restlessly about the room. He paused in front of the telegraph set and stared longingly at it. Then he turned to Skinsale, his voice warm and friendly. 'I don't suppose you learned anything useful in the army, Jimmy? Like how to use one of these gadgets?'

'And you surely don't suppose I'd send a message to your brokers for you?'

'We could make a real killing, old boy,' said Palmerdale persuasively. 'Tell you what, not only will I forget your IOUs, I'll even split the profits with you. What could be fairer than that?'

Skinsale stared at him in astonishment. You could say one thing for Palmerdale, he was consistent. Even in the middle of the dangers that surrounded them, he still had his mind fixed firmly on making a profit. 'Look, Henry, if the word got out I'd given you that information, I'd be ruined, and you know it. Money isn't everything, you know!'

Palmerdale was still trying to grapple with this novel thought when the Doctor appeared in the doorway. 'Where is he?'

'Who?'

'Reuben.'

'Saw him on the stairs a few minutes ago,' said Skinsale.

'Doctor, what's happening?' demanded Palmerdale indignantly. 'I insist on an explanation.'

The Doctor ignored him. 'How did Reuben look?'

Skinsale considered. 'Groggy,' he said finally.

'Groggy?'

'Yes, Doctor. Decidedly groggy.'

Adelaide sat up. 'Doctor, what was that terrible cry we heard?'

The Doctor said, 'Thanks very much, Colonel. Come on, Leela.' They hurried off.

Adelaide was indignant. 'Really! That man's manners are quite insufferable.'

'Things on his mind by the look of him,' said Skinsale thoughtfully. 'Eh, Henry?'

'We all have!' said Palmerdale shortly, and went abruptly out of the room.

Adelaide was still concerned with the social short comings of the Doctor and his companion. 'As for that girl, it's disgraceful the way she follows him about. You'd think she was tied to him by a piece of string ...'

Skinsale stared after Palmerdale. 'Where would you say his lordship's off to, Adelaide?'

'Is it important? None of us can go far on this dreadful place.'

'You know, some people make me nervous when I'm with 'em. Your employer has the opposite effect. I get nervous when he's out of my sight!' He made for the door.

'Colonel, you're not going to leave me here, alone?'

'Don't worry, my dear, back in a minute.'

Skinsale hurried out.

Adelaide rose to follow him, thought of the gloomy staircase and decided to stay where she was. She sat down again, huddling inside the blanket. Would morning never come? And why was it so cold ...

The Doctor and Leela looked for Reuben in the lamp room, but Vince had seen no sign of him. He suggested the old man might be in Ben's room. They went back downstairs, and along a short corridor, which ended in a closed door. The Doctor hammered on it with his fist. 'Reuben! Reuben, can you hear me? Are you in there? Are you all right?'

There was no reply.

Reuben was standing quite motionless, staring at the window. The Doctor's voice could be heard quite clearly, but it produced no reaction.

Reuben went over to the window and flung it open. Cold air and fog flooded into the little room. Reuben's body seemed to blur and glow in the darkness ...

8

THE BRIBE

The Doctor abandoned his banging and shouting and turned away.

Leela stared at the closed door. 'Why doesn't the old one answer?'

'He's not listening!'

'Not listening? Why not? We wish only to help him.'

'If he saw the creature and escaped from it, he'll have had a terrible shock—and shock can close the mind. He could stay like this for hours.'

'What shall we do?'

'For a start, somebody's got to keep the lighthouse running. You go down and tell Harker to keep the boiler-pressure up.'

'Keep the boiler-pressure up,' repeated Leela dutifully. She went back along the corridor and down the stairs chanting, 'Keep the boiler-pressure up. Keep the boiler-pressure up …'

'Lonely life you chaps lead here, eh?'

Vince jumped. Palmerdale was in the lamp-room doorway, smiling affably.

Vince was always uneasy with the gentry, but he was glad of company, even Lord Palmerdale's. 'That it is, sir. Still you soon get used to it.'

Palmerdale came into the room. 'Don't suppose they pay you much either.'

'Oh, it's not so bad. You get your keep, and it's steady work.'

'But you wouldn't mind earning a little extra—fifty pounds, say?'

'Fifty pounds!' It was as much as Vince could do to imagine such a huge amount of money.

Palmerdale moved closer and spoke in a confidential whisper. 'I need to send an urgent message to London. I assume you know how to use the telegraph?'

Vince nodded. 'Ben taught me, sir. But it can only be used for official business. Strict rule, that is.'

Palmerdale believed firmly that every man had his price. If the first offer was refused, you simply increased the size of the bribe. He pulled a wad of notes from his pocket, and riffled them persuasively under Vince's nose. 'Look, when I say fifty pounds, I mean fifty pounds now. It's all I happen to be carrying. There'll be another fifty pounds for you, as soon as I get back to London.'

Skinsale came quietly up the stairs and looked into the lamp room. He took in the scene at a glance; Palmerdale's low persuasive voice, the wad of money in his hand, Vince listening as if hypnotised.

There was a big streak of caution in Vince—no one gave you money for nothing. 'I don't want to get mixed up in nothing wrong, sir. It's a fortune, a hundred pounds.'

'Not to a man like me,' boasted Palmerdale. 'See here, my lad.' He thrust his hand under his shirt, fumbled with a hidden fastening, and brought out a handful of gleaming stones. 'Diamonds, worth thousands of pounds. I call 'em my insurance. That's the kind of man I am. You'll get your money, never fear.' He put the diamonds away, and held out the money. 'Here, take it. I'm a businessman. How could there be anything wrong?'

In the shadows of the staircase, Skinsale's face was cold and hard. He'd underestimated Palmerdale's persistence. Something would have to be done.

Something was moving up the outside of the lighthouse. It was shapeless, glowing, and it slithered up the smooth stone walls, higher and higher until it was just beneath the high gallery of the lamp room. There, it waited ...

Palmerdale scribbled in a leather-covered notebook with a silver pencil. He tore out the page and handed it to Vince. 'Here's the message, it's in my private business code ...'

They heard the Doctor's cheerful voice. 'Vince! Are you up there?'

Palmerdale put a finger to his lips. 'Send the message as soon as you get a chance. And remember, say nothing to anyone. I'll step out on the gallery until the Doctor's gone.'

Palmerdale slipped out on to the darkened gallery. Vince stuffed money and message into his pocket and gave a hasty blast on the foghorn, just as the Doctor entered.

'Are you all right, Vince? We've left you alone up here for quite a time.'

'I'm right enough, sir,' said Vince. But his face was white, and his voice quivered with nerves.

The Doctor put a hand on his shoulder. 'Good lad. Now then, I've got something important to tell you ...'

Harker found tools and some old lumber in a corner of the coal store. He chopped a plank into a number of rough wedges, and hammered them into place around the edges of the main door. He drove the last one home just as Leela came in. 'There, that should do the trick, eh, miss?'

Leela was chanting, 'Keep the boipressure up keep the boipressure up ...' Somehow her message had got a bit garbled on the way.

'What's that, again, miss?'

'It is a message from the Doctor. The old one Reuben is not listening, so you must keep the boipressure up.'

'Ah,' said Harker thoughtfully. 'Would that be boiler-pressure, now?'

'That is what I said.'

"Course it is, miss. Tell the Doctor not to worry, I'll see to it.'

Harker found the shovel and began shovelling coal into the boiler.

Leela picked up the hammer Harker had been using. She hefted it thoughtfully and slipped from the room.

The Doctor was engaged in the difficult task of putting Vince on his guard without scaring him to death. He told him of the cry from the generator room, and Reuben's strange behaviour.

Vince's eyes widened with terror. 'What do you reckon Reuben saw then, Doctor?'

'I don't know yet. But I think we'll find out before sunrise.'

'It's the Beast come back,' said Vince fearfully. 'Last time they found two keepers dead, and one mad with fear. Well, Ben's dead, isn't he, and Reuben's mad ... Only me left now ...' He clutched the Doctor's arm. 'It'll come for me next!'

'That's superstitious nonsense, Vince.'

'Is it? Look what happened to Ben—and now Reuben!'

'Whatever happened all those years ago, Vince, things are very different now. There's something dangerous on the rock, I don't deny. But there are eight of us here now, Vince. If it attacks again, we'll all be ready and waiting. All the advantages are with us. Remember, it's eight to one!'

The glowing shape paused underneath the gallery, gathering its strength. Its glow pulsed, then grew steadily brighter.

Coat collar turned up round his neck, Palmerdale shivered in the darkness of the gallery. Inside the lamp room, he could see the Doctor talking earnestly to Vince. Would the fellow never shut up and go away? He considered going back into the lamp room. What did it matter if the Doctor saw him? Vince had been well paid, he'd keep his mouth shut. Still, better not to arouse any curiosity. He decided to hang on for a little longer.

Lord Palmerdale put his hands on the guard-rail and peered out into the darkness. Still this confounded fog. He noticed a strange greenish glow from somewhere below him. A kind of phosphorescence ... He leaned over the guard-rail to get a better look—and a glowing tentacle whipped up from out of the darkness and took him round the neck.

Palmerdale went rigid, mouth distorted in a silent scream. Blue lightning flashed round his body as the tentacle snatched him over the guard-rail.

The glowing shape slid down the tower, towards an open window just below.

Skinsale and Adelaide were locked in furious argument. Skinsale had begun it, apparently quite deliberately. On his return to the crew room he had began making a series of disparaging remarks about Lord Palmerdale. Although Adelaide was prepared to admit to herself that his lordship's manners left much to be desired, he was a generous employer, and she felt obliged to come to his defence.

'You've no right to say such things. Lord Palmerdale is the kindest and most considerate of men.'

'To you no doubt,' sneered Skinsale. 'My experience has been somewhat different.'

'You've enjoyed his friendship—and the financial advantages of your association with him. I happen to know he has been most generous ...'

'A sprat to catch a mackerel! He plans to make far more money out of me than I ever had from him.'

'Indeed?' said Adelaide loftily. 'We both know that Lord Palmerdale is already a millionaire. How could you bring him any financial advantage?'

'He plied me with drink, encouraged me to gamble until I was almost ruined, then persuaded me to give him secret government information, information which he can turn to profit. Your precious employer is a crook and a skunk, my dear!'

'How dare you!' stormed Adelaide. 'I refuse to listen to another word. I shall go and find his lordship and tell him what a perfidious so-called friend you are.'

'Yes, somehow I thought you might,' said Skinsale softly. With a smile of satisfaction he watched Adelaide run from the room.

Leela marched determinedly up to Reuben's door, the heavy coal hammer over her shoulder. The trouble with the Doctor, she thought, was that he was too considerate. If the old man had information they needed, then he must come out and give it to them.

She came to a halt outside Reuben's door. 'Old one, hear me,' she shouted. 'If you do not open this door now I shall smash it down. Do you understand?'

Silence. Leela stepped back and raised the hammer.

The Doctor clapped Vince encouragingly on the shoulder. 'So, Harker will keep the boiler stoked, you look after the light and keep the siren going, and I'll organise the others to keep watch.'

'All right, Doctor, if you think that's best. You're sure it'd be no good me having a word with Reuben?'

'No good at all, Vince. You stay here, you've got your job to do.'

A splintering crash came from below. They listened. The crash came again, and again. 'Stay here,' ordered the Doctor. 'I'll go down and take a look.'

The door to Reuben's room was made of solid oak, and for all her efforts Leela was unable to smash it down. However, by hammering at the same spot, she managed to bash a hole in it. She peered through it, and saw Reuben standing motionless in the middle of the room. His face was white, his eyes stared blankly ahead.

Leela shouted through the gap. 'Come out, old one!' Reuben ignored her.

She stepped back, raising the hammer for another swing. She was about to bring it smashing down when a hand caught the hammer just below the head and held it still. The Doctor had come up behind her. 'That'll be quite enough of that, Leela.'

'You do not want the old one?'

The Doctor peered through the hole. 'He'll come out when he's ready. He's in a kind of coma at the moment. He probably couldn't tell us much, even if we did get him out.'

They heard agitated footsteps behind them, and saw Adelaide running towards them. 'Have you seen Lord Palmerdale? I've looked everywhere for him. I thought he might have come up here to rest.'

The Doctor shook his head. 'Old Reuben's locked himself in his room, and there's nobody in the lamp room except young Vince.' He took Adelaide by the shoulders and turned her round. 'Get back to the crew room.'

'But I must find Lord Palmerdale,' protested Adelaide.

'Get back to the crew room,' repeated the Doctor firmly.

Somewhat to her own surprise, Adelaide turned and walked meekly away.

The Doctor looked at the battered door and shook his head. 'Malicious damage to a lighthouse! That's a very serious business, Leela!'

When the Doctor left the lamp room Vince waited for a few minutes and then went to the gallery door. 'He's gone, sir. You can come in now.'

There was no answer. 'Your lordship?' Thinking Palmerdale must be on the other side, Vince walked right round the gallery, ending up back where he'd started.

Lord Palmerdale was gone. In total amazement, Vince stared down into the darkness.

9

THE CHAMELEON FACTOR

Vince gave a gasp of horror and ran back into the lamp room. Palmerdale had gone over the edge—and he had a bundle of his lordship's money in his pocket. They'd say he'd robbed him and pushed him over. He tugged the roll of five-pound notes from his pocket, crumpled them up on the floor. He screwed up Palmerdale's code message and put it with the money, struck a match with shaking hands and set light to the little heap of paper.

It was more money than he'd ever see again in his lifetime—but there was nothing but relief in Vince's heart as he watched it burn.

The Doctor and Leela found Skinsale and Adelaide in the crew room. They were sat with their backs to each other, ostentatiously not talking. The Doctor said, 'Ask Harker to come up here, Leela, and then see if you can find Lord Palmerdale.'

'The fat cowardly one?'

'That's right!'

Leela moved silently away, and the Doctor turned to the others. 'Now then, I want to have a little talk with you two.'

'Really, Doctor,' drawled Skinsale.'What about?'

'Survival, Colonel. Yours, mine, all of us here on this lighthouse.'

'You're not still worried about this mysterious sea-beast that eats lighthouse keepers?'

'You find the idea of such a creature hard to accept, Colonel?'

'Come now, Doctor, we're both men of intelligence and education ...'

'Quite so, Colonel. I don't believe in Reuben's sea monster either.'

'Then why do you consistently suggest we are in danger?'

The Doctor said calmly, 'Somewhere out there is an intelligent, hostile alien from a distant planet. I believe it intends to destroy us all.'

An unbelieving smile spread over Skinsale's face. 'An intelligent, hostile alien from a distant planet?'

Adelaide was equally scornful. 'That is the most ridiculous suggestion I have ever heard in my life. And you are supposed to be a scientist!'

Leela appeared with Harker close behind her. 'I cannot find the cowardly one, Doctor.'

The Doctor nodded, and went on trying to convince Skinsale. 'I've never been more serious in my life, Colonel. We're facing an enemy with greater powers than you can imagine.'

Skinsale rose and stretched. 'My dear Doctor, I too enjoy the scientific romances of Mr Wells but—'

'Old Herbert George may get a few of his facts wrong, but his basic supposition is sound enough!' said the Doctor heatedly. 'Do you really think your little speck in the galaxy is the only one with intelligent life?'

He was interrupted by a blast from the voice-pipe. The Doctor picked it up, listened for a moment and said, 'All right, stay where you are.' He put back the tube. 'That was young Vince. He says Lord Palmerdale has fallen from the lamp gallery.'

Adelaide let out a piercing shriek and immediately Leela slapped her face.

Skinsale said, 'Fallen? But you *can't* fall, there's a perfectly good safety-rail,'

The Doctor nodded.'I quite agree. But Vince says he was on the gallery, and now he's gone. The question is, do we go outside to look for him?'

Skinsale studied the Doctor's grim face. 'You really believe in this—alien, don't you?'

'Yes, I do. Leela, stay here and look after Adelaide.'

The Doctor, Harker and Skinsale moved off. As they went down the stairs, they didn't realise that Reuben was watching them from the stairway above. His face was twisted, and his dead eyes stared glassily down at them.

*

Leela stood warily by the door, while Adelaide sobbed quietly in her chair. 'I told Lord Palmerdale we shouldn't come, but he wouldn't listen. He laughed when I told him Miss Nethercott had seen danger in the stars. I knew something ghastly would happen. Her predictions are never wrong.'

'Your stars?' said Leela.'Ah, I understand. She is your shaman.'

'My astrologer,' corrected Adelaide. 'I consult her regularly and—'

'A waste of time,' interrupted Leela.'I too used to believe in magic, but that was before the Doctor taught me about science. It is better to believe in science.'

Harker knocked out the wedges and they all went outside, with lanterns, making a circuit of the lighthouse. It didn't take them long to find Palmerdale's body, lying at the base of the tower. They picked the body up and carried it into the generator room.

While Harker began knocking the wedges back into place, the Doctor and Skinsale carried the body upstairs to the crew room, and laid it on a bunk. Adelaide gave a cry of horror. 'Be quiet,' ordered Leela.'Have you never seen death before?'

'I can't bear it,' sobbed Adelaide.

Skinsale patted her awkwardly on the back. 'Now, be brave, my dear.'

'Keep away from me!' she screamed. 'You did this. You pushed him over!'

'Don't be ridiculous!'

'You went out of this room after him, not long ago. You followed him to the gallery, and pushed him over.'

'I was never even in the lamp room, let alone the gallery,' protested Skinsale.'It's true I followed him, but only to see what he was up to!'

'You did it, I know you did it,' screamed Adelaide. 'You killed him!' She began to sob hysterically.

Leela raised a threatening hand. 'Enough!'

Adelaide fell into a chair and buried her face in her hands.

The Doctor looked up from his examination of Palmerdale's body. 'And what was his lordship up to?'

'He was bribing that young keeper to send a message—'

354

'So you came back down here and wrecked the telegraph!' The Doctor pointed to the Morse apparatus. It was smashed beyond all chance of repair, wiring ripped out, telegraph key wrenched off.

'It was the only way I could think of to stop him,' admitted Skinsale. 'I'd have been dishonoured, ruined, if he'd got that message out.'

'So to protect your precious honour you put all our lives in danger.'

Suddenly Adelaide realised what the Doctor meant. 'There's no way of contacting the mainland!'

'None at all. We're on our own now.'

Harker hammered the last wedge back into place and straightened up. Sensing that there was someone behind him, he turned. Reuben was standing at the bottom of the stairs.

Poor old fellow looked terrible, thought Harker. With that white skin and those glaring eyes he seemed scarcely human. Best try to get him back to bed. 'Hullo, shipmate,' he said soothingly. 'How are you feeling then?'

Reuben's face twisted into a ghastly smile, as he shuffled slowly towards Harker, hands outstretched ...

Pacing nervously about the lamp room, Vince recollected guiltily that he hadn't sounded the siren for quite some time. He tugged at the lever. The booming note rang out—then died away in a kind of tired bleat ...

The Doctor resumed his examination of Palmerdale's body and Skinsale began talking earnestly to Adelaide. 'I swear to you, I didn't harm him.'

'Then who did?'

'I don't know. Could have been Harker, I suppose. He blamed Henry for losing the ship, actually attacked him earlier.'

'Oh, that's absurd.'

'Is it? No more absurd than saying that I murdered him.'

The Doctor straightened up. 'I almost wish you had, Colonel—it would all be so simple then. Unfortunately he was dead before he hit the ground. Lord Palmerdale was killed by a massive electric shock. Ben, the engineer, died in exactly the same way.'

'Electrocuted on the lamp gallery?' said Skinsale incredulously.

The Doctor nodded. 'While Vince was in the lamp room—I was there myself part of the time.'

'But it's not possible, Doctor. That would mean this—creature can climb sheer walls.'

'It can do considerably more than that, Colonel. It's amphibious, it has a natural affinity with electricity and it has the technological ability to adapt its environment. Do you follow me?'

'No,' said Skinsale frankly. 'Not a word, Doctor.'

'It likes the cold. Not enough data yet to place the species—but heat could be a useful method of defence.'

The voice-pipe whistled and Leela went to answer it. She listened then said urgently, 'Doctor, Vince says the boipressure has fallen—and the siren will not sound.'

'Harker,' said the Doctor. He set off at a run, and the others followed.

They found Harker's body sprawled by the generator. The Doctor knelt beside it, the others crowding into the room behind him. Adelaide caught sight of the body and started to scream again. 'Get her out of here,' said the Doctor impatiently. Skinsale hurried her away.

Leela looked at the body. 'He is like the others?'

The Doctor nodded. He rose slowly then looked at the door. Harker's wedges were still all in place. The Doctor stood thinking for a moment. He went over to the coal store, flung open the door and went inside. A moment later he emerged, dragging Reuben's body. He bent and tried to flex an arm. It was as stiff as an iron bar. 'Rigor mortis. He's been dead for hours.'

'Hours, Doctor? That's impossible. Less than an hour ago, Harker saw him go upstairs. I saw him standing in his room.'

'You saw something, Leela. But it wasn't Reuben. He was lying dead down here all the time.'

'But I saw him ...'

The Doctor's face was grim. 'Shape changing, Leela. Sometimes called the chameleon factor. Several species have developed it, and our alien must belong to one of them.' He looked at the door, still firmly barred by Harker's wedges. 'I've made a terrible mistake, Leela. I thought I'd locked the enemy out. Instead, I've locked it in here—with us!'

10

THE RUTAN

Vince tried the siren foghorn again, but it gave only the faintest of moans. He wondered vaguely why Harker didn't get on with stoking the boilers.

There was a dragging footstep from the doorway. He saw Reuben shuffling slowly towards him. Vince was shocked by, the old man's ghastly appearance. 'You shouldn't be out of bed, Reuben. Don't you worry about me, I'll hang on here till morning. You get some rest.'

Reuben said nothing. His face twisted in a horrible parody of a grin as he lurched slowly forward, arms reaching out.

Alarmed, Vince started to back away. 'Reuben, what's wrong? No, Reuben ... No ...'

Reuben lunged forward with terrifying speed, and grabbed Vince's shoulders. Immediately Vince went rigid, and blue sparks arced around his body.

Working at frantic speed, the Doctor shovelled in all the coal the boiler would hold. 'Don't want the lights failing now, do we?' He closed the boiler doors, and checked the pressure gauges.

'This alien has great powers. Doctor. To change its shape at will ...'

'Yes, it has ... though first it needed to analyse the human life pattern.'

That is why it stole the body of the engineer?'

'That's right. After that it was simply a matter of organic restructuring. Elementary biology for Time Lords.'

'But if the creature is a Time Lord, there is nothing we can do.'

357

'I didn't mean it was a Time Lord,' explained the Doctor patiently. 'Certainly not! But elementary biology for us is something a lesser species might master after a few thousand centuries or so.'

Leela swung from despair to total confidence. 'Then we have nothing to worry about.'

'We don't? That's nice to hear.'

'You will easily dispose of this primitive creature.'

'I will?'

'Of course! After all, you are a Time Lord!'

'I admire your confidence,' said the Doctor ruefully. 'You know, it must have taken Reuben's form for a reason.'

'So that it could kill us stealthily, one by one! Doctor, suppose we pretend that we think Reuben is still Reuben and not the alien ... could we not get close to it and kill it?'

'No, no, Leela. If we get close to it, then it gets close to us. Once it gets within touching distance, we're dead. It packs too many volts.' The Doctor was prowling thoughtfully around the generator. Suddenly he dropped to the ground, and reached under the machine. 'Aha, I thought so!'

'What is it?'

The Doctor got up and held out a complicated-looking metallic spiral of strange and alien design. 'It's a power relay!'

'It was placed there by the alien?'

'Of course! Rule One, on surviving a crash landing, send up some kind of distress beacon. Its ship was damaged so it needed another power-source.' The Doctor tapped the generator. 'That's why it came here. There must be a signal modulator as well, probably somewhere higher up the tower. That will be transmitting the actual message. I've got to find it ... Leela, you take the others up to the lamp room.'

'Why there?'

'It's the easiest place to defend.'

'Then we look for this ... mognal sigulator?'

'I'll do the looking. Now hurry, we haven't much time.'

Adelaide sat hunched by the dying fire while Skinsale paced nervously about the crew room. 'Oh, do keep still,' she snapped.

Skinsale looked at her in surprise. 'I'm sorry,' she said hastily. 'It's just that I'm so frightened. This is all like some terrible dream.'

'Pity it's not, we might stand some chance of waking up!' Skinsale turned as Leela came into the room. 'I suppose Harker's dead too?'

Leela nodded. 'Yes, like the others.'

Adelaide jumped to her feet, opening her mouth to scream. Leela glared warningly at her. 'There is no time for weeping. The creature has got into the lighthouse. Now we must fight for our lives—and everyone must play their part.'

Adelaide fainted.

When the Doctor arrived outside the little cabin, Reuben's door was standing open. He slipped into the empty room and began a rapid search. Even without the power relay, the signal modulator would transmit for some time. It was essential to find and destroy it.

The room was tiny and the Doctor's search thorough—but he found nothing. Suddenly he heard slow dragging footsteps coming along the corridor. Immediately he switched off the lights and looked for a hiding place. But the room was too small—there was nowhere to go.

The creature in Reuben's shape came along the landing and paused on the threshold as if sensing danger. It came into the room and switched on the light, looking round suspiciously. The room was empty. It moved over to the window and drew the curtain.

Outside the window, the Doctor was plastered flat against the sheer side of the lighthouse, high above the rocky ground. His toes were on a tiny ledge and his fingers clasped a shallow ridge between the stone blocks. He clung to the side of the lighthouse like a fly on the wall. All at once the Doctor saw a glint of alien metal just above the window ledge. He had found the signal modulator. Suddenly he felt his fingers beginning to slip and wondered how much longer he could hold on ...

Leela watched impatiently as Skinsale held a glass of water to Adelaide's lips. 'Drink this, Adelaide. Come along, drink it.'

'Hurry,' snapped Leela. 'The Doctor wants us to go to the lamp room

'Why the lamp room?'

'He says it is the easiest place to defend. If she cannot walk then we must carry her.'

Skinsale helped Adelaide to rise. Come along now.'

She clung to him in blind panic. 'No ... no ...'

Skinsale lifted Adelaide to her feet and half carried her towards the door. There was a dragging footstep outside the room and Leela shouted, 'Back! Get back!'

Reuben appeared in the doorway. He stared at them for a moment. His white face twisted in a ghastly smile.

The Doctor heard Reuben leave the little room, and started edging his way slowly towards the window. He reached it at last, heaving a great sigh of relief when his feet were on the sill. He rested for a moment and then reached upwards, wrenched the signal modulator from its niche in the stonework and climbed thankfully back into the room,

Leela, Skinsale and Adelaide backed away as Reuben advanced slowly towards them, the horrible grimace still fixed on his deathly-white face.

The monster sprang with terrifying speed, choosing Adelaide for its target. It clasped her in its arms in a deadly embrace. Her back arched, she went rigid and blue sparks flamed round her body.

Leela snatched the knife from her boot and hurled it with all her strength. It struck the monster's chest and rebounded harmlessly.

The monster's lunge for Adelaide had left clear the path to the doorway. 'Run!' shouted Leela, and fled up the stairs. Skinsale hesitated for an agonised moment and then followed.

The Reuben creature let go of Adelaide, who slumped lifeless to the floor.

The Doctor, Leela and Skinsale collided on the stairs. 'The creature is close behind us,' panted Leela.'We must find weapons.'

'I know,' said the Doctor calmly. He gripped Skinsale by his arm. 'Listen carefully, Colonel. Just below the lamp room is the service room. It's full of maroons and rockets. I want you to break them open and scatter the powder on the lamp-room steps. Have you got that?'

Skinsale nodded. 'Right, Doctor, leave it to me.'

There was a dragging footstep on the stair. 'It's coming,' called Leela.

The Doctor gave her a shove. 'Off you go, then, both of you!'

Leela and Skinsale dashed away.

The Doctor stood waiting.

The Reuben creature came slowly onwards. It stopped when it saw the Doctor, as if sensing a trap.

'Can I help you?' said the Doctor politely. 'You don't look very well. Are you having trouble? Not too easy holding the human form for so long, is it?'

The creature spoke, but its voice was not that of Reuben. It was weird, high, shrill, totally alien. 'It is no longer necessary. We can now abandon this unpleasantly primitive shape.'

'Why don't you do that?' suggested the Doctor. 'You'll find it much comfier, I'm sure.'

Reuben's body began to glow and melt and change … The human form warped and twisted and finally disappeared. In its place was a glowing shapeless mass. The creature was resuming its natural form.

Leela and Skinsale dashed into the lamp room, their arms full of rockets and maroons, and immediately stumbled over Vince's body. Skinsale examined it. 'Dead, like all the others.'

'Then there is nothing we can do,' said Leela practically. 'Let us move the body out of the way and then prepare the weapons.'

Skinsale was staring at Vince's body. The sudden spate of violent deaths had shaken him badly. 'That ghastly creature plans to kill us all—just like poor Vince …'

'You must forget him now,' said Leela practically. 'Now it is time for us to fight!'

A shrill alien howl came from below.

The howl was the triumphant cry of the alien, now back in its natural shape. The Doctor, who had been watching the transformation with detached scientific interest, was able to see the true shape of his enemy at last.

To be frank, he thought, it wasn't a pretty sight. In place of Reuben's form there was a huge, dimly glowing gelatinous mass, internal organs pulsing gently inside the semi-transparent body. Somewhere near the centre were huge many-faceted eyes, and a shapeless orifice that could have been a mouth. The Doctor nodded. 'Well, well, well, I should have guessed. Reuben the Rutan, eh?'

'We are a Rutan scout, specially trained in the newly-developed shape-shifting techniques.' (Rutans have little concept of individual identity, seeing themselves as units of the all-conquering Rutan race. Hence they always speak in the plural.)

'Never mind,' said the Doctor consolingly. 'I expect you'll get better with practice. What are you doing in this part of the galaxy, anyway?'

'That does not concern you. You are to be destroyed.'

'Got it. You're losing that interminable war of yours with the Sontarans.'

The Sontaran–Rutan war had raged through the cosmos for untold centuries. An insane struggle to the death between two fiercely militaristic species, it had swept to and fro over hundreds of planets, first one side winning and then the other. 'I should have realised I was dealing with a Rutan,' thought the Doctor. But they were a strange savage species with an implacable hatred for all life-forms other than their own. Even the Sontarans were preferable—and that was saying something!

The Doctor's charge provoked a fierce crackle of rage from the Rutan.'That is a lie!'

'Is it? You used to hold the whole of Mutters Spiral once. Now the Sontarans must have driven you to the far fringes of the galaxy.'

'The glorious Rutan Army is making a planned series of strategic withdrawals to selected strong-points …'

'That's the empty rhetoric of a defeated dictatorship, Rutan,' mocked the Doctor. 'And I don't like your face either!'

'Your mockery will end with your race, Earthling, when the mighty Rutan Battle Fleet occupies this planet.'

Suddenly the Doctor realised that the fate of the whole Earth was at stake in this struggle. 'Why bother to invade a planet like Earth? It's of no possible value to you.'

'The planet is obscure, but its strategic position is sound. We shall use it as a launch-point for our final assault on the Sontarans.'

'If you set up a power-base here, the Sontarans will bombard the planet with photonic missiles. Between the two of you, you'll destroy the Earth in your struggle.'

'That is unimportant. The sacrifice of the planet will serve the cause of the final glorious Rutan victory!'

'And what about its people?'

'Primitive bipeds of no value. We have scouted all the planets of this solar system. Only this one is suitable for our purpose.'

The Doctor had a ghastly vision of Earth as the battlefield in a vast interplanetary conflict. Whoever won, the people of Earth would lose. 'I can understand your military purpose. But why are you bothering to murder a handful of harmless people?'

'It is necessary. Until we return to our Mother Ship, and the Mother Ship informs the Fleet that a suitable planet has been found, no one must know of our visit to Earth.'

'But you crashed, didn't you, Rutan? Just as you made your discovery. You've failed.'

'We are sending a signal to the Mother Ship, with the power from the primitive mechanism below.'

'You're not, you know.' The Doctor tossed the gleaming alien spiral down the stairs.

There was a crackle of anger. 'It is of no importance. The Ship will still home in on the primary signal.'

The Doctor threw the larger spiral after the first. 'I'm sorry to disappoint you, but I fixed that too!'

'All your interference is useless. The beam was transmitting long enough for the Mother Ship to trace the signal and fix our position.'

The Rutan was probably quite right, thought the Doctor. But he refused to admit defeat. 'You can't be sure of that, can you—oyster-face?'

There was total confidence in the Rutan's voice. 'The Ship will come.'

'Perhaps. But long before that you will be dead!'

'We are Rutan! What could you Earthlings possibly do to harm us?'

'Just step this way and I'll show you,' said the Doctor politely—and sprinted back up the stairs.

Unhurriedly the glowing mass of the Rutan flowed after him. There was no need for haste. The stairs led only to the lamp room, the highest point of the lighthouse tower. After that there was nowhere to go.

The Doctor was trapped.

11

AMBUSH

The Doctor ran up the last few stairs, his feet crunching on the thick black powder underfoot. He had managed to delay the Rutan long enough for Leela and Skinsale to do their work. They were waiting for him just inside the lamp-room doorway.

'I've brought someone to see you,' said the Doctor. 'I hope you're ready for visitors, he'll be here any minute. Pass me one of those fuses, Colonel.'

Skinsale passed him the fuse, a short piece of soft rope, frayed at both ends. The Doctor was patting his pockets. 'I'm sorry to bother you,' he said politely. 'Could you oblige me with a light?'

'Yes, of course!' Skinsale produced some matches, lit one and held it to the Doctor's fuse, much as if he were lighting a friend's cigar. 'I say. Doctor, do you really think this is advisable? So much powder in a confined space?'

'Probably not. But we've no other choice.' A faint crackling came from the stairs below. 'I think our guest is coming.'

The crackling grew louder, and a faint greenish glow appeared round the turn of the stairs. 'How did you manage to hold it back for so long?' whispered Leela.

'Just a little military chit-chat. You know what these old soldiers are once they get talking.'

The Rutan moved round the bend of the stairs and came into full view. At the sight of the glowing, pulsating mass, Skinsale gave a gasp of horror, and even Leela took an involuntary pace back. Only the Doctor was unimpressed. 'Ah, there you are. What took you so long?'

'The time for talk is over now,' shrilled the weird, high-pitched voice.

'Correct!' The Doctor threw the fizzing fuse.

It landed close to the Rutan, on the powder-strewn stairway. There was a blinding flash and the stairway disappeared in a sheet of flame. The Rutan sprang back with a high-pitched shriek of agony. When the smoke cleared it had gone.

'Where is it, Doctor?' demanded Leela fiercely. 'Have we killed the thing?'

'Unlikely, I'm afraid!'

Skinsale was sweating with relief. 'I've never seen anything so horrible! What the devil was it?'

'An intelligent, highly-aggressive alien life-form from the planet Ruta 3.'

'Was it a sea-creature?' asked Leela.

'Evolved in the sea, adapted to land. Now then, Colonel, what about some more gunpowder?' Skinsale ran down into the service room.

Leela's eyes were fixed on the stairs. 'We are lucky that the beast fears the flame, Doctor.'

'Ruta 3 is an icy planet. The inhabitants find heat intensely painful. What we really need is a flame-thrower!'

Skinsale came out of the service room lugging what looked like a small oddly-shaped camion. 'What about this thing, Doctor? Some sort of mortar by the look of it.'

The Doctor helped Skinsale carry the device up to the lamp-room doorway. 'It's an early Schemurly!' he exclaimed delightedly.

'It's a what?'

The Doctor repeated the tongue-twisting phrase. 'An early Schemurly. It fires a rocket and line.'

'Then we could fire it at the monster.'

'We could, but it wouldn't do any good. Projectile weapons are useless against a Rutan. They go straight through and it simply seals the wound. The only way to dispose of a Rutan is to blow it to bits.'

Skinsale looked nervously at the stairs. 'Then what are we going to do?'

'Stay calm,' said the Doctor. 'I'll see what I can find.' He went dourly into the service room and began rooting through lockers and shelves. A few minutes later he emerged carrying a gun-like device mounted on a tripod. 'Rocket-launcher,' he explained. 'Now, loaded with a few extra odds and ends this could cover the stairs.' The Doctor went over to the tool-locker and came back with an assortment of rusty tins, filled with nuts and bolts, nails, cogs and other engineering debris. He began picking out the biggest and sharpest objects and arranging them in a little pile. 'Mind you,' the Doctor went on, 'it's not just this Rutan I'm concerned about. It's the others.'

Skinsale went pale. 'Others? You mean there are more of the creatures?'

Briefly the Doctor explained the background of the Rutan–Sontaran conflict, and the Rutan plans for Earth. 'By the time the Rutans and Sontarans have finished with it, this planet will be a dead cinder hanging in space.'

'Is there nothing we can do?'

The Doctor considered. 'The Battle Fleet won't come here unless the Rutan Mother Ship reports back with the news that their scout has found a suitable planet. If we could kill the Rutan, and knock out the Mother Ship as well … The Rutans are a cautious species. They'd simply conclude that this sector of space was too dangerous.'

'Then that is what we must do,' said Leela firmly. She looked expectantly at the Doctor. 'How?'

'How indeed. We've nothing here that would stop a Rutan spaceship in its tracks …' The Doctor struggled to recall what he knew of Rutan technology. 'Rutan ships have a crystalline infrastructure. They're shielded of course, but landing on a primitive planet like this they might risk cutting the protective energy-fields to save power.' The Doctor looked at his two companions, who hadn't understood a word of what he'd said. 'What we really need is an amplified carbon-oscillator.'

Leela frowned. 'Doctor, what exactly is a—whatever-you-said?'

'Something like a laser-beam, but far more destructive.'

Leela struggled to remember the science lectures which the Doctor occasionally delivered during their journeys in the TARDIS.

'A laser … that's some kind of very powerful light, isn't it?'

'Well, yes, putting it in the very simplest terms—'

Leela pointed to the lighthouse reflector lamp. 'Then why don't we use this?'

The Doctor stared hard at the lamp and then looked back at Leela. 'You mean convert the carbon-arc beam? Leela, that's a beautiful notion …'

'It is?'

The Doctor's face fell. 'Unfortunately I'd need a focusing device. A fairly large chunk of crystalline carbon.'

Skinsale seized eagerly on the first words he'd understood. 'Crystalline carbon? A diamond you mean?'

He held up his wrist and light glinted on his diamond cuff-links.

'Yes, that's right, but I'm afraid those are far too small. I'd need a fairly large one for the primary beam oscillator.'

'Palmerdale was carrying diamonds. He called them his insurance.'

'Then they'd still be on his body—in the crew room?'

'Yes.'

'Yes,' said the Doctor thoughtfully. 'Well, let's get this rocket-launcher ready first.'

Recovered now from the shock of the searing explosion, the Rutan flowed out of the generator room and up the stairs. It was cautious now, fearing more Earthling attacks, and it moved very slowly.

The Doctor packed the last few nails down the muzzle of the rocket-launcher. 'Right, that should do it. Sure you know how to work it?' Leela nodded and the Doctor rose, 'Then I'll be off.'

Skinsale got up too. 'I'm coming with you.'

'It isn't necessary, you know.'

'I want to. You'll need some help. Two will stand a better chance than one.'

'All right. Remember, Leela, don't fire until you see the green of its tentacles.'

They moved towards the door.

'How will you get past the Rutan?' asked Leela.

'With great discretion,' said the Doctor solemnly. 'With any luck it'll have retreated to the lower levels. Come on, Colonel.'

They crept cautiously down the stairs, past the smoke-blackened area of the explosion. They rounded the turn and came on to the crew-room landing. There was no sign of the Rutan.

The Doctor waved Skinsale forward and they slipped into the deserted crew room—empty except for Adelaide huddled where she had fallen, and the body of Palmerdale on the bunk.

The Doctor stood waiting by the door, waving Skinsale over to the body. Skinsale pulled back the blanket and began searching Palmerdale's pockets. He looked up at the Doctor and shook his head. 'Body-belt?' suggested the Doctor.

Skinsale felt inside Palmerdale's shirt and felt the stiff canvas belt with its pouch. He fumbled with the fastenings, his fingers stiff and clumsy.

The Rutan moved slowly up the staircase, all its senses alert. At the faint sounds of movement from the crew room it paused, and the pulsing glow became brighter as it gathered its energies. Moving faster now, it flowed on up the steps towards the crew-room landing.

Skinsale wrenched open the pouch, clawed out the handful of diamonds and went to join the Doctor. He tipped the pile of diamonds into the Doctor's cupped hands. The Doctor selected one diamond, the largest and finest, and tossed the rest carelessly on the floor. 'Come on,' he said and hurried off.

Skinsale stared down at the gleaming stones at his feet. There was a fortune there, enough to keep him in comfort for the rest of his life. He couldn't leave them ... Quickly he bent down—and began scrabbling for the gleaming stones.

There was a glow from the stairs as the Rutan flowed on to the landing and sprang forward into the crew room. A tentacle lashed out, curling round Skinsale's body and there was a crackle of blue sparks. Skinsale screamed ...

Just up the stairs the Doctor heard the sound and turned back. He ran down to the landing, looked into the crew room and saw the Rutan clasping its victim. Realising he could do nothing he turned and ran.

The Rutan dropped Skinsale's dead body and flowed after the Doctor with appalling speed. This time it was risking no Earthling traps. It would catch the Doctor and kill him now. Then there would only be the female.

The Doctor shot up the stairs three at a time, the angry crackling of the Rutan close behind him. If it got near enough to reach him with a tentacle he was finished—and so was Earth ...

As the Doctor ran up the last few steps the Rutan was close on his heels. It was almost upon him as he rounded the bend and saw Leela crouched behind the rocket-launcher.

As the Doctor dashed for the lamp-room doorway, the Rutan gathered all its energies for a final effort. With a shrill cry of triumph it sprang ...

12

THE LAST BATTLE

Leela crouched behind the rocket-launcher, frozen with horror. With the Doctor directly in front of her, how could she fire? Yet if she didn't shoot, the Rutan would surely catch him ...

One tremendous flying leap took the Doctor over the rocket-launcher, and clear over Leela's head.

With the Doctor in mid-air the Rutan surged forward—and Leela fired.

There was an ear-splitting crash as several pounds of assorted ironmongery ripped into the Rutan's body, blasting it back down the staircase.

Leela shook her head, half dazed by the noise. She turned and saw the Doctor sprawled in a heap on the other side of the room. 'Are you all right?'

The Doctor picked himself up, patted himself carefully here and there 'I think so—you singed the end of my scarf!'

'Where is the Colonel?'

'Dead, I'm afraid.'

'With honour?'

The Doctor hesitated, thinking of Skinsale scrabbling for the diamonds. It was no way for a man to be remembered.'Yes,' he said firmly.'With honour.'

'Then we have avenged him. Did you get the diamond?'

The Doctor held out his hand. The pride of Palmerdale's collection was gleaming in his palm.

'I'd better get to work.' The Doctor climbed up to the level of the arc-lamp, feeling for his sonic screwdriver. Soon he was absorbed in dismantling and reassembling the complex machinery. Leela watched him for a moment then went down the stairs. She wanted to be quite sure that their enemy was dead.

She found the Rutan on the landing below, a feebly glowing, jelly-like mass. It crackled faintly at the sight of her, and glowed a little brighter, but it was too weak to do her any harm. Leela called up the stairs. 'It is here, Doctor. I did it. The beast is finished!'

She looked down at the shattered body of her foe.

'Your triumph will be short-lived, Earthling,' whispered the Rutan. 'Soon our Mother Ship will blast this island to molten rock ...'

'Empty threats, Rutan. Enjoy your death, as I enjoyed killing you!'

The Rutan quivered and pulsed weakly. 'We die for the glory of our race. Long live the Rutan Empire ...'

The glow faded and died, and the Rutan died with it.

With a savage grin of triumph, Leela turned and went back to the lamp room.

The Doctor had rigged together one of his amazing contraptions, taking apart the reflector lamp and the giant telescope and re-assembling them in an entirely different order. As far as Leela could make out, the power of the carbon-arc lamp would be reflected through the telescope and finally focused through Palmerdale's diamond, which the Doctor was now fitting somewhere inside the telescope. He made a careful, final adjustment and looked up.

'They are hard to kill, these Rutans,' said Leela.

'Been celebrating, have you?'

'Of course. It is fitting to celebrate the death of an enemy.'

'Not in my opinion, but we haven't time to discuss morality. Look over there.'

A streak of light, like a giant fireball, had appeared in the night sky. It was moving steadily towards them ...

Leela shaded her eyes with her hand. 'Is that the Rutan ship?'

'It is,' said the Doctor grimly. 'Now, I've set this contraption to operate automatically. Once the ship is in range the beam will lock on to its resonator and fire, and we will then have exactly one hundred and seventeen seconds to get clear. Understand?'

'Perfectly!'

'So as soon as I switch on we run for it. All right?'

Leela stared up at the sky. The fireball was approaching with terrifying speed now. It was a moving sun hurtling straight towards them. Its fiery radiance lit up the lamp room like broad daylight, and the throbbing of its power-source grew louder and louder. 'I think you should switch on soon, Doctor. It's getting very near.'

'Nearly ready,' said the Doctor. He snapped a last connection into place and climbed down. The fireball was almost on them now. The noise of its approach was deafening, and its radiance hurt the eyes. The Doctor pulled the switch. The rickety-looking set-up began to throb with power …

'Come on, Leela. And whatever you do, don't look back!'

The humming of the Doctor's machine blended with the shattering roar of the approaching Rutan spaceship. Leela couldn't resist turning back for a final look. The fireball was so close it seemed about to smash through the lamp-room window. Its brightness almost blinded her … The Doctor pulled her towards the stairs. 'I said don't look back. Now run!'

They hurtled down the winding stairs, the Doctor in the lead. Outside the crew room, Leela paused again. She'd lost a good knife in there, when she'd thrown it at the Rutan. It was not good to lose such a fine weapon. She ran into the crew room and looked round.

The Doctor sped on, not realising that Leela was no longer with him. By now the whole lighthouse was shaking with the roar of the Rutan ship's power-source.

Luckily the knife had fallen fairly close to the door. Leela snatched it up and hurried on.

The Doctor ran down the long flights of stairs, finally reaching the generator room, where the generator was throbbing wildly. The door was still closed, and it took him precious seconds to knock out the wedges with the shovel. He flung the door open—ran outside and suddenly realised he was on his own. 'Leela!' he yelled and ran back into the generator room.

Leela paused to tuck her knife away in her boot, ran down the stairs into the generator room and bumped straight into the Doctor who was just coming in to look for her. He grabbed her wrist and yanked her outside. 'Leela, come on!'

They ran across the little island, slipping and sliding on the wet rocks, and finally flung themselves down behind a jagged rock, not far from where they'd left the TARDIS. By now the whole island was throbbing and shaking with the noise of the Rutan ship's approach.

Leela peeped over the rock. The fireball seemed to be hovering over the lighthouse tower … A thin beam of light speared out from the tower at the Rutan ship. The fireball glowed brighter and brighter, the noise rose to a screaming crescendo—there was a blinding flash, a colossal explosion, and Leela fell back, her hands over her eyes. The ground convulsed beneath them, and shattered rocks came down from the sky like rain. At last the rumbling echoes of the explosion died away, and all was silent.

The Doctor stood up. The lighthouse was still standing, but the Rutan spaceship had disappeared, blasted to atoms by the force of its own exploding power-drive.

Leela was still crouching down, her hands over her face. Gently he helped her up.

She took her hands from her face and moved her head to and fro. 'Slay me, Doctor!'

'I beg your pardon?' said the Doctor in some astonishment.

'I am blind,' said Leela stoically. 'Slay me now. It is the fate of the old and crippled.'

The Doctor took Leela's face in his hands and stared hard into her eyes. For a moment he looked worried, but then he smiled. 'You're neither old nor crippled, Leela. You were just dazzled by the flash. The effect will pass.'

'You're sure?'

'Yes. Just blink!'

Leela blinked rapidly several times. A hazy shape appeared before her eyes. It cleared, became the Doctor looking down at her. She noticed that he was staring into her eyes.

'That's strange!' he said.

'What is?'

'Pigmentation dispersal caused by the flash.' Leela looked at him in alarm and the Doctor said. 'It's all right. It just means your eyes have changed colour. You can stop blinking now, Leela. It's time to go.'

As they walked towards the TARDIS, Leela asked curiously, 'What colour are my eyes now?'

'Blue,' said the Doctor. 'Don't worry, it looks very nice.'

She turned for a last look at the lighthouse. 'Doctor, what will the people of this time say about all this? What will they think happened here?'

The Doctor shrugged. 'Who knows? Someone will probably write a poem about it. "Aye though we hunted high and low, and hunted everywhere" ...'

'What litany is that?'

The Doctor smiled. 'The Ballad of Flannen Isle. Wilfred Gibson.' He opened the TARDIS door.

> ' "Aye, though we hunted high and low.
> And hunted everywhere,
> Of the three men's fate we found no trace
> Of any kind, in any place,
> But a door ajar, and an untouched meal
> And an overtoppled chair ... " '

The Doctor ushered Leela into the TARDIS, followed her and closed the door behind them.

There was a wheezing groaning noise, and the TARDIS vanished. The only sound was the thundering of the waves as they crashed on the jagged coastline of Fang Rock ...

No one was left alive to hear them.

DOCTOR WHO – THE FIVE DOCTORS

1

THE GAME BEGINS

It was a place of ancient evil.

Somehow the evil seemed to hang in the air, like smoke or fog that long centuries had been unable to disperse. Along the length of one wall ran a massive control console with a monitor screen at its centre. The console's instrumentation was at once clumsy and complex. A scientist would have guessed it to be an early, primitive model of some highly sophisticated device. A huge Game Table dominated the centre of the room. It held a contoured model of a bleak and desolate landscape. In the centre, there was a Tower. Even in model form it looked sinister, threatening.

On a nearby table stood a carved, ivory box. Black-robed, black-gloved, the Player sat at the console operating controls untouched for many long years. The monitor screen lit up, filled only with the swirling mists of the temporal vortex. The black-robed Player worked with obsessive concentration, and at last his efforts met with some success. The swirling mists on the monitor screen resolved themselves into a blurred picture – a picture of a man. An old white-haired man in an old-fashioned frock-coat.

The Player leaned forward eagerly, tuning the controls, bringing the picture into clear focus.

It was time for the Game to begin.

The Doctor stepped back from the refurbished TARDIS console, surveying the results of his work with pride. Now in his fifth incarnation, he was a slender fair-haired young man, with a pleasant open face. As usual, he wore the costume of an Edwardian cricketer: striped trousers, fawn blazer with red piping, white cricketing sweater and an open-necked shirt. There was a fresh sprig of celery in his buttonhole.

One of the Doctor's two companions stood watching him suspiciously. Her name was Tegan Jovanka and she was an Australian air hostess. Tegan's experience of travelling with the Doctor had convinced her that (a) he didn't know what was going on most of the time, and (b) when he did get things right it was more by luck than judgement.

The Doctor had been repairing the TARDIS console which had suffered badly in a recent Cybermen attack. He had assured Tegan that the TARDIS was now even better than new, a claim Tegan viewed with her usual scepticism.

Feeling Tegan's eyes on the back of his neck, the Doctor turned. 'There we are then!'

'Finished?'

Proudly the Doctor patted the gleaming console. 'Yes. Looks rather splendid, doesn't it?'

Tegan had more practical concern. 'Will the TARDIS work properly now?'

'Of course,' said the Doctor airily. Catching Tegan's eye he added. 'Once everything's run in, that is ...'

'Did you repair the TARDIS or didn't you?'

'The TARDIS is more than just a machine, you know. It's like a person. It needs coaxing, persuading, encouraging.'

'In other words, the TARDIS is just as unreliable?'

'You have so little faith, Tegan.'

'Do you blame me?' asked Tegan bitterly. 'The amount of trouble you've landed me in, one way and another.'

Hurriedly the Doctor opened the main doors and slipped out of the TARDIS.

Once outside, the Doctor stood looking around him, surveying the peaceful scene with quiet enjoyment. The TARDIS stood amidst picturesque ivy-covered ruins. There was scarcely a breeze to stir the leaves and the tall grass. It might almost have been a fine summer afternoon on Earth, thought the Doctor. Except for the faint purple haze that hung in the air. Even this, exotic though it was, seemed somehow to add to the atmosphere of reassuring calm.

Turlough, the Doctor's other companion, sat with his back against a ruined wall, peacefully sketching. He was a thin-faced, sandy-haired young man, in the blazer and flannels of his public school, good-looking in a faintly untrustworthy way. For the moment, however, Turlough appeared to be in an exceptionally good mood. 'It really is marvellous here. I feel so calm and relaxed!'

'It's the high bombardment of positive ions in the atmosphere,' said the Doctor.

Tegan had followed the Doctor from the TARDIS and she came over to join them, sniffing the air. 'It's like Earth, after a thunderstorm.'

'Same cause, same reason.'

Tegan looked round, her irritation fading in the peaceful atmosphere. 'It's beautiful here.'

The Doctor nodded. 'For some, the Eye of Orion is the most tranquil place in the Universe.'

Turlough yawned and stretched. 'Can't we stay here, Doctor?'

'Why not – for a while at least. We could all do with a rest.'

They stood for a moment in a companionable silence, drinking in the atmosphere of peace and tranquillity. It was the last peace of mind they were to enjoy for a very long time.

The Player made a final adjustment and the picture on the monitor sprang sharply into focus. It showed a white-haired frock-coated old man, bending over a rose-bush, secateurs in hand, face totally absorbed. It was an old face, lined and wrinkled, yet somehow alert and vital at the same time. The blue eyes were bright with intelligence. The commanding beak of the nose gave the old man a haughty, imperious air.

The Player smiled in cruel satisfaction.

The old man in the garden was known as the Doctor – a Doctor nearing the end of his first incarnation. The Doctor sensed that the end was near. He had come to this place to prepare himself, to say farewell to a body and a personality almost worn out by now, to prepare himself for the birth of a new self. Here in this peaceful garden he could prune his roses, and care for his bees. He could enjoy a time of peace, of semi-retirement, before returning to the mainstream of his life and preparing to face the coming change.

Suddenly the old man tensed. Something was wrong. Something evil, some alien presence had come into his peaceful retreat. It seemed to be some kind of obelisk, rolling and tumbling towards him, growing larger and larger ...

Suddenly it was almost upon him.

He turned to run but it was too late, far too late. 'No! No!' he shouted. The obelisk rolled forward, swallowing him up, absorbing him completely.

For a moment his distorted screaming face peered out from inside the obelisk. Then the obelisk rolled away, disappearing as rapidly as it had arrived.

The Player rose from the console, and went over to the Game Table. From the ivory box he took a tiny, beautifully carved figure. It represented a white-haired old man in an old-fashioned frock-coat. The Player put the little figure of Doctor One onto the board, pushing it towards the centre with a long rake.

The first piece was on the board.

In the Eye of Orion, the current Doctor, the fair-haired young man in the cricketer's blazer, gave a sudden involuntary cry, his face twisted in pain.

'Are you all right?' asked Turlough.

'Just a twinge of cosmic angst.'

Tegan stared at him. 'Cosmic how much?'

The Doctor looked puzzled. 'As if I'd – lost something ...'

Brigadier Alastair Lethbridge-Stewart (Retired), one-time Commanding Officer of the United Nations Intelligence Taskforce, looked round the room that had once been his office. The annual UNIT Reunion was soon to take place. The Brigadier had mixed feelings about this sort of thing. Nice to see old friends of course, but odd to see them so changed.

Charlie Crichton came across the room towards the Brigadier, whisky bottle in hand. Strange to think he was now in command of UNIT. Bit stiff and formal old Charlie, thought the Brigadier, not realising how much he himself had mellowed over the years. Still, Charlie would learn – if he lived. In UNIT you encountered problems that weren't in anyone's rule book.

Crichton refilled the Brigadier's glass. 'Can't have our guest of honour running dry.'

Crichton raised his glass. 'To civilian life!'

'Hear, hear,' said the Brigadier. 'You know, I can't tell you how much I am looking forward to this reunion. The chance to meet old friends again.'

Brigadier Crichton put down his glass. 'There's one chap we've been trying to get hold of for ages. Mysterious sort of fellow. Used to be your Unpaid Scientific Adviser.'

The Brigadier smiled. 'Ah, the Doctor.'

'That's right. The Doctor!'

The Brigadier smiled reminiscently. 'Wonderful chap. All of them.'

Crichton looked curiously at him. 'Them? More than one, was there?'

'Well, yes and no,' said the Brigadier.

To his relief, they were interrupted by the buzz of the desk intercom. Crichton flicked the switch. 'Yes?'

The voice of the duty-sergeant crackled out. 'Excuse me, sir. Sorry to interrupt. Someone's arrived.'

'I'm not expecting anyone. Who is it?'

There was a tinge of desperation in the sergeant's voice. 'I'm not sure, sir. He insists on seeing Brigadier Lethbridge-Stewart.' The tone of the sergeant's voice changed, as he addressed the unseen intruder. 'I'm sorry, sir, you're not allowed in there.'

'What?' said a familiar voice indignantly. 'Me? Not allowed? I'm allowed everywhere. Just get out of the way, will you? Thank you!'

The office door was flung open and a little figure popped inside eluding the grasp of the UNIT sergeant. The newcomer looked swiftly round the room. 'Brigadier!' He rushed across to them and shook hands warmly.

'Good heavens,' said the Brigadier faintly. 'Is it really you?'

'For once I've been able to steer the TARDIS correctly, and here I am!'

Brigadier Crichton caught the duty-sergeant's eye. 'It's all right, Sergeant.'

'Yessir,' said the sergeant woodenly and withdrew.

Crichton studied the newcomer curiously. He saw an odd-looking little fellow in a shabby old frock coat and rather baggy check trousers. Untidy black hair hung in a fringe over his forehead, and his dark brown eyes seemed humorous and sad at the same time.

The little man looked hopefully up at the Brigadier. 'I'm not too late, am I?'

'What for?'

'Your speech, as guest of honour.'

Brigadier Crichton looked at him in astonishment. 'How did you know the Brigadier would be here?'

'Saw it in *The Times.*'

'Impossible. The reporter's still here.'

'Tomorrow's *Times* ,' said the little man witheringly. He turned to the Brigadier. 'Who is this fellow?'

'Colonel Crichton. My replacement.'

The little man sniffed. 'Mine was pretty unpromising too!'

Hastily, the Brigadier took the newcomer's arm. 'Come along, Doctor, we'll just take a stroll around the grounds.' He looked apologetically at Crichton. 'Excuse us for a moment. I'm awfully sorry about this.' He urged the newcomer to the door.

The little man stopped on the threshold and glanced around the office. 'You've had the place redecorated, haven't you. I don't like it!'

'Come on, Doctor,' said the Brigadier, and dragged him away.

As they went out, the UNIT sergeant came into the room. 'Everything all right, sir?'

'What the blazes is going on, Sergeant? Who was that strange little man?'

The sergeant answered. 'That was the Doctor.'

The Doctor and the Brigadier strolled through the formal grounds of UNIT HQ talking animatedly. To the Brigadier, this was the first, the original Doctor. The one he'd encountered in the London Underground during that terrible adventure with the Yeti. The one who had helped him defeat the invasion of the Cybermen. The Doctor who had reappeared one day, to defeat the menace of Omega in uneasy collaboration with his other selves. They were discussing these adventures and more as they strolled round the stiffly formal grounds with their neatly raked gravel paths and flowers that seemed to be standing to attention.

'Yes indeed, Doctor,' the Brigadier was saying. 'Yeti, Cybermen. We've seen some times ...'

'And Omega! Don't forget Omega!'

'As if I could.'

'And the terrible Zodin.'

'Who?'

'No, of course, you weren't concerned with her, were you? She happened in your future.' The Doctor came to a halt. 'I think it's time I said goodbye, Brigadier. I really shouldn't be here at all. I'm not exactly breaking the Laws of Time, but I'm bending them a little.'

'You never did bother very much about rules, Doctor, not as I remember.' The Brigadier noticed that the Doctor was staring fixedly at something over his shoulder. 'What's the matter?'

The Doctor pointed. 'Look!'

The Brigadier turned. A black obelisk was tumbling down the path towards them. 'What is it, Doctor?'

'I think our past is catching up with us, Brigadier. Or maybe it's our future. Come on, run!'

They began haring down the path. The obelisk tumbled after them at terrifying speed. The Doctor ran faster, the Brigadier panting along after him. 'Dammit, Doctor, I'm too old for this sort of thing.'

'Hurry Brigadier! We must get to the TARDIS before it's too late.'

The Doctor turned a corner, and found himself in a cul-de-sac. The path ended in a high wall. He turned, bumped into the Brigadier and the obelisk was upon them. It swallowed them up. For a moment their distorted faces could be seen inside it, then the obelisk tumbled rapidly into the distance, and disappeared.

The black-gloved hand of the Player took two more pieces from the box. A tiny figure in frock-coat and baggy trousers and a military-looking man with a neat moustache. The rake pushed the two pieces out onto the board. The Player returned to the console.

The Game was under way now.

But there was more, much more, to be done.

2

PAWNS IN THE GAME

'Over here, Tegan,' called Turlough. 'Quickly – the Doctor's ill!'

The Doctor was leaning against a ruined wall, his face twisted with pain.

Tegan ran up to him. 'Doctor, what is it?'

He stared at her – or rather, through her.

'Fading,' he whispered. 'All fading.'

'What's fading?'

'Great chunks of my past. Detaching themselves, like melting icebergs.'

Tegan turned almost angrily to Turlough. 'Don't just stand there. Do something to help him!'

'What am I supposed to do?'

Tegan saw from Turlough's face that he was as confused and frightened as she was herself.

Dimly aware of the wrangle, the Doctor managed a weak smile. 'Don't look so worried, you two. I'll have it all worked out soon. Everything's all right, you know. Everything is quite all right.' He fainted.

Elsewhere in space and time, on the planet Earth, the Doctor's third incarnation was driving very fast along a long straight road. This particular Doctor was a tall figure with a young-old face and a mane of prematurely white hair. He wore a velvet smoking-jacket and an open-necked shirt. The outfit was completed by a rather flamboyant checkered cloak. Doctor Three was something of a dandy.

The car he was driving was a vintage Edwardian roadster nicknamed 'Bessie'. It was moving at an impossible speed for so ancient a vehicle.

This was because, over the years, the Doctor had tinkered with the engine to such an extent that he had virtually rebuilt it. Bessie now had a turn of speed that left racing cars standing. Indeed, at this very moment, the Doctor was driving Bessie on a privately owned stretch of road used to test racing engines. Just as well, since every possible speed limit had been well and truly shattered.

Suddenly, the Doctor spotted what looked like an obstruction in the road ahead. The obstruction, which appeared to be some kind of obelisk, was actually speeding down the road towards him.

'Great balls of fire!' said the Doctor. He threw the car into a spectacular skid-turn which made the tyres shriek protestingly.

Seconds later, the Doctor was streaking down the road in the opposite direction, leaving a black skid-mark on the road behind him, and a smell of burning rubber in the air. He checked his driving mirror and saw, with indignant surprise, that the obelisk was tumbling rapidly down the road in pursuit – and it was gaining fast.

'Right!' said the Doctor. He put Bessie into overdrive. The car shot off down the road, accelerating at an incredible rate. The Doctor looked in his mirror, noting with grim satisfaction that the obelisk was now dwindling back into the distance. It became smaller, smaller, and then disappeared.

He slowed the car, patting the dashboard. 'Good old Bessie.' He glanced over his shoulder, but the road behind him was reassuringly empty. 'I wonder what it was … He returned his attention to the road ahead. And there was the obelisk – bearing down upon him.

He spun the wheel for another turn, but far too late this time.

Car and Doctor disappeared inside the obelisk.

The black-gloved hand put another piece on the board.

In the Eye of Orion Tegan and Turlough knelt worriedly by the Doctor. To their immense relief he opened his eyes and stared vacantly up at them.

'What's happening to him?' whispered Tegan. 'What are we going to do?'

'Search me. He doesn't seem to be ill exactly. It's more like some kind of psychic attack.'

'I am being diminished,' said the Doctor suddenly. 'Whittled away, piece by piece.' His voice was faint but calm, as if making some interesting scientific observation. 'A man is the sum of his memories, you know, and a Time Lord even more so.'

He struggled to sit up, and! Tegan supported him. 'Doctor, what can we do to help you?'

'Get me into the TARDIS … I have to find … to find …'

Between them, Tegan and Turlough got the Doctor to his feet.

'Find what?' asked Turlough.

'My other selves …'

The Doctor slumped back in their arms.

Tegan looked at Turlough. 'What does he mean?'

Turlough shrugged.

Half dragging, half carrying, they helped the Doctor towards the TARDIS

The Player sat back. Three of the main pieces were now on the board – two more to go. But first he would allow himself a little diversion. He would pick up a pawn. Insignificant, valueless, fit only for sacrifice. It could be quite amusing …

The Player's hands glided over the controls. The swirling time-mists cleared, revealing the face of an attractive dark-haired girl.

Sarah Jane Smith, freelance journalist, opened the front door of her flat and looked out at the day. Not particularly bright, but at least it wasn't actually raining. She was on her way to see a magazine editor to discuss an important assignment. Her little car had chosen the previous evening to stage a total breakdown. She'd have to travel by bus, which meant a walk and a wait at the bus stop. She didn't want to arrive at the meeting all soggy …

Sarah's rambling thoughts were interrupted by the appearance of a sort of squared-off metal dog with disc aerials for ears and a long thin antenna for a tail.

K9 was, in reality, a mobile self-powered computer with defensive capabilities. He was a souvenir of Sarah's former association with that traveller in time and space known as the Doctor.

Looking down Sarah saw that K9 was on full alert.

'What's the matter, K9?'

'Danger, Mistress.'

'What?'

'I sense danger, Mistress. Telepathic trace faint, but rapidly increasing in strength. Do not go out!'

Sarah knelt beside K9. 'What *kind* of danger?'

'Regret – more positive data not available.'

'I can't just stay at home all day,' said Sarah helplessly. 'Can't you give me some reason?'

'Negative, Mistress. Data analysis shows too many variables.' K9's voice became urgent. 'Danger readings now becoming much higher. Suggestion, Mistress: take me with you.'

'Honestly, I can't. The car's in dock and I'm going on the bus.'

Sarah turned to leave.

K9 glided forward. 'There *is* danger, Mistress,' he insisted. 'My sensors tell me it is now extreme. The Doctor is involved.'

Sarah frowned. Her parting with the Doctor had been abrupt, and as far as she was concerned, final. 'Now I know you're imagining things, K9. I'll see you later.'

Stepping quickly past K9 she closed the door.

K9's voice came faintly from behind the door. 'Doctor … danger … Doctor … Mistress …'

Hardening her heart, Sarah ignored it, and set off for the bus stop.

Doctor, indeed, she thought as she walked down the quiet suburban road. After years of companionship and innumerable shared dangers, the Doctor had suddenly rushed off to Gallifrey in response to some mysterious summons, leaving Sarah behind. She had been insisting for some time that all she wanted was to return to Earth and lead a quiet life, but the abruptness of the parting had left Sarah feeling abandoned, and more than a little resentful.

And he needn't think he can get round me by sending me a crated-up K9 either, thought Sarah as she peered down the road in search of her bus. She seemed to be in luck, for there was something moving ahead. It came nearer and nearer.

Too late, Sarah saw that it wasn't a bus at all, but a strange, tumbling black obelisk. She screamed, and turned to run, but it was much too late ...

The woman called Susan Campbell, who had once been known as Susan Foreman, walked through the streets of New London on the way to market. Looking about her she marvelled at how swiftly the city had recovered from the devastation of the Dalek attack.

Gleaming new buildings were everywhere, the old bombed sites had all been cleared. Those which hadn't been used as sites for new buildings had been turned into parks and gardens. It was a smaller London – it would be many years before population rose anywhere near its old levels – but it was a greener, far more attractive one.

Life had been hard at first. For many years she had seen very little of her husband David, who was a prominent figure in the Reconstruction Government. But gradually life had returned to normal. Now Susan and David and their three children could look forward to a more peaceful life. These days it seldom occurred to Susan that this wasn't really her world at all, that she had originally come here almost by chance in the company of the old man she sometimes called Grandfather, and everyone else called the Doctor.

It was still early, and the street was deserted.

Susan stopped dead, staring ahead of her.

Something very odd had appeared at the far end of the street.

A strange alien shape, tumbling over and over, was rushing straight towards her.

Susan felt the kind of terror she had not felt for many years. Somehow the unknown had come to claim her, shattering her normal life once again. As the obelisk swallowed her up, her last despairing thoughts were of the Doctor.

The Player stepped back from the Game Table, smiling coldly. Two more pawns in place.

The three main pieces were already on the board.

He had only to add the fourth and the fifth would follow, drawn by the attraction of his other selves, by the need to be whole.

He must find and transfer the fourth piece ...

He returned to the console and leaned forward, his face tense with concentration. The swirling time-mists on the monitor cleared at last, to show a river and a boat.

The tall curly-haired man with the wide staring eyes propelled the punt along the backwaters of the river Cam with steady thrusts of the long pole. He wore comfortable Bohemian-looking clothes, a loose coat with an open-necked shirt. A broad-brimmed soft hat was jammed on the back of his head, and an incredibly long scarf looped about his neck. This was the Doctor in his fourth incarnation. As might have been expected, he had something of all his previous selves about him: the intellectual arrogance of the first, the humour of the second, and something of the elegance of the third, though in a more relaxed and informal style.

Lolling back on cushions in the front of the boat, a girl was watching the Doctor's efforts with amused admiration. She was on the small side, aristocratically beautiful, with long fair hair above a high forehead. This was Romana, the Doctor's Time Lady companion.

They were gliding along the part of the river known as the Backs, so called because the river ran between the backs of the various Cambridge colleges. On either side, green lawns sloped up to elegant old buildings.

The Doctor made an expansive gesture, almost overbalancing in the process. 'Wordsworth!' he said dramatically. 'Rutherford, Christoper Smart, Andrew Marvell, Judge Jeffries, Owen Chadwick ...'

Romana trailed a hand in the cool water. 'Who?'

'Owen Chadwick. Economist, I think. They were all here, you know, some of the finest minds, the greatest intellectual labourers in the history of Earth.'

Romana nodded. 'Isaac Newton, of course.'

'Oh yes, definitely Newton.'

The Doctor thrust the pole into the river bed, and the punt shot forward.

'For every action there must be an equal and opposite re-action,' quoted Romana solemnly.

'Quite right!'

'So Newton invented punting?'

'Oh yes, there was no limit to old Isaac's genius.'

The punt glided smoothly forwards and Romana said, 'Isn't it wonderful how something so primitive can be so …'

'Civilised?'

'No, simple. You just push in one direction and the boat moves in the other.' She looked about her. 'I do love the Earth in spring. The leaves, the colours …'

'It's almost October,' said the Doctor apologetically.

'I thought you said we were coming here for May week?'

'I did – though mind you, May week's in June.'

'I'm confused.'

'So was the TARDIS.'

Romana tried again. 'I do love the autumn,' she said poetically. 'The leaves, the colours …'

'Well, never mind! If only the TARDIS was as simple as a punt! No co-ordinates, no dimensional stabilisers. Just the water, the punt, a strong pair of hands and a pole. Nothing can possibly go wrong.'

Romana was peering ahead. 'What's that under the bridge, Doctor. Another boat?'

The Doctor leaned forward to look, at the same time thrusting the pole hard into the river bed. It stuck fast in a soft patch. Distracted by the sight of a black obelisk rolling across the water towards him, the Doctor let go of the pole. The boat drifted helplessly on and the obelisk swallowed up both its occupants.

Slowly the empty punt drifted beneath the bridge.

Lights flashed on the console. A warning siren hooted, shattering the silence. The Player worked frantically at the controls. Something had gone wrong – badly wrong. Unless he could stabilise the situation there was grave danger of temporal instability. He worked feverishly, and at last the siren was stilled and the warning lights ceased to flash. The Player leaned back, exhausted.

On the monitor screen he could see the distorted, slowly rotating shapes of the Doctor and Romana. They were trapped in a freak eddy in the vortex – and he had neither the skill nor the energy to free them. But although it was a set-back, it was by no means complete disaster. There were already three Doctors on the board. And there were the companions, those luckless pawns in the game. Enemies, old and new, were already in place. One more piece on the board, and the game could enter the next, most vital phase.

The Player leaned forwards and worked on the controls. The trapped fourth Doctor faded and the fifth appeared ...

3

DEATH ZONE

Once inside the TARDIS, the Doctor pulled free from Tegan and Turlough, and staggered over to the centre console. Eyes staring blankly ahead, he punched up co-ordinates and set the TARDIS in motion. It seemed almost as if he was operating the TARDIS in his sleep. As the time rotor began its rise and fall, the Doctor slid gently to the ground.

'Oh no!' gasped Tegan.

Turlough knelt beside the Doctor, taking his pulse. It was strong and steady. For confirmation, Turlough put a hand on the Doctor's chest and felt a steady thump-thump. He moved his hand to the other side, and felt another heartbeat, equally strong. He looked up in astonishment at Tegan who said briefly, 'Two hearts!'

Turlough straightened up. 'I see. Well, his body seems to be all right, as far as I can tell … He seems to be just … fading away.' He looked angrily at Tegan. 'Why did he have to set the TARDIS moving? We were safe before he did that.'

Tegan wasn't listening. She was staring in horror at the Doctor's unconscious body. The Doctor really was fading away – quite literally.

His body was actually becoming transparent, as he faded slowly out of existence.

Tegan knelt and grasped the already insubstantial hand. '*Doctor!*'

The Doctor responded, and she felt his hand become solid and real inside her own.

She looked in anguish up at Turlough. 'What's going on?'

Turlough pointed to the time rotor. It had stopped moving. 'We've landed.'

He switched on the scanner. They saw a stretch of bleak and threatening landscape. At its centre, not far away, there loomed a dark and sinister tower.

The Player gave a great sigh of relief. As he had hoped, the presence of three of the Doctor's selves had been powerful enough to draw him to their side, even though the fourth Doctor was still missing. Drawn irresistibly by his need to be whole again, the Doctor had delivered himself and his companions into the trap.

The Player took a model Doctor, and a model Tegan and Turlough from the box and pushed them on to the Game Table.

While Tegan kept a watchful eye on the Doctor, Turlough carried out a quick check on the TARDIS control console.

'As far as I can make out from the instruments, we're nowhere and no-time.'

'The Doctor probably forgot to reconnect something,' said Tegan gloomily.

Turlough shook his head. 'The instruments appear to be working perfectly. They just won't tell us anything. The TARDIS is paralysed.'

'So how did we get here? And what do we do now?'

Turlough looked sombrely down at the Doctor. He was still unconscious, and breathing heavily, but at least he was *there*.

'I suppose we just wait, till the Doctor recovers.'

'And if he doesn't?' asked Tegan.

Turlough had no answer.

Magnificent in full presidential regalia, President Borusa strode through the corridors of the Capitol, acknowledging the respectful greetings of passing Time Lords with the briefest of nods. The expression on the long intellectual face was positively thunderous. Lord President Borusa was in a very bad mood indeed.

He reached the presidential conference room, swept past the guards at the door and paused on the threshold. The conference room was small, but furnished with the greatest luxury. There was a transmat booth, discreetly tucked away in one corner. A highly polished oval conference table occupied the centre of the room with high-backed chairs ranged around it. The only ornaments were an antique harp on a stand, and an ancient painting on the wall. Two of the chairs were already occupied, one by Chancellor Flavia, the other by the Castellan.

Borusa surveyed them coldly, then took his place in the throne-like presidential chair at the head of the conference table. 'Well?'

The Castellan said respectfully, 'He has arrived, Lord President.'

The news gave Borusa no pleasure. 'Involving this – person does not please me.'

The Castellan's voice was still respectful, but it held an underlying firmness. 'The Constitution clearly states that when, in Emergency Session, the Members of the Inner Council are unanimous –'

'As indeed we are,' interrupted Chancellor Flavia crisply. She was a small neat woman, with an immensely strong will.

Borusa waved them both to silence. 'Yes, yes, in such an event, the President can be overruled. I know that ridiculous clause.' Borusa sighed with exaggerated weariness. 'Very well, have him enter.'

The Castellan touched the mini-control console built into the arm of his chair. Everyone looked expectantly at the door.

Seconds later it opened. A figure stood in the doorway. A tall figure, elegant in black velvet, his arrogantly handsome features set off by a neatly pointed black beard.

The Master.

He stood looking at the three Time Lords for a moment, then gave an exaggeratedly courtly bow. 'Lord President, Castellan, Chancellor Flavia. This is a very great, may I say, a most unexpected honour.'

The deep musical voice had an insolently amused undertone like the purr of a great black cat. It was with catlike litheness that the Master strolled across the room. 'I may be seated?' Without waiting for either permission or reply, the Master dropped gracefully into the vacant chair and looked insolently around the little group. 'Now what can I do for you?'

Borusa leaned forward, fixing the Master with the piercing look that had reduced many a Time Lord opponent to terrified silence. 'You are one of the most evil and corrupt beings our Time Lord race has ever produced. Your crimes are without number, your villainy without end.'

The Master nodded graciously, like someone receiving a well deserved compliment.

Restraining himself with a visible effort, Borusa continued, 'Nevertheless, we are prepared to offer you a full and free pardon.'

If Borusa expected surprise or gratitude, he was to be disappointed. The Master raised an eyebrow. 'What makes you think I want your forgiveness?'

'We can offer you an alternative to your renegade existence,' said the Castellan bluntly.

Indeed?' The Master raised an eyebrow. Beneath the assumed calm his mind was racing furiously. The Time Lords needed him, that was obvious. And if that was the case, they must know that no ordinary reward would persuade him to serve them. Could it be …

Borusa spoke, completing the Master's thought. 'Regeneration. A whole new life cycle.'

It was all that the Master could do not to show his excitement. Regeneration! In the course of a spectacularly criminal existence, the Master had used up all his allotted regenerations with record speed. He had only survived in his present form by ruthlessly hijacking the body of another. Unfortunately it was not a Time Lord body. When it began to age and decay, as it inevitably would, the Master would be forced to steal another body, and then another. It was a ghoulish sort of existence at best, and the Master wanted desperately to be free of it. With a fierce effort of will, he forced himself to remain calm. 'I see … And what must I do?'

Borusa blurted out the incredible truth. 'Rescue the Doctor.'

The first Doctor was wandering in a nightmare. Old, white-haired and frail, yet somehow indomitable, he staggered on through endless metal corridors. The silver, polished walls seemed to be set at odd, disconcerting angles, presenting a mind-bending sense of unreality. All around him he saw distorted versions of his own reflection. He plodded on. There was an answer somewhere, a reason behind this mystery, and eventually he would find it. He had never given up yet, and he was too old to change.

Suddenly he paused, peering ahead.

Someone was moving towards him.

The Doctor stepped back, flattening himself against an angle of wall. A towering distorted shape moved along the corridors. The shape came nearer, the twisted reflections danced – and suddenly a slender dark-haired young woman appeared from round the corner.

The Doctor looked at her in astonishment for a moment, and then stepped forward, 'Susan? Surely it's Susan?'

The young woman threw herself into his arms with a force that almost knocked him over. 'Grandfather! Thank goodness I've found you! How did we get here? What's happening?'

Gently the Doctor disengaged himself. 'I wish I knew, my dear.'

'As soon as I found myself in this horrible place I started looking for you. Somehow I knew you were here.'

'Yes, yes,' said the Doctor, with a touch of his old tetchiness. 'The important question now is, where are we and why?'

Susan looked despairingly around. There was a patch of light at the corridor junction behind them, and suddenly a shadow fell across it.

The shadow of a Dalek.

Susan pointed. 'Look! We must be on Skaro!'

The Doctor, as usual, refused to take anything for granted. 'We were brought here. Perhaps the Dalek was brought here too.'

Before Susan could answer the Dalek glided round the corner. She gave a gasp of horror at the sight of the squat metal-studded pepper-pot shape, with the jutting sucker arm and gun stick. The constantly swivelling eye-stalk registered their presence immediately.

The harsh grating Dalek voice echoed through the metal corridors. 'Halt! Halt at once or you will be exterminated!'

'Run, Doctor!' shouted Susan.

Separating to present smaller targets, ducking and weaving and zigzagging, the Doctor and Susan fled. As they ran, their distorted reflections moved with them.

Confused by the constantly changing images, the Dalek fired again and again, the blasts echoing along the metal corridors. Unfortunately, it had registered Susan's use of the Doctor's name. As it pursued them along the corridors, the metallic voice grated, 'It is the Doctor! The Doctor must be destroyed! Exterminate! Exterminate! Exterminate!'

*

A monitor screen lit up on one wall of the conference room. It showed the Mountains of Gallifrey. At the inaccessible centre was a patch of sinister blackness.

'The Death Zone,' said Borusa simply.

The Master stroked his beard. 'Ah yes. The black secret at the centre of your Time Lord paradise.'

'Recently,' said the Castellan, 'the Death Zone has become – reactivated. Somehow it is draining energy from the Eye of Harmony.'

'To such an extent,' said Chancellor Flavia, 'that all Gallifrey is endangered.'

The Eye of Harmony was the precious Time Lord energy source, formed from the nucleus of a Black Hole, stabilised by Rassilon untold years ago.

Borusa stared broodingly at the map of the Zone. 'We must know what is happening there.'

'Did it occur to you to go and look?'

'Two of the High Council entered the Zone to investigate. Neither one returned,'

'So you sent for the Doctor.' The Master knew that for many years the Time Lords had used the Doctor, often against his will, as a kind of cosmic troubleshooter.

'We *looked* for the Doctor,' corrected the Castellan.

'But we discovered that the Doctor no longer existed, in any, of his regenerations,' Borusa said flatly. 'It appears that the Doctor has been taken out of space and time.'

The Castellan touched a control in his chair. The map of the Death Zone was replaced by a distorted, swirling vision of the fourth Doctor, whose punting trip had been so suddenly interrupted. 'We believe that the attempt to lift *this* regeneration from his time-stream was unsuccessful. He is trapped in a time-eddy, and there he must stay until we find and free his other selves.'

'And if you cannot?' There was no reply, and the Master laughed softly. 'A cosmos without the Doctor. It scarcely bears thinking about!' He considered for a moment. 'You can get me into the Zone?'

The Castellan nodded to the transmat booth in the corner. 'We have a power-boosted open-ended transmat beam.'

'What makes you believe the Doctor's other selves are in the Zone?'

Borusa shrugged. 'Their time-traces converge there.'

The Master nodded thoughtfully. 'Why me?'

'We needed someone cunning, ruthless, experienced, determined ...'

'And disposable?' suggested the Master.

'Not at all,' said the Castellan blandly. 'You would be useless to us dead.'

Chancellor Flavia was becoming impatient. 'Will you go?'

For a long moment the Master made no reply.

Borusa leaned forward. *'Will you?'*

'And rescue the Doctor ...' The Master smiled.

4

UNEXPECTED MEETING

The Doctor was fading again. For some time now he had been pulsing in and out of existence, sometimes completely real and solid, at others insubstantial as a ghost. Tegan and Turlough knelt beside him, doing their best to will him back into being. It appeared that the Doctor could arrest the process by some kind of mental effort. The problem was to keep him conscious, and to persuade him to exert his will. In the Doctor's weakened condition, it wasn't easy.

'Come on, Doctor,' urged Tegan.

'Hold on,' shouted Turlough. 'Hold on!'

As if responding to the urgency in their voices, the Doctor opened his eyes, suddenly becoming real and solid again.

'Doctor, what's happening to you?' asked Tegan desperately.

The Doctor's voice was faint. 'Being sucked into the time vortex … Part of me there already … pulling the rest.'

He began to fade again.

'No!' shouted Tegan.

Suddenly the Doctor became solid again.

He started struggling to his feet. 'I mustn't sleep. Don't let me sleep …'

Susan and the first Doctor were still running through endless metal corridors, the angry Dalek at their heels. Its metallic voice echoed close behind them, shrieking orders, threats and warnings. 'Halt at once! You will be exterminated. Obey the Daleks!' And always the old, chilling battle-cry. 'Exterminate! Exterminate! Exterminate!'

They had been running for what seemed a very long time now, and the old man was almost exhausted. For the later stages of their flight,

Susan had been helping, almost dragging him along. Sometimes the Dalek was close enough to fire at them, at others they managed to shake it off for a while. But Susan was all too aware that in the long run it was steadily gaining on them. The end was only a matter of time.

They turned a corner, only to find themselves in a kind of cul-de-sac, a metal wall barring the way ahead.

'It's a blind alley,' gasped Susan. 'Turn back, quickly.'

The old man's body might be exhausted, but his mind was as alert and active as ever. 'That may be precisely what we need.'

Susan tugged at his sleeve. 'Grandfather, let's get out of here. Please!'

The Doctor refused to move. 'Don't argue, there isn't time,' he said imperiously. 'Now, listen carefully, Susan. When I shout "Now!" help me to shove the Dalek down that alley. And when I shout "Drop!" – then *drop*. Understood?'

Susan opened her mouth to argue, caught the old man's eye and said meekly, 'Understood.'

The Doctor flattened himself against the wall, drawing Susan beside him.

The monotonous ranting of the Dalek was very close now. 'Halt! You will be exterminated!'

Suddenly it glided around the corner, very fast, moving a little way past them.

'Now!' shouted the Doctor.

They sprang out of hiding, ran up behind the Dalek and shoved it down the little blind alley with all their combined strength. The Dalek shot forward, eye-stalk swivelling to find its attackers, trying desperately to turn and bring its blaster to bear. 'Under attack. Under attack!' it screeched. Catching a distorted glimpse of the Doctor and Susan it began firing wildly.

'Drop!' shouted the Doctor.

They dropped, flattening themselves on to the floor, while energy-bolts roared and ricocheted over their heads. Then the inevitable happened. One of the energy-bolts ricocheting about the tiny blind alley bounced back and scored a direct hit on the Dalek itself, and it exploded in smoke and flame, blasting a substantial hole in the metal wall. They kept their heads down, waiting for the rain of fiery debris to subside. Finally the Doctor rose a little creakily to his feet, and helped Susan to stand up. The Dalek was no more than a pile of smoking metallic fragments.

The Doctor surveyed the remains with some satisfaction. 'It's very dangerous to fire energy weapons in an enclosed space,' he observed mildly. Not that it would have been any good warning the Dalek, he thought, even if he'd wanted to. Daleks never listen.

Susan was staring through the jagged hole in the wall. 'Look!'

The hole revealed a bleak and barren landscape, scarred and pitted like some ancient battlefield. In the distance there were jagged mountains, and in the middle of them, a dark and sinister tower. Both Susan and the Doctor recognised the Tower and landscape immediately, and looked at each other in horror. If there was a place worse than Skaro to find yourself in, this was it.

'The Dark Tower,' whispered the old man.

'We're on Gallifrey,' said Susan unbelievingly.

'In the Death Zone.'

'But why? Why were we brought here?'

The Doctor rallied, straightening up, and tugging at his lapels. 'Instinct, my dear, tells me that the answer to that question lies in the Tower. Come!'

Indomitable as ever, the old man led the way forward.

The Brigadier looked down at his little companion with an air of bitter reproach. 'Charming spot, Doctor!'

After their sudden abduction from the grounds of UNIT HQ, the second Doctor and the Brigadier had found themselves, apparently unharmed, in what looked like the ruins of some once-great city. A city that had been flattened, devastated by some long-past catastrophe, leaving behind only patches of rubble and the occasional broken wall. The whole area was dark and overcast. Occasionally there was a rumble of distant thunder, and jagged lightning bolts streaked across the sky. Thick patches of drifting fog added a sinister touch to the terrifying landscape.

Pushing back his fringe of untidy black hair, the little Doctor peered cautiously around him. 'My dear Brigadier, it's no use blaming me!'

'You attract trouble, Doctor,' said the Brigadier grimly. 'You always did! Where the devil are we?'

'I'm not sure yet,' said the Doctor mysteriously. 'But I have some very nasty suspicions.' Suddenly he pointed. 'What's that? Over there!'

The Brigadier shaded his eyes with his hands. He caught a fleeting glimpse of huge shapes, moving stealthily through the fog. The instincts of long-ago battlefields made him pull the Doctor into the shelter of a nearby wall. 'Something moving up ahead.'

'Keep down,' hissed the Doctor, and immediately popped his own head up for a better look.

They both crouched low, careful to keep close to the remains of the delapidated wall. So intent were they both on the threat out there in the distance that neither noticed when an enormous hand appeared through a hole in the wall and groped stealthily towards them.

It moved closer … closer … Suddenly it seized the Brigadier by the arm in a grip like that of a steel clamp. The Brigadier gave a yell of alarm. He leaped to his feet, and began desperately trying to pull himself free. The Doctor jumped up, and grabbed the Brigadier's other arm, pulling hard. But the unseen owner of the hand and arm was incredibly strong. Both Doctor and Brigadier were dragged remorselessly towards the hole.

Letting go of the Brigadier's arm, the Doctor looked round for a weapon. To his delight he spotted a chunk of metal piping half buried in the mud. Wrenching it free, he used it as a club, smashing again and again at the wrist of the unseen attacker. The great hand was jarred open, and the Brigadier was free. The Doctor tossed the length of piping aside and yelled, 'Run, Brigadier!'

They ran, stumbling across the rough ground, away from the threat behind the wall and the menacing shapes that lurked in the mist.

In the TARDIS, the fifth Doctor staggered towards the console. 'Signal,' he muttered. 'Must send signal …' He reeled, and Turlough caught him just in time. Doctor wake up! We need you to get us out of here.'

Gently Tegan shook the Doctor's shoulder. 'What signal, Doctor?'

The Doctor opened his eyes and stared blankly at her. 'Must send signal … find them. Must be … *whole*.' He stared at her in anguish. 'Help me!'

*

The tall man with the shock of white hair drove cautiously through the drifting mists. It was considerate of his unknown kidnapper to hijack Bessie as well, he thought. Thanks to the Doctor's many modifications, the little roadster was making good progress, even over this rough ground. Suddenly the fog thickened.' The Doctor stopped the car for a moment. 'Now what?' He peered ahead, pulling his cloak collar up around his ears.

It was a bleak and barren landscape, churned and broken, and the road was little more than a rough track. There were mountains ahead, and the looming shape of some kind of tower. Grim suspicions were beginning to form in the Doctor's mind. He narrowed his eyes. Had he seen something moving in the dense patch of fog ahead?

Sarah Jane Smith stumbled miserably through the fog, picking her way through rough ground, broken up only by the occasional stunted tree. Black clouds rolled overhead, and lightning bolts seared across the sky. It was, thought Sarah, as unattractive a piece of landscape as she had ever seen. 'Oh, K9, why didn't I listen to you?' she moaned.

The fog pressed in on her threateningly. Somehow Sarah was convinced that there was something waiting in ambush, out there in the fog. She tripped over a chunk of broken branch and snatched it up, thinking it might serve as a weapon. Clutching her club, she took a cautious step forwards – and suddenly the ground vanished from beneath her feet. She had stepped clean over the edge of a ravine.

Sarah screamed, dropping the stick, and flailed out desperately in an attempt to regain her balance, but it was too late. She hurtled over the edge, scrabbling desperately for some kind of handhold. She managed to arrest her fall by clutching at a shrub growing from the cliff edge. But it was too slight to bear her weight. She felt it beginning to pull away. Sarah looked below. The ravine appeared to be bottomless, a deep fissure in the earth. If she fell she would probably be killed. Even if she survived, she would never get out again. The roots began to tear …

Then as if from nowhere a voice called, 'Hang on a minute. Catch hold of this!', and something dropped past her face. It was a rope!

Sarah grabbed it, saving herself just as the roots pulled free.

She looked up and saw a tall, white-haired figure looking down at her from the cliff edge. 'Hang on!'

Sarah heard the growl of an engine. Then came a steady pull on the rope, miraculously drawing her upwards.

She scrambled over the cliff-edge, and fell into the arms of the Doctor. 'I've never been so pleased to see anyone!'

'Me too,' said the familiar voice. 'But I really think we should move away from the edge!'

He drew her back towards safety. Sarah saw that the Doctor had tied the rope to Bessie and used the car to pull her up. He unfastened the rope and began coiling it neatly.

Sarah stared unbelievingly at him. 'Wait a minute – it's you!'

'Of course it's me. Hello, Sarah Jane.'

'No, but it's the *you* you!'

'That's right!'

This was undoubtedly the Doctor as Sarah had known him first, before that ghastly business with the spiders had triggered his regeneration.

'But you changed!'

The Doctor smiled. 'Did I?'

'Don't you remember? You became – all teeth and curls.'

The Doctor shuddered, visibly appalled by the prospect. 'Teeth and curls? Well, maybe I did – but I haven't yet.'

Suddenly Sarah could feel herself becoming very angry. 'I see. No, I don't – but never mind. Well, thanks very much for rescuing me, Doctor. Now maybe you'll explain just why I'm here to need rescuing?'

The Doctor smiled, thinking that Sarah hadn't changed. She had never been ready to accept the traditional role of the maiden in distress. 'Steady on, Sarah Jane. I'm not exactly here by choice myself.'

She gaped at him. 'You're not? Then what are we both doing here?'

'I'm not sure, yet,' said the Doctor darkly, 'though I have my suspicions.' He tossed the coiled rope into the back of the car. 'Come along, Sarah Jane, get in the car. I'll try to explain on the way.'

Supported by Tegan and Turlough, the fifth Doctor stared at the TARDIS console as if he had never seen it before in all his lives. 'I've got to … got to …' He looked almost indignantly at Tegan and Turlough – as if it was all their fault. 'What is it I've got to do?'

Tegan said, 'You were going on about some kind of signal.'

'And about being whole,' added Turlough.

'The signal. Yes, of course!'

'What's the signal *for*, Doctor?' asked Tegan. 'Who is it to?

'Recall signal,' said the Doctor with almost pathetic eagerness. 'They'll hear it. Yes, that'll bring them …'

He staggered again, clutching at the console for support and staring vaguely at the maze of controls. It was all too obvious that the Doctor didn't have the slightest idea what to do next.

Tegan spoke urgently. 'Listen, Doctor, tell us where the signal control is, so we can send it for you.'

The Doctor stared wildly at her. 'It's … it's …'

His hands groped blindly over the console for a moment, then he crashed to the floor.

5

TWO DOCTORS

As she helped the tired old man across the rough ground, Susan was beginning to wonder if their situation had really improved very much. They had exchanged endless metal corridors for endless barren countryside. At the moment they were making their way through a desolate area strewn with boulders. Still, at least they'd got rid of the Dalek – though it was very possible that more Daleks waited in ambush somewhere ahead. The Doctor came to a sudden halt. He leaned gasping against a boulder.

'It's no good, Susan,' he said angrily, hating to admit his weakness. 'I shall have to rest.'

'Yes, of course, Grandfather, you stay there. I'll just go and see what things look like past these boulders.'

Susan walked a little way forwards to where the clump of boulders ended. The land sloped downwards a little. To her delight, there in a little hollow she saw a familiar square blue shape. She turned and called, 'Grandfather, look. Come and see!'

Wearily the Doctor heaved himself upright and came to join her. 'What is it?' He stared. 'Goodness me! The TARDIS!'

'What's the TARDIS doing here?'

The discovery had revived the old man's flagging energies. 'I suggest we go and find out,' he said sharply, and set off down the path.

The Doctor moaned and stirred and opened his eyes. 'He's conscious,' said Turlough gloomily. 'But only just.'

Tegan nodded. 'If only he'd recovered long enough to send that signal.'

Then to her utter astonishment, the outer door of the TARDIS opened. In marched a white-haired old man, key in hand. A slim dark-haired woman was close behind him.

Tegan and Turlough stared.

The newcomers stared back at them with an astonishment equal to their own.

Tegan jumped to her feet. 'Who are you?'

The old man snapped, 'More to the point, young woman, who are you?' He surveyed the little group with obvious disapproval. 'What are all you young people doing inside my TARDIS?'

Tegan pointed to the slight fair-haired figure stretched out on the floor. 'It's *his* TARDIS.'

'And who might he be?' asked the old man disdainfully.

Turlough got to his feet. 'He happens to be the Doctor.'

The old man gave a gasp of sheer astonishment. '*He's* the Doctor? Good grief!'

A little stiffly, he went down on one knee beside the unconscious Doctor, looking curiously into his face. The Doctor opened his eyes, and saw the lined old face looking down at him. 'You're here!' he said delightedly. 'You're here!' Reaching out to clasp the old man's outstretched hands, he struggled into a sitting position.

'Evidently, evidently,' said the old man gruffly. 'Now, take it steadily, my boy. Let me help you up.'

It was as though the younger man was actually drawing strength from the elder, thought Tegan. You could almost see the life flooding back into the Doctor's body.

The Doctor hung onto the old man's hand for a moment, steadying himself. 'I was trying to send you the recall signal …'

'Never mind about that. How do you come to be here?'

The Doctor looked puzzled. 'I'm not sure … the TARDIS … I was drawn here, I think. I don't really know.'

'Well, it doesn't matter. The point is, we're here.'

Susan put a hand on the old man's arm. She was looking in astonishment at the Doctor's youthful face. 'Is he really …'

The old man said wryly, 'Me? Yes, I'm afraid so.' He turned to the Doctor. 'Regeneration?'

'Fourth.'

'Goodness me. So, there are five of us now! By the way, this is Susan.'

'Yes,' said the Doctor gently. 'I know.' He smiled affectionately at Susan, a face from a past so far away it seemed hardly real.

The old man looked at the Doctor's two companions. 'And you are?'

'Turlough,' said Turlough briefly, not sure what was going on.

Tegan said, 'And I'm Tegan Jovanka. And who might you be?'

'I might be any number of things, young lady. As it happens, I am the Doctor. The original, you might say. Number One!'

He drew himself up proudly, hands tugging at his lapels.

It wasn't so much the first Doctor's existence that puzzled Tegan. By now she was familiar with the concept of regeneration. It was his presence, here and now. 'But you shouldn't be here, with him, at the same time – should you?'

Vigorously the old man shook his head. 'Certainly not!'

The Doctor said, 'It only happens in the gravest of emergencies –'

'Like now,' completed Doctor One. 'Now, just make yourself useful, will you, young woman. This young fellow looks as if he needs some refreshment, and I know Susan and I do.'

Tegan glared at him in sheer disbelief. 'Now just you hang on a minute,' she began dangerously.

Hurriedly the Doctor intervened. 'Tegan, *please*. He gets a bit – tetchy, sometimes. Turlough will help – won't you, Turlough?'

Exchanging mutinous glances, Tegan and Turlough left by the inner door.

The old man put his hand on the Doctor's shoulder. 'Now then, young fellow, tell me all about it.'

There was an elaborate golden badge in Chancellor Flavia's hand. She held it out to the Master. 'The Seal of the High Council. It will help convince the Doctors of your good faith.'

It would take a lot more than a seal, however eminent, to do that, thought the Master wryly. 'Perhaps,' he said.

The Castellan was busy at the controls of the transmat booth. 'It is time to go.'

The Master rose and crossed to the booth, and the Castellan gave him a flat metallic disc with a button set into the centre. 'When you have learned something worth telling us, activate this. We'll pick up your signal and transmat you back.'

The Master took the recall device and put it away. He looked round the little group. 'Isn't anyone going to wish me luck?'

Borusa replied coldly. 'Naturally, we wish you success. For all our sakes.'

The Master smiled cynically, and stepped into the booth.

As if afraid that he would change his mind, the Castellan operated the transmat controls with impatient speed. In a matter of seconds the Master faded away. The Castellan stepped back. 'And now, we wait, my Lord President.'

'I should prefer to wait alone.'

Accepting the dismissal, the Castellan and Chancellor Flavia went silently from the conference room.

Somewhere in the Death Zone, the Master blinked into existence. He stood on a little knoll, surveying the forbidden landscape around him with marked displeasure. Thunder rumbled, and lightning bolts flashed across the sky. The Death Zone. A place known to every Time Lord, but never mentioned, never visited. Closed off, forbidden, sealed behind an impenetrable forcefield from the rest of Gallifrey. Custodian of the Dark Tower – and of the most horrifying secret in Time Lord history.

The Master looked around him, at mist-covered barren wasteland stretching as far as the eye could see. Over there in the distance loomed the mountains and the Tower.

The Master took a few steps forwards and his foot struck against something dry and brittle. Glancing down, he saw what appeared to be a large charred log. The Master frowned, and bent to look at it. On closer examination, the burnt log turned out to be a corpse, twisted and blackened, white teeth gleaming from the blackened skull. 'One of my predecessors!'

Charred by what, the Master wondered – and found his answer when a vicious lightning bolt sizzled from the sky towards him.

Warned by some instinct, the Master flung himself aside. The bolt struck the corpse, making it dance and twitch in a ghastly parody of life. The Master regarded the grisly sight unmoved.

'Not the most hospitable of environments,' he observed thoughtfully, and hurried on his way.

The mists cleared for a moment and the Tower appeared, quite close now, surrounded by its ring of mountains. The unassuming little figure of the second Doctor stood staring up at its threatening bulk. 'You see, Brigadier, it's just as I feared. We're on Gallifrey, my home planet. In the Death Zone.'

The Brigadier frowned. 'You know this place?'

With sudden unexpected passion the Doctor shouted, 'Yes! To my shame, Brigadier.'

'*Your* shame?'

'Yes, mine, and the shame of every other Time Lord.'

Seeing the Brigadier's puzzled face, he went on more gently, 'In the days before Rassilon my ancestors already had tremendous powers – which they misused disgracefully. They set up this place, the Death Zone, walled it round with an impenetrable forcefield. Then they kidnapped other life forms from all over the cosmos, and set them down here.'

'What for?'

'To fight, and to die, for the amusement of the Time Lords,' said the little man. It was clear that he found the subject almost too distasteful to talk about. 'Come along, Brigadier, I'll explain as we go.'

'Where are we going?'

'To the Dark Tower, of course. To Rassilon. The greatest single figure in Time Lord history.'

The Brigadier looked up at the Tower, with a noticeable lack of enthusiasm. 'I see. And is that Tower where Rassilon lives?'

'Not exactly *lives*, Brigadier. It's his Tomb.'

A simple meal of fruit cordial and food concentrates was over, and now, watched by their companions, the two Doctors were concluding their conference.

It was a conference that looked very like turning into a quarrel.

'You're talking nonsense, my boy,' said the old man vigorously. 'What we have to do is quite clear. We must send the signal as you planned, wait for the rest of me, and then act together.'

The Doctor was equally determined. 'I'm sorry, but there simply isn't time. I'm already being affected by temporal instability. I can resist for a while, now you're here – but you know the danger?'

The old man nodded gravely. The segment of the Doctor that was trapped in the vortex was exerting a fateful pull. As next in line, this Doctor was most affected. He formed a kind of thumb in the temporal dike. If he gave way, *all* the Doctors would be swept away, dispersed in a temporal limbo.

'Even so, my boy – without our other selves, we stand little chance out there.'

'We daren't wait for the others,' said the Doctor. 'We daren't. After all, they may never make it here. There is evil at work.'

'Evil,' said Tegan. 'What kind of evil? Isn't it time we had a few explanations – such as where are we?'

Doctor One snapped, 'We're in the Death Zone on Gallifrey.'

'How do you know?'

It was the Doctor who answered, pointing to the picture of the Tower on the scanner. 'Because that's the Dark Tower. The Tomb of Rassilon.' He turned back to the old man. 'Do you really think we can afford to wait – especially if someone has tapped his power?'

'Very well. What do you intend to do, young man?'

'Go to the Tower.'

'There will be great danger.'

The Doctor nodded, accepting the risks. 'Help me to set up the computer scan. At least we can see what's out there.'

Sarah looked around her as Bessie jolted along. 'So that's why it's all so desolated!'

The third Doctor nodded. 'All this was the setting for the Game, Sarah. It's a place of evil.'

Sarah shuddered. 'It's horrible, Doctor. Kidnapping different life forms, setting them to kill each other, setting traps – and then coming to watch it all from a safe distance. It's worse than the Roman arena.'

The Doctor nodded his agreement. 'Mind you, it's all in the distant past. Old Rassilon put a stop to it in the end. Sealed off the entire Zone, forbade the use of the Timescoop. That's the way things stayed for generations – until now.'

'If the Time Lords brought you here to deal with some problem in the Zone, why don't they tell you why you're here?'

'They delight in deviousness, that's why!' said the Doctor angrily. 'It amuses them, chucking us in the deep end, watching us sink or swim.'

He stopped the car.

'Why've we stopped, Doctor?'

'Just getting my bearings.' The Doctor stood up, scanning the horizon. 'Ah yes, there it is!'

'There what is?'

The Doctor pointed and Sarah saw a tower, silhouetted in a gap between mountains. 'What is it?'

'The Tomb of Rassilon. I'm pretty sure our enemy will be using it as a base – so that's where we're going.'

'Are you sure that's a good idea, Doctor? From what you say, whatever's in that tower must have enormous powers. What can you do against them?'

The Doctor smiled down at her, his mane of white hair ruffled by the wind. 'What I've always done, Sarah Jane. Improvise!'

He sat down, gathering his cloak around him, and was just about to drive on when a black-clad figure appeared, standing on a low hillock beside the road. 'Wait, Doctor!'

The newcomer was a tall man clad in black, with a neatly pointed black beard.

'Who is it, Doctor?' whispered Sarah.

'I don't know … it looks very like …'

The Doctor drove Bessie a little closer, then stopped, peering incredulously at the black-clad man on the mount. 'Jehosophat!' he said explosively. 'It really is you! I should have known you'd be behind all this!'

'Doctor, who *is* it?'

The Doctor replied, 'Allow me to introduce my best enemy, Sarah. He likes to be known as the Master!'

6

ABOVE, BETWEEN, BELOW!

The third Doctor stared thoughtfully at his old enemy. 'My, my, my, you've changed! Another regeneration?'

'Not exactly.'

'I take it you're responsible for our presence in the Death Zone?'

'No, Doctor, for once I'm innocent, here at the High Council's request – to help you, and your other selves.'

The Doctor exploded with laughter. '*You?* Sent here, by the Time Lords, to help *me?* I never heard such arrant nonsense.'

'I happen to be telling the truth, Doctor.' The Master held out his hand. 'I carry the Seal of the High Council.'

The Doctor glanced briefly at the Seal. 'Forged, no doubt.'

'Geniune, Doctor. See for yourself.'

The Master tossed the Seal and the Doctor caught it. He examined the device with a puzzled frown. It was undoubtedly genuine. The Doctor's face cleared.

'Stolen, then,' he said cheerfully, and slipped the Seal into his pocket. 'I'll return it at the first opportunity.'

'Doctor, if you will only listen! I'm here to help you.'

'You help me? Rubbish! This is some kind of trap.'

'I knew this was going to be difficult, Doctor – but I didn't realise that even you would be so stupid as to make it impossible. For the last time, I am here to help you.'

Despite the sneering words, the sincerity in the Master's voice was unmistakable. Just for a moment, the Doctor began to wonder if he was being too hasty. Could it be possible –

A thunderbolt sizzled down from the sky and the Master's hillock exploded in flames.

'I knew it!' yelled the Doctor. 'A trap!'

He threw the little car into a racing start, swinging around the Master and heading off into the distance. The Master's despairing voice called out behind them. 'Doctor, wait! Those thunderbolts are everywhere in the Zone ...'

Sarah turned and saw another thunderbolt strike the ground close to the Master, blowing him off his feet. She saw him roll over, scramble to his feet and run for cover. Sarah frowned. If the thunderbolts were attacking the Master as well ... 'Doctor, wait! Suppose you're wrong? We can't just leave him.'

'Just watch me!'

Suddenly a thunderbolt struck the rear of the car, exploding one of the back tyres, and the car screeched to a halt.

'You see,' said the Doctor triumphantly. 'What did I tell you? A trap! Come on Sarah Jane, run for it!'

They set off towards the mountains.

There was a picture of the Tower on the TARDIS console screen, but it was a computer graphics picture showing the whole of the Tower and a proportion of the countryside around it. Mysterious symbols flowed across the screen, and it seemed that this computer-scan provided the two Doctors with a great deal of useful information.

'As far as I can make out,' said the Doctor, 'there are three possible ways in. From above – climb the mountain and somehow cross to the Tower.' He pointed to the base of the picture. 'From below – there seems to be some kind of cave system.' The Doctor pointed a little higher. 'Or there's the main door – here!'

The old man nodded. 'And which approach do *you* plan to use?'

'The main door. The nearest and the simplest.'

'And very possibly the most dangerous! I still think you should wait.'

'I daren't. Remember – there may be very little time.'

'Of course,' said the second Doctor thoughtfully, 'it's always possible that Rassilon himself could have brought us here.'

The Brigadier came to a halt, and looked disapprovingly down at him. They had been on the move for quite some time. The mountains, and the Tower, were very close – too close for the Brigadier's liking.

'Hang on a minute, Doctor. You did say this chap Rassilon was dead, didn't you?' He pointed up at the Tower. 'You said *that* was his tomb.'

'Oh yes, it is,' said the little man innocently. 'But there are all sorts of legends about Rassilon you know. No one knows how extensive his powers really were.' The Doctor lowered his voice. 'Some say he never really died at all!'

'He could still be alive then?'

'Watching us – at this very moment.'

The Brigadier looked round uneasily. 'Still, didn't you say Rassilon was supposed to be rather a good type?'

'So the official history tells us. But there are many rumours, many legends to the contrary. Some say Rassilon was really a cruel and bloodthirsty tyrant. Far from banning the Game, Rassilon really invented it. In that particular version of the legend, his fellow Time Lords are supposed to have rebelled against his cruelty and locked him in the Tower bound in eternal sleep.'

'So you think he's woken up again, getting up to his old tricks?'

'It would certainly explain a great deal.' The Doctor looked alarmed. 'Oh dear! We could be playing the Game of Rassilon at this very moment!'

'Your tone doesn't inspire confidence, Doctor,' said the Brigadier dryly. 'I take it we're not expected to win?'

The Doctor didn't answer.

'Come along, Brigadier,' he said at last.

They moved on, towards the Dark Tower.

The distorted faces of the fourth Doctor and his companion, the Lady Romana, swirled and twisted endlessly on the screen in the conference room. A young Time Technician, an eminent Time Lord scientist in his own right, was reporting to the Inner Council. Borusa nodded at the figures on the screen. 'You can do nothing to retrieve him?'

'Nothing, my Lord President. With the existing energy-drain from the Death Zone, it is beyond our resources!'

'We must do something,' protested Chancellor Flavia. 'As long as *he* is trapped, all the Doctors are endangered.'

Borusa considered for a moment. 'Use whatever energy you can spare to stabilise that portion of the vortex. At least that will give the remaining Doctors a little more time.'

'Lord President.' The scientist bowed and withdrew.

The Castellan joined the conference. 'I take it there is no news from the Master?'

Borusa gave him a scornful glance. 'Did you really think there would be?'

It seemed to Turlough, who had a strong streak of caution, that the Doctor was proposing to risk his life for no good reason. And if anything happened to the Doctor, things would look bad for Turlough as well. 'Even if you reach the Tower, Doctor, what are you going to do?'

'Release the TARDIS, for a start.'

Doctor One nodded towards the scanner. 'The computer scan has located the generator of the forcefield paralysing the TARDIS, young man. Not surprisingly, the generator is located in the Tower, very close to the Tomb itself.'

The Doctor said, 'Well, I'd better be off.'

It had already been established that the old man would stay in the TARDIS, following the Doctor's progress on the scanner.

As the Doctor headed for the door, Tegan said, 'Wait. I'll come with you.'

Susan said, 'I'd like to come too.'

Turlough said nothing.

The Doctor looked questioningly at his other self. The old man frowned. 'It would be safer if you both remained here with me.'

'I want to come,' said Tegan determinedly.

Susan said, 'Me too!'

'Oh, very well,' said the Doctor. He looked at the old man. 'And you'll bring the TARDIS to the Tower the moment I've switched off the forcefield.'

'Of course, my boy!'

The Doctor braced himself. 'Then we'd better get started. Time is running out.'

*

Meanwhile Sarah and the third Doctor were toiling up a mountain path which wound steeply, and apparently endlessly, upwards.

'I thought we were going to the Tower,' protested Sarah.

The Doctor stopped, his cloak blowing in the chill mountain wind. 'We are.'

'Then why are we going this way?'

'Because,' said the Doctor patiently, 'the mountains happen to be between us and the Tower. That's why.'

'Can't we find an easier route?'

'It would take far too long – besides ...' The Doctor pointed.

Sarah looked. At the foot of the mountain, far, far below them, a group of tall silver figures was moving after them.

'It seems that the Master has used the Timescoop to bring others here as well as us,' said the Doctor sombrely.

Sarah was still not sure that the Doctor's theory about the Master was correct. But there was no doubt at all about the group of Cybermen moving purposefully after them. Wearily she resumed her climb.

Left with nothing to do but wait, Turlough and the first Doctor were hovering anxiously over the scanner. A small point of light represented the Doctor and, presumably, his two companions. It seemed to be moving with agonising slowness. Turlough kept moving away from the screen, and then coming impatiently back to it. 'Do you think it will take them very much longer to reach the Tower?'

'Depends on what may try to stop them, my boy. It's not called the Death Zone without reason, you know.' Suddenly the old man leaned forward excitedly. 'Great Heavens! Two more traces.'

'Two more Time Lords?'

'Two more Doctors,' said the old man triumphantly. 'The scanner-trace is keyed to my – our – brain-patterns. Well, well, well, so two of them made it! I wonder what happened to the other one ...'

The Brigadier and the second Doctor had reached the very base of the mountains by now. The ground sloped sharply upwards above them. Shading his eyes, the Brigadier could see nothing ahead but a very nasty, and very dangerous climb. Then he heard a strange, plaintive sound.

The Doctor was singing in a high quavery voice.

'Who unto Rassilon's Tower would go,' he warbled. 'Must choose – Above, Between, Below!'

'Are you in pain, Doctor?' enquired the Brigadier sarcastically.

The Doctor looked offended. 'I see that age has not mellowed you, Brigadier. I was recalling, in point of fact, an old Gallifreyan nursery rhyme – about the Dark Tower.'

'I see. Does it help?'

'Considerably more than you do! It describes three different ways to enter the Dark Tower.'

'You mean we're going to be guided by a nursery rhyme? I've never heard anything so ridiculous.'

'Nevertheless, Brigadier, I propose to put the matter to the test. And I choose – Below! Come along!'

'Come along where?'

The Doctor led the way to a cave mouth so tiny that the Brigadier hadn't even registered it.

'Down here,' said the Doctor, and popped into the tiny opening like a rabbit down a hole.

Groaning, the Brigadier squeezed through after him.

7

THE DOCTOR
DISAPPEARS

The Doctor, Tegan and Susan were hurrying over the rocky ground, heading towards the Tower. The Doctor was setting a tremendous pace. Tegan guessed he was haunted by the fear that temporal instability would set in again before he could complete his task. It must be very worrying, she thought, wondering if you were suddenly going to fade away.

Susan was struggling on bravely. After years of quiet, domestic life she found she was enjoying the adventure. 'I'm finding this quite exhilarating!'

Tegan had had more than her fair share of adventure in recent years. 'Oh, are you? I wish I was!'

The ground was beginning to fall away a little before them, descending into a kind of shallow valley which ran between them and the Tower, when a familiar black-clad figure appeared at the foot of the path ahead.

'The Master!' gasped Tegan.

'Wait here,' ordered the Doctor.

He began moving down the path towards the Master. They met in the centre of the little valley. The Doctor stopped when he felt he was near enough to talk, but still far enough from the Master for safety. He stood waiting, forcing the Master to speak first. The Master's voice was almost diffident. 'I know this is hard to believe, Doctor, but for once I mean you no harm.'

The Doctor said lightly, 'Wasn't it Alice who was told to believe three impossible things before breakfast? Go on.'

The Master drew a deep breath. 'I have been sent here by the High Council of the Time Lords – to help you.'

From their vantage-point on the high ground, Tegan could see the Master talking earnestly. She could even hear the rumble of his voice though she was too far away to make out what was actually being said.

If Tegan was suspicious, Susan was baffled. 'Is that man a friend of the Doctor – Doctors?'

'Anything but!'

'They're talking as if they were old friends.'

'I know,' said Tegan tersely. 'That's what worries me.'

At a point beyond the valley, out of sight of both Tegan and Susan, a group of silver figures were waiting in ambush. They were extremely tall, humanoid in shape with terrifyingly blank faces, small round eyes and slits for mouths. Two handle-like projections took the place of ears, and a complicated chest-unit occupied the front of the massive bodies. Human, or at least humanoid in origin, their bodies were part organic, but mostly metal and plastic. Immensely strong, they were passionless, emotionless, tireless, and almost invulnerable, interested only in power and in conquest.

They were Cybermen.

The Cyber Lieutenant was reporting to his Leader. 'Two aliens have been detected climbing the mountain. A patrol has been despatched in pursuit. We have located the party from the TARDIS. They have reached the valley close by. They have joined forces with another alien. Shall I take the patrol and destroy them?'

The Cyberleader considered. 'Capture them alive. They must be interrogated before they are destroyed.'

'Yes, Leader.'

'Remember also that we will need the Time Lord to pilot the TARDIS. Now go.'

The Cyber Lieutenant turned and stalked over to the group of waiting Cybermen. 'Here are your orders.'

The Cyberleader watched as the little group moved away. Things were going well.

He was uncertain as to how he and his troops came to be in this strange place, but that was unimportant. Now that they were here, they would act in a way that befitted Cybermen. They would conquer, destroying all opposition.

The Master had talked himself almost hoarse. Still the Doctor listened with that same infuriating air of silent scepticism. 'Be reasonable, Doctor!'

'I am. I'm listening.'

The Master changed his tactics, producing his Tissue Compression Eliminator, a hideous weapon that left only a tiny shrunken corpse. 'As you see, I am armed. I could kill you easily – if I wanted to.'

'Just like that – without humiliating me first?' The Doctor shook his head. 'Not your style at all.'

The Master took out the recall device and held it out. 'I also have this – a recall device that will take me back to the Inner Council's conference room in the heart of the Capitol.'

'So you say,' said the Doctor infuriatingly. 'I would prefer something more positive in the way of credentials.'

'Not long ago I had the Seal of the High Council,' said the Master bitterly.

'Then where is it?'

'One of your other selves took it from me.'

'All in all you really have told me the most fantastic tale,' said the Doctor thoughtfully. 'Do you expect me to believe it, I wonder? Or have you some other reason for delaying me here?'

Giant silver figures appeared on the skyline. Engrossed in their conversation, neither of the adversaries saw them. But Tegan did. Jumping to her feet she yelled, 'Doctor, look out! Cybermen!'

The Doctor cupped his hands to his lips. 'Go back!'

Susan looked in anguish at Tegan. 'We can't just leave him!'

'We can't help him either,' said Tegan practically. 'Come on, do as he says. We must warn the others.'

She began heading back to the TARDIS. Susan started to follow but she couldn't resist turning back to see what was happening ...

*

423

The Doctor and the Master were both running by now, trying to evade a rapidly-closing circle of Cybermen. There seemed to be only one gap in the ring and naturally enough they found themselves both running towards it, almost bumping into each other. 'After you,' said the Doctor politely.

The Master sprinted ahead.

'Halt, or you will be destroyed,' roared the Cyber Lieutenant. He fired a warning shot. It disintegrated a rock close to the Master's fleeing figure. Fragments of rock flew through the air, and one of them took the Master on the forehead. He reeled and fell.

The Doctor ran up to him, instinctively kneeling to see if he could help. He saw the trickle of blood on the Master's forehead. 'Zapped!' He saw the recall device, in the Master's outflung hand. He looked up, and saw the ring of Cybermen closing in.

Although she knew it was almost suicidally dangerous, Susan still couldn't resist hanging back.

She saw the Master fall.

She saw the Doctor kneeling by his body.

She saw the Cybermen closing in.

Recall device in his hand, the Doctor looked up and saw the Cyber Lieutenant standing over him. The eerie mechanical voice said, 'You will accompany me.'

'Sorry, must dash,' said the Doctor.

A reddish halo surrounded his body and he faded away.

Susan looked on in astonishment, as the Doctor faded out of existence. She heard Tegan's voice. 'What are you *doing*, Susan. Come on!' She ran towards the waiting Tegan – but even as she ran she turned again to look over her shoulder. Her foot turned on a chunk of loose rock and she stumbled and fell. Tegan ran back, helping Susan to her feet. 'Can you walk?'

'Just about …'

'Then get moving. Here, let me help you.'

Her arm round Tegan's shoulders, Susan hobbled away.

*

A figure materialised in the haze of light in the transmat booth. The Doctor stepped out and glanced around the table. President Borusa, Chancellor Flavia and the Castellan gazed at him in blank astonishment.

'Well, well,' said the Doctor. 'Quite a reception committee!'

The Master recovered consciousness, stabbing frantically at the button on the recall device – until he realised it was no longer in his hand. Looking up, he saw himself surrounded by a ring of Cybermen.

The Cyberleader approached and studied the Master. 'This is not the Doctor.'

The Master scrambled to his feet, brushing himself down. 'I'm glad you're here at last,' he said calmly. 'I've been looking for you.'

'Kill him,' said the Cyberleader.

The Cybermen raised their weapons.

The Master shouted, 'Wait! I am here as your friend. I can help you.'

The Cyberleader raised a hand to check his men. 'Who are you?'

The Master bowed. 'The Master – and your loyal servant.'

Back in the TARDIS, Tegan was binding Susan's ankle. Susan was telling the first Doctor the story of their ill-fated expedition. 'Then the Doctor just disappeared,' she concluded.

'Vanished?' said Turlough. 'How? What could have happened?'

'From the way Susan described it, young man,' snapped the first Doctor, 'Through the operation of some kind of transmat device.'

Tegan said, 'But the Doctor didn't ... of course! He must have got it from the Master. Thing is, where did it take him?'

Susan shook her head. 'No idea. I just hope he's all right.'

The first Doctor drew himself up. 'Well, wherever our young friend may have got to – I shall have to go to the Dark Tower!'

The old boy might be tetchy and domineering, thought Tegan, but you had to admire his spirit.

'Good for you,' she said. 'I'll come with you.'

The old man actually smiled. 'Thank you, my dear.'

The Doctor had given a brief report on his adventures to the Inner Council. Now he was listening to the Castellan's account of recent events on Gallifrey – the re-activation of the Death Zone, the energy-drain from the Eye of Harmony, the abduction of his other selves. Finally, the decision to despatch the Master as an agent of the Council. A decision which the Castellan freely admitted had been taken against President Borusa's advice.

When the Castellan had finished, the Doctor said, 'It seems I have done the Master an injustice.'

'Should he survive, I'm sure he will learn to live with your misjudgement,' said Borusa.

'This changes things,' the Doctor went on. 'If the Master isn't responsible – then who is misusing the Death Zone?'

The Castellan said, 'We were hoping you could tell us that, Doctor. After all, you have just been there.'

'Who has control of the Timescoop?'

'No one,' said Borusa crisply. 'Its use has long been prohibited.'

'But the machinery still exists?'

Borusa shrugged. 'Presumably. It has been unused so long that even the location of the Game control room is now unknown.'

'Not presumably to everyone!'

'You seemed to be implying that the Timescoop was used to bring you here?' said Borusa coldly.

'Yes, I am rather.'

Chancellor Flavia looked keenly at him. 'Then since the machinery, if it still exists, is somewhere here, in the Capitol – you accuse a Time Lord?'

'Yes. I should think it would be quite an important one as well. Probably one of the High Council.'

Borusa sat back in his Presidential chair. 'You have evidence, of course, Doctor?'

'Not yet.'

'Then on what do you base this outrageous accusation?'

'This and that,' said the Doctor vaguely. 'I thought at first someone was simply trying to revive the Game. But then, there are the Cybermen … Whoever brought me and my other selves here, brought them as well. You know the legends well enough. Even in our most corrupt period, our ancestors never allowed the Cybermen to play the Game.

Like the Daleks, they fight too well. Yet the Cybermen are in the Zone – and a Dalek too, I gather.'

The Castellan leaned forward angrily. 'You admit then that you have no proof that there is a traitor on the High Council?'

'Well, there's this,' said the Doctor mildly. He held out the recall device. 'The Death Zone is a very big place, yet the Cybermen found us very quickly. Almost as if they were supposed to.'

'They are highly skilled in such matters,' said Borusa wearily.

'Especially when helped?' The Doctor held up the device. 'Remember, this is the one thing the Master would be sure to keep on him at all times.' The Doctor took a penknife from his pocket and prised off the base plate of the device, revealing a small brightly pulsing light. 'A powerful homing device – transmitting a signal that would easily be picked up by Cybermen ground-scanners.'

Borusa leaned forward, fixing the Castellan with his piercing gaze. 'A homing device … which you gave him, Castellan!'

8

CONDEMNED

The Castellan leaped to his feet. 'It's a lie! The Doctor is after revenge.' He was referring to an occasion, not so very long ago, when with the best possible motives the Castellan had been instrumental in having the Doctor sentenced to death.

'Sit down, Castellan,' said Borusa coldly.

'I will not submit to these wild accusations.'

'Sit down.'

Trembling with rage, the Castellan resumed his seat.

Borusa touched the control in his chair arm, and a burly Guard Commander appeared. The Commander crashed to attention. 'Lord President?'

'You will institute an immediate and rigorous search of the offices and living quarters of the Castellan.' The Commander wheeled and stamped away.

The Castellan sat staring ahead of him, his face a ghastly white. He looked, thought the Doctor, like a man condemned to death.

In the hollow that the Cybermen used as their base, the Master stood before the Cyberleader. He was talking for his life.

'I do not believe your lies,' said the Cyberleader flatly.

'What I have told you is the truth. Do you know how you come to be here? Do you?' There was no reply. The Master smiled triumphantly. 'You were brought here, just as I was. We've all been brought here, and for the same reason.'

'To fight?'

'To fight and die, for the amusement of the Time Lords.' The Master leaned forward urgently. 'But you don't have to play their game. You can defeat them, gain your revenge – but only with my help!'

'Explain.'

'You have seen the Tower, close by? It is a fortress. The fortress of your enemies – the Time Lords. It is well defended, but I can help you to conquer it.'

'What do you ask in return?'

The Master shrugged. 'My life. My freedom. A chance to share in your revenge – to destroy the Time Lords.'

The Cyberleader gestured to one of his troops. 'Guard him.'

The Cyberleader moved a little apart, and his Lieutenant followed.

'You will send a patrol to capture the TARDIS,' ordered the Cyberleader. 'The remaining patrol will go with the Master to the Tower.'

'He is an Alien. Aliens are not to be trusted.'

'It is not necessary to trust him.'

'Will you give him his freedom?'

The Cyberleader said, 'Promises made to Aliens have no validity. Once the Tower is in our hands he will be destroyed.'

The Cyberleader turned and strode back to the Master. 'You will guide us to the Tower!' Well satisfied, the Master smiled and bowed. He had told the Cybermen a carefully simplified story – by now the Master too was convinced that something far more complex was going on than a simple revival of the Game. The truth, whatever it was, lay in the Tower.

Now it was Susan and Turlough who stood peering into the scanner, tracing the tiny dot that registered the first Doctor's progress.

'They're moving so slowly,' said Susan.

Turlough shrugged. 'Don't worry. Tegan will look after the old man.'

Suddenly they heard a scuffling sound from outside. A great thump shook the TARDIS. Hurriedly Turlough switched the scanner back on to normal picture. The screen was filled with giant silver shapes.

'Oh no,' gasped Susan. 'Cybermen!'

*

To the Brigadier's surprise, the little cave mouth led into a narrow tunnel – a tunnel that seemed to wind steadily upwards. Unfortunately the tunnel was narrow and low-ceilinged. It served well enough for a little chap like the Doctor, but a man of the Brigadier's impressive bulk had to move along it doubled up like a hoop, cursing his aching back, and scraping knees and elbows. The Brigadier struggled on, infuriated more than encouraged by the cheerful voice ahead of him.

'Come along, Brigadier. Come along. This way! Mind your head!'

Cursing, the Brigadier struggled through a particularly narrow gap to find the Doctor waiting for him in a slightly wider section. 'Dammit, Doctor, I'm just not built for this kind of thing any more.'

'You never were,' said the Doctor unkindly. 'Cheer up – we're getting along very nicely. The tunnel's rising all the time. We should be at the Tower very soon.'

'Is that supposed to cheer me up?'

A low, sinister growling came out of the darkness behind them.

The Brigadier spun round. 'What was that?'

There came another scraping, shuffling sound. Then a bloodthirsty growl. The Doctor said thoughtfully, 'It sounded to me like something very large, very fierce and probably very hungry. Come on, Brigadier – run!'

High up on the mountain path, Sarah and the third Doctor found themselves facing a dead end. The path ran between high rock walls and disappeared into a cave. Before the cave a wider, flatter area, strewn with rocks and giant boulders, made a sort of pass.

'It's a dead end,' said Sarah despairingly.

The Doctor shook his head. 'No it's not. It's a pass. Look!'

Just beyond the cave was the beginning of an incredibly steep and narrow path that seemed to wind up to the summit.

'I couldn't go up there,' protested Sarah. 'I'll get vertigo.'

'Don't worry, I'll help you!'

Sarah wasn't convinced. 'Let's just go back, Doctor, for an easier way.'

'We can't go back.'

'Why not? We seem to have shaken off the Cybermen.'

'No we haven't. Cybermen don't shake off. They never get tired and they never give up!'

'All right, all right, I remember,' said Sarah wearily. 'Okay, let's go then. If I don't fall off that path, I'll probably die of fright anyway.'

She was about to move forward when an astonishing sight appeared in the cave mouth. It was some kind of robot. Basically man-shaped and very tall and thin, it had a smooth, shining body surface in gleaming metal. Its head was completely blank, a metal egg, with no eyes or mouth. Its movements were lithe and graceful, like those of a trained athlete.

'What is it?' whispered Sarah.

'A Raston Warrior Robot – the most perfect killing-machine ever devised.'

'But it's not armed.'

Sarah must have spoken a fraction too loudly. The Robot wheeled round in her direction. One hand went back over its shoulder and then flashed forwards. A thin steel rod, like a javelin, flashed through the air and stuck quivering at Sarah's feet.

'Quick, over there,' whispered the Doctor. He dragged her behind the shelter of another boulder. Lips close to her ear he whispered, 'The armaments are built in and the sensors detect movement. Any movement.'

'Anything else I shouldn't like to know,' whispered Sarah.

'Yes,' the Doctor whispered. 'It can move like –'

The Robot blurred and vanished.

'Lightning,' concluded the Doctor.

They looked cautiously around, and saw the Robot standing quite motionless among the rocks, some way behind them.

The Doctor and Sarah ducked down.

'What's it doing?' whispered Sarah.

The Doctor said, 'It's playing with us.'

Slowly, very slowly, they moved into cover. 'Freeze, Sarah Jane,' whispered the Doctor. 'If we move – we're dead.'

Susan and Turlough staggered as the TARDIS shook and rocked under the repeated hammering of giant metal fists. The noise was deafening.

431

'If only we could get away from here,' muttered Turlough. He looked accusingly at Susan. 'You told me you travelled with the Doctor for ages. Can't you operate the controls?'

'You forget – the TARDIS is paralysed. We're still trapped by the forcefield from the Tower. We can't move till the Doctor neutralises it.'

Tegan and the first Doctor were very close to the Tower now, but the going was rough, and Tegan had to give the old man quite a lot of help.

'Come on, Doc, you can make it,' she said encouragingly.

The old man scowled at her. 'Of course I can, young woman. And kindly refrain from addressing me as Doc!'

They struggled on.

The Guard Commander put an ornately-decorated metal casket on the conference room table, and stepped back as if he was afraid it might contaminate him.

'This is the casket, Lord President. As you see, it bears the Seal of Rassilon.'

Borusa nodded. 'And where did you find it?'

'In the Castellan's room – well hidden.'

Carefully Borusa opened the lid. The casket was filled with rolled parchment scrolls, bound with black silk ribbon, sealed with the same seal that was on the casket. Chancellor Flavia drew back in horror. 'The Black Scrolls of Rassilon! This is forbidden knowledge!'

'How very interesting,' said the Doctor. 'I thought they were out of print!' He reached for the casket, but Borusa snatched it away, slamming shut the lid.

'No, Doctor. This is forbidden knowledge, from the Dark Times.'

The Doctor was the first to notice the faint wisp of smoke coming from the casket. Before he could even shout a warning the wisp became a black plume, the plume became a stream and suddenly something inside the casket flared white and exploded.

When the smoke cleared, Borusa lifted the lid. The Black Scrolls had been totally incinerated, leaving nothing but a box of fine ash. Borusa turned his cold gaze on the Castellan. 'You were taking no chances.'

The Castellan licked dry lips. 'I am innocent. I have never seen that casket before.'

Borusa nodded to the Guard Commander. 'Take him to Security and get the truth out of him.' The Commander put a hand on the Castellan's shoulder. Numbly he rose and allowed himself to be led away. As he reached the door, Borusa called, 'Commander! You are authorised to use the mind probe.' The Castellan shouted, 'No!' but the protest was quelled and the guards dragged him roughly away.

The Doctor shuddered. The mind probe worked quickly, or not at all. Resist too long and you were left a mindless idiot. 'Let me speak to him. Perhaps I can persuade –'

Borusa shook his head. 'The mind probe will provide us with all the answers we require.'

Suddenly there was an outbreak of shouting from the corridor outside. They heard sounds of struggle and the unmistakable crack of a staser blast. The Doctor leaped up and ran out into the corridor. There he saw a kind of frozen tableau. The Castellan lay face down some little way along the corridor. A blaster lay close to his outstretched hand. The Commander was standing over him – reholstering his phaser. Nearby the other guards stood frozen like waxworks.

The Doctor looked down at the Castellan's body, then up at the Commander. 'Was that necessary?'

'He was armed,' said the Commander impassively. 'Armed, and trying to escape.'

The Doctor turned and went back into the conference room. No one seemed to have moved since he had left. The Doctor dropped wearily into a chair. 'It seems you have been saved the embarrassment of a trial, Lord President.'

'And you have found your traitor, Doctor,' said Borusa. 'We can only hope that the task of your other selves will now be simplified.'

The Doctor rose. 'I'd better be getting back to them.' He moved towards the transmat booth.

'No, Doctor,' said Borusa firmly. 'I admire your courage, but I cannot allow you to return. I still need your help and advice.'

'But my companions are in the Death Zone. I can't abandon them.'

'I am sure your other selves will be able to cope.'

'Are they all in the Zone?'

'All but one!' Borusa touched a control and the distorted features of the fourth Doctor and Romana appeared on the screen. 'As you see, he is trapped in the vortex.' The screen went dark. 'I am sorry, Doctor, but I must insist that you remain here in the Capitol. Chancellor Flavia, perhaps you would escort the Doctor to a place of rest. I'm sure he must be exhausted.'

'Of course. If you will accompany me, Doctor?'

Chancellor Flavia led the Doctor from the conference room.

The second Doctor and the Brigadier hurried along the tunnels, the snuffling, grunting and roaring of the creature very close behind them.

'Whatever that thing is, Doctor,' panted the Brigadier, 'it's got our scent now. It's *hunting* us.'

The Doctor saw a small opening in the tunnel wall and nipped inside. 'Quick, Brigadier. In here.'

The Doctor had slipped through the gap, and the Brigadier, with a good deal more effort, squeezed through after him. They found themselves in a tiny cave, just big enough to hold them both. There was a shattering roar from outside, and something very large hurled itself against the gap through which they'd come. Luckily it was much too large, its massive bulk filling the gap.

'It's all right,' said the Doctor. 'It can't get in. It's much too big!'

'Maybe it can't get in,' said the Brigadier, 'but we can't get out. It's got us trapped!'

9

THE DARK TOWER

The little Doctor stood quite still for a moment, considering the situation. He began searching frantically through his pockets. 'There must be something useful here …'

There came a fierce scrabbling from outside, and the rattle of falling rock. Either the local stone was exceptionally soft or the creature outside was quite inconceivably strong.

'Better hurry, Doctor,' said the Brigadier. 'It's trying to dig us out!'

'Aha!' said the Doctor triumphantly. 'Here we are!' There was a slender tube-shaped object in his hand. 'Have you got a light, Brigadier?' The Brigadier fished a lighter out of his pocket and handed it over. The Doctor lit the end of the tube and tossed it through the gap.

'What was that?' whispered the Brigadier. 'A bomb?'

'A Giant Galactic Glitter!'

'Well, it doesn't seem to be working.'

'Wait!'

Suddenly a fountain of golden sparks shot up in the air outside the little cave, illuminating in its golden glow the giant shaggy form of the creature that was pursuing them.

'It's a Yeti!' said the Doctor happily. He sounded almost as if he was welcoming an old friend. The Brigadier shuddered, remembering the days when the shaggy robot-beasts had terrorised London. It was then that he had first met the Doctor. 'Where did it come from?'

The Doctor shrugged. 'Left over from the Game perhaps. Or maybe it was brought here for our benefit.'

The shower of sparks ended in a very loud bang – and an even louder roar of rage from the Yeti.

'You've maddened it!' shouted the Brigadier.

Scrabbling claws appeared in the gap and the whole cave seemed to shudder as the monster hurled itself against the rock wall, followed by the rumbling sound of a rock fall. The creature must have dislodged loose rock, somewhere up above. The Doctor and the Brigadier leaped back as a curtain of rock fell, blocking their escape completely.

For a moment there was only silence and darkness. The Brigadier snapped on his lighter. The flame flared high, revealing the rock pile blocking the entrance, and the guilty face of the Doctor. He looked apologetically at the Brigadier. 'Well, at least the Yeti can't get at us now.'

'We're trapped,' said the Brigadier grimly. 'Buried alive.'

The Doctor stared worriedly at the lighter flame. 'Yes, I'm afraid we are …'

The flame flickered wildly and almost went out. It recovered, but it was still streaming over to one side. The Doctor said, 'On the other hand – where there's a wind, there's a way!' He scrabbled his way to the back of the little cave and called 'Over here, Brigadier. There's another gap!'

And so there was. They crawled through it and up into a still narrower tunnel, sloping even more steeply upwards.

'Well, well,' said the Doctor suddenly. 'I think we've arrived.'

He pointed ahead. The tunnel ended suddenly in a smooth stone wall, into which there was set a small metal door. The Brigadier gave the door a tentative push. To his surprise, it swung smoothly open. The Doctor frowned. 'I don't like that. I don't like that at all.'

'Why not?'

'Someone or something *wants* us to go inside. After you, Brigadier.'

'No, Doctor,' said the Brigadier, with equal politeness. 'After you!'

Turlough adjusted the scanner lens, trying to follow the movements of the little group of Cybermen moving about outside the TARDIS. Susan was doing her best to be cheerful.

'Well, at least that terrible banging's stopped.'

'That's what worries me,' said Turlough gloomily. He peered up at the screen. The Cybermen appeared to be bringing up some kind of device. Something metallic, and very large.

'What's that they're carrying?' asked Susan. 'What are they planning to do?'

Turlough said wearily, 'Well I don't actually *know*. But I would think their intention is to break in – wouldn't you?'

The end of Sarah's nose itched. She had agonising cramp in her left toe. She shifted her position ever so slightly, and the tall silver figure of the Robot swung round. Sarah froze again.

'I can't take much more of this!'

The tall, white-haired figure of the third Doctor might have been carved from solid rock. Even when he spoke, his lips didn't move. 'Hang on, Sarah Jane. Hang on. I think we've got just one hope.'

'What?'

The Doctor drew in his breath. 'Look, Sarah. Here it comes!'

A Cyberman stalked arrogantly into the space before the cave. The Cyber patrol had caught up with them. The Cyberman stared at the Robot, raised its weapon – and was immediately transfixed with a metal lance. This time there was a slender thread attached to the lance. The Cyberman staggered, and raised its weapon again. The Robot twitched the thread and the Cyberman crashed to the ground. It staggered to its feet and advanced once more. The Robot blurred, reappeared in a different position and hurled a silver disc which sliced the Cyberman's head from its body. The headless Cyberman staggered a few steps, firing wildly, and crashed to the ground.

More Cybermen came pouring into the pass. The first of them raised his weapon. A silver disc sliced his arm from his body. The arm fell, the weapon still firing. The Cybermen crowded closer, trying to surround the Robot. They never stood a chance. The Robot blurred and reappeared changing its position every time a Cyberman fired. It sliced off arms and legs and heads with silver discs, sending Cybermen reeling to the ground. It transfixed them with steel lances, and enmeshed them in fine metallic thread. If a Cyberman came too close, the Robot extruded a sword-blade from its hand and sliced it to pieces.

The Doctor and Sarah watched the massacre with fascinated horror. It was hard to feel sorry for a Cyberman, but Sarah found herself watching the slaughter of the silver giants with something very like pity. Before the flashing quicksilver movements of the Robot they were clumsy and helpless. When the battle was at its height, the Doctor tapped her shoulder. 'Come on, Sarah Jane. Now's our chance.' They ran round the edge of the battle and headed up the narrow path.

A Cyberman, wounded and weaponless, saw their escape and staggered determinedly after them.

As they hurried up the precipitous mountain path, the Doctor paused for a moment.

Stacked neatly against the rock wall was some of the Robot's spare equipment: steel lances, razor-edged throwing discs, and coils of metallic thread. The Doctor grabbed a handful of lances. 'At least we'll have something to fight with. Hang on a minute, this might come in handy as well.' He snatched up several coils of metallic thread and hurried after Sarah.

As the Doctor turned a corner and disappeared, the wounded Cyberman came staggering up the path after him.

By now only one Cyberman was still on its feet, facing the Robot. As the Cyberman raised its weapon, the Robot flicked out its sword-blade and sliced off its arm. It blurred and shifted position, and lopped off the Cyberman's head. A series of swift flashing strokes reduced the Cyberman to scattered chunks of metal and plastic. Retracting the blade the Robot stood poised, motionless, surrounded by the bodies of its enemies.

The Doctor and Sarah struggled up the last few feet of path and found themselves on the edge of a precipice, lined with massive boulders. Looking over the edge, Sarah was astonished to see how far they had climbed. Below, very close to them, was the top of the Dark Tower, shrouded in mists.

Sarah turned to the Doctor. 'What do we do now? Fly?'

'What a splendid idea, Sarah Jane!'

Washed and brushed and wined and dined, the fifth Doctor was his usual neat self again. Nevertheless, his face was sombre and preoccupied as he strolled along the corridors of the Capitol beside

Chancellor Flavia. Noticing his expression, Chancellor Flavia came to a halt. 'You look worried, Doctor,' she said. 'Your friends and your other selves will come safely through their dangers, I am sure.'

'At the moment I'm almost more concerned for the High Council, and for Gallifrey.'

'Surely, the traitor has been found?'

'Has he? I've known the Castellan for a very long time. He was limited, a little narrow, and ruthless when he thought it his duty. But he was always fiercely loyal to his oath of office. Any mention of the Dark Days, of the Forbidden Knowledge, filled him with horror. You saw his reaction to the Black Scrolls?'

Chancellor Flavia nodded slowly.

'Not so much the reaction of a guilty man discovered,' said the Doctor. 'More sheer disbelief.'

As they walked on the Doctor said, 'I am convinced that the traitor is still at large.'

Although she could be obstinate, Chancellor Flavia was a shrewd and intelligent woman, and the Doctor had spelled out her own hidden fears. 'I agree that there is still cause for concern, Doctor. I shall speak to the Commander who killed the Castellan. I have a suspicion that there may be much to be learnt from him.

The Doctor said slowly, 'I must speak to the Lord President.'

After a few more words, they separated, going their different ways. Now it was Chancellor Flavia who looked worried.

Sarah looked on appalled as the Doctor fashioned one end of his coil of steel wire into a kind of lasso. She glanced down the steep path and saw a Cyberman lumbering towards them. 'Doctor, look out! There's a Cyberman coming.' The Doctor didn't even look up.

'See if you can hold it off, will you? I won't be a second.' Sarah gave him a withering look. Hold it off, indeed! She picked up the biggest rock she could manage, and lobbed it down the path towards the Cyberman. Wounded as it was, it managed to step aside, and the rock rolled harmlessly by.

'I missed, Doctor!'

The Doctor finished his noose and looked up. 'What? There, that should do it.'

Sarah looked at the loop, and then down at the Tower. 'You're crazy. It'll never work!'

The Doctor looked down at the Cyberman labouring towards them. 'Maybe not. But unless you've got a better suggestion?'

Sarah hadn't.

'Right, then,' said the Doctor. 'Stand back!' Whirling the loop around his head the Doctor cast it towards the Tower. The loop dropped over one of the turrets and pulled itself tight. Following the Doctor's instructions, Sarah wrapped the other end of the metal wire around the biggest of the boulders, a massive column of rock.

The Doctor meanwhile was busily making a kind of stirrup arrangement, which he attached to the wire rope linking them to the Tower. 'It's quite simple, Sarah Jane. You put your foot in here, hold on here, jump off and away you go!'

Sarah didn't believe it for one moment. What decided her was the wounded Cyberman still lumbering to the top of the path. Luckily it seemed to have lost its weapon, but even wounded and unarmed it could tear them to pieces.

The Doctor called, 'Come on, Sarah Jane.' He put his foot in his stirrup, held tin tight and leaped into space.

Numb with terror, Sarah did the same. She found herself flying through the foggy air at terrifying speed. The Cyberman grabbed at her, missed, staggered and almost fell. Determined to the last it struggled to the boulder and tried to unfasten the rope. Its strength gave out at last and it fell dying at the foot of the boulder.

Leading his new-found allies to the Tower, the Master glanced casually upwards – and saw the Doctor and Sarah apparently flying through the air. The Master smiled. 'Ever resourceful, Doctor.'

Looking back, he saw the Cybermen too were gazing upwards in astonishment. Seizing his chance, the Master drew ahead.

The Doctor thumped onto the Tower roof, swung himself over the edge, and reached out to catch Sarah, who arrived almost on top of him. 'All right, Sarah. Hold tight. Try to find a foothold, that's right. Don't look down, I've got you.' Somehow or other he managed to heave her over the battlements. 'Well done, Sarah Jane. Enjoy the flight?'

'Great!' Sarah looked around the flat stone roof. 'All right, we're here. How do we get in?'

The Doctor searched round and spotted a ring-bolt set into the roof. He heaved on it, and found it attached to a trapdoor, which lifted smoothly upwards. 'Well, would you believe it,' said the Doctor thoughtfully. 'Come on Sarah Jane. In here!'

Tegan and the Doctor – the first Doctor – reached the Dark Tower at last. They climbed up a massive stone staircase, and found themselves facing a set of colossal doors. They were firmly closed.

'Now what?' demanded Tegan. 'You're not going to suggest we batter them down, I hope?'

The old man stood looking about him getting his breath back after the steep climb. He noticed a thick rope hanging down by the side of the doors and pottered over to examine it.

Tegan followed. 'What's that?'

'It looks very like a bell to me!'

'I suppose we just pull it and the door opens?'

'We can but try.'

The Doctor grabbed the bell-rope and gave a hefty tug.

There was a deep and sonorous clanging, which faded away into silence. Then to Tegan's utter astonishment, the doors creaked slowly open. Dwarfed by the immense size of the doors, the Doctor and Tegan went inside.

Three Doctors had entered the Dark Tower. Now the real danger would begin.

10

DEADLY COMPANIONS

Outside the TARDIS, the Cybermen were busier than ever.

Susan and Turlough watched helplessly on the scanner as a group of Cybermen carried an enormous metal cylinder and set it down by the TARDIS door. Susan looked at Turlough. 'It's a bomb – isn't it?'

He nodded, making an unsuccessful attempt to sound casual. 'I imagine so. Big, isn't it?'

The enormous doors gave on to an enormous hall. Tegan blinked. She had been bracing herself to meet all kinds of horrors, and instead there was – nothing. The hall was vast, cavernous and gloomy, empty except for the occasional pillar. In the distance, on the far side, she could just make out a huge staircase, leading upwards. Immediately in front of them, on the floor, alternating squares of black and white were laid out in a chess-board design.

Tegan was about to set off for the staircase when the old man put a hand on her arm. 'Don't be in such a hurry, my dear.' He fished a handful of coins from out of his pocket, oddly shaped coins from many times and many planets. Tegan looked at him in surprise. 'We have to pay to get in?'

'It could cost you your life,' said the Doctor cryptically. He tossed a coin onto the first row of the chess-board. Nothing happened.

He tossed another coin on the second row.

Still nothing.

Nothing happened on the third row, or the fourth.

Tegan was getting impatient.

'How long do you plan to stand here playing pitch and toss?'

Ignoring her, the Doctor tossed a coin onto the fifth row – and the chess-board seemed to explode. A kind of lightning bolt flashed down from the high ceiling, again and again and again, striking square after square with incredible speed. It seemed to range over the entire board, striking many, but by no means all of the squares, in turn. So, thought Tegan, some squares were safe, for some of the time – but which?

'Diabolical ingenuity,' muttered the Doctor. 'You see? Nothing happens until you reach the fifth row, half-way. Then the entire board becomes a death-trap.'

'Our ancestors had such a wonderful sense of humour,' said a smooth voice from the doorway behind them.

They turned and saw the Master striding into the hall. The first Doctor peered suspiciously at him. 'Do I know you, young man?' The Master came to join them, at the edge of the board.

'Believe it or not, we were at the Academy together.'

'What do you want?' asked Tegan suspiciously.

The Master spread his hands. 'To help.'

'Oh really? That's the funniest thing I've heard all day.'

'Believe what you like, but I should advise you to hide. I have some very suspicious allies close behind me.'

'Allies? What –'

She broke off as a massive silver figure loomed up in the doorway.

'Come on,' whispered Tegan. Grabbing the old Doctor's hand she dragged him behind the nearest pillar.

The Master turned towards the doorway. 'Enter – but be careful.' The Cyberleader marched into the hall, his patrol behind him. The Master waved his hand, gesturing around the vast hall. 'The fortress of the Time Lords is at your mercy.' The Cybermen gathered in the doorway, a tightly bunched, suspicious group.

The Cyber Lieutenant looked round the hall. 'Why was the main gate unguarded?'

'The Time Lords believe that no one could survive in the Death Zone. It's the kind of woolly thinking that will bring about their destruction.' The Master pointed to the great stairway at the other end of the hall. 'There lies your way!'

The Cybermen moved forward as far as the edge of the chess-board, and then stopped. The Master looked at them in surprise. 'Do you fear an empty room? Shall I lead the way?'

Tegan and the Doctor watched from hiding as the Master moved on to the board. First row, second row, third row ... he stopped, looking expectantly at the Cybermen. The Cyberleader raised his weapon. 'You will cross to the far side.' The Master shrugged. 'Very well.'

To their astonishment he strolled across the rest of the board – though Tegan noticed he followed a slightly eccentric path, never quite moving in a straight line. On the far side of the board, the Master turned, and made the return journey. But the path he followed this time was slightly different. He returned to stand by the Cybermen. 'You see?'

The Cyberleader turned to his Lieutenant. 'Take the patrol across.' Very slowly, weapons at the ready, the giant silver figures moved across the chess-board. The Doctor and Tegan saw them reach the first square, the second, the third and the fourth ... As the Cyberleader's foot touched the fifth row, the lightning bolts struck. Again and again and again they flashed down from the ceiling, and each time a Cyberman was struck it reeled and fell, smoke pouring from its chest-unit.

By pure chance one or two of the Cybermen survived for a time, but there was nothing they could do to fight back. They staggered disorientated about the board, firing wildly, sometimes hitting their fellows. One by one the lightning bolts found them and they were smashed burning to the ground. The Cyber Lieutenant was the last to fall. Struggling desperately to return to his Leader he was struck down at the very edge of the board. His gun skidded across the floor landing almost at the Cyberleader's feet.

The Cyberleader had watched the slaughter of his men with no apparent emotion. He turned to the Master. 'You betrayed us. Why?'

The Master looked hurt. 'Betrayed? I may have misled you a little, unintentionally of course. You see the safe path across the board changes with every journey.'

The Cyberleader's weapon was covering the Master. 'Show me the safe route, or I shall destroy you.'

'As you wish.' The Master bowed, and suddenly converted the bow into a dive. He hit the floor, rolled over, and came up firing, the fallen Cyberweapon in his hand. Before the Cyberleader realised what was happening, the Master's first blast struck him full in the chest-unit. The Cyberleader staggered back, on to the board. The Master blasted him again and again, driving him further onto the board. Smoke pouring from his chest, the dying Cyberleader staggered on to the fifth row, triggering another sequence of the deadly lightning bolts. Seconds later, a bolt smashed him to the ground, to lie amongst the slaughtered bodies of his patrol. The Master threw back his head and laughed.

Tegan and the first Doctor came out of hiding. Tegan glared indignantly at the Master. 'Wasn't that a little ruthless, even for you?'

The Master smiled. 'In one of the many wars on your miserable little planet, they used to drive sheep across minefields. The principle is the same.'

'Not quite. This minefield is still just as dangerous.'

'You think so?'

The Master strolled across the board, apparently casually – though again, Tegan noticed, he picked his route with great care. On the other side of the board, the Master turned and waved. 'Try it, Doctor,' he invited. 'It's as easy as pie!' He turned and disappeared up the giant staircase.

The old Doctor stared after him indignantly. 'What an extraordinary fellow! Easy as pie? Easy as pie ...'

Tegan shrugged. 'That's what he said.'

Suddenly the Doctor chuckled. 'No he didn't. He said easy as pi. Greek letter pi. Surely you know some basic mathematics, child?'

'Of course I do,' said Tegan indignantly. Closing her eyes she began reciting a long-ago lesson. '"The ratio of the circumference of a circle to its diameter is represented by the Greek letter pi."' She opened her eyes. 'Right?'

'Exactly. You work out the safe path, by using the mathematical term pi, that's clear enough. But the application, the application ...'

The Doctor frowned, studying the board. 'A hundred squares, ten by ten ... So, using the first hundred terms of pi as *co-ordinates* – Yes, that's it, it must be. Let me see now, three point one, four ...' The

Doctor began mumbling a long stream of figures, faster and faster. At last he stopped. 'Yes, that'll be it!'

Tegan never did understand quite how the 'safe' sequence worked, even when the Doctor (her Doctor) explained it to her later. All she could gather was that *if* you could observe exactly where the lightning bolts struck each time, and *if* you could then carry out some terrifyingly complex mathematical calculation at blinding speed, you *might* then be able to work out a way of crossing the second part of the board without setting off the trap.

All that concerned her at the moment was that the Doctor seemed to have got the hang of it, never mind how. He walked slowly across the board, first half then second half, and arrived safe on the other side.

'Come along, my child,' he said briskly. 'But once you pass the fifth row, be careful to tread exactly where I tell you.'

Tegan stepped cautiously on to the board. 'Don't worry. I will. I just hope you've got your sums right!'

President Borusa had left orders that he was not to be disturbed, but the Doctor could be very persuasive when he wanted to be. Convinced that the entire fate of Gallifrey depended on the Doctor being admitted to the Inner Council conference room, the bemused guard threw open the door. The Doctor stepped into the room. 'Lord President – ' He broke off, looking round in astonishment. The conference room was empty.

He turned accusingly to the equally astonished guard. 'You said the Lord President was here.'

'He is – or at least, he was, not long ago.'

'You're sure about that, are you?'

'Positive. I saw him go in – and this conference room has only one entrance. There isn't any way he could have left without me seeing him.'

Struck by a sudden thought, the Doctor went over to the transmat booth and tried the console. 'No power. He couldn't have left that way … Guard, go to Chancellor Flavia and inform her, discreetly, that the Lord President seems to have disappeared.'

Impelled by the sudden authority in the Doctor's tone, the guard hurried away, closing the door behind him.

The Doctor stood looking round the room. There was little to see. Just the conference table, the chairs, the wall screen, the transmat booth, and the antique harp on its stand in the corner with the portrait behind it. Shaking his head in bafflement the Doctor began a methodical search for some kind of secret door.

Sarah and the third Doctor had descended from the trapdoor into a long gloomy corridor. Dark-panelled, with occasional musty wall-hangings, the place had an atmosphere that was. decidedly sinister. They went along corridors, down staircases, along more corridors, and down more staircases. Sarah found she couldn't go on. Suddenly she stopped.

The Doctor stopped too. 'What is it, Sarah Jane?'

'I'm not sure. I feel as if something was … pushing me back.'

'I can feel it too,' said the Doctor gently. 'It's a kind of mental attack – from the mind of Rassilon. We must be getting close to the Tomb. You must fight it, keep your mind under control.'

Sarah shook her head. 'I can't. I feel as if there was something absolutely terrible waiting, just round the next corner.'

The Doctor smiled reassuringly. 'I'll just take a look, and make sure there isn't. You rest here for a moment.'

'All right. Don't be too long!'

The Doctor went round the corner, and found, as he expected, an identical corridor stretching ahead. Then, quite suddenly a tall thin-faced young man stepped out of an alcove, further down the corridor. 'Doctor!' he called urgently. 'Doctor, this way!'

The Doctor hurried forward. 'Mike? Mike Yates? How did you get here?' Mike Yates was an old friend, the Brigadier's number two for much of the Doctor's association with UNIT.

'Same way as you, I imagine,' said Mike. 'Quickly, Doctor, this way. Liz Shaw is here.'

Liz had been part of UNIT too, the Doctor's assistant when he started his exile on Earth. And there she was, waving from further down the corridor.

'Good heavens,' said the Doctor. 'Hullo, Liz. Anyone else here?'

'Come and see,' said Liz Shaw invitingly. 'You'll be delighted.'

The Doctor moved on down the corridor. 'Have you seen anything of a little chap in an old frock-coat and check trousers?'

Liz Shaw smiled. 'Him, and lots of others. There are five of you now, you know.'

'Good grief!'

'And they're all waiting for you, Doctor,' said Mike Yates.

The Doctor stopped dead. 'Hang on a minute, I must get Sarah.'

'I'll fetch her for you,' suggested Mike.

'I think I'd better go, she's scared enough already.'

Liz Shaw stepped in front of him. 'Let Mike go, Doctor. Your other selves need you, urgently.'

'No, I think I should go!'

Mike Yates stepped up beside Liz so that they barred his way. 'No, Doctor.'

The Doctor stared hard at them both, thinking that his old friends were acting very strangely. Suddenly he noticed that they were looking strange too, skins white and waxen, eyes burning fanatically. Hands out-stretched like claws, they stalked slowly towards him.

'No, Doctor,' screamed Liz Shaw.

'No, Doctor,' howled Mike Yates ...

Their voices rose, distorted into unearthly screeches.

11

RASSILON'S SECRET

The Doctor moved determinedly forward.

'Stop him, stop him,' howled Mike Yateş and Liz Shaw. Their voices blended eerily and they seemed to float towards him. The Doctor poised himself to meet their attack – then suddenly he laughed.

'Stop me? How can you stop me? You're not Liz and Mike, you're just phantoms, illusions, projections from someone's mind. You can't harm me.' He strode past – or was it through? – the two illusions, and they disappeared.

The Doctor hurried back round the corner to Sarah, where she was waiting. She looked up eagerly.

'There you are Doctor? What's happening?'

The Doctor hurried towards her, and then stopped. 'It is Sarah – isn't it?'

'Well of course it is! What's happening? Why did you leave me so long? What was that scream?'

The Doctor smiled at the stream of questions. 'Just phantoms from the past.'

'Well, I'm in the present. How about worrying about me?'

The Doctor put an arm around her shoulders. 'Yes, you're real enough Sarah Jane. Let's be on our way.'

'I don't like it, Doctor,' said the Brigadier. 'I feel strange. Nauseated.'

The second Doctor looked up at him. 'What you feel is fear, Brigadier. Fear projected from the mind of Rassilon.'

'Fear?' The Brigadier frowned, not sure that this was an admissible emotion for an old soldier.

The second Doctor and the Brigadier had been engaged in a very similar journey to that of the third Doctor and Sarah – except, of course, that they had been moving upwards, rather than downwards. Now that they were approaching the Tomb, at the centre of the Tower, they were feeling the same terrifying effects.

Suddenly a piercing scream rang out. 'Doctor! Doctor, help me!'

'It may be a trap,' said the Doctor. 'I'll go, you wait here.'

'I'll do nothing of the kind, Doctor!'

'Oh all right. But don't get in the way!'

They ran on together, rounding the bend and reached some more steps. At the bottom of them, one each side, were two figures flattened against the wall, apparently pinioned by some kind of light-beam. One of the prisoners was a very small girl with an attractive elfin face, the other a brawny Highlander in a kilt.

'It's Zoe,' said the Doctor. 'Zoe and Jamie!'

Both had been the third Doctor's companions on his travels for many years.

'Stay back, Doctor,' shouted Jamie.

'Why? What's happening?'

The Doctor moved nearer.

Zoe called, 'Don't come any closer! There's a forcefield, Doctor.'

The Doctor started rummaging through his pockets. 'Forcefield? I'll soon fix that! Where's my sonic screwdriver?'

'No, Doctor,' called Jamie desperately. 'If the forcefield is disturbed, it will destroy us, and you as well.'

'You've got to go back,' sobbed Zoe.

The Brigadier looked down at the Doctor. 'What are we going to do?'

The little man fished out his sonic screwdriver and brandished it. 'Get them out, of course!'

'No, please don't Doctor,' said Jamie.

'If you try to go on you'll kill all of us,' said Zoe. 'Please, go back, save yourselves.'

'I can't leave you here.'

'We could try to find another way to the Tomb,' suggested the Brigadier uneasily.

The Doctor shook his head. 'Jamie and Zoe would still be prisoners.'

'Turn back, Doctor,' urged Zoe. 'The Brigadier's right!'

'Is he? Perhaps he is,' said the little Doctor sadly, and turned away. Then he turned back. 'Is he? Wait a minute.'

The Brigadier stared at him. 'Now what?'

'A matter of memory, Brigadier.'

He moved back towards the stairway.

'A step nearer and we're both dead,' warned Jamie.

'Brigadier, stop him,' screamed Zoe.

'It's all right, Brigadier,' said the Doctor cheerfully. 'You can't kill illusions. You two aren't real. When I was exiled to Earth, you were both returned to your own people, your own times – and the Time Lords erased the memory of the time you'd spent with me. *So how do you know who we are? Answer!*'

The Doctor marched determinedly forwards – and the phantoms faded away.

'Good heavens,' said the Brigadier dazedly, and followed the Doctor up the stairs.

They hurried on their way.

The first Doctor and Tegan too were nearing the Tomb.

'Do you feel odd, Doctor?' asked Tegan suddenly.

'Full of strange fears and mysterious forebodings, you mean?'

'That's it, exactly. You feel it too?'

The old man chuckled. 'As a matter of fact, I don't! It's all illusion, my child. We're getting close to the domain of Rassilon, and his mind is reaching out to attack us. Just ignore it as I do.'

'How?'

'Tell yourself it's an illusion. All fear is largely illusion – and at my time of life, there's little left to fear!' The old man walked serenely on. 'There's nothing here to harm us, child.'

For once, the old Doctor was wrong. As they walked on down the corridor, the Master emerged from his hiding place behind a musty arras, and moved stealthily after them.

The Doctor stood in the centre of the Inner Council conference room, totally baffled. He had tapped and rapped on every possible surface. He had twiddled every ornamental moulding and projection and decoration he could lay his hands on. All to no avail.

The Doctor knew that just because he hadn't found a secret door it didn't mean that there wasn't one. A secret door could be padded so that it wouldn't give off a hollow sound when tapped. The way into a hidden chamber on Gallifrey might well be more complex than pressing the third carved moulding on the right. The Doctor scratched his head.

The guard had returned with a note from Chancellor Flavia. The Commander showed every sign of having some guilty secret, and was expected to confess his involvement in conspiracy very soon.

Meanwhile President Borusa was nowhere to be found. The Doctor considered calling in a security squad with electronic equipment. But that might cause a scandal – something he still hoped to avoid. Hands in pockets, the Doctor wandered around the little chamber, coming to a halt before the antique harp on its stand. He read the inscription. *Here is the Harp of Rassilon.* The Doctor rubbed his chin. 'Never knew he was musical – or Borusa either, come to that!' The Doctor gave the harp an idle twang – and there was a grinding of machinery, somewhere behind the wall. 'Interesting,' He twanged again. More grinding. 'A musical key,' said the Doctor. 'A particular note … a combination of notes … a tune!'

The Doctor began strumming on the harp.

Appropriately enough, the first Doctor was the first to reach the Tomb of Rassilon. He stood, with Tegan at his side, in the doorway of a tomb as big as a cathedral. A cathedral with just one occupant.

In the centre of the enormous chamber was a richly decorated bier. On it lay a motionless form, dressed in ceremonial robes. Close by there was the incongruous shape of an antiquated but complex control console, and a transmat booth. And that was all. Echoing space, silence, and the one still figure.

Tegan moved to the bier and studied the occupant. He had a face that was strong rather than handsome. He looked wise and kindly. Set into the wall by the great arched doorway there was a plinth, bearing a long inscription in some complex script. The old man spotted it immediately and began studying it. Tegan stood gazing about her in awe. Then she heard footsteps, whirled round and saw a tall white-haired man and a dark-haired young woman.

They stood in the doorway, looking wonderingly around them. The first Doctor saw them too. He stared hard at the tall man for a moment and then nodded. 'There you are at last, my dear fellow. First regeneration?'

'Second. I'm the third Doctor.'

'Yes, of course. Well, what kept you?'

The tall man drew himself up. 'Well, of all the confounded arrogance.'

'Never mind, never mind, you can tell me later. Come and take a look at this!'

A little huffily the tall man went over to look at the inscription. It caught his interest immediately. 'Fascinating,' he said and began studying it absorbedly.

Tegan smiled at the girl. 'I'm Tegan Jovanka.'

The girl smiled back. 'Sarah Jane Smith.'

It occurred to Tegan that she'd better work out some way of keeping track of the Doctors in her mind. She knew that her Doctor, *the* Doctor, was the fifth.

The old man who'd accompanied her to the Tower was the first – call him Doctor One. Now it appeared that this tall white-haired bloke was Doctor Three. In that case, what about …

Doctor One looked up and said suddenly. 'By the way, what's happened to the little fellow?'

Before Doctor Three could reply an indignant voice said, 'The little fellow is perfectly all right, thank you very much!' A little man in a battered old frock-coat and baggy check trousers came into the room, followed closely by an old friend, the Brigadier.

'Ah, you're here,' said Doctor Three. 'About time!'

'Of course we're here,' said the little man impatiently. 'You don't imagine anything you two can cope with would stump *me*, do you?' He spotted the inscription. 'What's all this then, eh? Let's have a look!' Pushing past his other selves, he hunched over the inscription. This, thought Tegan, just had to be Doctor Two.

The Brigadier came over to the two girls.

'Brigadier!' said Sarah, and promptly hugged him.

The Brigadier flushed, and cleared his throat. 'Nice to see you, Miss Smith … Miss Jovanka. Don't ask me how we got here. Like a cross between Guy Fawkes and Halloween!'

453

The tall white-haired man came hurrying over and shook the Brigadier hastily by the hand. 'My dear Brigadier! How very nice to see you again!'

The Brigadier said dazedly, 'Good Heavens, you as well! Nice to see you too, Doctor – though I can't exactly say it's nice to be here.'

Doctor Three glanced over his shoulder. 'Excuse me, will you, old chap? Only we've got a rather important inscription to translate, and those two will get it all wrong without me!' He hurried back to the plinth.

'Typical,' said the Brigadier. 'Absolutely typical.'

'I know,' said Sarah sympathetically. 'They haul you through space and time without so much as a by-your-leave, then leave you stuck on the sidelines just when things get interesting!'

Tegan nodded. 'My one's no better.'

'Which one's yours?' asked Sarah, and they began comparing notes.

Once they'd got things sorted out, Sarah asked, 'What's happened to the other one. The one after him,' she pointed to Doctor Three, 'and before your one?'

'The one with the hair and the scarf and the funny hat?' That would be Doctor Four, thought Tegan. 'He doesn't seem to be here. They were saying something about one of them not making it, getting trapped in the time-vortex.'

'Trust him to get himself in trouble,' said Sarah. 'Pity, I'd have liked to see him again.'

While they were talking, the three Doctors had concluded their study of the inscription. They looked at each other, clearly shaken, their faces grave. 'So that's what it's all about,' whispered Doctor Two. 'I never dreamed …'

'Then don't,' commanded Doctor One. 'This changes nothing. Absolutely nothing. We lower the forcefield, get the young fellow back from Gallifrey, and all go home. This doesn't concern us. It mustn't.'

Tegan caught the end of their conversation. 'What does the inscription say?'

'You really needn't trouble yourself …'

'I'd like to know as well,' said the Brigadier firmly.

'And me,' said Sarah. 'We've all gone through quite a lot just getting here, you know.'

The Doctors exchanged glances.

Doctor One snapped, 'Tell them!'

Doctor Two said gently, 'It's in Old High Gallifreyan, the ancient language of the Time Lords. Very few people understand it these days ...'

'Fortunately, I do,' interjected Doctor One complacently.

'Very interesting I'm sure,' said the Brigadier. 'Never mind what it's written in, what does it say?'

Doctor Three glanced at the inscription. 'It says, Brigadier, that this is the Tomb of Rassilon – where Rassilon himself lies in eternal sleep.'

Doctor Two said, 'It also says that anyone who has got this far has passed many dangers and shown great courage and determination ... Like me!' He pointed to the inscription, looking up at Doctor Three. 'What does that bit mean?'

Doctor Three stooped to look. 'To lose is to win – and he who wins shall lose!' He shrugged baffled.

Doctor One said quietly. 'The inscription promises that whoever takes the Ring from Rassilon's finger and puts it on shall have the reward he seeks.'

'What reward?' asked Sarah.

Gravely the old man said, 'Immortality.'

There was an astonished silence.

'Immortality,' said the Brigadier. 'Live for ever? Never die?'

The old man sniffed. 'That is what the word means, young man.'

Sarah said, 'But that's impossible!'

'Apparently not,' said Doctor Three.

'Thank you, gentlemen,' said the Master.

He was standing in the doorway with the Tissue Compression Eliminator in his hand. He moved the weapon to cover the little group of Doctors. 'I came here to help you, Doctor – Doctors! A little unwillingly, but I came. My services were scorned, my help refused. Now I shall help myself – to Immortality!'

Doctor One shook his head. 'Out of the question!'

'You're hardly a suitable candidate,' pointed out Doctor Three.

'For anything,' concluded Doctor Two.

The Master smiled. 'You think not? But then, the decision is scarcely yours. Killing you once was never enough for me, Doctor. How gratifying to do it three times over!' Stepping back, the Master raised the weapon, and took careful aim.

12

THE GAME OF RASSILON

In his eagerness to destroy the Doctors, the Master had forgotten their companions. Or perhaps he had thought them unworthy of his consideration. It was a serious mistake.

Moving very silently for such a big man, the Brigadier crept up behind the Master. He tapped him on the shoulder. 'Nice to see you again!'

The Master spun round, snarling, weapon raised. The Brigadier delivered a right uppercut that would have dropped anyone else cold. The force of the blow sent the Master staggering back. He raised his blaster – and Doctor Three kicked it out of his hand. The Master disappeared beneath a pile of Doctors.

It had taken a very long time, but the Cybermen were ready at last. The Patrol's Lieutenant held up a remote-control device. 'The bomb is ready, Leader.'

'Excellent. Prepare for detonation.'

The Cyber Lieutenant raised his arm in signal. 'Patrol! Your orders are, move back.'

The Cybermen began to disperse.

Turlough watched them on the scanner, cursing the caution that had trapped him here in the TARDIS. He had no faith in the TARDIS's invulnerability. Not against a bomb of such colossal size. He looked bleakly at Susan. 'You realise what's happening?'

She nodded. 'What are we going to do?'

Turlough essayed a last, black joke. 'Die, it seems.'

*

The Doctor gave a final despairing twang on the harp. He had tried every tune in his repertoire, without success.

'If it's a tune, what tune can it be. A tune like … a tune like …' The Doctor gazed up at the picture for inspiration. It showed a mysterious cowled figure – Rassilon himself presumably – playing a harp exactly like the one on the stand. There was a music-stand in the picture, with a sheet of music on it. The music was painted in such detail that you could actually read it. 'A tune like the one that's been here under my nose all this time!'

His eyes on the painted music, the Doctor started to pick out the simple tune. It was a strange haunting air, an old Gallifreyan ballad now almost forgotten. As the Doctor played the final note, the hidden door beneath the picture slid quietly open.

The Doctor went down a flight of steep and narrow steps, and found himself in an underground control room – the ancient, long-forgotten Game Control.

He looked at the great Game Table with its model of the Death Zone with the central Tower. He saw the little figures dotted about, the Doctors, the companions, the Master. Only then did the Doctor turn and look at the Timescoop Control console.

Hunched over the ancient instrument there was a black-clad figure, wearing the old black cloak and head-dress of the early Time Lords. The tall figure turned and the Doctor saw with more sadness than surprise that it was Borusa, Lord President of Gallifrey. He was pulling off black gauntlets, and a jewelled coronet blazed on his forehead. His eyes seemed to burn with feverish excitement. 'Welcome, Doctor.'

The Doctor bowed his head. 'Lord President.'

'You show little surprise.' Borusa's tone was almost petulant, as if the Doctor had spoiled his fun. 'Can it be you already suspected me?'

'Not immediately. Your little charade fooled me – for a while.'

'It *was* rather neat, I thought,' said Borusa modestly. 'Pity about the Castellan – but I had to use someone as a diversion.'

The Doctor looked sadly at his old teacher. 'Oh, Borusa, what's happened to you?'

Borusa became serious, matter-of-fact, almost like his old self. 'You know how long I have ruled Gallifrey, Doctor – openly, or from behind the scenes?'

'You have done great service. It was only right that you should become President.'

'President!' said Borusa scornfully. 'How long before I must retire with my work half done! If I could only continue …'

'You want to be Perpetual President, throughout all your remaining regenerations?'

'Do you think my ambition so limited, Doctor? I shall be President Eternal, and rule forever!'

The Doctor shook his head. 'Immortality? That's impossible, even for Time Lords.'

'No! Rassilon achieved it. Timeless, perpetual bodily regeneration. True Immortality. Rassilon lives, Doctor. He cannot die. *He is Immortal!*'

The Master lay in a corner, firmly bound with ropes made from a torn-up wall-hanging.

Doctor Three was hard at work on the console that controlled the forcefield. He looked up. 'There, that's done. I've reversed the polarity of the neutron flow. The TARDIS should be free now.'

Doctor Two was standing ready at the communications area of the console. 'About time! I'll try to get through to the Capitol!'

The massive Cyberbomb stood jammed by the TARDIS door. The Cybermen were gathered at the edge of the little hollow. The Cyber Lieutenant held the remote-control detonator. 'All is prepared.'

The Cyberleader said, 'Excellent. Detonate!'

The Lieutenant depressed the plunger. The bomb exploded, sending a fountain of stones and dirt high into the air. When the smoke and dust cleared, the TARDIS was nowhere to be seen.

Inside the TARDIS, the time rotor was rising and falling.

Susan and Turlough hugged one another joyfully.

'They made it,' shouted Susan. 'They made it!'

Turlough was grinning broadly. 'So where are we going – the Tower?'

Susan nodded. 'We must be, the Doctor pre-set the co-ordinates ...'

Pleased to have an audience at last, Borusa was pouring out all his secrets.

'Before Rassilon was bound, he left clues for the successor he knew would one day follow him. I have discovered much, Doctor. This Game Control, the Black Scrolls, the Coronet of Rassilon.' He tapped his forehead.

'But not the final secret?'

Borusa gave him a cunning look. 'The secret of Immortality is hidden in the Dark Tower, in the Tomb of Rassilon itself. There are many dangers, many traps.'

'So you transported me to the Death Zone to deal with them for you?'

Borusa was clearly proud of his ruthless scheme. 'I even provided companions to help, old enemies to fight. A Game within a Game!'

'Only you botched it rather, didn't you?' accused the Doctor. 'One of my selves is trapped in the time-vortex, endangering my very existence.'

Borusa laughed. 'Have no fear, Doctor. Your temporal stability will be maintained. I need you to serve me.'

The Doctor shook his head. 'I will not serve you, Borusa. Not now.'

Again Borusa tapped his forehead. 'You have no choice, Doctor. I wear the Coronet of Rassilon.'

'And very fetching it is too!'

Borusa ignored the taunt. 'The Coronet emphasises the power of my will. It allows me to control the mind of others. Bow down to me, Doctor.'

The Doctor resisted with every atom of his will, but the power of Borusa's amplified mind clamped down on him with irresistible strength. Slowly, very slowly, fighting every inch of the way, the Doctor sank to his knees.

A low signal chimed. Borusa adjusted controls. 'Come, Doctor.' He mounted the stairs. Helplessly, the Doctor rose and followed.

When they reached the conference room, a light was flashing on the console beside the transmat booth. A monitor screen on the console lit up, showing a quizzical face crowned by a mop of straight black hair. 'This is the Doctor – well one of them – calling the Capitol. Are you there? Are you there, Doctor?'

The Doctor found himself moving to the console. 'Yes, I'm here.'

The TARDIS materialised in the Tomb of Rassilon. Turlough and Susan rushed out – and found everyone crouched round Doctor Two, who was talking into the communications console.

'What's going on?' demanded Turlough.

No one took any notice of him.

'Can you hear me, old fellow?' Doctor Two was saying. 'We've reached the Tower, we're all safe, the barriers are down and, oh yes, the TARDIS is here. I say, we've made the most extraordinary discovery …'

The face of the fifth Doctor appeared on the monitor. 'I know what you have discovered. Do not transmit further. Stay where you are. Touch nothing. President Borusa is arriving to take full charge.' The screen went dead.

Doctor Two looked up. 'Touch nothing,' said the little man indignantly. 'Touch nothing, indeed. Who does he think he is?'

Doctor One said slowly, 'Perhaps he didn't want you babbling about the Ring of Rassilon on an open channel. Even so, his manner …'

Doctor Three said slowly, 'You know, I think there's something wrong.'

'Oh rubbish,' said Doctor Two rudely. 'You haven't changed, I see – still finding menace in your own shadow!'

Doctor One said, 'He's right. There is something wrong. I feel it too.'

'We'll soon see,' said Doctor Two. 'They're here!' The transmat booth lit up, and the Doctor and Borusa stepped out. Borusa looked exultant. The Doctor's face was utterly expressionless.

Tegan ran forwards. 'Doctor, are you all right?'

'Be silent,' hissed Borusa furiously. Tegan stopped dead, as if she had run into an invisible wall.

Borusa made a sweeping gesture towards the companions. 'Be silent, all of you. Do not move or speak until I give you leave.'

The companions froze, like living statues.

Borusa turned back to the Doctors. 'Gentlemen, I owe you my thanks. You have served the purpose for which I brought you here.'

'*You* brought us here? said Doctor Three.

Doctor Two said, 'He's after the Ring of Rassilon. He wants Immortality.'

Doctor Three shook his head. 'And you were the one who didn't sense that there was anything wrong.'

Doctor Two scowled at him.

Doctor One said sternly to Borusa. 'You're a renegade, no better than that villain over there.' He nodded towards the Master, bound and struggling in his corner.

'I'm afraid we can't allow this, you know,' said Doctor Two.

Doctor Three supported him. 'This Tomb was sealed for the best of reasons.'

Doctor One nodded vigorously. 'As soon as we're back to our own time-streams it must be sealed again – permanently.'

The Doctors ranged themselves before Borusa, barring his way to the Tomb. Doctor Two glanced at the still silent Doctor. 'Quickly, old chap, join us. Over here!'

The Doctor didn't move.

Doctor One stared hard at him. 'He can't. Some kind of mind-lock.' He raised his voice. 'Fight it, my boy, *fight it.*'

'We'll help you. Concentrate, all of you!'

Suddenly the Doctor felt the power of the linked minds of his other selves – his own mind amplified – tugging him free. With a sudden effort, he stepped away from Borusa and aligned himself with the other three Doctors.

The companions too found that they were free again. The Doctor was his old self. 'It's no good, Borusa! Together we're a match for you.'

Borusa said angrily, 'Perhaps. But you can never overcome me.'

'We don't need to. Your accomplice the Commander will have confessed by now. Soon Chancellor Flavia will be here with her guards. Can you overcome the whole High Council?'

'Why not? I am Lord President of Gallifrey, and you are a notorious renegade. We will see who is believed.'

A giant voice boomed, 'This is the Game of Rassilon.'

Borusa turned and took a step towards the Tomb. Instinctively the Doctor moved to stop him, but Doctor One whispered, 'Wait my boy. That's the voice of Rassilon. It's out of our hands now.'

They all turned. Rassilon had arisen from his Tomb.

Not the physical Rassilon, who slept on undisturbed, but a giant spectral presence, looming over them. The voice boomed out again. 'Who comes to disturb the long Sleep of Rassilon?'

Borusa stepped forward. 'I am Borusa, Lord President of Gallifrey.'

'Why do you come here?'

'I come to claim that which is promised.'

'You seek Immortality?'

'I do.'

'Be sure!' thundered Rassilon. 'Be very sure. Even now it is not too late to turn back.'

'I am sure,' said Borusa steadily.

'And these others?'

'They are my servants.'

The phantom's gaze turned towards them. 'Is this so?'

'It most certainly is not,' said Doctor Three indignantly.

'Don't believe him,' shouted Doctor Two.

Doctor One was silent for a moment.

Then he stepped forward and said loudly, 'Ignore them, Lord Rassilon. President Borusa speaks the truth.'

The other Doctors looked at Doctor One in horror.

'You believe that Borusa deserves the Immortality he seeks?' demanded Rassilon.

'Indeed I do,' said Doctor One loudly.

'Then he shall have it. Lord Borusa, take the Ring.'

Borusa crossed to the Tomb and took the Ring from the sleeping Rassilon's finger.

The ghostly Rassilon spoke again. 'You still claim Immortality, Lord Borusa? You will not turn back?'

'Never!'

'Then put on the Ring.'

Borusa slipped the great jewelled Ring on to his finger.

Rassilon's voice echoed through the Tomb. 'Others have come to claim Immortality through the ages, Lord Borusa. It was given to them – as it shall be given to you!'

*

Suddenly the side of the Tomb, which featured three stone carvings of Time Lords, came alive, eyes darting furiously, their faces frozen and dead. A central space was empty.

In a terrible voice, Rassilon said, 'Your place is prepared, Lord President.'

Suddenly, magically, the Ring left Borusa's finger, and returned to Rassilon. Suddenly there stood Borusa, amongst the other immortal Time Lords. His body stiffened. His face became frozen and dead. Only the eyes remained alive – alive and pleading. Borusa had achieved his Immortality. An eternity of living death.

The side of the tomb darkened and Borusa and his fellow Immortals once more became stone.

'And what of you, Doctor?' asked Rassilon sardonically. 'Do you claim Immortality too?'

'No my Lord. I ask only that we all be returned to our proper places in space and time.'

'It shall be so.'

'My Lord, one of us is trapped in the vortex.'

'He too shall be freed.'

Suddenly the fourth Doctor and Lady Romana were continuing their boating trip.

The Doctor frowned, shifting his grip on the pole. Had there been something? Some odd dislocation? Imagination, he decided. 'Now then, Romana, as I was saying ...'

The punt glided on.

Rassilon turned his attention to the Master. 'The one who is bound shall also be freed. His sins will find their punishment in due time.' The Master vanished, leaving only his bonds behind. For the moment Tegan actually thought she could see his snarl hanging in the air like the smile of the Cheshire Cat in *Alice in Wonderland*.

'Now it is time for your other selves to depart, Doctor,' said Rassilon. 'Let them make their farewells and go.' The Presence drew itself up. 'You have chosen wisely, Doctor. Farewell!'

With a crack of thunder that echoed around the Tomb, the Rassilon spectre vanished. There was left only the stillness and the silence, and the peaceful sleeping form.

The Doctor turned to Doctor One. 'You knew what would happen to Borusa!'

'I guessed,' said the old man simply. 'I suddenly realised what that proverb meant. "To lose is to win, and he who wins shall lose." Rassilon knew Immortality was a curse, not a blessing. Those who seek it are dangerous madmen, potential tyrants. This whole thing was Rassilon's trap to detect them, lure them here, and then put them out of the way.'

The Doctor looked regretfully at his other selves. 'It seems we must say goodbye. And I was just getting to know me.' He shook hands with Doctor One.

'Goodbye my boy,' said the old man. 'You did quite well. Quite well. It's reassuring to know my future is in safe hands. Come along, Susan, say goodbye.'

'Goodbye, everyone,' said Susan obediently.

Taking her by the arm, the old man led her into the TARDIS.

Doctor Two tugged at the Brigadier's sleeve. 'Time to go, Brigadier.' He shook hands warmly with the Doctor and grinned mischievously at Doctor Three. 'Goodbye – fancy pants!' Looking very pleased with his parting shot, the little man popped inside the TARDIS.

The Brigadier came to attention and did one of his formal little bows. 'Goodbye Miss Smith, Miss Jovanka. Goodbye, Doctor – Doctors. Splendid fellows, all of you!' The Brigadier strode briskly into the TARAIS.

Doctor Three shook hands warmly with the Doctor. 'Goodbye, my dear chap. I've had the time of my lives. Haven't we, Sarah Jane?'

'Have we?' Sarah smiled wryly. 'I've only got one life, and I think it's had too much of a time!' She looked curiously at the Doctor. 'Is that …'

Doctor Three nodded. 'Me!' he said proudly; and bustled Sarah into the TARDIS.

The Doctor gave a sigh of relief. 'I'm not the man I was,' he said. 'Thank Goodness!'

'Why all these goodbyes?' asked Turlough. 'If we're all going home together …'

'Watch,' said the Doctor.

As Tegan and Turlough watched they saw one, two, then three TARDISes split off from their own TARDIS and dematerialise, leaving their original TARDIS still there.

'Temporal fission,' said the Doctor. 'Very clever chap, old Rassilon.'

The transmat booth lit up and an agitated Chancellor Flavia appeared. There were guards at her heels, phasers in hand, alert for trouble. As the little group stepped out, more guards materialised in the booth and followed them out. Chancellor Flavia was taking no chances. Glancing quickly round she hurried over to the Doctor. 'You are safe, Doctor? The Commander confessed everything. I feared Borusa might have – ' She broke off, looking about her. 'Where is President Borusa?'

'Unavailable,' said the Doctor. 'Permanently I'm afraid. It seems the old legends about Rassilon are true. He was – he is – the greatest Time Lord of all.'

'You must make a full statement to the High Council,' said Chancellor Flavia sternly.

The Doctor looked dismayed. 'Must I really?'

'It can form part of your Inaugural Address.'

The Doctor backed away in alarm. 'My what?'

Chancellor Flavia marched up to him, taking him arm. It felt, thought the Doctor, rather like being arrested.

'Doctor,' she said firmly. 'You have evaded your responsibilities for far too long. The – disqualification of President Borusa leaves a gap at the very summit of our Time Lord hierarchy. We feel that there is only one who can fill this place.' She paused impressively. 'Yet again, Doctor, it is my duty and my pleasure to inform you that the Full Council has exercised its emergency powers to appoint you to the position of President – to take office immediately.'

The Doctor buried his face in his hands. 'Oh no!'

'This is a summons no Time Lord dare refuse,' warned Chancellor Flavia. She glanced meaningly at the phaser-carrying guards. 'To disobey the will of the High Council will attract the severest penalties.'

The Doctor bowed his head, apparently accepting the inevitable.

'Very well. Chancellor Flavia, you will go back to Gallifrey immediately, and summon the High Council. You have full deputy powers until I return. I shall travel in my TARDIS.'

'But Doctor,' protested Chancellor Flavia.

'You will address me by my proper title!'

Chancellor Flavia bit her lip. 'But my Lord President – '

'I *am* the President, am I not?' thundered the Doctor. 'Obey my commands at once!' He glared at the guards. 'You! Return Chancellor Flavia to her duties!'

Instinctively the guards snapped to attention – and escorted the unwilling Chancellor Flavia back to the transmat booth.

The Doctor said, 'Quickly, you – into the TARDIS!' He bustled them inside. They heard Chancellor Flavia's anguished voice. 'Doctor – my Lord President – *wait!*' The TARDIS door closed behind them.

The Doctor dashed to the central console, and soon the time rotor began its steady rise and fall. To Tegan, it seemed he was acting with almost indecent haste. 'It'll soon be goodbye then?'

The Doctor looked up from the controls. 'Will it? Why?'

'You're going off to Gallifrey to be President, aren't you?' said Turlough sulkily. 'I suppose your Time Lord subjects will find us a TARDIS that really works and pack us both off home.'

The Doctor looked at him wide-eyed. 'Who said anything about going to Gallifrey?'

'But you told Chancellor Flavia –'

'I told Chancellor Flavia she had full deputy powers till I got back,' said the Doctor cheerfully. 'She'll be the longest-serving Deputy President in Time Lord history!'

Tegan and Turlough looked at each other, then back at the Doctor.

'You're not going back?' asked Tegan.

'Exactly.'

Turlough said dubiously. 'Won't the Time Lords be very angry?'

'Furious! said the Doctor happily.

Tegan gave him one of her disapproving looks. 'You really mean to say, you're deliberately choosing to go on the run from your own people in a rackety old TARDIS?'

'Why not?' said the Doctor cheerfully. 'After all – that's how it all started!'